Ma

Book One of
By J.L.Mullins

Copyright © 2023 by J.L.Mullins

All rights reserved.

No part of this publication may be reproduced, distributed, or transmitted in any form or by any means, including photocopying, recording, or other electronic or mechanical methods, without the prior written permission of the author, except as permitted by U.S. copyright law.

The story, all names, characters, and incidents portrayed in this production are fictitious. No identification with actual persons (living or deceased), places, buildings, and products is intended or should be inferred.

Contents

Chapter: 1 - New Beginnings 7
Chapter: 2 - The Caravanner's Guild 23
Chapter: 3 - Dinner 35
Chapter: 4 - A Simple Home 53
Chapter: 5 - A Day of Preparation 65
Chapter: 6 - In Holly's Workshop 79
Chapter: 7 - The Old Made New 91
Chapter: 8 - Delivery and New Sight 103
Chapter: 9 - It's Just Glue 105
Chapter: 10 - Don't Let Them Poach You 133
Chapter: 11 - Mysteries and Chowder 147
Chapter: 12 - One Has to Dream 161
Chapter: 13 - Late-Night Meetings 173
Chapter: 14 - An Auspicious Start 187
Chapter: 15 - The Journey Begins 201
Chapter: 16 - Arcanous Beasts 215
Chapter: 17 - The Evening Encampment 227
Chapter: 18 - The Wilds Are My Workout 241
Chapter: 19 - Not Soon Enough 255
Chapter: 20 - Around the 'Death' Tree 267
Chapter: 21 - Berries and Jerky 281
Chapter: 22 - A Frustratingly Fitting Name 295
Chapter: 23 - Around the Dinner Table 309
Chapter: 24 - There Would Be a Next Time 323
Chapter: 25 - A Blood Star 337
Chapter: 26 - Please Don't Kill Us 349

Chapter: 27 - That's… a Big Bull 363
Chapter: 28 - Messy Work 377
Chapter: 29 - You're a Mage, Figure It Out 391
Chapter: 30 - A Morning to Decide 405
Chapter: 31 - The Foundation of Any Fighting Art 417
Chapter: 32 - Terribly Wrong 431
Chapter: 33 - Creature of Magic 443
Chapter: 34 - Aftermath 457
Chapter: 35 - Power Aplenty 471
Chapter: 36 - Through the Gatehouse 483
Chapter: 37 - A Spinner of Tales 497
Chapter: 38 - Little Shop of Wonders 509
Chapter: 39 - The Wandering Magician 521
Chapter: 40 - The Beginning of True Magehood 535
Author's Note 549

Chapter: 1
New Beginnings

Frost licked over Tala's already sensitive skin, accompanied by the static tension of power rippling through her from an outside source.

With a pulse of darkness, she left her old life, her adolescence of learning and exploration, behind.

She crouched low in the center of a large, white-speckled, granite room. It was the shape of a half-sphere, each block sculpted and placed so precisely that had she not known better, she'd have believed it was carved from a single piece.

Though, I suppose a Material Creator could have summoned the room into being, fully formed. That was unlikely. If her schooling had taught her anything, it was that magic was expensive; why would anyone do something with it, which could be done by hand?

Beneath her were the empty grooves of a spell-form, an anchor used to draw a target in and recombine them.

Everyone said teleportation was tricky, and that was true, in part. Disintegration and expulsion of a person was incredibly simple. Calling that person, and all their requisite pieces, back from the ether and putting them all back where they belonged, now that was tricky business.

She shivered, as much from the fading cold as from the existentially terrifying thoughts. *A person's soul does most of the work, Tala. It's not like the scripts could get your insides wrong.*

Millennial Mage 1 - Mageling

She glanced down at her hands and saw fading red traces where her spell-lines should have been. She let out a short groan. *Well, that didn't work...*

Blessedly, she saw her own dark hair, roughly shoulder length, swaying in her peripheral vision. The inscribers at the academy shaved all the students' heads to allow for the easier adding of spell-lines, but in her soul—how she viewed herself—Tala had hair. Thus, somehow, her recombination had returned it to her. *Now, I just have to find an inscriber capable of leaving it be.*

Huh... my skin is still raw. Shouldn't it be as healed and complete as my hair? She supposed that some things just didn't make sense.

Tala heard several of the guards gasp as one voice stuttered out, "She's... She's naked!"

A commanding voice cracked out. "Go check her! If the teleportation acolytes at the academy managed to leave her clothes behind, who knows what else was forgotten."

Take charge of your life, Tala. She sighed, standing fully upright, back straight.

An uninscribed guard, a tall, broad-shouldered and grizzled man, stepped back in surprise at the sudden movement.

Tala looked around the room, ignoring the man. A waist-high stone wall stood in a circle halfway between her and the smooth granite of the outer walls. It was broken only in one place, allowing access to the inner circle.

Everyone—six guards and two Mages—was staring at her.

One of the Mages, heavens bless him, was coloring so that the red was easily visible, even under his spell-lines. He was sparsely clad, as befit an on-duty Mage, and he was, somehow, blushing nearly down to his navel.

Tala cleared her throat, speaking softly but letting her voice carry. "Nothing's for sale, gents, so please stop window shopping."

Three of the guards turned away, blushing in turn. The two others grinned but averted their eyes. The one already in the circle with her huffed something near a laugh but turned slightly away, keeping his eyes to himself.

That poor mageling flushed even redder and turned, putting his face against the outer wall. The female Mage, likely his sponsor, rolled her eyes and walked forward with a blanket taken from a pile that rested on a shelf laden with supplies.

She was practically naked herself, cloth covering as little as possible, while maintaining the semblance of modesty. Her lines were proudly on display, their magic unhindered by covering. She was not young, but wrinkles had yet to render her inscriptions faulty. Both Mages were fit, if not well-muscled—as most Mages had to be. Changing size or shape would almost universally ruin your spell-lines, as well as force your inscriber to rebuild your spell-work from scratch. That was assuming the distortions didn't make such work impossible.

Make no mistake, Mages, one and all, were vain creatures, but it wasn't their vanity that inspired scrupulous attention to their own bodies, so much as devotion to their art.

The older Mage moved with practiced grace and fluidity, obviously aware of her every gesture, careful not to brush any of her lines against others. Such contact would usually be safe, but so would juggling knives; it was the unexpected that killed, and when spell-lines were involved, there was far more than a cut hand on the line.

The older guard walked beside her as Tala strode to meet the Mage. If she had to guess, he had strategically placed himself between her and some of the other guards, blocking their view of her. *Thoughtful of him.*

A furnace blazed on the opposite side of the room, and its heat was slowly taking the teleportation chill from her. *Quickly, now. Don't let them see how embarrassed you are.* She found herself blessing the chill, which had kept the flush from the surface.

As the Mage drew close, she lowered her tone to keep it from carrying. "The chill does many things, dear, but it doesn't hide *every* sign of your embarrassment, at least not from those who know to look." She draped the blanket over Tala's shoulders. "Now, how did you arrive in such a state?" She frowned. "Why does it look like someone put you through a sandblaster? You've raw, new skin across your whole body."

Tala gave a formal half-bow, clutching the blanket close, while trying to affect a nonchalance that she did not feel. Though it was soft, the blanket still chafed lightly on her skin. The rawness had little to do with the unclad teleport, though it was still her own doing. "I'm Tala, Mistress, newly graduated from the academy."

"Yes, dear. You may call me Phoen. You have not answered my questions."

Tala cleared her throat, glancing away. "Well, you see, Mistress Phoen. Our current teleportation spells strip away spell-lines and won't take any gear, save the clothes on your back."

"Hmmm?"

"In studying the formula, it looked like it might be some factor of mass, beyond the organic being teleported, that is why at least a modicum of clothing always comes. Metal only comes if the person was wearing armor, and then not very much of it."

Phoen sighed. "So, you thought to, what? Modify the spell somehow? Child, you are lucky you didn't scatter yourself across half of inner-solar space!"

Tala's eyes widened. "Oh, no! Absolutely not!"

Phoen narrowed her eyes. "Then, what?"

"I guessed that, without clothes to teleport, other material would be brought along." She held up her hands. The red marks were already faded into bare visibility. "But I missed something."

"...Wait..."

"Hmmm?"

"Do you mean to tell me that you went *into* the teleportation circle... naked?"

Tala cleared her throat and looked away. As she did so, she was able to see two guards using heavy metal tongs to move a crucible from the furnace to the short wall. They then poured the contents, liquid silver, down a funnel set into that stone.

She knew the formulas needed for this spell-form well. *Precisely two pounds of silver.*

The metal flowed out of a spout low in the wall and washed through the grooved lines of the spell form, which was set into the floor.

She didn't know what preparations had been laid into the stone to ensure the silver would always distribute evenly and cleanly. She hadn't studied the Builder Arts, after all. Nonetheless, the Mages' work was flawless, and the spell-form was filled once more, allowing the silver to cool evenly, creating strong, solid spell-lines.

Tala had found variations of this catching spell that used a combination of metals, thus making them much more efficient from the perspective of materials, but the difficulty in casting interlacing liquids quickly meant that the uniform version was vastly easier to use, and thus the most pervasive.

Millennial Mage 1 - Mageling

Phoen sighed. "Mact!"

The young mageling jumped, turning around. "Mistress?"

"The spell-lines are reset. Take your place."

"Yes, Mistress!" He scurried around the women and went to sit in the center of the spell-lines, a hand resting within hand-sized outlines to either side of him. He sat straight, his core tight, his limbs carefully aligned. He took a deep breath and exhaled.

Tala felt the power ripple out from the boy, activating and resetting this teleportation receiver.

Without delay, Mact stood and returned to his master.

"Well done, Mact."

"Thank you." He smiled happily, almost to himself.

"Now, girl. You are beginning to tire me."

Tala sighed. "Yes, I went into the circle naked. Yes, I was lectured by the Mages on the other end about the folly of it. Yes, I know that teleportation magic isn't intended to work on naked subjects." She pulled the blanket closer together in front, and the top billowed out slightly, causing it to fall from her shoulders, exposing her back.

The grizzled guard let out a little startled exhalation, then started to laugh.

Tala spun on him. "What's so funny?"

Phoen let out a similar sound and barked a laugh of her own.

Tala turned back. "Mistress Phoen?"

"You seem to be cleverer than I'd thought." After a moment's pause, she amended, "Or, your cleverness bore more fruit than we'd guessed."

Tala frowned. Then, her eyes widened in realization. "My keystone?"

"Yes, your keystone looks intact. Come, I'll examine it."

Tala thanked the guard and followed Phoen from the room.

Mact tried to follow, but Phoen sent him back with several stern words.

Less than two minutes later, Tala was sitting in a small side room, a blanket covering herself strategically while leaving her back exposed. She was naturally straight-backed, her feet flat on the floor, knees bent at as close to right angles as the seat allowed—as she'd been trained.

Phoen took nearly five minutes examining the spell-lines in excruciating detail. "Child, what type of Mage are you?"

"Immaterial Guide, Mistress."

She grunted. "That explains it. I'm a Material Creator. None of these mean a thing to me. Though, they do look intact. You'll need an inscriber to look these over." She sighed. "Fresh from the academy, right?"

"Yes."

"If you're here, I assume you've signed a contract with the Caravanners, or maybe the Constructionists or Wainwrights? Though, I didn't think the latter two took on magelings, here…"

Tala grinned. "Not yet."

Phoen blinked at her, cocked her head to one side, and then sighed. "Oh, child."

"What? It's the law."

"*If* that inscription is still viable, you have a case, but they may not be happy about it. They might just turn you away."

"I…" Tala hadn't thought of that. Magelings got such poor pay until they could buy some spell-lines themselves. In addition, they had to operate under a full Mage, bound to obey them, subject to their schedule and whims. Once the mageling had scraped together enough to afford their own spell-lines, though, they were a Mage, and it was common law that a Mage commanded a much higher salary. She'd not considered that, given a choice of paying her a high salary or not hiring her, they might simply not hire her. She cursed.

Phoen quirked a small smile. "You must have been a joy to your teachers."

Tala bristled. "My teachers loved me." After a moment, she amended, "Most of them, anyways."

Phoen just grinned.

"Well, what can I do?"

"You have to decide whether or not to gamble. Don't tell them you have inscriptions until after the contract is signed and accept the lower wage; or tell them, and possibly lose any chance at work. No one else is hiring those of your quadrant in this city... that I know of." She smiled ruefully. "If you were a Material Creator, I'd throw you out on your ear for hubris." Even so, her eyes twinkled. "But not everyone's as crotchety as I. Perhaps you'll be lucky."

Tala frowned. "So, I'm naked, likely for nothing... Lovely."

Phoen opened her mouth to comment, but Tala held up a hand.

"Please... I know I'm asking for it, but please don't."

Phoen patted her on the shoulder. "I'll get you some clothes, dear. I have a friend who's an inscriber, and she should be able to verify your spell-lines. Then, you can make your own choice."

"Thank you... for everything."

* * *

Half an hour later, Tala was dressed in surprisingly soft, simple clothes and heading out of the great doors, several floors below the teleportation receiving areas.

She wore no shoes for two reasons. First, shoes were expensive and should be custom-made to be more help than harm. Second, some Mages preferred going barefoot, and in this, Tala's oddities were no exception.

Phoen's inscriber had verified that Tala's keystone spell-lines were intact and functional. Blessedly, the trickiest portion of her inscriptions had been maintained.

While most spell-lines were scripted thin to avoid interference, the keystone was always made as robust as possible. As a result, the keystone only had to be refreshed every year or so, with normal casting. Heavy casters still only had to have that work redone every six months, at the most often.

In contrast, the ancillary spell-lines could be used up in days—faster with heavy casting. Even standard amounts of magical work forced many inscriptions to be refreshed every couple of weeks.

As a result, the work and materials required for the keystone were tremendous. In general, Mages spent as much on the once- or twice-a-year keystone work as on all the ancillary inscriptions for the rest of the year combined. In many cases, the keystone work could cost as much as two years of ancillary lines.

Ahh, math. How I hate how much I need thee.

She paused before exiting the tower fully, taking a moment to admire the craftsmanship of the arch and doors that stood open, allowing entrance into the teleportation tower. *Magic rarely makes beauty.* And the beauty of this work spoke of human labor.

Tala shook her head. *I can't imagine striving to add embellishments to buildings that won't last even four centuries.* Even so, she enjoyed them. She idly wondered how many passersby had already gained a measure of pleasure from the elaborations. *Maybe, that's enough.*

Millennial Mage 1 - Mageling

Turning her gaze outward, she looked out on Bandfast for the first time.

The sky above the city was the deep blue of a clear autumn day, with a scattering of thin, high clouds. She loved such days, such skies.

Below the clear blue beauty, from this high vantage, she could easily see six layers of the city's defenses. All but the outermost were still in place, making the burgeoning nature of the city even more apparent. *It's in the farming phase.*

Indeed, the city's outermost active defenses encompassed vast tracts of farmland. Those defensive scripts were enormously taxing and would only last for the first hundred and fifty years of a city's life. By the growth on the land, the city was close to halfway between leaving the first and entering the third phase.

The only ring beyond the farmland was the mines, but those would have been abandoned in this second phase city, their defenses already depleted.

When the farmland's defenses faltered, the workers would move inward to the foundries, ore processing plants, and raw-goods refineries of the third ring.

Inside of that were factories, workshops, and artisan shops, which stood ready within the next layer of defenses.

The next layer contained the clerks and organizers of the city.

Inside that, the final layer of defenses held the homes and services like the teleportation tower.

The fifth phase of every city simply allowed for the buttoning up of all loose ends, and the sixth kept those remaining people comfortable as they prepared to leave and then left. She'd heard mention of other tasks and opportunities surrounding the final years of a waning city, but had never delved too deeply. As a new Mage, she knew better than to consider work for the Harvesters Guild, at least for now.

One hundred years of mining, an additional fifty years of farming, fifty more of refining, fifty of manufacturing, then twenty-five years each of closing down and departing.

Three hundred years: the lifespan of a city, with only the last twenty-five years of waning to lament the end.

All of this to keep humanity safe.

As if on cue, she felt a thrum of power and saw a lance of lightning strike from one of the outermost towers into the sky. The piercing scream of an eagle split the air, despite the great distance, and she was able to see the great beast spiraling downward to crash into some poor farmer's field. *Not too poor.* That large corpse would bring substantial payment to the one who had lucked into receiving it. *Assuming it didn't drop on their heads.*

She sighed, contemplating the slain creature. *I have not missed that.* The academy, for some inexplicable reason, did not have to deal with arcanous or magical beasts. *Yet more unknowns.*

Tala shook her head, coming back from her reverie. *This city still has at least a hundred and fifty years.* Probably closer to two hundred, if she had to guess. She would be long dead before it was fully abandoned. *Unless I go back to the academy...*

For reasons that no one had been able to explain to her, the longer someone stayed at the academy, the slower they aged, but also the weaker their abilities with magic became. Finally, after endless pestering, Tala had determined that even the faculty had no idea why it worked as it did.

She smiled to herself, realizing that she'd fallen back into musings. *To the Caravanner's main office.* That would be in the ring one out from where she stood, with the other bureaucratic and guild offices.

The inscribers would be here, in the innermost ring, and she itched to have her spell-lines refreshed, but she lacked the funds to pay for such services. Like most students, she left the academy not with accounts bursting, but indebted to the institution for her training. She, herself, had… other debts, as well.

I'm delaying again.

With no further introspections, she strode through the archway and down the front steps, allowing herself to enjoy the artistry of the carvings as she passed.

The streets were busy but nowhere near capacity. After all, this section contained the housing for nearly the city's entire population—as well as several of the smaller market areas—and had been built accordingly. The majority of the population would be about their work—mostly farming, given the city's phase.

Even so, the streets were far from empty.

Several large arcanous animals trudged through the streets, led by handlers. There were oxen, whose shoulders stood twice her height; horses, both massive and diminutive, pulling loads that seemed comically overlarge for them; and even several clearly arcanous pets padding alongside their owners. In every case, a simple scripted collar enclosed the arcanous animal's neck, denoting them as tamed or domesticated, exempting them from the city's defensive magics.

Thankfully, Mages didn't need to wear any such thing, as human magic seemed to function differently enough that wards could differentiate.

As her eyes scanned those she passed, she was able to pick out the occasional Mage by their bearing and fluid manner of movement, not to mention the spell-lines evident across their exposed skin. Most also wore Mage's robes, but not all.

To her surprise, she also saw an arcane, a humanoid arcanous creature.

What had caught her attention at first was the leather collar he wore, though it was tucked low, almost entirely hidden by his shirt's collar. As she'd looked closer, ensuring that her eyes hadn't deceived her and that it wasn't just an odd fashion choice, he'd turned to regard her. She hadn't noticed his gaze until after she'd seen the metallic spell-lines on the leather collar.

When she had felt his gaze, her eyes flicked up, meeting his, and she felt frozen to the spot.

His eyes were blood.

No comparison held the weight of truth save to say that his eyes were spheres of fresh, liquid blood, unbroken save for small circular scabs in place of pupils.

Tala swallowed involuntarily. *He's looking at me.* She tried to smile politely and turn away, but she found she couldn't force herself to turn.

Around his eyes, true-black, smooth skin forced the orbs into starker contrast, making their deep shades seem almost to glow. Subtle hints of grey lines ran under that skin in patterns very like spell-lines but somehow utterly different. Like seeing her own language written with the phonetic alphabet. The concepts seemed familiar while remaining utterly opaque to her interpretation.

She tried to turn away, again, and actually felt resistance like she was fighting herself. A tingle of her own power, emanating from her keystone, proceeded the answer: *Allure. He's somehow manipulating the conceptual nature of reality, forcing my attention to remain locked on him.*

As an Immaterial Mage, she could work with non-substance aspects of the world, such as gravity, dimensionality, and molecular cohesion, but warping the magnitude of *concepts*? That… that had disturbing implications.

As if in response to her thoughts, a different set of lines seemed to flicker into prominence around those wounding eyes, and she found herself turning away in confusion.

Millennial Mage 1 - Mageling

What is wrong with me? I stare at something I've never seen before and suddenly insist that it must be magic.

She shook her head at her own foolishness. Then, another prickle rippled out from her keystone, a subtle warning, and she froze. *Conceptual manipulation... would the concept of believability count?* She spun, her eyes ripping across the crowds, trying desperately to find the arcane once more. She had the flickering impression of an amused smile but nothing more.

After another few moments of frenzied searching, she was left with a subtle, low-level itch from her keystone and the growing concern that she'd somehow imagined the brief encounter. *I... I need to get to the Caravanner's Guild.*

Why had she allowed herself to get lost in her own musings once more?

Tala huffed. *I'm never going to get anywhere if I don't get going.*

Without a backward glance, she passed through tremendous gates, the southernmost of eight sets, to breach the gargantuan innermost walls.

Those walls were also carved with beautiful, intriguing reliefs, showing the Builder's attention to detail. *When building a cage, make it a pretty one.*

She sighed, pushing those thoughts away, along with her others. *A cage with doors flung wide hardly counts.* At least, that was what she wanted herself to believe; what she needed to believe if she were going to maintain her own sanity. *Human cities are to keep violence out, not humans in.* She did *not* contemplate that the results were virtually indistinguishable.

She strode purposely onward, now, and though she had to ask for directions twice, it took her less than an hour to find the building that she sought. When she did, she hesitated, standing across the street and observing the flow of traffic in and out of the building, itself.

This is it, Tala. You need to decide. Will you take the easy way? Or risk it all? She laughed. It was hardly a risk. Even if no one would hire her, the academy wanted her to pay them back, plus she had her parents' debts, which had led to her sale into the academy's tutelage. No, they wouldn't let her stay unemployed, though who knew what pittance they'd give her if they were forced to find employment on her behalf...

Not helping, Tala.

She took a deep breath and let it out slowly. *Now or never.*

Without further delay, she strode through the wide, double doors.

Chapter: 2
The Caravanner's Guild

Tala took a deep breath as her feet carried her through the front door of the Caravanners' main office.

The doors were simple, if wide, and they stood open, allowing for easy foot-traffic in and out, of which there was a steady flow. The arch which held the doors was easily wide enough for four people—five of Tala's size—to come through shoulder to shoulder, with a bit of room to spare.

The room she entered was a wide receiving hall, with clerks working in alcoves around the outside, as well as some more senior workers moving through the shifting groups of their prospective clients.

Here, almost every business was represented.

Restaurants negotiated food shipments either for more specialized crops not grown within this city or beginning to establish contracts for when the city's farming phase ended; artisans similarly negotiated for materials and to ship their goods to other cities; and countless others sought or negotiated similar services.

The Caravanners also carried mail from city to city, along with other goods, and they did a brisk trade in that respect.

In truth, this guild was one of the pillars of human civilization. They were unique in the quantity and regularity of their ventures through the arcanous wilds. Only the Builders dealt with beasts more often than the Caravanners, and they didn't do trips *through* the wilds so much as they fielded vast, long-term expeditions *into* them, building the continuous wave of cities. Well, there was the Harvesters' Guild, but their goal was slaying beasts and taking from them, so it was hardly a fair comparison.

She returned her mind to her present time and place. *There is power within these walls.* She felt a growing sense of excitement at the prospect of working for such an important group.

She had barely taken five steps through the door before she was noticed by a clerk with copper and silver spell-lines covering her face, clearly focused around her eyes. "You! Mage. Can I help you?"

Tala smiled and strode over to the young woman, where she waited behind a high counter. The clerk was not wearing Mage's robes, opting instead for a simple, if elegant, single-piece dress. It allowed her freedom of movement, without being a distraction for those she worked with. She had long, dark-blonde hair, pulled into a loose braid. Tala almost frowned at that. *I'm seeing a lot of inscribed with hair. Is there something different about the inscribers in this city?* Now was hardly the time for that line of thinking, however. Tala smiled. "Yes, I am looking for work." If Tala had to guess, the clerk was only a few years older than she, herself.

The woman nodded. "I'd hoped so. May I?" She tapped the scribing around her eyes.

Be decisive. Tala nodded once.

The clerk blinked, seemingly with specific intent, and her spell-lines pulsed with power.

As before, Tala's keystone let her know that she was in close proximity to, or the target of, magic, but the feeling wasn't unpleasant. *A simple inspection.*

As before? She had the stuttering impression of blood and darkness but couldn't pull a coherent memory together.

Must have been a bad dream. She dismissed the fractured recollection without further thought.

To Tala's unenhanced eyes, the effect on the clerk's face looked very similar to a heat haze, though with a little more light to it. Even that indication was a vast improvement on what Tala had seen before her time at the academy. *My body is acclimating to magic detection.*

Her instructors had said that, in time, she wouldn't need to continue getting inscriptions for the magesight at all. Her body would learn how to see the signs for itself, and her mind would interpret the input in ways that mimicked the spell-line-granted vision.

It was, in truth, another thing those teachers didn't truly understand, but they likened it to a skilled merchant learning to know weights and measures without the need of a scale over time. He could simply pick up a sack and know the weight of its contents. No magic involved.

Tala had always been skeptical, but it seemed she might have been wrong, again. The tell-tale signs *were* there. *It would be nice to forgo that expense...* Magesight was so often used that the inscriptions around a Mage's eyes were almost always the most often refreshed.

She was letting her mind wander, again. She focused back on the clerk, just as the woman nodded and blinked again, deactivating her magesight.

"Yes, you will do nicely, Mage. Indications suggest an intact keystone." She smiled widely. "You must have had quite the run of bad luck to so completely deplete the rest of your inscriptions; I can't detect even a single ripple of non-natural magic from anything *except* your keystone."

Tala laughed, nervously. "Yeah, well. I'm alive, and here, so…" She smiled, trying to put forward confidence. *So much for being able to decide whether or not to be considered a Mage...* She hadn't considered a magesight inspection this early in the process. *More the fool, me.*

The clerk waved a hand. "I don't need the details. You are an Immaterial Guide, yes?"

"Yes..." Tala cleared her throat. "I apologize, but I didn't catch your name."

"Oh! How silly of me. You may call me Lyn Clerkson."

"Mistress Lyn, a pleasure to meet you. I'm Tala."

"Tala...?"

"No family name."

"Mistress Tala, then." Lyn smiled.

Tala extended her hand.

Lyn shook it happily. As she did so, her sleeve pulled up, and Tala was able to get a better look at the extensive spell-lines twining about Lyn's forearm, wrist, and hand. *So, a full Mage?* Or she was just more heavily inscribed than the non-Mages Tala was used to.

"Are all the clerks here Mages?"

"Oh, no. I'm one of the Senior Exchequers, here. Specifically, I'm in charge of the recruiting and handling of new recruits." She made a motion with her arms that mimed excitement. "Yay! Right? I'm glad I was here when you wandered in."

Tala blinked at Lyn several times, trying to figure out what to make of the girl. "Yeah. I suppose I'm glad, too."

"So, have you ever empowered bigger boxes?"

She blinked several times, trying to make sense of the question. "What?"

"Apologies. That's how I always think of them. I mean have you ever empowered spatial enlargement scripts? Not many Mages have, outside the Caravanners' Guild, but I figure it's good to ask."

"Oh! You mean expanding the available space within a given container?"

Lyn brightened. "Yes! Do you have experience?"

"Some, but not on any large scale." The idea had fascinated Tala enough that she'd pestered a teacher into giving her extra lessons and materials on the subject. Even so, she'd only empowered the spell-lines involved a few times.

Lyn's smile grew, genuine excitement evident in the expression. "Oh, that's just wonderful! Teaching new Mages how to twist their mind 'just so' can be a… time-consuming process."

Tala nodded in acknowledgment. "Yeah, it took me nearly a month before I was able to get past the mental blocks."

Lyn laughed, and her tone took on that of someone quoting an oft-heard refrain. "If you don't believe it's possible, it isn't."

Tala smiled in return. *I just might like working with you, Lyn.*

"But only a month? That is quite quick!" She paused, then cleared her throat. "You don't have to answer this, but I have a pet theory I'd like to test."

Tala tilted her head, curious herself. "Oh?"

"Did you have any background in physics or geometry before your first attempt?"

She laughed. "No! And having spatial distortion theory in my head definitely made those harder to tackle."

A small, knowingly contented smile tugged at Lyn's lips. "I'd thought so! It always seems that the more ignorant Mages are able to master more obscure aspects faster." She paled, her smile faltering. "I am so sorry! I didn't mean—"

Tala held up a hand, grinning. "No harm meant; no harm done. I *was* ignorant."

Lyn cleared her throat. "Even so. I apologize." She took a deep breath and let it out quickly. "Now, then. We really should get to business. Are you looking for work on your way to a particular city, work within this city, or were you hoping for a longer-term contract?"

Tala's grin slipped back to a casual smile. Her research had not been in vain. *Once I've enough to fund my own inscriptions, I can just do piecework to get between cities.* That would leave her free to do as she pleased… *Once my debts are paid off…* Her smile weakened, just slightly.

"Longer term is better paid, and we do offer signing bonuses for certain contracts, and an Immaterial Guide with spatial distortion experience is definitely in that wagon!" After a brief pause, she added, "At least for certain contract lengths."

"What is the shortest contract with a signing bonus?"

"Hmmm… Let me see." She pulled out a stone slate and began manipulating the text on the surface, seemingly flipping through magically stored pages. "It looks like, for your quadrant, we can offer a contract of one year or ten trips, whichever is completed sooner. You are obligated to take a minimum of one trip every other month, including within a week of first signing."

"And the rate?"

"Four ounces per trip, and the signing bonus is four ounces."

Tala deflated. One ounce of silver would buy a good meal, but not much more than that. That was lower than an average worker's day wage, and she doubted the trips only took a day. *How do people survive on so little?* "How often could I take trips? Is there a minimum waiting time?"

Lyn blinked, seemingly confused at Tala's dour tone. "No… but even the shortest trips take nearly a week, and most Mages like to have time to spend their earnings in whichever city they arrive in. That, on top of getting re-inscribed and allowing any change to the scribings to set… I've known very few to make a trip every month." She wobbled her head slightly, seeming to hedge. "Well, excepting those who do 'out and back' work. Those tend to do two trip blocks, then take longer breaks in between."

"Time to spend..." She was frowning.

Lyn opened her mouth in an understanding 'Oh!' "Apologies, again, Mistress Tala. Four ounces *gold.*"

Tala found herself frozen in surprise. *Four ounces... gold.* An ounce of gold was a hundred times as valuable as one of silver. *Yeah, a month to relax after each trip would be quite nice.* That, and her debt to the academy, on top of her parents' debt... *Now, also mine...* was 487 ounces gold, twenty ounces silver. *One hundred twenty-two trips. Ten years.* She'd been expecting the debt to follow her for her entire life unless she found alternate means of paying it off. *I can make ten years work.* Though, she wasn't accounting for expenses.

Lyn quirked a questioning smile. "You haven't done much contract work, have you? You don't seem to have a good idea of your value."

"Clearly not." No one had been willing to give her solid data.

"Well, that is our fault. If we advertised better, maybe we'd have gotten you in here sooner!" Her smile firmed up. "And I can assure you, with as well-traveled as you'll be after even a short contract, we wouldn't dream of underpaying you. We'd never hold onto Mages if we tried that." She gave a little chuckle.

Tala nodded distractedly, not really hearing Lyn's continued dialogue. "Maybe... Is there a slightly longer contract available? Could I negotiate better rates for two years or twenty trips? A higher signing bonus? Oh! And after the contracted trips, what is the piece job rate, going one way?"

"All great questions. If you aren't on a contract, and we have a caravan in need of a Mage of your type, your rate would be three-and-a-half ounces gold, though that can vary slightly from trip to trip. For a three-year, twenty-trip contract, the best I can offer is a trip rate of four-and-a-half ounces, with a one-trip-value signing bonus."

Ninety-four-and-a-half ounces gold... Tala was speechless. Even with her inscriptions, that should cover over a sixth of her debt, with some to spare. She *thought* she had a good guess of how much her spell-lines would cost. She hesitated.

Lyn's smile grew. "It won't increase the signing bonus beyond four-and-a-half ounces, but if you sign a five-year or thirty-trip contract, I can give you five ounces per trip. You won't be as free to choose your destinations, as those rates are a bit too much except on more lucrative runs."

"What about frequency?"

"There are *many* of those leaving every week, but they tend to be a bit longer, closer to two weeks on average." She hesitated. "I should be clear, even at the lower rates, the trips will range from one to four weeks. You could always choose the shorter trips, but that is frowned upon—as you can imagine. We try to give as much freedom as possible, but we don't like to see that abused."

Tala nodded. *Five years.* She hesitated. *No, thirty trips. Each around two weeks...* She could fulfill her contract in less than half the prescribed time. *Just about thirty percent of my debt gone in a year and a half, in one contract? That's a great start, Tala.* She grinned. "I'm interested in a thirty-trip contract, but let's talk terms. What all is provided on the trips? Do I need to bring my own supplies, shelter, gear? What expenses should I expect to bear, and what ancillary support will the guild be providing?"

Lyn's smile turned slightly predatory. "Let's see what we can work out."

* * *

Nearly two hours later, Lyn and Tala sat across from each other in comfortable chairs, sequestered in a back room of the Caravanner's headquarters.

Empty mugs of tea stood on the table between them, alongside a contract.

"Here." Lyn turned the scripted stone tablet around, passing it back to Tala. "I think this represents everything we've agreed to."

The text was not written on the stone, though it seemed to be. The words were manifest there from the contract archive, and once Tala willingly put a drop of her blood to the slate, with the intent to confirm the agreement, it would be logged as officially binding. Lyn had already placed her own blood in one corner, using a small, sharp protrusion on the tablet, in place for that purpose.

Tala scanned the document quickly. It outlined a statement of her own qualifications; those that were verified within the system, such as her certification as a Mage, were highlighted, while those based on her word were set apart. The wording, and the magic in the contract, would annul any obligation from the Caravanner's Guild if she had been false. Indeed, there were steep penalties if that were to be the case. Thankfully, she'd avoided any falsehoods.

Beyond her own merit, the agreed-to payments were outlined, along with other restrictions and benefits.

She was required to have a certain level of preparedness before accepting an assignment, as well as to modify her preparations to meet any specific requirements for the given trip. She would additionally be granted food for the duration of any voyage. She had forgone the standard offerings of an attached servant, to manage the day-to-day responsibilities, and a private wagon for her personal residence while outside city walls.

Millennial Mage 1 - Mageling

Her magics, once she was reinscribed, were mostly bent towards survival, so safety shouldn't be a concern. As to the convenience of it, she could bear a little discomfort to pay off her debt more quickly.

That in mind, she'd negotiated for greater pay in exchange for less convenience and a bit more danger.

Thus, the agreed to per-trip payment, as well as her advance, had been raised to five-and-a-half ounces gold, and she would not be limited to the high-value or longer missions. Apparently, most Mages expected a luxuriously appointed carriage and highly skilled servant, and Tala had gotten Lyn to admit that those items easily cost the guild upwards of one-and-a-half ounces gold per trip. Thus, Tala was offering them a bargain.

Everything on the contract was, indeed, as they'd agreed, and it was written with plain, easy-to-understand language, as Common Law demanded.

Tala pricked her finger on the sharp nub, and it retracted immediately after.

With an effort of will, she allowed her gate to open, and magic flickered through her body, infusing her blood just as she touched the cool stone. The drop of blood that had been building on her finger vanished into the stone, and the tablet turned a pleasant, emerald green, denoting full confirmation.

Without an inscription to direct and release its power, the magic still flowing through her left Tala with a nervous energy. She wanted to get up and run. Her keystone didn't help, as it wasn't meant to use up excess power.

Lyn had been watching the contract, and when she noted the change to green, she smiled. "Your consent, as well as your words, have been accepted." She looked up at Tala. "Welcome!" Her smile spread with genuine enthusiasm. "I'm so glad that you came to us." She tilted her head, seeming to consider for a moment. "Do you have an inscriber in the city, yet?"

Tala thought about Phoen's friend, but she didn't really know them well, so she shook her head. "No."

Lyn's smile seemed to settle into one of satisfaction. "I figured not. Now, no self-respecting inscriber would dare get handsy with a Mage of *our* guild, but I know of one who's better than average."

Tala... hadn't thought of the issue of finding an inscriber herself. She nodded gratefully. "Thank you. Are they your inscriber?"

"She is, yes." Lyn nodded. "Though it's one of her apprentices that does the work on me, directly. She'll have closed up for the evening, but I know where she likes to grab dinner. We can join her if you'd like, and if you two get on, you can have your spell-lines inscribed tomorrow."

Tala's eyes flicked to Lyn's hair. Though it was held up in a utilitarian style, it was clearly quite long. Even so, Tala thought she saw hints of spell-lines among the roots, confirming her suspicion that something was different about this city's inscribers. A smile tugged at her lips. "That sounds like a great plan." She hesitated, her smile faltering, but after a moment's indecision, she decided to push forward. "When would I get my advance?"

Lyn's smile shifted, again, becoming a knowing smirk. "We can grab it for you on the way out. I'm off anyways."

"Oh! I held you up?"

Lyn waved away the concern. "Not really. I always have to finish up my work, regardless of the time. Today? Getting this contract worked out was the priority." She stood, smoothing out her simple dress.

For the most part, Mages' robes had quick-release ties so that the Mage could shed the garment with speed. Most Mages expressed their power from many locations, so cloth coverings added difficulty and expense when the spells breached the cloth to escape.

There was also the danger, in more restrictive clothing, that a garment could pull the skin in an unexpected manner, altering a Mage's spell-lines in unexpected or dangerous ways. The net result was that most Mages wore as little as they could manage while casting and covered themselves with Mage's robes in between such workings.

Tala… well, she ascribed to a different philosophy of casting. She ensured that the manifestations of all outward expressions of power originated from her hands. It was a weakness if she were ever truly hampered, but she'd seen that as an acceptable tradeoff.

Lyn's own choice of a simple dress spoke volumes about her life, as well as her work as a Mage. She did not expect, or have need, for quick, complicated castings, nor did she seem to have any concern about having to remain mobile. In short, she led a safe life.

"Tala?"

"Hmm?"

Lyn was standing, half turned away, seeming to be waiting. "Are you coming?"

"Oh!" Tala stood in a rush. She'd allowed her mind to wander, again. "Yes. Let's go."

Tala followed as Lyn led her through the now mostly empty main hall of the guild. They came to a small counter, tucked into a back corner, where an unlined clerk asked Tala for a drop of blood.

The clerk confirmed her contract and that money was owed. He frowned when he saw the amount, and Lyn was forced to take him aside for a quick, quiet conversation. Apparently, no one had received a signing bonus as high as Tala's during his time working this station.

Finally, he was satisfied, and he presented Tala with a small pouch of coins. She counted it, at his prompting, and when she had verified the amount, he marked her as having been paid. That complete, he hesitated. "I know it isn't my place, but may I offer a word of advice?"

Tala had already begun to turn away but hesitated at his question. "Umm... sure? I'm happy to learn, where I can." As she responded, she'd turned back towards the middle-aged man.

"Always count your pay. No one *should* ever try to short you, but mistakes happen, and after you confirm receipt, even the best-intentioned pay clerks can't give you more."

She contemplated that for a long moment, then nodded. "I see."

He quirked a smile. "If anyone gives you grief for counting, it is reasonable for you to remind them that you are giving your word that you received the full amount. The only honorable thing for you to do is check before so swearing."

She smiled in turn. "Clever. I'll remember that. Thank you."

He gave a small bow. "Welcome to the guild, Mistress Tala."

She gave a nod in return. "Thank you." She hesitated. "I'm sorry, I didn't catch your name."

He blinked at her a few times, then looked down at his tunic.

Tala followed his gaze, then flushed. A small wooden placard was affixed on the left side of his tunic's chest, his name clearly written out in white lettering.

He cleared his throat. "You can call me Gram."

"Gram... A pleasure to meet you."

He quirked another smile. "And you, Mistress Tala."

Lyn let out a small laugh, leading Tala away, across the hall, and out the doors.

Chapter: 3
Dinner

The sun was setting as Tala and Lyn walked the city streets towards food and introductions.

Tala had the comforting weight of money in a pouch at her belt, while still retaining the hesitancy of the recently destitute. This money would have to provide for her until her first trip, as well as outfit her for that venture, and she still had no idea exactly what that entailed.

Thankfully, Lyn was leading them purposefully towards their goal, so Tala wasn't delayed or sidetracked by her many musings. *I really do need to focus on my surroundings more...* In school, her introspections had kept her away from too much notice and allowed her to skirt the attention of many who might otherwise have called upon her or used conflict with her to elevate their own positions. Out in the real world? It was likely to get her killed.

As if to highlight the very lack of awareness she was contemplating, Tala was suddenly led from the busy, if relatively quiet, main streets into a crowded courtyard, filled with people, tables, and portable kitchens.

Mature trees stood, pleasingly distributed throughout the space. She noticed several braziers as well, though they were unlit since it was a warmer autumn evening. Ceramic plates, magically altered to release gathered sunlight in an even glow, provided a comfortable, if not bright, illumination.

Millennial Mage 1 - Mageling

There were people at every table, but no table was truly full. While the seating was biased towards the center of the space, the food carts—for that was what the cart-bound kitchens were—encircled the lot, doing brisk business.

Many passersby ducked into the area to buy food before continuing on their way, but some stayed, grabbing a seat as others vacated it, creating a slowly rotating, constant group of people.

It reminded Tala of the academy's dining hall—if the people had been excited to be there and the food had ever smelled this *good*.

She inhaled deeply, instantly imprisoned by the rapture of succulent smells.

She couldn't distinguish the smell of any one dish, or even one stall, among the milieu, but the combination was a joy and a half.

Lyn was staring at her again. "Are you okay? You look like a starving dog presented with a steak."

Tala grinned. "It has been *far* too long since I've had a meal that smelled this good."

Lyn quirked an eyebrow. "You still haven't."

Tala's grin broadened. "What do you recommend?"

They made their way over to a particularly overburdened cart, lorded over by a large, but not truly rotund, woman. "Mistress Lyn! Good to see you!" The woman came around to the front of her cart to enfold the much-smaller Lyn. "And who is this waif you bring to my kitchen?"

Her reply came out muffled. "This is Mistress Tala. She's new to the city." As Lyn was released, she turned towards Tala. "Mistress Tala, this is Gretel."

Tala began to bow. "It is a pleasure to meet you, Gret—" But she was cut off as Gretel scooped her up in an overpowering embrace.

"Welcome, child." She turned and picked up a meat pie, thrusting it at Tala.

Tala took it, marveling at how thick and sturdy the crust felt. Not a drop of filling was evident on the outside as she took the proffered food. "Oh! Ah… What do I owe you for this?"

Gretel laughed. "Girl, that one's on me. If you aren't compelled to buy more after you eat it, well, that's my fault for making them too resistible." She winked.

Tala smiled and took a bite.

There were no words for the culinary delight, which the pie encompassed. It was a light cream, vegetable, and poultry mixture, with *exactly* the right blend and ratio of spices.

Gretel served several other customers while Tala devoured her own acquisition.

When she was, once again, up in the queue, Tala sang her praises of the offering.

"I like this one, Mistress Lyn. Will she be about for long?"

"I hope she will be, at least every so often."

Tala nodded her assent. "I can promise I'll be back. How much for another?"

"Five copper."

Five ounces copper. *So cheap? How?* "How? These are amazing!"

Gretel smiled in response. "My customers usually get five or six." She gestured to the other carts in the area. "We try to make our portions small so that our patrons can enjoy a large variety." She leaned in close as if sharing a secret. "But, tell you the truth, most who try mine just fill up right here." She straightened and winked again.

"Mistress Lyn, can I buy you a few?"

"Oh! Sure? That really isn't necessary, Mistress Tala."

Millennial Mage 1 - Mageling

She waved away the objection. "Nonsense. I'll take ten." She dug around in her money pouch before pulling out a one ounce silver coin. "Can you make change?"

"Easily." Gretel took the silver, verifying the weight, and returned four much smaller silver coins, a tenth of an ounce each, and ten one ounce coppers. "So, you can easily try some of the other stalls if you'd like. I can't hog all the good customers, now can I?" She winked yet again.

After tucking the coins away, Tala gave a slight bow. "Thank you."

Gretel handed over the ten small pies on a wooden platter. "Mistress Lyn knows what to do with that when you're done. I look forward to seeing you again, girl!"

Tala gave a wave as she followed Lyn towards one side of the courtyard. As they approached, Tala was able to guess where they were heading.

One table was a bit emptier than the others. A striking woman sat on one short side of the long, rectangular table.

Tala could not tell her age, or much else about her, because most of her features were obscured by the most all-encompassing, intricate set of spell-lines Tala had ever beheld. The woman, herself, was clothed as if she were expecting to cast, meaning with as little covered as possible. In all fairness, however, the intricacy of her inscriptions, and their pervasive nature, left the woman looking as if she wore a skintight outfit of woven silver, copper, and gold.

It was beautiful.

They approached, and Tala set their tray down in front of a couple of empty seats beside the woman. The inscriber lifted her gaze from her own platter of simple foods to regard Lyn and Tala, and Tala felt the telltale tingle of magic. Her eyes showed her minute ripples of power across the woman's face, indicating that she'd activated her magesight.

"Mistress Holly, this is Mistress Tala." Lyn gestured to the seated woman. "Mistress Tala, Mistress Holly."

Tala bowed slightly. "A pleasure to meet you."

"You're cast quite dry, aren't you?"

Tala hesitated, then quirked a smile. "I suppose I am."

Holly's head tilted to an inquisitive angle. "No? Interesting. If casting didn't strip you of your ancillary lines, what did?" She leaned closer, even as Tala sat. "You *must* tell me."

Tala cleared her throat. "I… um…" She swallowed and glanced to Lyn. "I was teleported here."

Lyn's eyes widened, slightly, but she didn't comment.

"Teleported. That seems to be true. But why would you only have your keystone replaced…?" Holly's eyes snapped back to Tala's own. "You didn't, did you?"

"No?"

"Be decisive. I can't see the truth of your words if you have no confidence."

"No. I did not have my keystone replaced. It was maintained through transport."

Holly pushed herself backward, just a bit, nodding happily. "I knew it. I knew it. There is an… ethereal aspect to your keystone, as if another's power was forced through it. Why it didn't break your gate I've no idea, but I suppose by Hethron's third law…" Her mutterings slowly faded below Tala's ability to hear them, and she turned to Lyn.

"Is she… always like this?"

"Hmmm? Oh, yes. She's quite brilliant, and so most of her conversations are with herself." Lyn shrugged. "But she's the best, and I quite like you."

Holly's eyes narrowed. "Still not giving you a discount."

Lyn rolled her eyes. "Let's eat. I'm *starving*."

Millennial Mage 1 - Mageling

Thus, as night truly fell upon the city, Tala sat with new acquaintances, surrounded by the sounds of revelry and the hum of conversation.

This just might be possible. I might just be able to work free of this burden.

* * *

Tala licked her fingers clean of her last meat pie and leaned back, comfortably stuffed.

Holly finished the last of her own food, savoring a fruit tart, which had been covered with fluffed cream.

"Now. Give me some blood."

Tala's lazy comfort flashed away in an instant. "What."

Holly held out her hand, palm down, revealing a circle of bare skin, surrounded by vaguely familiar silver scripts. "Your blood, Mage. I need it to access your scripting records."

Tala looked to Lyn, but the woman just shrugged. "It's how she operates. My understanding is that it allows her to directly overlay the schema on her client within her vision, instead of having to do comparisons."

Tala found herself nodding. "That does sound easier." She glanced at the hand, still extended her way. "If a bit… gross."

Holly rolled her eyes. "Well? Mistress Lyn did bring you here for this, right? Let's see what we have to work with."

Reluctantly, Tala pricked her own finger, willing a spark of power into the blood just as she pressed a drop down upon the empty circle of Holly's flesh.

She had a moment of feeling oddly disjointed, but it passed as quickly as it had come. *Her skin is much tougher to the touch than I'd have guessed.*

As the blood came into the circle, silver scripts all over Holly's body flickered to life, their power then flowing into lines of copper or gold. "I see." The older woman stood. "Come, now. Stand up. Let me get a good look."

Feeling incredibly self-conscious, and aware that they were in a highly public place, Tala stood.

Holly began moving her about, looking at various parts of her like an alchemist deciding if an herb was worth processing. Holly made an appreciative sound as she inspected Tala's hands but scoffed as she looked elsewhere.

Finally, Holly poked her in the side of her left breast, just softly enough to avoid leaving a bruise. "Whoever designed these was a gifted idiot." She snorted a laugh as Tala rubbed the side of her chest discreetly. "And he was likely in love with you."

Tala froze. "What?"

Holly waved away the question but then seemed to answer it anyway. "Much of this is incredibly clever and well-structured; the majority of your surface inscription is interlinking hexagons of protection, each of three parts: first, a strengthening of the inter- and intra-cellular bonds, silver to sense for stress on those bonds with copper to be activated to counter the stress; second, inscription to reform bonds if they are broken despite the aforementioned work, again with silver and copper acting in concert; and finally, a mild enhancement of signal speed through your nervous system, when your heart rate rises, again silver to copper." She shook her head. "Such a stupid trigger. That should be passively on, all the time, with gold so that it lasts longer. That way would actually take less material on average, and we could increase the effect… though you'd have to get used to it…"

Tala blinked. "But the other two features?"

Millennial Mage 1 - Mageling

"Hmmm? Oh, those are quite well executed, but you've no obvious defense against magic."

Tala glanced away. "I've found a different method for handling that."

"Care to share?"

"Not at the moment." She looked down. Something shifted subtly in the air around Holly, and Tala felt an odd, subtle pressure from the woman's presence.

"Fine, fine." She looked back down at Tala, and the pressure faded. "The poor boy seems to have been afraid to take your feminine curves into account. It is almost like he built it around a man's body, roughly your size, and slapped it onto your skin." She shook her head, again, before poking the side of Tala's breast once more. "So much unused surface area! And, in this case, unprotected." She scowled. "He likely didn't want to be seen as focusing on your chest." She glanced down. "Or your hips, so he ignored them." Another huff escaped her. "All it did was highlight his attention all the more."

Tala was quite flushed with embarrassment but decided to press on. "And the rest?"

"Hmmm? Oh, no human is a flat plane, so he had to account for curves in the hexagonal connections, and he did quite well in modifying the scripts for rotational orientations."

Tala blinked, trying to follow. She only had the most basic understanding of inscription theory.

"And... I'm losing you." Holly sighed. "He did a good job." She glanced at Tala's head, clearly focusing on something only she could see. "Good use of standard mental enhancements, here, but again with the heartbeat trigger." She sighed, once more. "His true genius came in the implementation of your hands!" She grasped Tala's hands. "I don't know why you only want your expressions to originate here, but I'm not here to judge."

Tala did *not* comment on the obvious contradiction.

Holly looked at Tala's right hand, obviously seeing inscriptions where there was only blank skin. "You focus on gravity manipulation for attack and submission but not area of effects!" She held the hand out towards Lyn for a moment before the latter's raised eyebrow seemed to remind Holly that there was nothing there for anyone else to see. "Oh, right." She looked to Tala. "Can you actually control this?"

"Yes? What do you mean?"

"The structure of these spell-lines is *incredibly* dependent on your ability to attenuate your focus. You must be a savant, incredibly lucky, or ridiculously stubborn."

"How would luck factor it?"

"To not have killed yourself with these or been killed as you tried to use them."

Tala cleared her throat. "Well, it did take quite a while to get them to work as I wanted…"

"So, stubborn, then. How many targets have you been able to indicate?"

She hesitated, not wanting to admit the truth. *Well, if I'm not willing to tell her the truth, I probably shouldn't let her work on my inscriptions…* "Three or four, at a practice range, but I have difficulty getting more than one while under pressure."

Holly nodded as if satisfied. "That makes sense. Especially with the odd methods of your mental enhancements. Imagine throwing a Mage's thinking to the wind as soon as they need to be at their most disciplined." She shook her head.

Tala frowned. "Wait, faster thinking made it harder?"

"*Different* thinking made it harder. Faster connection speed doesn't speed up your mind so much as reduce the time between thoughts. That will change *how* you think as much as how fast."

Tala... actually understood that. "So, you can improve on this?"

Holly snorted. "Can a fish swim?"

I suppose that's a yes...

But Holly had already returned her attention to Tala's hands. "Despite the... flaws, it's genius how he got around the difficulties of..."

Tala stopped listening. She knew how her magic worked and that it had been a pain to learn how to use the unusual style of spell-craft, but she had never regretted the choice. Her magic was precise and efficient. She was a scalpel next to the headsman's axe of most gravity manipulators, and she sipped metals.

Tala's mind returned to Holly when the woman snapped her fingers in front of Tala's nose. "You aren't listening at all, are you?"

Tala cleared her throat. "Well, I do know what my scriptings do." She sat back down at the table, as Holly didn't seem to need to inspect her directly anymore.

Holly sighed. "We have a lot to discuss, and there is much we can improve. Your designer only thought of your inscriptions as multilayered, without truly embracing the potential of three-dimensional workings. I see other layers for muscle and bone spell-lines, and that shows a depth of thinking." Holly smiled briefly at her own pun. "But they could, and should, be intertwined, unified."

"I've... I've never actually been able to test out those other layers." She glanced to Lyn, who was staring at her with shocked fascination. Deeper inscriptions weren't rare, per se, but they were unpopular because they could be *very* painful, and if they weren't done perfectly, they led to magic poisoning at a much faster pace than even the most frivolous Material Creator would experience. "I hadn't decided to commit to using them, yet."

Holly waved the objection aside. "Don't be foolish, of course you'd never get these as they are. You'd be dead in a week."

Tala hesitated. *They aren't that crude... Are they?*

"No, no. I'll get this worked up for you in just a day or so." There was a strange light in Holly's eyes.

Tala leaned back, suddenly wary. "Ummm… What will this cost me?"

"Hmm?" Holly was already moving her fingers through the air as if manipulating something Tala couldn't see. "Oh, my alterations to your pattern won't be cheap, but they will be worth it. The spell-lines themselves should only cost four or five ounces gold, but with the modifications, I wouldn't be surprised if you only need refreshing for your passive scripts every year or so, but I'll know more after I finish the changes." She glanced to Tala's hands. "Though, of course, your own use of the active abilities will force more regular inscription of the lines around the functions for your hands."

Tala blanched. *Five ounces gold.* Just for the inscriptions? How much would this crazy person charge for the schematic? "I only have five-and-a-half ounces of gold for inscriptions and to outfit myself for my first job." She glanced at the empty wooden platter. "Well, five-and-a-half ounces, less fifty ounces copper."

Holly paused, glancing to Lyn. "What rate will she get?"

Lyn cleared her throat. "That is confidential."

Holly waved a frustrated hand. "Fine, fine." She turned back to Tala. "I'll get you the basics for your first two jobs if you swear to come straight back here and not let another inscriber muck up my work. I'll take a day to finalize the schema, and then three days to do the actual inking…" She began muttering to herself again, but Tala had, once again, hit a mental block.

Three days *of inscription work?* She supposed if it were really only required every year or so, that would total less than she had been expecting. It was the same with the cost of the work, itself, but it was front-loaded, and she did not have enough money as it was. She cleared her throat, drawing Holly's attention back. "I will need at least half an ounce of gold for another necessity."

Holly's eyes narrowed. "More secrets, eh?" She drummed her fingers on the table as she finally sat down once more. "Or, perhaps, the same secret." She looked into Tala's eyes, but Tala glanced away. "Fine. Five ounces gold, with a promise of prompt return, and"—she glanced to Lyn, then back to Tala—"eight ounces gold upon your return. Fair? I'll finalize your inscriptions, then."

After two trips, Tala should have an additional eleven ounces gold, before any expenses, so she *should* be able to afford it, but… She looked to Lyn.

The other woman sighed and shrugged. "She's the best, honestly. Most of our Mages won't let anyone else work on them if they can help it." After a moment's hesitation, she added, "Well, in truth, most are satisfied with her apprentices."

Holly scoffed. "Of course they are. Most just want to throw fireballs or some other simple nonsense." She gestured to Tala. "This creature wishes to do true magic." She grinned. "You will play a golden harp beside their hide drums!"

A harp is easily drowned by the sound of drums… Tala opened her mouth to reply, but Holly cut her off.

"A long bow beside a wooden club, then, if instruments aren't well known to you."

Tala tried to object again, as the instruments in question were so basic the assumed lack of knowledge on her part could only be insulting, but Holly overrode her, again.

"But as I was saying, you will need at least three days to adjust to even the first stage of enhanced signal speed, both in your own head and in your nervous system as a whole." She scratched an itch behind her left ear. "I bet you'll have at least three cardiac arrests before your brain and heart work out a new rhythm. Expect *lots* of hiccups, too."

Tala's face hardened. "Excuse me."

"What did you expect? I'd leave your involuntary mental functions alone? That would be dangerous! Imagine enhancing only a portion of your mind. You'd be lucky not to fry within your own skull."

"That is not what I—"

"And moving! I can't wait to see you try to walk."—She patted Tala's arm. — "You're young, though, that part should acclimate in a matter of minutes."

"Hold on a mo—"

"Yes, this will be a work of art, my next masterpiece will reside on the canvas of your power. Lesser Mages will not be able to comprehend your majesty when I'm done." She stood, in a rush, turning and striding away.

"Wait a minute!"

Holly ignored her but called over her shoulder. "Mistress Lyn, you're her handler, right? Book her two jobs, leaving in a week, and returning as soon thereafter as possible. Make them safe, or I'll never get my money. Bring her by the shop tomorrow evening."

Lyn called a vague sound of affirmation.

Tala spun on the woman. "What do you mean, okay? I didn't agree to anything!"

Lyn shrugged. "You won't get a better deal, and honestly, I'd be surprised if any other inscriber would take you now that Holly is interested."

Tala glowered. "You've tricked me."

"Into the best inscriptions this side of heaven? Yes, yes, I did." The clerk looked almost smug.

"She's going to kill me! You heard her."

"She won't leave you dead. It's not hard to restart a heart if it actually goes that far."

Tala growled. "I don't like being backed into things."

"This is for your own good."

"You didn't understand any more of what she said than I did."

"I didn't need to. She has never failed to improve the magic of the Mages she works on. And I figured that she would be fascinated by your… unusualness."

Tala's eyes narrowed. "You said she was better than average." A dawning sense of understanding was growing within her. "You *knew* that she'd be like this."

Lyn quirked a smile. "And you knew that a fresh graduate shouldn't really be getting a Mage's rates." She winked. "I've got to ensure we get your true worth from you, or I'll look bad."

Tala's mouth dropped open. "You… knew?"

"Suspected. You know, one of the reasons a mageling is paid less is that their inscriptions, and their use of them, aren't fully worked out yet." She shrugged. "Mistress Holly will take care of that." Lyn smiled, again, patting Tala on the shoulder. "I've just helped you become who you wanted me to believe you were."

Tala groaned and put her head into her hands. "I suppose I deserved that."

Lyn's voice had just a hint of sympathy in it. "It won't be so bad, Mistress Tala. Come on. Let me buy dessert. You can stay at my place tonight."

Tala looked up hopefully. "Are you sure?"

"Absolutely. You've a busy week ahead."

Reluctantly, Tala followed the other woman to a nearby food cart to select a consolation.

Chapter: 4
A Simple Home

Tala and Lyn walked together through the nighttime, city streets.

Regularly spaced lights made it easy to see, and the lit windows in the residences they passed assured Tala that it wasn't too late.

I'm going to die tomorrow night.

She'd been assured many, many times, that if she did die, it wouldn't stick, but that was hardly a comfort.

The dessert, compliments of Lyn's own coin pouch, had been fantastic, but Tala hadn't been able to fully enjoy it.

She didn't really take in the spectacular examples of a dozen types of architecture that they passed as they wound through the meandering streets.

They circumnavigated construction zones where the owner, or the needs of the same, had changed, and a home was being altered or rebuilt entirely.

They passed parks and shuttered businesses, vacant for the evening.

To her distracted mind, it reminded her of home, her life with her parents, and the time before the academy.

Her father had been an herbalist or an alchemist—they were variations on the same idea. *I suppose he still is.*

He'd helped treat minor injuries, those either beneath the notice of magical healing, or those that would be too expensive to heal with magic, especially those that would pass with time if some discomfort.

Millennial Mage 1 - Mageling

As a result, Tala had been raised around the manufacture of salves, teas, simple splints, and other varied treatments. It had been a happy childhood, and she'd thought that such would be her life, her shop, when she grew up.

She'd been too young to recognize her father's addictions.

Later, looking back on it, she'd been able to piece together the sequence of events: a growing pain in his joints had led him to increasingly strong remedies. A desire to use his own methods had kept him from seeking magical assistance. The painkillers had moved into true opiates, and the cost of those had created a compulsive need for money, and thus, gambling.

To his credit, her father had finally realized the disaster he was creating, put aside his pride, and gotten magical healing. Unfortunately, the physical and mental reconstructions required had been expensive. Hence the family debts.

The only way to pay off the debt had been to sell a promising student into the career of Mage, as such were *always* of value to humanity, and the Mage's guild often paid simply to have a child choose that profession. It was also common practice for a family's debts to be moved to a promising up-and-coming member. Supposedly, it added motivation. It also protected the family if one member turned out to be a failure. Things seemed to sort themselves out from there.

And so, as the eldest, at the confused age of twelve, Tala had been given into the indenture of strangers, never to see her parents again.

Make no mistake, they'd sent letters, but she'd never written back. Teleportation was expensive, so visits were out. Likely, they'd assumed she would choose to return to her home city when her training was complete.

She hadn't.

And now, nearly eight years later, I'm going to die without ever seeing them again. She didn't know how she felt about that, but something in her rebelled at the thought, though she couldn't have said if it was at that of never seeing her family again or that of dying.

Lyn, again, pulled Tala out of her musings with a simple sentence. "We're here."

Tala looked up to see a small home, across the street from a large park.

"It isn't much, but I've a spare room you can use for the next few days." Lyn glanced her way. "I won't charge you, not for just one night."

Tala snorted. "I paid in pies."

Lyn laughed. "I don't have enough house to warrant such a payment. Let's call it reciprocal kindness and leave it there."

"Says the woman who threw me to the wolves."

Lyn used a brass key to unlock her front door, pushing it open. "Your soul-deep rage will pass, and this will be nothing but a quirky story of how we first met."

Tala followed her inside, closing the solid wooden door behind her. "If you write that on my tombstone, I'll haunt you."

"You're a bit dramatic, aren't you?" Lyn glanced over her shoulder before snapping her fingers, causing lights to flare around the entry hall. "Shoes off. This isn't the wilds."

Tala cleared her throat and glanced down.

Lyn followed the gesture and paused, staring at Tala's bare feet. "Oh... Not sure how I missed that." She glanced up. "You do take your magery seriously, don't you." Lyn's own feet were clad in simple, if sturdy, slippers, which she casually removed and tucked to one side.

"So... do you have a basin and some water? If you keep shoes out of your house, I don't want to muck it up."

Millennial Mage 1 - Mageling

Lyn gestured to a door off to their right. "Washroom's there. I'll be in the sitting room when you're done." She gestured again, but this time to the arch directly opposite the main door.

Tala nodded her thanks and went into the washroom. It was simple but well cared for. Running water and citywide sewage systems weren't new to Tala. No one lived outside of cities, so there really wasn't a possibility of being 'uncivilized.'

She carefully washed the dust from her feet with cool water, cleaned her hands with the aid of a bar of scented lye soap, and dried both feet and hands on a cloth hanging on the wall for the purpose.

She'd heard of running hot water, but that was a luxury that few had, and one that she'd never experienced, even at the academy. *Would have been nice, though.* Apparently, someone had decided that hauling water and chopping wood built character. *I'm up to my eyeballs in character if that's true.*

Thankfully, the cool water and well-made soap were surprisingly refreshing, even on her still-sensitive skin. *And I'll be signing up for much more of that...* Though, the less frequent inscriptions would mean that she wouldn't have to scrub off her outer skin so often. *Or, I could find a different solution to magical defenses...*

Her defense was so effective, though, it made any thoughts of seeking other means seem almost laughable. *I'll have to sort that out before I depart.* Iron dust, bee's wax, and a few other odds and ends. *Along with an herbalist's tools to properly combine them...*

She walked out, into the sitting room, and hesitated. There were three comfortable-looking reading chairs, a bookshelf, and a couple of rugs on the floor, but that was it. The walls were almost entirely bare, and Lyn was already reading in the central chair.

The place had a lived-in feel, but it didn't feel like a home.

Tala frowned.

Lyn glanced up. "Ready to grab some sleep?"

"I suppose. Is this your house?"

"Yes? Why?"

"The walls are bare. It just seems…"

"Like I don't care much?" Lyn smiled. "Somewhat accurate. I'm rarely here, to be honest. I don't use the kitchen, and when I get back here at night, I sleep." She shrugged. "Or I read a bit. I'm not really a big one for guests."

"…You have three chairs…"

Lyn grinned. "And each is comfortable in a different position. I don't like to be constrained."

"So… are you sure I'm not intruding?"

"Absolutely, come on." She set her book aside and led Tala to a back room.

There was a bed, just bigger than Tala thought necessary for one person. Besides the bed, a set of drawers were the only furnishings.

"It's very little, but it's free!" Lyn grinned.

"Thank you, Mistress Lyn."

"Glad to have a place to offer." She looked around, seeming almost awkward for a moment. "Umm… Need anything else?"

"I should be fine. Thank you. I'll go shopping for some necessities tomorrow while you're at work."

"Sounds reasonable. Don't make any plans after tomorrow, though. I imagine Mistress Holly's got you booked solid."

Tala grunted. "Yay."

"I'll get your jobs booked, too." She hesitated. "Just so you know, Mages normally do their own bookings or pay a service fee to the guild if we do it for them." She held up her hands, forestalling Tala. "But! But I'm happy to do it this time and walk you through it the next couple times. Your master would have taught you the ropes if you'd been hired as a mageling, so the least I can do is fill that role." She smiled. "At least in part. You've chosen a bit of a hard road. A master can help a new graduate in a thousand little ways that I just can't." Her smile turned a bit sad, but she continued. "I will do what I can, though. And I'll get you some documents on the dimensional manipulation spell-forms you'll be empowering as well. No reason to set you up for failure."

On that happy note, Lyn turned and left.

Tala hadn't really considered her own tiredness, but when she lay down to briefly check the comfort of the bed, she fell asleep instead.

* * *

Tala woke slowly, stretching on her borrowed bed.

The temperature was just right, though she couldn't have said whether that was due to magical climate control or simply the current weather of this city. As she thought about it, she doubted Lyn would have sprung for the exorbitant expense of magical temperature manipulation.

Tala opened her eyes and stared at the simple ceiling. *Today, I have to buy the supplies for my venture, as well as my magical defense, and then put my life in the hands of a madwoman, trusting that she can repair the inevitable fractures.*

That soured her mood, just a little.

She slid from the bed, stripped, and ran through some quick, full-ranging movements. She'd missed her nightly stretches, so she lingered through her morning set. When her body was fully limbered, she worked through a set of twelve exercises, doing each for a slow count of thirty, maximizing reps during that time.

Having finished her morning activities, she picked up her borrowed clothes, opened her door, and glanced up and down the hall. *Looks clear.*

She darted across the way to what she *hoped* was an indoor bath. The academy had such, and even her parent's home had had such luxuries, but she wasn't one-hundred-percent sure that Lyn's much smaller residence would.

Blessedly, she'd been right in her guess and found a large tub with a hearth below the empty basin. Wood was carefully arranged for easy lighting, and a chest to the side revealed about three times as much fuel.

Tala filled the vessel halfway but forwent the heat. *I'll be in the wilds soon enough. No reason I shouldn't move towards cold washings now.*

Thankfully, there was a clean brush near the tub, along with several towels, and she was able to work out the night's tangles with relative ease despite the fact that she hadn't bound it up before sleep.

Her speedy self-cleaning was hastened by the cool water but slowed by refamiliarizing herself with her hair. *I'd almost forgotten how much of a pain it is to manage.*

Soon, she was out and drying herself off. That done, she pulled on her borrowed clothes and stood. *So, a brush and some changes of clothes.* She looked around, thinking to begin writing her shopping list. After a moment, she smiled wryly. *And notebooks and pencils.* She was too used to having her notebooks close at hand.

With a sigh, she strode out of the washroom and towards the sitting room. By the light coming in through various windows, it was late morning. Lyn should be at work. *I wonder when we'll meet up.*

Millennial Mage 1 - Mageling

Tala saw a note on a small table, off to one side, just before she entered the sitting room. It was written in a neat, flowing hand that immediately reminded Tala of Lyn.

> Mistress Tala,
> I'm at work, but I will be off by fifth bell. Meet me at the Guild Hall, where you found me yesterday. I've written up a simple list of items I think it wise for you to buy, given what will be provided for you. Have fun!
> -Lyn

Got the author in one. The location had also been a giveaway. Who else would have come into Lyn's house?

Tala glanced down and found a second piece of paper on the table as well, containing a list of some basic supplies. The page was held down by a pencil. *I'm borrowing that.*

A slight noise caught her attention, and she turned to see a man staring quizzically at her.

"Gah!" She gasped out, flicking her right hand forward in a practiced gesture. Palm towards her target, fingers together, pinky and ring finger tucked down.

He would be incapacitated, and she could... Her inscriptions were gone. She felt a brief pulse of power from her gate and keystone, but no magic extended from her body. She was left with a mildly uncomfortable tingling itchiness.

The man, for his part, had stepped back, raising a forearm as if to block her incoming attack, even as he, too, gasped out a surprised sound. "Wah!"

He tripped over one of the chairs but managed to turn the fall into a roll, coming back to his feet, both arms raised in a practiced guard.

They stared at each other for a long moment. Tala didn't lower her hand, though she felt rather embarrassed at the ineffectual gesture.

Take charge, Tala. "Who are you? Why are you in Mistress Lyn's house?" The man was young, probably close to her own age, and he wore clean, well-maintained clothes. They had a look about them, which made her think they might be a uniform or meant to serve that purpose.

The man hesitated. "Mistress Tala, right?"

"...Yes? You haven't answered my questions."

"Mistress Lyn sent me. Please, don't light me on fire or crush my... soul, or anything."

She hesitantly lowered her hand. "Crush your soul?"

He straightened, brushing himself off. "I'm no Mage. You people are crazy."

She quirked a smile. "So, unnamed stranger. Why are you here?"

He narrowed his eyes, but his gaze flicked towards her now-relaxed hand. "I'm Ashin. Mistress Lyn thought you could use a guide for your shopping day."

"And she sent *you*?" Tala emphasized the last to make her skepticism clear.

He straightened. "She felt that we should get to know one another."

"Oh?"

"I'm to be one of the guards on your next trip."

"Oh! You're a caravan guard?"

"Yes, Mistress."

Tala waved a hand. "None of that. Call me Tala."

"Yes, Mistress Tala."

"You're being a bit stereotypical."

"You could kill me with a gesture. Respect and courtesy are simple and reasonable safeguards on my life. Especially since most Mages desire supplication."

Millennial Mage 1 - Mageling

She grinned. "I think I'm going to like you, Ashin." She glanced down to his waist. "Where are your weapons?"

He shifted uncomfortably. "I left them outside. Most Mages don't particularly like iron. 'Iron Reflects' and all that."

Tala's grin widened. "I think you'll find I'm not like other Mages, in many ways."

He shrugged. "Does that mean that I can be armed for our venture?"

She hadn't actually decided to let him accompany her, but the more she considered it, the more sense it made. "I suppose so, yes. Do you know this city well?"

"Yes, I grew up here."

That settles it. Having a local would be infinitely more efficient than simply wandering around on her own. "Very well. Let's be off."

Ashin backed up, allowing her to pass by with a large amount of room to spare. They walked outside, him keeping a wary distance from her, even as he locked the door behind them. He strapped on a sword belt, which had been leaning against the outer wall, before picking up a round, iron-bound shield and slinging it across his back. His final piece was a padded, steel cap, which he fastened onto his head. "You're sure? All this iron doesn't put you off?"

She chuckled. "My magic doesn't have to act *through* objects as if I were throwing fire or such, so it is no hindrance to me."

Ashin paled, swallowing visibly.

Tala cleared her throat and continued in a rush, trying to placate him. "And I actually quite like the smell of iron and leather. You are fine. Really."

Ashin regained some of his coloring but didn't close the distance between them. "So... where to?"

"I will need to pick up a few things, as I am sure you are aware. I think the first should be either a satchel or a set of notebooks. Which would be closer?" Her stomach rumbled slightly. "And, we should probably grab some food. Are you hungry?"

*   *   *

An hour later, Tala was checking off the last item from Lyn's short list, which she had transposed into her own new notebook. She had both a small satchel, containing the bare necessities such as her notebooks and pencils, as well as a few other items she thought wise to have within easy reach, and a rucksack for her other belongings.

She had commissioned four sets of clothes, and the tailor had premade clothing ready to hand, so he expected the alterations to her sizing would be done by midafternoon. She'd also picked up a small host of other odds and ends to make her trips better. *I imagine I'll refine this setup after my first few outings.*

Ashin had refrained from commenting, though he had raised an eyebrow when she'd bought a heavy magnet.

He had maintained a paranoid distance from her, preferring to keep her in sight at all times. Thus, they'd had the comical interactions of him telling her where to turn, while he stubbornly stayed at least a pace behind.

All their stops considered, her stomach was now quite empty and unhappy at that fact, so Tala had asked Ashin to direct them to food.

A full morning requires a full breakfast. And it was time to deliver.

Chapter: 5
A Day of Preparation

Tala and Ashin approached the counter of a small restaurant, tucked a little back from the main thoroughfares. It was a busy place, doing brisk business with customers ranging from clerks and errand boys to what looked to be a few Mages.

Tala stepped up first when they reached the front of the line. "I'll take a sausage pasty. And whatever he wants."

"Ummm… No. I cannot possibly let you pay for me."

"Why?"

"Because you're a Mage!"

"And you're acting as my guide. Order."

"No."

"Guardsman Ashin, I caused you to miss breakfast, and it is easily time for lunch. Let me buy you food."

He looked away, seeming uncomfortable, but he didn't answer.

"Are you defying the will of a Mage?" She had a twinkle in her eye as she asked that, but either he didn't notice, or he took it for malevolence.

He swallowed visibly, then turned to the bemused clerk. "I'll have the same."

Tala paid, received their food, and picked a table off to one side.

They ate in silence.

The pasties were much larger than Gretel's meat pies had been, but Tala supposed that was because they were intended as full meals in their own right. They weren't *quite* as good, but they were different enough that she didn't begrudge the variation.

As Ashin finished his meal, wiping his crumb-covered hands off on his pants, he nodded his head towards her. "Thank you, Mistress Tala."

"You are quite welcome, Guardsman Ashin."

He frowned but didn't otherwise object. "Where else do we need to go?"

"I need to get a serviceable camp knife and also drop through a working forge."

Ashin cocked his head. "Wouldn't those be the same place?"

"Not necessarily. I don't want to go to a simple seller of knives. I need to go where metal is worked. And I don't want to go to a forge that doesn't sell such knives."

He shrugged. "Very well. Are you ready?"

She nodded, finishing her own pasty and brushing her hands together to free them of the crumbs. "Let's go."

They wound through the streets out of the inner city, through the second ring, and into the artisan circle. While most workshops had attached stores, there weren't many merchants actively hawking their wares, so it made for a much quieter, more relaxing stroll.

Over the course of the morning, Ashin had slowly narrowed the distance he kept from her while remaining out of easy reach, and that bothered her—if only just.

Did I fear Mages before I became one? It wasn't really a fair question. She'd been a child and had never had to deal with one directly.

Will everyone, aside from other Mages, treat me like this? No, servers and merchants had been nothing but polite to her.

Because, to them, a Mage is a wealthy customer… Ashin had always been *quite* certain to introduce her as a Mage, wherever they went.

Likely because I don't have any visible spell-lines at the moment. She sighed, continuing her inward contemplations.

Though there was the sound of hammer on metal coming from many directions, Ashin directed them unerringly through the sparse crowds until they came to a smithy, tucked in a side alley.

As they approach, Ashin raised his voice. "Heyho! In the smithy."

The sound of hammer on steel paused, and a response floated out. "Enter!"

Ashin led her through the broad arch, into a warm space where organized tools were affixed to almost every surface.

An older man strode out to greet them. "Ashin! Good to see you, sir. Is the new blade holding up?"

Ashin patted his sword. "Haven't had to test her, yet."

"Glad to hear that! Better a safe man, than a drawn blade. But do let me know if you have any trouble." He turned towards Tala, nodding slightly. "And who is your friend, Ashin?"

Ashin cleared his throat. "Master Aniv, this is Mage Tala."

Master Aniv hesitated for a moment. "Mage?" He glanced around. "Mistress. This is a smithy… I don't mean to be insulting, but isn't iron…"

Tala grinned. "Exactly why I'm here. I'm in need of a camp knife and your permission to fill a bag with iron dust."

"Iron… dust? I don't exactly collect—" He broke off as she pulled out the magnet she'd purchased. He frowned. "Is that an ingot?" He scratched the side of his face. "No, if you're wanting iron dust, that'll be a magnet. Right?"

"Yes."

He scratched the back of his head next. "I've no use for the dust in my shop, I suppose. I'll see what I have in stock for the knife, and you're welcome to the iron you can gather with that." He hesitated. "Iron dust, that is. I imagine that could grab some of my tools." He smiled, kindly.

Tala gave a slight bow towards him. "Thank you, Master Aniv." Without further comment, she knelt and ran the magnet across the hardpacked floor, immediately collecting iron dust. As she worked, she heard the mutterings of Ashin and Aniv's conversation but didn't bother to attempt to listen in. She was used to people finding her methods unusual.

When the magnet was well loaded, she scraped off the iron dust into one of her canvas sacks, which she'd purchased for the purpose. Within five minutes, she'd collected close to seven pounds of the stuff. If it had been solid, it would have been a bar roughly an inch square and two feet long. *That should be enough.*

Standing, she brushed her hands and knees off and placed the newly cleaned magnet back in her pack. The bag of iron dust, she kept out.

True to his word, Master Aniv had a sturdy-looking, simple camp knife set out for her.

They haggled on the price for a bit but not vehemently.

After the knife was securely on her belt, she turned to go, but Master Aniv cleared his throat. "Mistress, if I may ask…"

"Yes?"

"Has something changed? Will Mages be seeking iron dust for… some new type of working?"

She grinned. "Oh, I doubt it, Master Aniv. You see, I'm quite mad." With a wink, she turned and strode from his shop, Ashin following behind.

* * *

Their final stop was at an apothecary, the local name for an herbalist, where Tala negotiated for use of the man's tools. She'd had to bargain quite strenuously to get the apothecary down to what she had remaining to spend, but as she looked around at the small workshop, she assured herself that it had been worth it.

Now alone in the back room, she dumped the iron dust into a shallow basin. First, she filled the basin with water, gently agitating the bowl to allow any flotsam to separate out. This, she swept from the water's surface.

Next, she carefully drained most of the water and added a harsh soap, gently agitating the mixture to free up even more contaminants. Finally, she went through a dozen cycles of filling the basin with clean water, swirling it together with the iron, then slowly removing the water. She continued this process until the water was no longer soapy, and she was left with a uniform, wet powder in the bottom of the large basin.

She had taken her time with each step. Though the iron had been free, she was loath to lose any, and if she left contaminants in the dust, they could spoil the end result. Because of that, the cleaning process had taken at least a couple of hours, though she didn't have a clock to watch the time. *I hope that Ashin isn't too bored.*

She then carefully spread the iron out on large drying trays, which the apothecary would use to dry herbs, separating off as much water as she could during the process. She then stuck them into the hot box, which was on the building's southern side. The air inside was uncomfortably hot to her fingers even as she quickly stuck the trays inside.

There, that will be dry in no time. It appeared to use a process similar to a solar oven that she'd seen some artisan bakers use. *The apothecary must have some way of lowering the temperature at need, or he's more likely to burn the herbs than dry them.* Still, she did not complain; it was perfect for her purposes.

While the iron was drying, she melted a large portion of beeswax, also purchased from the apothecary, adding in several oils, and, oh so slowly, she brought it up to temperature. While that was happening, she prepared the molds that were ready to hand. These particular molds were used for making soap integrated with, and affixed to, a wooden handle, so a less flexible user could lather up their own back with ease.

The iron still wasn't dry.

She cleaned the basin, and the other items she had used and wasn't still using, and then checked the iron again.

Still damp.

The academy had magically powered dehydrators, which removed all traces of moisture almost instantly. It was mainly intended for medicinal or preservation purposes, but she'd happily implemented it for her own designs.

I've already been here for too long. If her estimates were correct, it was at least the third hour after noon.

Irritated, she walked back to the front of the shop and discussed the issue with the apothecary. He was quite bemused, explaining that he'd assumed she needed his workshop for the next couple of days, given her description of her project.

His heated haggling and irritated capitulation made much more sense in that light.

After further discussion, the man happily agreed to finish the process on her behalf, following her specifications exactly, in exchange for her departing now and only returning to claim the end product: six large, iron salve bars on sticks. He even promised to put the extra iron dust into small bags, with five ounces of iron in each.

He guessed that he would have her products ready for her in two days, three at the most. He also assured her that he would happily do the entire process for her, in the future, if she provided the iron.

All in all, she was quite happy with how it turned out. *Now, I'm ready.*

But she was broke... again.

*   *   *

Tala was not, in fact, *quite* ready. She and Ashin had to practically run back to the tailor; thankfully, she'd paid in advance. Then, they hurried back to Lyn's house, where Tala quickly, and self-consciously, scrubbed herself clean, hoping to the heavens that she'd removed all traces of the iron dust. And *then,* clad in her new clothes, she was ready.

She planned to have her borrowed clothes cleaned and returned to Phoen, along with a thank you note, but she didn't have time, or funds, for that just now. So, she left them in the room in Lyn's house for the time being.

They arrived at the doors to the Caravanner's Guild, not quite out of breath, just as a bell tower resounded for the fifth time, and Lyn stepped out. "Oh! Good, you're here." She smiled easily. Her eyes flicked over Tala's outfit. "I like that. Non-traditional for a Mage but pretty, in a simple sort of way."

Tala looked down at her linen blouse and loose pants. "Thank you. I quite like them." The top was light grey, the pants dark, and each was tightened to her figure, held in place with simple cloth ties, monkey's fist knots, and braided loops. These were not meant for quick removal, and the tailor had done an excellent job fitting them to her for easy, free movement.

Lyn glanced towards Ashin. "How was the day?"

Ashin gave a shallow bow towards Lyn. "It was… interesting, Mistress Lyn. Thank you for allowing me to assist."

Lyn nodded to the man but then turned to Tala, eyebrow quirked.

Tala gave a small smile. "He was quite helpful. Another taste of 'guild benefits?'"

Lyn's smile grew just slightly predatory. "And don't you forget it. I want you begging to renew your contract once you're done." She held out a small book. "This is an overview of what you need to know to empower guild-specific dimensional expansion spell-forms for our wagons. For any trip, you will have to begin work on that front at least two days before departure. That way, the wagons can be loaded before the day of departure."

Tala nodded. She'd been wondering about that. "That explains it. I was curious how you'd addressed the issue of switching out who empowered them."

"Exactly. Aside from the standard issues of any empowered magic item, each Mage visualizes the changes differently. Even if we could, changing casters while cargo is inside would be… problematic."

"I can imagine." She took the small book and examined it. "This is a ridiculous title…"

Lyn turned and walked away as she replied, Tala and Ashin falling in step. "Oh? You don't like 'Why Organize When You Can Expand?'" Ashin seemed much less hesitant about being close to Lyn than to Tala.

Tala sighed. "Seems like someone's flawed attempt at humor."

"Not everyone excels at Meta-Naming, dear." Lyn glanced at the little book, even as Tala was flicking through it. "There isn't enough in there for you to recreate the spell on your own, but I don't know why the Wainwrights bother with that precaution. You will be in sole charge of the wagons for your entire trip. I doubt that even a half-wit of a Mage would miss the 'hidden' aspects of the working." She sighed. "But, I suppose, we have to maintain the illusion of secrecy. Honestly, they are just a marginal modification on any number of dimensional storage items used throughout the cities." She shrugged. "That book is yours now, by the way. Feel free to take notes in it or modify it as you see fit."

Tala held up the book, even as she began reading snippets. "Thank you. I can already tell I'll glean a lot from it."

Lyn's eyes twinkled. "Oh, I hope so. I have high expectations for you, little Tala."

Tala decided to ignore that and absently let her feet follow where Lyn led, her eyes ravenously consuming the spell-lines, theory, and concepts outlined in the little book. *I should dedicate one of my notebooks to spell-workings and copy out the relevant sections, adding in what was redacted once I can examine the wagons themselves.*

The workings were actually vastly more complicated than simple dimensional expansion. They also prevented gravity from affecting the container based on the contents, while allowing the same to act on the contents within the expanded space, as normal. It was delicate work, but, in the end, it meant that the wagons would function as if unloaded, while the cargo would still be held in place as expected.

Clever. I'm glad I've an understanding of gravity, too, or this would be vastly more difficult. She supposed that it was easier to educate a lacking Mage on the basics of gravity than on dimensional distortion. *And I am familiar with both.* She smiled happily to herself.

A criminally short time later, Lyn pulled Tala's attention back up. "Here we are!"

Tala's eyes reluctantly left the page before her, but as they did, she hesitated. "Is Mistress Holly's shop in there?"

Before them rose a colossal, three-story building with a warehouse aesthetic. It wasn't dilapidated, but it was clear that very little care had been taken for the outward appearance of the place.

"It doesn't look like a great place to establish a business in…"

Lyn chuckled. "No, Tala. *This* is Mistress Holly's place."

Tala turned to her in confusion. "How can she possibly need this much space?"

"She has over a hundred apprentices, and there are ten full inscribers who also work under her direction with their own apprentices."

Tala almost gaped.

"She isn't the only inscription business in town, but nearly so. She has developed a special means of applying inscriptions, which she manufactures here and sells to inscribers in each of the fourteen cities." Lyn brushed back her hair. "It has changed what is possible for Mages."

No wonder Lyn was confident I couldn't go elsewhere…

"Shall we?"

The three of them walked through the front door into a cozy waiting room, but before they could sit, an assistant bustled out from behind a sturdy desk. "Mistress Tala?"

"Um, yes?"

The assistant muttered something under her breath that Tala thought was, "Heaven's be praised." Then, she smiled widely. "Welcome! The Mistress has been expecting you." Tala thought she saw a bit of manic stress in that look.

"Please, right this way." She paused. "I'm to take your payment?"

Tala was hesitant, once again. Nonetheless, she took out five golden coins and handed them over.

"Thank you." The assistant placed the coins through a slot in a strongbox mounted to the wall. "This way, please."

Tala followed the woman down a wide, brightly lit hallway. The inside of this facility was a good deal nicer than the outside. *I suppose Holly isn't concerned with attracting clients so much as keeping them happy once they're here?*

Doors stood open to either side, and Tala was able to glimpse inscription application chambers, as well as what looked like planning rooms. Several of the latter had large blackboards, covered with multicolored lines, depicting dozens of slight variations of different spell-lines. Some were crossed out, and others had pieces circled, showing clear progressions through versions of possible schema. *How much effort do they put into each set of inscriptions?* If she understood the scaling correctly, one of those rooms had been devoted to the discussion of spell-lines for a single shoulder. *Do those lines look familiar?*

The implications were staggering. *And Holly said she would have my schema modified and ready in one day?* If she'd succeeded, Tala's opinion of Holly would drastically rise above its already lofty heights.

The assistant stopped outside the door at the end of the hall and gestured for them to enter.

The room was fairly standard for an inscriber's workroom. A comfortable-looking chair sat in the center, surrounded by lenses and lights to give the inscriber better vantage for their work. That said, there were a couple differences that were immediately apparent.

First, the chair didn't seem to be set up to allow the occupant to be face down, which was odd. *How will she inscribe my back?* Her keystone, the largest set of spell-lines, encompassing and overlaying her magical gate, was intact, between her shoulder blades, but she would still need other work done across her back.

Second, along the wall were racks upon racks of needles from half an inch long to nearly two feet in length. Each looked to be made of an intricate, if irregular, braiding of silver, gold, and copper.

What?

Holly was already in there, sitting on a stool in the corner where she hadn't been obvious. She stood immediately. "Good! Finally. Mistress Tala, have a seat."

Tala glanced towards Ashin. "Um… don't I need to undress?"

Holly waved a dismissive hand. "Of course not… unless you want to? Just set your things, especially anything iron, over to the side there." She hesitated before adding. "Clothes are fine, iron is not." She indicated an empty shelf. "Make sure to get it all. No buckles forgotten, dear!"

The assistant was already gone, though Ashin and Lyn had followed Tala inside.

Tala obeyed, leaving her pack, satchel, and belt to the side. Her belt held her knife, so that was easy, and she had opted not to get shoes, so those, likewise, couldn't be an issue.

"Simple cloth fasteners on the garments? Good. That makes this easier. I'm glad you found an adequate tailor. Sit!"

Tala sat.

"Now"—she glanced at Lyn and Ashin—"this will take a while. I assume all night, in fact. Do you really want to stay?"

Ashin cleared his throat. "No, Mistress. I will take my leave." He bowed slightly to each of them in turn.

Tala waved to him, just before he departed. "Wait, why did you stay so long, then?"

He gave her a quizzical look. "I was asked to accompany you and had not been dismissed."

She opened her mouth, then hesitated. *I'm going to have to learn better what is expected of me.* "Ahh… Well, thank you, Ashin. I appreciated the guidance today."

He gave her a second nod and a smile. Then, he was gone.

Chapter: 6
In Holly's Workshop

"Now then, dear." Holly seemed to be ignoring Lyn. "We need to test you."

Tala frowned. "I was tested for magic compatibility before I went to the academy."

Holly sighed. "Your previous inscribers were either lazy or uninterested. You should have had whoever designed the work on your hand do the inscription. He would have taken the time to test you."

Tala cleared her throat. "I'm clearly missing something. Can you explain what you mean, then?"

"In order to ensure your inscriptions are perfectly suited and tailored to you, I need to test your abilities. For some Mages, I'd check their power flow: how fast they draw magic through their gate. Others, I would be most concerned about their aspect control: how many distinct aspects they can affect with one working. Others still, the thing I'd need is power spread: the area or number of distinct targets they can affect with one working."

She was nodding. "And for me?"

"For you, I need to check power density: how much power you can innately hold within your physical form. You are quite young, so I assume we won't have too much to work with, but it is the most important aspect of your power for the inscriptions you've selected. I've worked up several schemas and inscription plans, based on what we find." She pulled out a small stone plate, carved and inlaid with silver spell-lines. "I need a drop of blood, here."

"Wouldn't it have been easier to test this before making the plans?"

Holly blinked at her. "Possibly? No. Not really. You are ignorant of my arts. Stop asking stupid questions."

Tala felt Holly's magesight settle on her, in preparation for the test. It was a perfectly valid question… Tala moved to prick her finger.

"Stop!"

Tala froze, the needle held just away from her finger. "What?"

"What are you doing?"

Tala frowned. "I'm going to get a drop of blood."

"No, silly girl, what are you doing in your body?"

Tala frowned, looking down at her finger. "I don't know?"

Holly reached out and snatched the needle from her, using her other hand to grab Tala's hand. "You don't want me to prick you with this needle."

"Okay…?"

Holly moved to stick Tala's finger, and she tried to pull away, confused at what game Holly was playing. To her surprise, she couldn't free herself from Holly's grip, and the woman didn't even seem to be struggling. The needle hit Tala's skin, pushing in to dimple the surrounding finger-pad… and stopped.

Holly frowned. "You don't have any inscriptions." She pushed harder, and the needle slipped in slowly.

"Ow!" Tala pulled back her hand and sucked her finger. Holly had, presumably, released her.

Holly handed the pin back to Tala, and Tala took it with a glare. "I don't see why I need…" She looked down at her finger. She'd sucked the blood off and revealed a clean finger. "What?"

Holly was nodding. "You were pulling power away from your finger on reflex, to allow the pin to stick you. I'm now very interested in the results of this test. It seems that your body is acclimating to your chosen magics already." She waved a hand to dismiss Tala's question, even as Tala opened her mouth to speak. "Many people have tough skin, and many more will have their skin seal up from such a little stick. Both are well within the range of normal human beings, but it is still something. Go on." She held out the stone tablet, again, awaiting the drop of blood.

Tala pricked her finger on the needle and held the finger over the stone.

"Now, put as much power into the blood as you are able, but please don't open your gate. We are measuring the power in your body, naturally. Don't hold back on me, now."

Tala almost opened her gate on instinct, to draw power through her keystone. She resisted the urge, and instead, she gathered up the lingering power she felt within herself. *Okay. This is like signing a contract or giving her access to my schema.* When her finger began to get uncomfortably tingly, she compressed the pad, and a single drop of blood fell to the proffered slate. *There we go.* She realized, after, that she hadn't wanted the pinprick to close this time, and it hadn't. She didn't really know how to feel about that.

As the drop touched the plate, it flashed with power and turned from the normal red to copper, then silver, then finally, it became a softly glowing gold.

Lyn blinked, seeming surprised, and she opened her mouth, but Holly held up her hand.

She seemed quite serious, all of a sudden. "I didn't ask for half-measures. Give me all you can." After a moment, she added, "This isn't like accessing your accounts, dear. The fools at the academy didn't do this test because they assumed they knew the results, but the nuance is important if I'm to inscribe you correctly. Open your gate for a moment, to equalize. Then, please, give it your all." She smiled, but Tala thought she saw a hesitancy in Holly's eyes.

Tala frowned. *Fine, then. Not like a contract.* She threw her gate open and waited, not pulling in power, but not keeping it out either. A moment later, she felt the power equalize, and she closed her gate. *Okay. Let's do this.* She began to draw all the power in her body towards her finger, trying to wring every bit free, leaving nothing behind. Exhaustion swept through her, left in the wake of the departed power. Even as exhaustion settled in some parts of her, the path towards her finger was practically vibrating with nervous energy.

You want everything? If she was being honest, Tala was curious, herself. Here it goes! She exerted her will and drew all the power that she'd gathered into her finger as she compressed it, releasing another drop of blood.

The action was much like throwing a perfect punch, kinesthetically connecting all the major muscle groups into a single blow. Except, in this case, she was doing it with her power.

The energy left her in a rush, and the drop of blood seemed almost to tremble as it fell.

Before it even reached the stone, it began to glow, shifting through copper, silver, and gold with barely a flicker of time presenting each metallic sheen, and as it struck beside the first drop, it became iridescent, leaving the metallic look and flickering through uncountable colors in indescribable patterns, glowing all the while.

Tala sagged back in her chair, exhausted. "Satisfied?" She opened her gate, allowing power to rush back into her, returning her body's magic levels to normal. It took an uncomfortably long time.

Lyn gaped openly.

Holly simply stared at the shimmering drops. "What did you do to yourself, child? Have you been casting in an iron coffin?"

Tala's eyes flicked to her pack, where the bars of iron dust salve would have been, had she not drastically underestimated the drying time. *That is... an uncomfortably close guess.* "Ummm... Why?"

Lyn stepped forward. "At your age, you should struggle to indicate silver. Such easy presentation of gold, as your first drop indicated, should only come after a couple of decades of casting. That." She pointed to the still glowing, perfectly spherical drop of blood. "That means that you are registering in the Archon range, for power density."

"The Archon range?" Tala frowned.

Holly gave Lyn a silencing look. "It doesn't matter, yet. The time it's taking you to re-equalize means that your power rate is vastly below your density. That is a weak point, it seems."

Tala was examining the drop of blood, still on the stone tablet held before her. *Is it hovering, slightly off the surface?*

Holly nodded, seeming to decide something as she looked at Tala. "Every Mage builds up power in their system with each casting, usually due to leakage or poorly applied inscriptions. That excess power acclimatizes your body to itself, and over time, it changes how much power you naturally hold. Higher power density results in more powerful spells but can lead directly to magic poisoning, depending on the type of magic involved." She gestured with the stone in her hand. "You seem to have kept most of the power of your castings inside of yourself. Forcing your body to drastically reshape its capacities." Her eyes narrowed. "Is this why you only express from your hands? Do you wear some strange iron suit?"

"Not exactly…" I suppose I don't really have a choice. She briefly explained about her iron dust concoction.

"So, you basically coat yourself in a salve, impregnated with iron."

"Yes."

"The iron then settles into the top layers of your skin, making you resistant to direct magical expressions?"

"That's how it seems to work, yes."

"And you keep it off your palms so that you can express your own magic from there?"

"That's the theory. In practice, spell-workings seem unable to affect me, directly. Something created by magic can, and if I enter into a region already altered, I am affected by that alteration."

Holly was nodding. "Thus, a Mage or arcanous creature would need to fight you as if you were in a suit of full plate armor, without the obvious visual clues or the burdensome weight on you." She began to laugh. "Child! You are either brilliant or lucky beyond count." She hesitated, her laughter faltering. "Given that this is the second facet of your magic to give me that feeling, I'm beginning to assume brilliant." She looked Tala straight in the eyes. "Any other type of Mage would have been dead from magic poisoning long before now with your little trick. Even another Immaterial Guide would have obliterated themselves if they expressed from anywhere covered by this salve of yours. The iron dust would have radiated a good portion of their spells back into their own body, causing havoc. You, though," —She shook her head.— "you only have internal enhancements, thus having that radiant effect reflect back into yourself is only a benefit." Her eyes narrowed. "This must have been excruciating and quite tedious to enact."

Tala laughed. "You've no idea."

Holly smiled. "Oh, child. I can guess. This required you to entirely scrub away the upper layers of your skin any time you needed your inscriptions refreshed. Yes?"

Tala grunted an affirmation.

"And before your teleportation?"

Another grunt.

"And you mentioned practice, so I imagine you were injured…" Holly sighed. "You had to scrub your wounds clean, removing the impregnated skin before they could heal you as well."

Tala glanced away. "Yeah. That was… unideal."

Holly was nodding again. "That's why you focused on the inscriptions you did. Minimize injury in the first place."

That's one of the reasons. She was not going to tell these two Mages that she'd been enamored by warriors of old and sought to imitate them. Tala sighed. "Fair enough. You clearly understand exactly what it took."

"Don't take my understanding as an insult, child. No one I've ever heard of has done this before, and even knowing it works, I doubt any would be willing to do as you have." Holly smiled slightly. "Only time will tell if it proves worth the pain." She turned to Lyn. "Well, I will have to do this in much smaller stages, and only half right now. If I were to fully inscribe Tala, her body would tear itself apart. She has too much power going into her activations."

Tala frowned.

Holly turned back to her. "Don't be like that. We'll get you fully inscribed." She patted Tala's shoulder. "We just need to do it in stages, to let your systems compensate." She smiled. "I was right to take this on personally. You will be perfect when I'm done."

"Okay… so, how will this work?"

Holly held up one of the myriad needles. "These"—she swiped it at her own hand, through which it passed effortlessly—"don't interact with normal matter, save at the handle." She wiggled it. "The metallic ink flows through the center, and I can deposit the metal exactly where I need, without having to poke you full of a thousand holes." She hesitated. "Millions of holes, actually."

Tala frowned. "That sounds…"

"Expensive? Yes. The needles do last for a full inscription session, once activated, but can't be used during more than one such. But it is the only way to work." She winked. "Besides. I'm not the one paying the bill."

Tala sighed. Still, though, not having to deal with the pain of all those punctures…

"We do need to discuss the alterations so that the activation will go smoothly once we're done here."

Tala nodded. She'd expected as much.

"The effects should be nearly identical to your previous set, except the quickened signal speed will be constant; the inter- and intra-cellular bond augmentation will be more focused, only strengthening the bonds that are under stress instead of all bonds in the area; and the regenerative effects have been similarly focused. This will increase the speed of repair and strengthening, along with reducing the cost to you in power and inscription integrity."

"Understood. And the work on my right hand?"

"Unchanged, save I'm giving you more uses between re-inscriptions. We'll discuss your mage sight spell-lines later. I will be adding in the deeper work on your head, too, but we can discuss the specifics as I work. The last major change of note is that I'll be altering your keystone away from standard."

"That sounds… dangerous?" And expensive. The keystone represented the majority of any Mage's inscriptions.

"Most keystones are designed to close when the Mage is unconscious. It protects from magic poisoning and accidental triggering. The way your spell-lines are set up, that would be foolish. It will still cut power to spell-forms that take activation, but your passive magics, such as your enhancements, will receive power whether you are awake, asleep, unconscious, or in any other state."

"That sounds dangerous."

"Not especially, and definitely not in comparison to the other risks we're taking." She smiled. "I won't modify your keystone beyond that, for now, but I imagine we'll have to tweak it a bit more when you come back."

Tala nodded, steeling her resolve. "Alright, then. So, how many of those needles will you be using?"

"As many as it takes for the various depths." Holly smiled before lifting the indicated tool. "Well, this one's been activated, so time's a wasting! Let us begin."

Without warning, Holly thrust the needle into Tala's neck. The needle itself didn't hurt, but as metallic ink was inserted within Tala's skin, there was a decidedly unpleasant feeling of swelling, near to bursting.

Tala almost whimpered.

It was going to be a long night.

* * *

Hours had passed in abject discomfort, and it was somewhere in the wee hours of the morning.

Tala lay with as much of herself under the water of her warm bath as she could manage, luxuriating in the heat and the subtle, pleasant smell of bath salts.

Even so, she was miserable. While the inscribed needles removed the need for her skin to be pierced, they also didn't allow for any release of pressure when the ink was injected. Thus, much of her body felt like it was swollen, and it hurt to move. The soak was helping.

Millennial Mage 1 - Mageling

She'd never truly understood why bath salt soaks helped with swelling, but she couldn't argue with the results.

In addition to the mild bloating from the minimal amounts of metallic ink involved in her inscriptions, her body was working to encapsulate such, isolating the foreign elements and, in essence, enclosing the new material. This also caused swelling. Worse, she couldn't allow her gate to open or any power to enter the inscriptions, or they would activate and begin, effectively, fighting the process, attempting to keep her body in the current state.

She had not needed Holly's warnings to know how bad of an idea that was. At the academy, they'd simply activated the healing portion of her spell-lines first, which sealed everything nicely.

There weren't perforations to restore in this case.

I might actually hate Holly's way more… Though, it was much more precise and quite a bit faster.

There was a rushing sound as the tub drained down to half, then refilled with new, hot, salted water, returning the temperature to her limit.

Tala floated, forcing herself to stay awake so that her body wouldn't subconsciously allow power to flow through her.

Two more cycles of renewing hot water came and went with no other discernible change.

Then, as the water drained once more, Tala's eyes opened, warily. *The tub is getting lower than before…*

She was about to sit up when what felt like a liquid snowbank was dropped upon her.

She would have screamed if her lungs would obey her.

All sense of relaxation vanished in a flash. Interestingly, the feeling of swelling drastically reduced as well.

She vaulted to her feet, fighting every instinct she had, and managed to keep her gate closed.

Arms clutched tightly around her torso and chest, and she turned and glared at the woman standing in the doorway.

"Impressive control, Tala. I'd have guessed you would open your gate at that."

"St... still t-t-testing me?" She began sloshing her way through flowing ice towards the side of the small basin, towards towels and warmth.

"I have to know your limits." Holly idly scratched at the indentation that lay at the base of her throat. "I think you're ready for round two."

Tala paused mid-drying. She looked down at herself.

Her chest, upper legs, arms, and the back of her hands were covered in an intricate latticework of subtly metallic lines. The back of her right hand also had thirty golden rings, easily visible for her own reference. That way she couldn't miss how many castings she had remaining of her offensive spells.

She could feel the lattice on her back due to the remaining sense of swelling. It surrounded and even overlaid her keystone spell-lines as well.

Holly noticed Tala's hesitation. "Come, dear, this round we're doing from your neck up. The session after we'll tackle your hips, waist, and lower legs. I think that is all your body will be able to handle this time. When you return from your venture, we'll tackle the deeper workings and those for your left hand."

Tala glanced at her bare left palm. "You'll leave me half-equipped?"

"You'll be fine, dear. I've increased your available castings for your primary magics, so as long as you aren't ridiculously unlucky, there won't be an issue. Besides, you can get those refreshed on the far end if you need."

Tala grumbled, but not very loudly. The price for magic. It is so much, yet so little. She felt much warmer now. "Well, then. Let's get to round two."

Chapter: 7
The Old Made New

Tala had lost all sense of time.

She was sure that they were done inscribing, for now, but she couldn't say how long that had taken, or how long it had been since that was complete.

She was surrounded by heat, however, so she did know that horror was coming.

That lessened the relaxing effects of the bath.

Sure enough, an indeterminate time later, she felt the bath fully drain, and she braced for the glacial baptism.

As it washed over her, she found that she didn't hate it quite as much as the first two times. Holly, however... Tala hated Holly.

When can I sleep?

She sluggishly rolled out of the basin and onto the awaiting towel pile. "Can I sleep, now?" Her voice barely chattered from the cold, though it was muffled by the towels.

"Not yet, dear. Soon, though. We need to keep your gate closed for another hour or so, then you can rest."

"How long...?"

Tala saw Holly frown out of the corner of her eyes. "I just said: another hour. Are you quite alright?"

"I heard you... rusted jerk... I meant"—she took several deep breaths, pulling her thoughts back to herself—"how long have we been at this?"

Millennial Mage 1 - Mageling

"Oh!" Holly seemed to consider for a moment. "It's been roughly a day since we began, and you've done splendidly. I feared that I'd have to send you out with only the first session complete, that's why I crammed so much into that one. But you surpassed my highest expectations!" She grinned down at Tala. "We were able to complete all surface level inscriptions, save your left hand, and all the inscriptions above your neck."

"Why are you standing over me…?"

"Why are you lying down?"

"I want to sleep."

"Precisely. You cannot sleep, yet. Your subconscious would activate your keystone, opening your gate and undoing a great deal of work from our last session. I will not allow that." She shook her head. "That is just unacceptable."

Tala grunted. "Food."

"Ahh, yes. Here it is." Holly gestured toward a small table off to one side.

Tala didn't move. Instead, she opened her mouth.

"You-you're serious, aren't you?"

"Feed me, or I sleep."

Holly sighed. "And just like that, you remind me how much of a child you still are."

Tala slandered Holly's good name, then added, "Not very child-like, eh?"

Holly sighed, again. "Oh, yes. I can think of nothing more mature than expressing your emotions via vulgarity." After a moment, she patted Tala on the shoulder. "But I'll get you food. You have been through *much*, and much of it is unique, due to your particular inscriptions and power density." She continued talking as she walked over to the table and retrieved a selection of food. "Rest assured, I am taking extensive notes, should anyone else consider this path."

Tala accepted the first bite of food gratefully but spoke around it. "If anyone considers it, slap them. Please?"

Holly snorted a laugh. She *snorted*. "I'll admit, even if the results are spectacular, I'm not sure I'll be willing to do this for anyone else." She frowned. "I don't like to see my clients suffer." She put another piece of pastry into Tala's mouth. "Can you please sit up? I don't like treating you like an invalid, and you are beginning to make me nervous... You can move, can't you?"

Tala grunted, then sat up, pulling up a mass of towels to drape over herself.

"There you go. Much better."

Tala glared, but then her eyes slid down to the plate of food in Holly's hand, and she sluggishly snatched it, devoting her limited thoughts to the consumption of the food. "Your offering is accepted." *For now.*

Holly smiled and patted her on the shoulder again, through the towels this time. "Glad you're up and moving. We can walk you to a back room where we have a bed once you're done."

Tala hesitated. "I thought you said an hour?"

Holly hesitated. "Hmmm... You're losing your perception of time, then? Definitely time to sleep."

Tala frowned, continuing to eat and speak around the food. "What does that mean?"

"That was nearly two hours ago, dear."

"Oh." *Articulate, Tala.* It made no sense. She'd only asked a moment ago... but she didn't really care. Holly was going to let her sleep.

She devoured the remaining food and stood, with Holly's help. They replaced the towels with a robe, and true to her word, Holly led her to a back room and a bed.

Tala was asleep before she laid down... literally. As they entered the room, Tala glanced at the bed and passed out. Thankfully, Holly was able to catch the other woman and lift her, bodily, into place.

"Sleep well, dear."

As if at the words, a pulse of power washed over Tala, originating from her back—from her keystone and the gate beneath.

The spell-lines across Tala's entire body flared briefly to life, resembling nothing so much as spider-web-thin stained glass before a sunrise. The ripple of power and accompanying light passed, then seemed to settle.

Tala gasped loudly at the initial flare but failed to rouse. As the power faded, reducing to a barely noticeable thrum, she breathed easier, seeming to drift into a deep, restful sleep.

* * *

Sleep left Tala slowly as she became aware of the world around her.

The soft murmur of dozens of voices tickled at the edges of her hearing, though they were overshadowed by a deep, regular *thump-thump*. The sound of great bellows filled the air around her every so often, almost seeming to be in sync with her breathing, and as she began to shift, wagonloads of fabric seemed to cascade around her.

Her skin was alive with the feel of ten thousand gaping cracks pressing against her flesh, and the alternating patterns of textured cloth and blessedly smooth air threatened to overwhelm her.

Her eyes were closed, she knew they were, but she was still forced to look upon a great latticework of intersecting lines, harshly backlit: a stained-glass masterpiece, knit from flesh.

The smell of her own clean skin could almost have been described as overwhelming, except that she could still easily discern the scents of linen, leather, wood, and oils from the bed in which she lay. The odor of a dozen meals, of metal, of dust, of *people* underpinned it all, and she suddenly felt the overarching need to plug her nose to keep it out.

She moved to do just that, but her arm responded too quickly, and she simply slapped herself across the face.

It *hurt*.

She'd also, with that simple slap, driven a minuscule amount of blood into her mouth. It *might* have been as much as a drop.

Even so, the taste of blood bloomed, and suddenly, she could taste the inside of her own mouth, taste her teeth, her gums, and her…

She couldn't take it.

She drew in on herself, curling into a ball.

Her knees slammed into her forehead quickly enough to send her mind spinning, but she didn't change position; she did not allow herself to uncurl. Even so, her surprise caused her eyes to pop open.

The world shattered into light.

The room before her was rendered within her own mind in still images, her brain struggling to process the overabundance of information deluging her from her eyes, and for just a moment, her other senses were thrust aside as too much.

She was still in the back room, in the spare bed on which Holly had laid her.

Blessedly, her knees were blocking nearly half of her vision, though the intricacy of the hexagonally arranged spell-lines inscribed into them was, in and of itself, an abject agony in its quantity of information.

Above her knees, she saw the door, closed but with light streaming around the edges and through minute gaps. It was the only light coming into the room, but it was still too much.

The wall was well-plastered and newly painted. There was some dust, here and there, but it seemed to have been cleaned recently. *Who dusts walls?*

Some deep, animalistic part of her grabbed onto that, her first, truly coherent thought. *Who dusts walls?*

Her eyes fixed on the door. Tala knew that it was opening, even though she didn't *see* it opening so much as notice that one side was suddenly slightly closer to her. And again closer. And closer.

Tala's other senses came crashing back, no longer able to be held back by her sight, and the light swelled as the door opened. Her mind, animalistic and sapient together, agreed: This was too much.

She fell into the blissful, total nothingness of sleep.

*   *   *

Tala slowly came back to herself, hearing snatches of a hushed conversation.

"…overwhelmed!"

"…compensating…"

"…can't believe…"

"…no choice now…"

"Let her…"

Tala groaned, and the sound was like the quaking of a mountain. Strangely, though, it didn't seem deafening. *How does that make sense?*

She blinked her eyes open, staring up at the wooden beams above her. She could see the tool marks from where each had been worked, though she didn't know enough about woodworking to guess at how. The ceiling they supported had been plastered and smoothed, but she could easily see the variations and textures in the surface.

How am I seeing so much detail? If that madwoman had inscribed her *eyes* there would be a reckoning... It was a ridiculous thought. She'd been conscious for the inscribing, and her eyes were untouched.

No... I'm not seeing more detail. It's more like... She hesitated. *It's like every instant is a painting that I've had a week to study and find the details and patterns within.*

This was *nothing* like it had been with her old inscriptions.

Voices reached her, loud enough that she felt like Lyn and Holly were each speaking straight into her ears. Strangely, there was a breathy quality to the words that made Tala think that they were whispering despite the volume.

"Did you hear that?"

"I think she's awake."

Tala groaned again and then shuddered at her own sound. *They must be sitting above my head.* She whispered back to them, her voice an avalanche. "I'm awake... and hungry."

They didn't respond.

"Should we go in? When I went in earlier, she reacted like it was a physical blow."

"I told you to give her more time." Tala could practically hear Holly rolling her eyes.

What in zeme? Go in? She twisted to look above herself, but somehow, the motion threw her out of her own bed. She slammed into the hard floor and swore as pain equivalent to stubbing a toe blossomed across her elbows, knees, and forehead. She yelped, then twitched away from the pulse of sound, slamming her head back against the bed that she'd just fallen out of.

Pain blossomed on the back of her skull, causing her to curl inward.

Millennial Mage 1 - Mageling

Somehow, she remembered kneeing herself in the head before and pulled up short.

The door burst open, flooding the room with harsh light, and Lyn's voice boomed through the small space.

"Mistress Tala? Are you awake?"

Tala could see one of Lyn's eyes, looking in through the slightly cracked door.

Tala groaned, again, but kept herself from moving. *If I don't move, I can't hurt myself. Don't move, no more pain.* That was good mantra. *Don't move, no more pain.*

Lyn put it to lie by opening the door wider and slapping Tala in the face with the full light of… nothing?

A lamp was lit on the far end of the hallway, but otherwise, there was no source that Tala could see.

Lyn seemed to see her on the floor, and she shrieked in horror and stomped across the floor to check on her.

Oh, she gasped… and is likely tip-toeing…

Holly stood in the doorway, lines of concern clear across her face.

"Mistress Tala? Are you okay?"

Tala knew, now, that Lyn wasn't shouting. It didn't hurt her ears like shouting would have, but it was still *loud*. She groaned again and found herself more used to the sound. "I'm…" Her own whispered voice sounded like a trumpet and seemed to rattle her skull. *Measured actions, Tala.* "…thirsty." *There, see? First steps.*

Holly immediately seemed to relax, if only just. She spoke incredibly softly but seemed to be intending for Tala to hear. "Your mind is reframing your senses, dear. It will not cause you harm, but it will feel incredibly overwhelming. You are doing very, very well. Be patient and move slowly."

Lyn had already stood, hurrying from the room. She returned shortly with a cup and pitcher of water.

The rushing, rumbling waterfall that resounded behind Lyn's filling of Tala's cup was incredibly soothing.

Tala tried to take the cup but almost slapped it from Lyn's hand instead.

"Mistress Lyn, why don't you help her drink it?"

Lyn nodded and did just that, helping Tala to sit up and pressing the cup to her lips.

What followed was, frankly, a humiliating night, in which the two women slowly helped Tala retrain her various senses and movements. Her system was thrown off, but it had also been enhanced, which allowed her to retrain it vastly more quickly than would otherwise have been possible.

By the time dawn broke, Tala was able to stand and shuffle-step without tripping. Her first great voyage without assistance was outside to see the sunrise.

"Hey!" Holly clapped Tala on the shoulder. "Your heart never stopped."

Tala turned and glared at the woman.

"Good for you, Mistress Tala."

Tala grunted and turned back to regard the city, softly glowing in the newborn, yellow-orange light. "I think I might be happy if you died."

Lyn laughed, and Holly snorted.

Lyn placed a hand on Tala's shoulder. "I'm impressed, Mistress Tala. With your magic saturation…" She shook her head. "I would not want to be under the influence of your enhancements. The fact that you are acclimating so quickly…"

Tala sighed. "Is testament to Mistress Holly's inscriptions on my mind."

Holly snorted, again. "Capacity does not equal capability, girl. Nor does it grant the ability to persevere."

"What does that even mean?"

Holly smiled. "It is like a carpenter in a fully functioning smithy: He has the strength to do the work; he has all the tools; but unless he is persistent, and practices, he will never make anything but a fool of himself."

Tala grunted. "I suppose."

Lyn chimed in again. "Besides! You didn't close your gate *once* while we were working, or even before we came to help you. That would have shut off the flow of power and greatly reduced what you were experiencing as your power density dropped."

Holly nodded and continued the thought. "It would have slowed your adjustment and likely would have made it worse for you in the long run, but it took strength to avoid that."

Tala stared at them for a long moment before looking away. "Umm… yeah. Thank you."

Lyn's mouth opened in a silent 'Oh,' and Holly laughed. "You completely forgot you could do that, didn't you."

Tala glared at her, again. "It wasn't exactly in the front of my thoughts, no." She grumbled, looking away.

When she looked back up, both Lyn and Holly were grinning at her.

"I kind of hate you two, right now."

"Oh, we know, dear." Holly patted her on the arm yet again.

"Let's get breakfast. Hate is always harder over breakfast." Lyn began leading Tala away, not waiting for a reply.

Blessedly, she was right. Everything seemed better over breakfast.

* * *

Tala, being broke, relied on the charity of her tormentors—or friends as they likely saw themselves.

They refused to help her walk, insisting that she needed to retrain the movements, and any further assistance on their part would slow her readjustment to her own body.

Her mood had not improved when it turned out they were seemingly correct. By the time they reached a cozy breakfast eatery, Tala was walking with her usual, steady, Mage's grace. In fact, it seemed easier to keep her balance than it had before now that she was more used to her passive enhancements.

The deep-fried, sausage-and-egg-filled donuts *did* improve her mood, as did the rich, smooth, black coffee. *Worth every copper I didn't pay.*

Coffee was a habit she'd avoided, as the crop required magical climate control of vast underground growing rooms to properly ripen. Grown on that scale, it wasn't *too* expensive, but it was still a delicacy. Some people did drink it every day, but she supposed that some drank wine every day, too, and the cost was roughly equivalent. She usually abstained from both, barring special occasions.

This was a special occasion.

Holly had not, in fact, inscribed Tala's tongue, but she had added spell-lines with increased communication speed and information density throughout her entire nervous system. Thus, she felt, smelled, tasted, and heard *more* without actually taking in additional input.

Lyn and Holly hadn't been feeding her gruel, but the breakfast donuts and coffee were so rich and full of wondrousness that Tala felt they might as well have been.

In retrospect, they had likely chosen to bring her more bland foods to reduce at least one aspect of her sensory overload. In that light, it was almost kind.

As the three of them sat around a small table, outside the little café, Tala did *not* grumble to herself, deciding, instead, to enjoy her food.

Millennial Mage 1 - Mageling

After long minutes of such enjoyment, she opted to break the silence. "So... how long has it been?"

Lyn smiled. "You 'missed' four full days. You're due to check in at the workyard tomorrow, for departure in three days from now."

Tala nodded. She'd lost fewer days than she'd feared and recovered much faster than she would have expected. "Why is everything so much... more intense than with the inscriptions I had before?"

Holly answered from Tala's other side. "Inscription design. First, by covering all your skin, curves included"—she quirked a smile—"the efficiency and power of the spells were increased. Additionally, those you had before only activated when your heart rate increased, which was usually accompanied by massive adrenaline spikes. The adrenaline would have both protected your mind from some of the harshness of the increase and convinced your body that it wasn't something to adapt to."

Tala nodded. "I think I can see that."

Holly rested her hand on her own upper chest. "In addition, I was able to make better use of your prodigious magical density. Your old schema was simply skimming off the surface. The new design funnels the majority into your workings. Our upper limit on the always-active scripts was still your power accumulation rate, otherwise we'd run you dry, but even so, there was room for a marked increase."

Tala frowned. "Wouldn't Mages always want their inscriptions to make use of all their power? Why would any design leave power unutilized?"

Lyn's smile shifted, just slightly, towards patronizing. "Mistress Tala, more power doesn't mean better, for most magics. Imagine throwing the full power at a Mage's disposal behind Magesight. I'd see every trace of magic within fifty miles, and my mind would overload."

Tala found herself nodding, again. "Right, precise use of power is much more important than the amount of power used."

"Except in your case." Holly took a bite of her own donut. "The inscriptions we worked for your enhancements are meant to be overtly powerful. The finesse is from you and how you learn to use your body, thus holding back in the empowerment really didn't make sense."

"Huh." Tala glanced to the two women. "I suppose that makes sense.

Chapter: 8
Delivery and New Sight

Tala looked from Lyn to Holly. "Speaking of magesight…"

"Ahh, yes. I left off the four connection points that will activate that portion of your inscriptions. I thought it better to not add that on top of everything else. Additionally, we still need to discuss the changes, adding to the wisdom of the delay."

"But I should just be able to activate…" She hesitated, then sighed. "You made that a passive enhancement as well, didn't you."

Holly grinned. "Of course! Once connected and activated, it will show you any magic source you focus on, but otherwise, it will only bring new, or changing, sources of magic to your awareness. It is really quite genius."

"If you do say so yourself," Lyn muttered under her breath just before taking a sip of coffee; Tala heard it perfectly.

Tala grinned but then turned back to Holly. "Why?"

"Many a Mage has been undone because they didn't know to activate their magesight or because they were overwhelmed by the information provided, as Lyn implied. This gets around that problem."

Tala was unconvinced. "So, why doesn't everyone use your method?"

"Because, without the mental enhancing inscriptions, which we added to you, their mind would pop like an egg thrown at a wall."

"Vivid."

Holly shrugged. "Accurate."

"So, my inscriptions will allow for this?"

"Based on my calculations."

Tala had been about to take another bite, but she paused. "Say again?"

"From everything I can determine, you should be fine."

"You could just say, 'Yes.'"

"That would be a lie. I strive for honesty with my clients."

Tala set her donut aside, cleaned off her hands, and then rubbed her face. "How can you not know?" She pointed at her own cheek, where she presumed that the spell-lines were awaiting activation. "They are already on my face, Mistress Holly. How can you not know?"

"Because no one else has been quite like you, dear. This is all new."

Tala groaned. She did have a moment of reflexive relief that groaning didn't cause any discomfort.

In a strange turn, Lyn patted Tala gently on the back. Based on the brief contact, Tala noticed a ring she hadn't taken note of before. Through Tala's distraction, she still heard Lyn's reassurance. "Think of it this way, Mistress Tala: Would you prefer someone who takes a risk, all the while assuring you it was perfectly safe, or someone who was perfectly aware of the risks, honest about them, and actively worked to reduce them?"

She sighed. "Fine." A moment's thought brought to mind a memory of Lyn's ring as she'd obviously seen it earlier. It was *incredibly* disconcerting for Tala to remember something, in vivid detail, that she hadn't noticed before. She twisted, looking at Lyn's hand and confirming the ring was as she'd expected. "What's with the ring?"

Lyn blinked at her. "It's... It's just a ring. I've had it for years." She frowned. "You've never seen me without it."

Holly was grinning. "She'll be noticing things she missed before. The ring is likely just the first she vocalized."

Tala was staring at the ring, seemingly unable to divert her attention as her mind showed her a dozen memories of Lyn, all including that ring. "How did I...?"

"Not notice, dear?"

"Yeah. It seems so obvious."

"Each of us is blind to some things. You just didn't take note of it."

Tala looked at the woman and was suddenly struck by the weariness in her. Holly's posture was good but not as perfect as when Tala had first met her. Her intricate inscriptions were darker beneath her eyes, and there were subtle lines across her features. "Mistress Holly? Are you alright?"

The older woman blinked at her. "Yes... Ahh... I see you are actually beginning to use your increased perception."

"You look exhausted."

She smiled. "Oh, I am. I've gotten some sleep since we began but not much. As soon as we discuss your magesight and activate it, I plan to sleep for..." She thought for a moment, then laughed. "For as long as I can, probably."

"Well, we should get to it, then." Tala took the last two bites of breakfast in a single mouthful and washed it down with the remains of her coffee. Tala's eyes swept over Lyn, and she noted that she could now take a better guess at the other woman's age. *Twenty-five. She has a full five years on me.* That was a funny thought; Lyn acted like a peer, but she also acted like she was Tala's mother.

Honestly, Tala felt a bit foolish. Any Mage, lacking a master as Lyn clearly did, would have had to finish their time as a mageling, which could take anywhere from three to ten years. The fact that Lyn was still so young, and a full Mage, spoke very well to her abilities.

How will I be perceived? I skipped that whole process... She wondered if she would ever learn all that she would have under a master. *No going back, now.*

Standing, Tala looked down at her two companions. "Shall we?"

They smiled up at her, and she could easily see their agreement and care in the expressions. *I am luckier than I knew.*

Holly and Lyn stood almost as one, their smiles still playing across their faces.

"Yes. The quicker we get back to my shop, the sooner I can sleep."

*   *   *

They were back at the front of Holly's warehouse, door open for re-entry, when a man's voice interrupted them, "Mistress Tala! Wait a moment." Tala heard a power behind the voice; the volume wasn't great, but the words carried clearly and easily across the distance. The tone and intonation denoted control and ready strength.

She turned and saw Ashin striding across the road, several packages in hand. *Noticing things that I haven't noticed before is... odd.* She quirked an eyebrow. "Guardsman?"

He smiled slightly, his eyes flicking to her face, arms, and bare feet, seeming to take in her new inscriptions. "Your apothecary was quite distraught when you didn't return to claim your items." He lifted the few small packages slightly, indicating their contents.

"Oh! Thank you." She stepped forward quickly to take them from him. Once the packages were in hand, she paused. He didn't leave or say anything, and her newly prominent senses were screaming at her that he was feeling suddenly awkward. Tala glanced at Lyn. "I'm... I'm not certain if anything else is required? I'd offer him a fee, for carrying the packages for me, but... I'm broke."

Ashin reddened. "I am right here, Mistress."

Tala turned back to him. "I'm hardly going to ask you if it's appropriate to give you money."

His red features darkened. "Are you implying that I would lie?" His hand seemed to be drifting towards his sword, but the motion struck her as subconscious. *Interesting. He has an unconscious reflex to be ready to defend his honor with violence but not an immediate drive towards such.*

"No, of course not. Just that..." She hesitated. *I had been concerned that he'd lie...* That was a bit uncharitable, she supposed. "I apologize for the offense. I've had a taxing few days. Is there anything else I can do for you?"

Ashin took a deep breath and seemed to wrangle down his own emotions, bringing his hands forward to clasp in front of his waist.

Tala began looking through the packages, moving paper wrapping aside to look in. She frowned. *This isn't right.* There were fewer parcels than there should have been.

After letting out his breath, Ashin bowed slightly. "He asked me to convey—"

Tala spoke over him. "These don't look right, the bars are too heavy, and there is far too little iron left. What did he do, add lead?"

Ashin's eyes tightened in clear irritation. "As I was *trying* to say"—he took another calming breath—"he asked me to convey that he has modified your recipe. He included several emulsifying agents to help the iron bind to the other ingredients more easily. Thus, he was able to increase the amount of dust in each bar, without changing the other properties of the end result. Therefore"—he emphasized that last word—"the bars will be heavier than expected, and more of your iron dust was used."

Tala closed her mouth and grunted. "Ahh."

He held out a slip of paper to her. "The altered recipe. He said that it should allow a greater amount of the iron dust to bind to your skin as well."

She took it and examined the careful, precise script. "Huh… clever." She nodded. "This *is* better." *I'll have to thank him personally… when I have funds to add to the words.* "Thank you, Ashin."

His smile was a bit strained. "I'm glad it meets with your approval, Mistress."

She rolled her eyes. "If that is all, we are about to complete our work for the day." She hesitated. "You are welcome to observe, I suppose."

He reddened visibly, again, but this time with obvious embarrassment as he tried to stammer out a reply.

Lyn sighed, giving a little wave to grab Ashin's attention. "The inscriptions are on her face, Ashin. No nakedness required."

Holly sighed. "No nakedness is ever required when I work."

Lyn shushed her with a dismissive hand wave. "Irrelevant."

"But true."

Lyn fixed Holly with a look that made it quite clear what Lyn thought of *that*.

Holly huffed. "Fine. He wants to watch Mistress Tala's mind pop, who am I to argue?"

Tala's head whipped back to face Holly. "What? You said that wouldn't happen."

"It won't, dear." She turned to Ashin. "Would you care to watch?"

Ashin was looking between the three women and slowly stepping backward. His offhand was resting, solidly, on his sword's hilt. "I… I think I will be about my business. Thank you, though." Then, as if fearing being forced to stay, he turned and strode away, clearly going as fast as he could without moving into a 'disrespectful' jog.

Lyn grinned. "He's such a good boy." She glanced towards Tala. "Don't you think so?"

Tala shrugged. "Don't know him that well." She looked to Holly. "Shall we?"

* * *

"So, Mistress Tala. You understand how your new magesight will work, as well as the other changes?"

"Everything will light up, and I will see all the magic around me in one brilliant instant, then it will fade, and only new or changing sources will be presented to me… or the initial burst will fry my brain."

Holly quirked a smile. "Unlikely. I need you to repay me for all this work, after all." She hesitated. "Also, we have reparative scripts that *should* repair any damage in your brain." She held up a forestalling hand. "But there won't be any, so they won't be needed." She smiled.

"I feel so loved."

"You should. No one loves you like your banker or your creditors." The inscriber winked.

Lyn leaned in. "Mistress Tala, we hardly know you. *Of course* we care more for you as an investment than as a person." Her eyes were twinkling, and Tala hoped that was meant to put the statement to lie. "I can assure you, I would be quite aggrieved to lose my investment."

"You two are kind of mean."

They smiled back at her. "You are quite a lovely person, dear, but friendship takes more than a few days."

Tala sighed. "Fine, but sometimes pretty lies are better than hard truth."

Lyn's smile widened. "Oh, they are *always* better, but never for the hearer, not in the end, and only a coward takes the easy way out."

Tala found herself oddly comforted by the sentiment. "I... uh... thank you, Mistress Lyn." She smiled.

Lyn glanced at Holly. "Go fast. I don't want to be overly distraught if this fails, and she's growing on me."

"I hate you."

"Like the older sister who stole your favorite dress?"

Tala didn't have a response to that, and Holly was quick to capitalize on her hesitation.

With four quick, painless jabs, Holly left Tala with four new, swelling additions to her spell-lines.

Power moved through the spell-forms on her face, and the world *rippled* before her sight.

Every stone in Holly's wall, behind the plaster, flickered with earthly power. The boards affixed to the stones seemed almost to grow before her vision, then settled down. They were not so old as to have lost their connection to nature, and the power of life was quite evident within, though dimmed by time. The plaster, coating and covering the wood, had flashes both of water and stone through it, just like the paint that finished the surface, though the latter had more water in the mix than the former did.

Each needle on Holly's wall screamed at Tala's sight, proclaiming their purpose, and as they were all made toward the same purpose, the unified voice was a chorus to shake the heavens.

Licks of power danced through the air: heat, movement, life, and so much more.

Then, her eyes fell upon Lyn, and she *knew* the woman's power.

As an Exchequer, Lyn had extensive networks of spell-lines across her entire body, all tuned towards the acquisition, processing, and storage of information. *Immaterial Creator.* The woman's quadrant was obvious.

None of her scriptings were active, but they were still readily apparent, even as the woman's life and magical power showed from between the spell-lines. The lines, themselves, had a familiarity to them, and Tala realized that they bore Holly's distinctive style.

Even so, the holistic view, coupled with Tala's own ease of intake and processing, left her with an uncomfortable realization.

If I struck there—her mind seemed to highlight a cluster of crossing lines, just inside of Lyn's right shoulder—*I could disable, or overwhelm, her entire network of spell-forms.*

Tala tried to turn her head but realized that she couldn't. Her perception was, momentarily, moving much more quickly than normal.

She was able to shift her focus, even so, and then her sight beheld Holly.

Thoughts bearing words paled, and any attempt at description was rendered utterly inadequate to convey the overpowering radiance of the woman's spell-lines and the power and intricacies therein. It was more than that, though. There almost seemed to be power in the air around Holly, which made no sense. *She has spell-lines that aren't a part of her body? How?* Taken as a whole, it was a tapestry of utter mastery, meticulously constructed on a bright yellow canvas.

Tala's mind simply couldn't hold, let alone understand, the complexity and depth.

That simple glance caused her consciousness to flicker, and she was left with a hole in her memory and a single-word impression.

Create.

Tala could not have stated what quadrant Holly was. Tala wondered if she'd ever find out if the woman didn't choose to share that information.

After the flicker of mental blackness, her perception seemed to return to a normal pace, and she was able to turn her head, scanning her surroundings more fully.

Each item was briefly highlighted, and their marginal magical affinities were noted.

Nothing was surprising to her, or even new, as she'd always known the inherent connections all things had to various aspects of power. She'd sometimes even seen those, in the past.

What did surprise her was that she could actually see the zeme, the magical currents in the air. There wasn't much, as cities kept their free-floating magic to a minimum, but the small inefficiencies in the inscriptions on the three Mages in this room let some power drift through the air before being pulled downward into the city's power collection grid.

After a long minute, during which Holly and Lyn regarded her carefully, if silently, Tala finally smiled. "I think... I think I'm adjusting."

Lyn let out what seemed to be a long-held breath. "Good. I like this robe." She gestured down at her cream-colored Mage's robe. "I'd hate to have it soiled by exploding heads." After a moment's hesitation, she amended, "Well, *an* exploding head."

Holly sighed. "As I explained, the bursting would have been entirely internal. The most we'd have seen was some bleeding from her eyes."

Tala cleared her throat. "So... we're clear?"

Holly smiled. "We are. We won't do the deeper dimensions of your inscriptions on the rest of your body until you return, and we'll save the tailored inscriptions on your internal organs for some time after that." She hesitated. "Maybe, we'll do it at the same time. We'll have to see." She smiled.

Tala spun her right forefinger in a circle in the air. "Yay! I can't wait."

Just then, a form walked into range of her magesight, across and behind the closed door. Tala could tell by the lack of strictly patterned, concentrated aura that they were un-inscribed, but even so, she was able to see traces of power looping through them in flowing circuits. The circuits had an odd look, as if they were spell-lines but of a different metal and design than any she'd yet seen. *Is that their circulatory system?*

She followed the form as it passed. Initially, it had begun to slowly fade, as her magesight determined that she'd seen it, but as she maintained her focus, keeping her gaze locked on the movements, it became clear once again.

"Huh."

Holly and Lyn were looking at her strangely. "Dear? Are you alright?"

Tala kept following the person with her sight as they continued on their way. "Yes. A person came into range, beyond the wall, and I could see them."

Holly glanced at the door, then back at Tala. "Through the wall? Are you sure?"

Tala nodded, still not turning. "And I'm still seeing them, even though they are close to three times as far away, now, as when they first came into sight."

"That part makes sense. If you focus on something, no matter the distance, your magesight will show the magic of it, but…" She hesitated. "Is it clear? Are you sure your eyes aren't tricking you?"

Tala quirked a smile. "I can count their heartbeats if you want." She nodded. "I'm sure."

"Focus on me, I'm going to go through the door, and I want to know if you can tell what I am doing."

Tala allowed her gaze to leave the target, and it immediately vanished. She glanced towards Holly but made sure not to focus on her. "Ummm... I'd rather not. You're kind of painful to look at."

Holly blinked. "I think I should be insulted."

Tala's smile grew. "I *meant* that your magic is incredibly bright. It overwhelmed me for a moment there. There's also a strange underlying hue to the whole thing. Do you have spell-lines in the air around you? How is that even possible?"

"Hmmmm..." Holly scratched the side of her face. "You were still adjusting... Would you be willing to try again?" She did not answer any of Tala's questions.

Tala hesitated, then nodded. *If I'm looking at it, I can ask more pointed questions.* "I suppose so." She allowed her focus to fall on Holly, and the woman immediately began to glow, her spell-lines becoming easily visible, even through her clothing. The light became painful, but something within Tala seemed to shift, and while she could tell the power, as she perceived it, was continuing to grow, it was no longer difficult to take in. "Interesting. I can see now." *It looks different than before, and it also seems a little hazy.* She smiled. "Material Creator? Are you doing something to shield your magic?"

"That's right, I began my career as a Material Creator. As to the second, that's not your concern right now."

There was too much in that answer to unpack at the moment, so Tala decided to press on with the matter at hand. "Are *all* your spell-lines bent towards the understanding and enacting of inscriptions?" *All those I can see. It sounds like she's masking or altering how she looks to me.*

"It is my life, dear."

It's more than that. Portions of Holly's magic were devoted to connecting with various knowledge archives. Most inscribers that Tala knew of would use tablets, or other such items, empowered for the purpose; Holly used herself. It was less materially efficient, for that specific task, but Tala would bet her last copper that it saved Holly a great deal overall in time, metal, and power. "I don't understand all the archive functions."

Holly's eyes widened, just slightly, and Tala saw power ripple through the lines around the older woman's eyes. "Those are on my ribs, dear. You can see them?"

"Yes. But what is the—"

Holly placed her hand over Tala's mouth, cutting her off. Holly then cleared her throat. "That is not something we should discuss. Maybe when we know each other better…" Her eyes flicked to Lyn, then to the door. "And when we can have time to talk alone."

Lyn's eyes narrowed, but she seemed to decide not to say anything.

Holly's hand came away, and Tala shrugged. "As you wish." She'd decided not to press. *The Core Archives does sound like something without wide access.* She found herself grinning. *If Holly inscribes administrative Mages, it would not have been difficult for her to give herself those same magics. I wonder how many such secrets she has made use of over the years?* There was something more. The fact that she'd seen something real, which Holly didn't expect, meant that she wasn't being deceived by what she saw, at least not entirely. *Maybe, Holly is just hiding the spell-lines in the air?* The underlying yellow hue was also missing, now. *I'll figure it out eventually, I suppose.*

Millennial Mage 1 - Mageling

Holly was watching Tala carefully, but when the younger girl didn't say more, Holly nodded. "Very well. It seems that your magesight will be even more useful than we'd thought if it can pick up power even through solid objects. You *should* receive some sort of signal if magic pops up, or changes, outside of your line of sight, but I've honestly no idea how that will manifest, or if there is some sort of threshold involved."

Tala nodded. "I was wondering about that. The schema we discussed seemed to have allowed that. It almost looked like it would take a threshold to open that portion of my sight, but afterward, it would function much the same as that within my normal vision."

"Could be. That was my hope, but poor is the fool who counts on hopes and wishes. If that is how you understood it, then that's the most likely way it will function."

Lyn cleared her throat. "As wonderful as this is, I think that Tala is due a good night of sleep in a normal bed." She glanced to Tala. "Can you apply your... iron at my house?" After a moment, she added, "I would prefer if there weren't any cleanup required when you are done."

Tala nodded. "Absolutely. I've gotten very practiced at keeping the iron contained. The masters at the academy were *quite* cross until I was able to perfect the process." In truth, they'd never approved, but at least they'd stopped slating her for punishment after she'd stopped contaminating random parts of the school.

"In that case, we should be off." Lyn turned and gave Holly a half bow. "Mistress."

Holly bowed tiredly in return. "Mistress. Until next time."

Tala bowed as well and came up smiling. "Thank you, Mistress Holly. I suppose I will see you in just over two weeks!"

"See that you do." Holly winked. "Take care, child."

"I will."

Without another word, Tala and Lyn departed, heading for Lyn's home and a good night's sleep.

Chapter: 9
It's Just Glue

Tala bid Lyn a good night and checked on her gear, which had been stored in Lyn's guest room. It rested in a small pile in one corner, on the poured stone floor.

Before she began sorting her items, she went to Lyn's washroom, filled the tub, and lit the prebuilt fire with her fire striker. The fire striker was a simple stone rod, as long as her finger, with copper scripting lines on the outside and a spark lizard tongue powering it. It was cunningly constructed so that she could expect close to three minutes of use. She could turn the device on or off by rotating a small wooden pin to either align, or breach, the scripting. When it was on, an eight-inch jet of flame was sustained from the tip.

It had cost three silver, but she'd never been good at starting fires with flint and steel, so it had seemed a reasonable expense.

With her bath heating, she returned to the room and sorted through her pack.

I should get my sleeping situation worked out. Estimating that it would be five minutes at least before the water was sufficiently warm, she got out the base for the bed she would use in the coming weeks.

A large tarp of overlapping, stitched, and waxed leather. It was two feet longer than she was tall and similarly wider than she needed, to provide a comfortable border around her in the night. *I want to get silver and gold inscriptions stitched into it, relying on my own gate, but that will be at least a gold ounce, or two... Holly could likely do it without the difficulty of stitching, just inscribing the leather as she would my skin, but I'd guess that that would be even more expensive...* The extra protection would likely be worth it, but she was racking up quite a few expenses that were 'worth it.'

She decided to ask and took out a loose piece of paper, penning the beginnings of a note to Holly, detailing her ideas.

Once the note was started, she turned her attention back to the fully spread tarp. She stepped around it, inspecting the craftsman's work. She'd not been able to fully look over the piece when she purchased it, but Ashin had spoken well of the man's products, so she hadn't quibbled. *He was right.* The seams were tight and subtle, meaning they wouldn't add to the bumps of the ground and shouldn't allow any water to come up through. The man had also stated that there was a layer of woolen batting inside the leather to aid in sleep on rough terrain. From the cushioned feel of the tarp, it was well made and evenly spread throughout, as well. The only exception was that, in the center of the tarp, just more than a foot from one edge, a portion of thicker padding was evident. It was a pillow of sorts, though much flatter than any she'd find in the cities.

As she considered her purchase, she realized that the leather was a bit wider than the bed, which stood beside it, and just a few inches longer. She frowned at that. *I'm not that* much *shorter than average...* She sighed. It wasn't important.

She pulled out a quilted woolen blanket and centered it on the leather, completing her padding. Above that, she had a linen-lined woolen blanket, sewn into a sort of envelope, so she didn't risk sticking out, regardless of her movements through the night. It was apparently a common design, used to compensate for the lack of any sort of mattress to tuck bedding around.

This might be a bit excessive... But it was coming into full autumn, and it might be quite cold. *I suppose I'll see how my preparations stack up.* Ashin had been skeptical, but he hadn't argued over any of her choices. *Does that mean they were wise, or he wasn't willing to speak up...?*

She sighed. No use second-guessing now.

I should get used to this before my trip. She glanced at the bed. *Besides, I don't want to get iron all over Lyn's linens.*

She stepped across the hall and verified that the water was close to the right temperature. She banked the fire, closed the window, and grabbed one of the bars of iron salve on its stick, along with a small jar.

Finally ready, she stripped and climbed into the bath, sinking down into the water and letting the heat seep deeply into her. Knowing that she'd not want to bathe too often until she reached the destination city, she took a long time to get thoroughly clean.

By the time she was done, the air in the washroom was quite warm as well, between the low-burning fire and the steam from the hot water.

She took great care to dry herself off. When that was complete, she took the little jar and removed the lid. Affixed inside the lid was a little brush, which she used to carefully spread the thick white liquid on her palms and the inside face of her fingers and thumbs. It was a glue that dried quickly and maintained flexibility once dry.

That complete, she placed the lid back on but couldn't seal it easily. Tala held her hands carefully spread, moving them through the air as the glue dried. It only took a few minutes before it was no longer tacky, and she was able to reseal the jar fully.

Millennial Mage 1 - Mageling

That done, she took up the salve bar by the handle and rubbed it across her back. Her warmth allowed the salve to spread across her skin easily in a thin layer, and she worked it in across all her skin, pressing it in and helping it get absorbed. She took care around her eyes to coat the skin without getting the salve in where it didn't belong.

Finally, she worked it through her hair, coating it lightly but making sure each strand stayed separate.

When that was complete, she opened the window and allowed the warm air to escape, cooling the washroom quickly.

As the air cooled, she continued to work the salve into her skin and hair, using a comb and brush to keep her hair from affixing to itself.

Nearly an hour after she had started, she was shivering from the cool air but finished.

She examined herself in the full-length mirror, taking in her darkened skin, now with a subtle grey tint, and her utterly black hair. Her hair had always been a deep brown that was *almost* black, but the iron-impregnated salve had finally tipped it into true black.

As she focused on herself, she felt her magesight activate, but though she could still see hints of her inscriptions beneath her skin, she couldn't see any magic flowing through her. Her gaze panned over herself from toe to head, and when her gaze met her own eyes, she stepped back in shock.

Her eyes were *blazing* with power as if the glow that should have been evident across her entire body had been collected and concentrated to shine from her eyes, alone.

She looked closely around her eyes, and she could see the spell-lines worked into her eyelids, which contained wards against magics acting on her through her sight. It was one-way, though, and didn't prevent her own magic from shining out.

The effect was... terrifying, if she was being honest. In the past, once she was coated in the iron salve, she'd been unable to see power in her own spell-lines, but her eyes had never glowed like this under her magesight. *Is this an increased sensitivity in my magesight, or is it an amplification of power in my inscriptions?* Likely, it was both.

Well, we're in it now, Tala. Let's hope no one mistakes us for an arcane. She grinned to herself.

There was a brief flicker of a memory, black skin, white teeth, and blood, but it was nothing more than a passing fancy, dismissed even before it had fully passed through her mind.

It was time to sleep. She dressed, crossed the hall, and slipped into her bedroll on the floor.

Tala was immediately glad for her purchases and quickly drifted off into a comfortable sleep.

* * *

Tala was poked.

She groaned and rolled over.

More pokes.

Tala pulled her blanket over her head and grunted. "Go away."

"Mistress Tala. Get up."

Is that Lyn? Tala sat up, glaring.

Lyn was near the door, a handkerchief over her nose and mouth.

"Mistress Lyn?"

"You reek of iron..."

Tala glanced down and saw that the other woman was holding a broom, the flicker of life magic momentarily evident, indicating that it had a wooden handle. Tala blinked several times, trying to process that. "Did... did you poke me with a broom?"

"I'm not going to touch you."

Tala looked at the window behind her, still dark. "Why are we awake?"

"You said you needed another hour or two this morning, before we left, for more iron... or something."

Tala scratched her forehead, trying to clear her thoughts. A healthy amount of iron dust trickled down into her lap.

"Thank you, by the way, for not using the bed."

Tala glared, but Lyn's smile seemed quite genuine. Finally, the younger woman grunted, again. "Happy to help."

Lyn chuckled to herself, but Tala heard it easily. "Well, I'm going to go grab us breakfast. When I get back, we can eat and head to the workyard."

Right! I need to empower the wagons today. With a sigh, she pushed herself to her feet and brushed herself off. She then shook out her clothes, allowing the dust to fall into her woolen envelope.

When the trickle had all but stopped, she did her best to empty the blankets onto her tarp, and from there, it poured easily into a little pouch.

Her magnet gathered up the remainder of what she could find.

That done, she stripped and moved through her stretches and workout. *Gotta keep in shape.* Heavens help her if Holly had to modify the inscriptions because of a few extra pounds.

Now sweaty, she re-lit the fire in the washroom and repeated her tasks from the night before. Though, this time, she only had to use a very small amount of the liquid glue to touch up the edges and cracks on her palms and fingers.

Roughly an hour later, she'd finished applying the next layer of iron salve and working it in. The now-open washroom window showed the barest hints of dawn's first light, and Tala thought she heard Lyn out in the front room.

Freshly ironed and dressed, Tala strode out into the sitting room to find breakfast, coffee, and Lyn.

Tala grinned. "I think I love you."

Lyn held out a mug and plate. "I get the feeling that your love and hate are rather freely given."

Tala took the offered sustenance and narrowed her eyes in an approximation of a glare, even as she kept her smile. "And quickly taken away, when appropriate."

"You better not leave. There is *no* way any other Mage would take your room now."

Tala paused only having taken a small sip. "I knew it."

"I don't know what you're talking about." Lyn took her own breakfast and sat.

"You normally rent out that room, don't you."

"I still do." Lyn grinned.

Tala sighed. "How much will it cost me?"

"For the room? Twenty silver a month—once you have funds. I'm not a monster. That said, food and delivery of such?" She lifted her own breakfast. "That's extra."

"You're trying to rob me blind."

Lyn laughed quietly, around her food. "Not at all. By all means, compare rates. I'm giving you a good deal." She smiled towards Tala, even as the latter took another chair. "I like you, and I'll be glad to have you around when you're in town."

"Hmm…" Tala kept her narrowed gaze on Lyn, even as she ate the nutritional offering. "Fine. But if you're overcharging me…"

"You should leave if you can find better accommodations or a better rate. It was an offer, Tala. I trust that you will find that it is a good one."

"So… I only have to pay when I'm in town?"

Lyn snorted. "Hardly. I'm holding the room for you, so you'll pay."

"But what if I go to other cities?"

Lyn shrugged. "Not my issue. Day rates in most cities are at least three to five silver a night. It would be hard to beat my rate, but you're welcome to check. I don't want you here if you'd rather be elsewhere."

Tala thought about it momentarily, then nodded before returning her attention to her food.

* * *

Less than an hour later, they were approaching the outer wall and a large workyard. Make no mistake, it wasn't the outside of the city, as the farms and their defensive towers and magics lay beyond, but this was the outer reaches of the urban area of the city.

As they approached, Lyn was explaining the procedure to Tala.

"Because we don't have a baseline for you, they will need you to empower several variations on the trade wagons. They'll start you on the smallest and simplest ones." She hesitated for a moment. "If you can, please try not to burn them out."

"What do you mean?"

"If you dump power into the activation, you'll likely fry the whole script. They aren't cheap to replace…"

"So, if I do this wrong, I'll have more debt?" Tala cocked an eyebrow in irritation.

"Not at all. I sent them a note to start higher up the chain, but I expect them to ignore that. When they do, if you burn out a wagon or two, the cost will fall on them…" Lyn seemed to realize something and clarified. "That would be bad, Tala."

Tala sighed. "I'm not a child. I won't break their toys just because *I* don't have to replace them."

Lyn quirked a smile. "And because you would do well to stay on the wainwrights' good side."

"How many tests am I going to need to do?"

"Shouldn't be more than six. Once they've determined your capabilities, you will have to empower at least ten spell-forms for the actual trip, likely more on the way back."

Tala was nodding. "And again, every morning until the trip, during the trip, and for at least two days after the trip."

"Exactly."

They came around the final turn, and Tala got a better look at what awaited them.

There were three fully enclosed, large wagons, each with a door in the back. The wagons stood nearly ten feet tall, from ground to mostly flat top. Beside the wagons stood three objects that seemed to be little more than freestanding back panels from wagons, similar to those they stood beside. All six awaiting objects were covered with deep lines, filled with copper. *Test pieces?* That made sense. The actual trade wagons would use gold, but it would be incredibly inefficient to activate gold scripts just for a test. They'd burn out without really being useful.

Even so, the copper meant that it would take more power to activate. After a moment's thought, Tala found herself nodding, and she spoke her realization under her breath. "It's mimicking the strain of multiple activations and fatigue from days on the road."

Lyn glanced at her. "Well reasoned. There are Archons who've never bothered to work that out."

Tala smiled. "Let's do this."

Two men and a woman were waiting for them.

As they came into range, their bodies flickered beneath Tala's magesight, showing their blood flowing through looping circuits, again seeming reminiscent of spell-lines but... not. The power of life and water and earth was intermixed with that of blood throughout their flesh, with their inscriptions glowing overtop it all.

They were, all three, Immaterial Guides. And all three had nearly identical spell-lines, only seeming to have been modified in consideration of their different body types, shapes, and heights. They were configurations that she would never have recognized herself, but her magesight seemed to help with translation.

The spell-lines were made to allow for the testing, analysis, and creation of inscribed items. The inscriptions had resemblances to those Holly bore but clearly had a different focus.

One of the three, clearly the oldest, seemed to have a different *depth* to his spell-lines, to his power, as if they were canyons and his were vastly deeper. Through those canyons, Tala thought she saw flickers of underlying orange light, but it wasn't steady or pervasive. In addition to the other oddities, a small glass bead hung around his neck, which positively radiated power. Something seemed to be diminishing it, though, as if someone had tried throwing a veil over the sun.

Is that an Archon's mark? None of her teachers at the academy had been Archons, but she'd heard of them. *I thought it was supposed to look like a star...* She sighed. *A question for another time, I suppose.*

As Tala didn't focus on any of the Mages, specifically, their power faded to her magesight, leaving them as they had been.

They each bowed slightly in greeting, and the older man gestured to the first wagon. "This schema is the simplest; it doubles the interior space and stabilizes the cargo therein."

Tala saw the outline of a right hand and strode forward to place her palm against it.

The Mage continued his explanation. "Most young Mages take close to ten minutes to fully recharge this scripting when they first encounter cargo wagons. Are you familiar enough with the concepts to activate it?"

Lyn spoke under her breath, but Tala heard easily. "Not your toys."

Tala grinned. Without a word, she opened her gate, and drew deeply on her power, shifting it to her hand as if she were going to prick a finger and confirm a contract. She was *very* careful not to activate any of her spell-lines. As the power flowed through her, from her gate, it gathered up more from her body, carrying it along and into the wagon.

She felt a strange resistance and had a realization. *I forgot to peel off the glue.* Likely, some of the iron dust had managed to get stuck in the glue, creating what amounted to a dampening filter for her power.

She was about to pull her hand back in embarrassment, to remove the barrier, when she saw three symbols above her hand blossom with light in quick succession. She pulled her hand back quickly to keep from overcharging the spells.

To her magesight, power rippled through the copper lines, and there was a twisting expansion before her sight, contained within the wagon. It had a similar look, under her magesight, to a pillowcase as the stuffing was shoved inside but without a physical change. In addition, the secondary and tertiary symbols each seemed to correspond with a well of power, which appeared to her magesight as knot-like bundles of scripting, connecting and feeding into the main functions.

The older Mage smiled, stepping forward. "Oh! That's wonderful. I can see that Mage Lyn did not oversell your ability." The two other Mages came forward and opened the door in the back of the wagon. They both stepped inside with ease and seemed to be measuring the space.

After a quick moment, their voices echoed out, clear for all to hear. "Correct empowering. Precisely doubled in size. She did not double the size of the indents and other imperfections in the outer shell, thus maintaining maximum efficiency." As they stepped out, the woman triggered a secondary portion of the spell-lines, deactivating the script.

They walked to the next wagon, and Tala pointed to a part of the spell-lines that lay above the activation point that resembled an outline for her hand and the three symbols, which would indicate the level of empowerment. The portion she'd indicated looked more like writing than true spell-lines, but it wasn't the alphabet used in books. "These are the specifications, correct?" She glanced to the older man. "This wagon's scripts triple the size, stabilize the cargo, and protect the wagon, itself, from the weight and jostling of said cargo, correct?"

He had opened his mouth to give exactly that explanation but seemed satisfied as he closed his mouth, nodded, and smiled.

She took a moment to catch the edge of the glue on her right hand and peel it free in one large piece. As Tala looked around for a place to dispose of her now-removed handprint, she saw several aghast looks. She smiled. "It's just glue."

They did *not* look mollified.

Tala sighed, then decided to just toss it aside. *Some people freak out much too easily.*

Chapter: 10
Don't Let Them Poach You

Hand now free of glue, Tala grinned. *Let's see what I can really do.*

She placed her hand on the activation panel and channeled power into it once more. Based on her previous activation, she channeled less power, so as not to overwhelm this next wagon.

The three lights flicked on at almost the same time, and she jerked her hand back as if she'd seen a snake. *Please don't be overloaded.* She felt a bit tired, given the power that had been pulled from her body towards the empowering, but her gate was open, and her stores were replenishing rapidly.

After a long pause, when nothing further happened, the two Mages came forward, verified her work, and deactivated the working, once again.

"Well, I think we can skip the third wagon." The older Mage smiled in an almost grandfatherly way. After a moment's thought, he added, "Let's skip the first cargo-slot as well."

Ahh, that's what they're called. Following his instructions, she walked up to the second free-standing door. *Cargo-slot.* More than anything, it looked like someone had taken off the back of one of the enclosed wagons and added another wall directly to the back before standing it up.

She frowned at the descriptive scripting for a long moment.

"Do you want me to give you the explanation?"

"I think I understand. It expands the small crevice between the two layers of wood into a large room, roughly twice the size of a mundane wagon's interior. It also stabilizes and isolates the weight of the cargo."

"Correct."

Tala placed her hand on the activation point and filled herself with power, carefully, pushing it into the cargo-slot's spell-lines.

Nothing happened.

Tala frowned and drew deeply, pushing more power forward. The first symbol slowly blossomed with light.

Tala found a low growl rippling up through her chest, and she threw her gate wide, holding nothing back, drawing more than before on her own reserves. The second and third symbols filled with light in quick succession over the following twenty seconds or so.

When the final symbol lit up, Tala was breathing hard. "Done!" Her voice was a bit breathless, and she felt quite tired, though that passed quickly as her body's power slowly returned to her standard density. In truth, she was surprised at how tired she'd felt, given her estimate that she'd only used about a quarter of her personal power. *I guess that's because my body is used to always having that power.*

The oldest Mage had a look of mild surprise but didn't comment as the other two opened the door and stepped into the obviously spacious interior.

It took only a moment for them to confirm her success.

She strode to the final test and analyzed the inscriptions. "Same as before, but four times the interior size. So, it would be eight times the space as a non-magical, cargo wagon. Right?"

"As you say. Begin when you are ready." After a moment, he added, "You are welcome to take a short break if you so desire."

She shook her head. "No need, but thank you." In retrospect, his offer had been a kind one. She was feeling a bit drained still, and she knew that while her density was high, her power accumulation rate was nothing special.

Tala threw her gate as wide as her keystone would allow and drew deeply, channeling all that she could into her hand, even as she slammed it against the activation location.

She felt a deep reverberation through her chest, though she was not consciously growling with the effort. Her gate was insufficient, so she pulled at her body for power, pulling every vestige she could yank free and throwing it at the cargo-slot's activation panel.

It felt like someone was pouring boiling water over her right arm, and her palm might as well have been on a stove, from the feel of it.

Finally, after what seemed like an eternity, the first symbol blossomed to life.

Is that all? You're mine, now. One symbol meant she could activate it, now she was just filling out the capacity, so it would keep running for a time.

A second eternity passed, but she wasn't growling anymore; she didn't have the strength. The next symbol faded into brilliance.

Sweat was pouring off her, and her eyes felt like she had been staring down a crucible for hours, but finally, the last inscribed symbol lit.

She sank to her knees despite her attempts to stay up.

No one spoke as the two junior Mages opened the door and entered the expanded space to measure.

When they returned, they simply nodded.

It had been done correctly.

Finally, Tala was able to speak but found her voice slightly hoarse. "How long?"

The older man stepped forward and spoke softly. "I have you at twelve minutes, Mistress."

"Oh… I failed then." She'd had ten minutes to charge them if she was to use ones like this on her venture. "Oh well." She smiled up at him.

He cleared his throat and glanced away. "That one is meant as an upper bound, Mistress Tala. We've never had one activated by a simple Mage during testing." He looked back to her and smiled.

Tala's eyes returned to the script she'd just empowered. *Maybe, I should try again? I bet I could do better the second time.* That… that would not be a good idea. She couldn't remember having this little power within herself. Even before she'd gone to the academy, she'd had magic within, like all humans did.

"Huh… so my failure was a success." She glanced to Lyn. The woman's face was an attempt at impassivity, but Tala could see pride and concern both clear and clearly mixed across her features. "Yay me." Then, Tala slipped into unconsciousness. Her last thought was oddly disconnected.

Wait a minute… we added an inscription to prevent me from falling unconscious, except to sleep. I guess it didn't quite work… Oh well.

*   *   *

A pulse of power exploded from the base of Tala's skull, and she returned to consciousness, violently.

She'd fallen too far to easily catch herself, but her heightened reflexes allowed her to tuck, turning the kneeling fall into a roll.

Thus, an instant after she'd fainted from overuse of power, she found herself standing fully upright, staring out across the workyard.

A shiver ran through her from head to toe, and a sense akin to her magesight picked up the signature of what had awoken her. It had been a silver inscription, set to watch for any loss of consciousness not due to falling asleep. *So, it did work?*

A sound, almost like a bell, hummed through her thoughts, and she found the note calming. Then, her own voice came to her as if she were thinking, though she never truly considered that the voice might be her own thoughts.

-Consciousness lost for 0.05 seconds due to Magical Overuse and Severe Internal Power Scarcity. The Keystone Inscription attempted to induce unconsciousness to allow for expedited recovery. Keystone flaw noted for correction.-

-Mild, targeted, electrical shock and hormone cocktail utilized for near-instant resuscitation.-

-No lasting effects detected.-

-Log complete.-

"What. Utter. Slag." Tala spun towards Lyn who was staring at her, open-mouthed. "Mistress Holly is a madwoman." Tala threw up her hands. "A madwoman!"

Lyn stepped forward but stopped before touching her. "Mistress Tala, are you okay? What just happened?"

"I… I can't even…" Tala had been about to explain that a voice in her head just revived her, but that sounded crazy, even to her, and she'd been the one to hear it. Finally, she sighed. "Never mind…" She turned back to the older Mage, who was still standing next to the last test. She bowed, slightly more than necessary. "My apologies. Might I have a minute to rest before empowering the scripts for loading?"

He seemed to gather himself at her words and smiled. "Of course. The tests are meant to be difficult, so that we may better ascertain a Mage's merit, but I must say, we rarely see anyone put quite as much effort into it as you have."

"That's Mistress Tala for you." Lyn glanced to Tala, then back to the Mage.

He turned to regard Lyn. "You speak on her behalf?"

"Yes, I am the arbiter of her indenture. You are Master Himmal, correct?"

"I am." He gave a nod of acknowledgment. "How does she stand on the road to Archon?"

"She is not yet trained in the creation of a star; she has no sponsor; and she lacks the requisite years of—"

He was waving his hand dismissively. "The lack of experience might be troublesome, but I doubt many would care." He looked at Tala. "But the star is crucial…" He seemed to be considering. "It is best for Mages to discover it on their own, but it isn't unheard of for someone to be taught instead. Still, her master didn't deem it a good idea, so I should not interfere." He turned towards Tala. "When the time comes, if you still lack a sponsor, I will speak on your behalf."

She was stunned. "I have no words… Thank you, Master Himmal." *I also have no idea what you are talking about…*

He simply smiled.

Tala smiled back. "I suppose I will have to seek out a star…" *I knew it was a star! But why does his look like a bead?* She bowed, once again. "Truly, thank you." Turning back towards their destination, Tala added, "Now, where may I sit until the scripts are ready?"

Master Himmal gave her a bemused look but didn't comment. Instead, he gave instruction to his two underlings, then led her, himself, to a shaded seating area and already waiting refreshments.

He was serious, then. They expect Mages to take a short break after the test. Once she had a drink in hand, and a few choice bites consumed, she turned to the man. "If I may ask, you are an Archon, correct?"

He smiled. "Yes. I am Glass Archon, Void Key."

Not a gem? I thought all Archons were some form of gem like Diamond Archon or some such.

As she was contemplating, he showed his palms, each of which held an inscription of a keyhole, and thoughts of his Archon title faded.

No, not an inscription. It looked like someone had done the work with regular ink as the keyholes were black. *How odd.* "How did you get the name? Do all Archons get such titles?"

"No, but many hope to. You have to excel in a particular area for the Council to give you a title beyond the designation. I am the 'key to the void' in that my empowerments of dimensional expansion were without equal."

Tala looked at him quizzically.

"Ah, I should explain: First, I am the discoverer of these scripts." He gestured back to the cargo-slots. "That is one part. Second, when I said no single Mage has ever empowered the one that you activated last in a test, I meant it. Outside of a test, however, any Archon of our order could do as you did—most could do it more quickly."

She nodded, understanding. "How large of a space can you create?"

He quirked a smile. "In my prime, a single one of my scripts opened a new storehouse for use in transportation. So"—he thought for a moment—"a hundred times the size of your final test?" He nodded. "Give or take."

She gaped. "How?"

"Discipline, a perfect mental focus and understanding of what was being done, and a reckless disregard for the longevity of my arts." He smiled again, sadly this time. "I'm not capable of half so much, now. My gate is overused and a bit abused." He glanced at her and seemed to read her thoughts. "No, it isn't near collapse. I was not *that* foolish, but my days of traveling are done."

"If I may ask, what did you do? My understanding was that our gates are incredibly resilient and flexible enough to grow with use."

He snorted a laugh. "True enough. I convinced an inscriber to alter my keystone to keep my gate under constant stress, forcing it open as wide as possible at all times, always straining for more." He shook his head, sadly. "It almost worked, but the wider the gate was open, the more the prying script put pressure on my gate. It was a feedback loop, and before the inscription ran its course, I'd irreparably damaged myself." He gave a sad smile.

"So... a lesser version of it would work?"

He barked out his laugh, this time. "Leave it to the young to ignore the true lesson." He grinned at her. "You aren't wrong though. My design was perfected and is now a part of every standard keystone, but to a *much* more restricted level." His smile shifted to one of pride. "My work will help every future Mage grow in power more quickly and with less effort."

"I'm sorry that it cost you what it did."

He shrugged. "It was probably for the best. Now, I get to *design*."

"And you enjoy that?"

"More than I ever thought possible." His smile settled into one of clear contentment.

Tala smiled. "I'm glad." She had a thought and returned to something he'd said earlier. "What mental focus do you bring to bear? I understand how the spell-forms function, else I couldn't empower them, but I don't do anything specific to..." She trailed off as Master Himmal was gaping at her. "What?"

"Mistress Tala. Without a mental framework, you would need orders of magnitude more power to activate any spell-form than truly necessary." He shook his head. "You are throwing a chuck-wagon at the cook, trusting him to find what he needs in the wreckage."

Chuck-wagon? "Is it really that bad?"

"Yes. You must funnel your power through a mental structure of whatever you attempt to do." His voice faded at the end, and he blinked several times then glanced back towards the yard. "Wait..." He looked back to her. "You empowered *that* via brute force? Are you insane?"

"Yes, I did, but no?"

"Did you crack your gate for a test, girl?" He was frowning, now. "Who taught you so negligently?"

Lyn stepped forward, interceding on Tala's behalf. "Her training was unusual, and not quite as thorough as it should have been. She has power and is perfecting its use."

Tala's magesight showed flickers of power around Master Himmal's eyes as he activated his own magesight. Immediately, he took a step back. "How are you doing that?"

"You'll have to be more specific?"

"You have no power about you, save in your eyes and palms, and those are blazing. Even your breath has less than usual. Is your gate thrown wide, even now?"

"It is open, but not widely. As to the rest—"

Lyn stepped forward. "Mistress Tala would gladly trade technique for technique, or her knowledge for items."

Master Himmal opened his mouth to object, then hesitated. After a long moment, he closed it and nodded. "That is fair, I suppose." He glanced to Tala. "I assume it has to do with the iron scent surrounding you, but I will not dig further, not at this moment. Your training must have been unusual indeed."

Tala quirked a smile. "Quite, yes."

With a last look at Tala, Master Himmal turned back towards the yard. "Now, I must ensure your cargo-slots are ready for empowerment and loading. You know to return each day just after dawn until your departure, yes?" He narrowed his eyes, seeming to bring the entirety of his focus to bear upon her.

"Yes, sir. I will."

While he returned to the yard, directing workmen and conversing with his underlings, Tala rested.

Lyn remained quiet, seeming contemplative.

After a short time, Tala glanced around and verified that the two of them were, indeed, alone. "So… why are you still here?"

Lyn started, turning to face her. "Do you want me to leave?"

"No, but I don't really know why you're here."

"To help you."

"Because I'm not really supposed to be more than a mageling?"

Lyn grinned. "You've proven yourself far beyond that, Tala."

"Then…?"

She shrugged. "I need to occasionally assess the various portions of our operations, both within the guild and within our partner organizations. This was as good a time as any to follow a new recruit through the process; I thought you could use a friendly face; and I am never bored around you." She smiled. "I think I'm beginning to like you." Her eyes flicked down Tala's length, then back to her eyes. "But please don't start rubbing off on me. That would be *quite* inconvenient. Iron dust and all that."

It was Tala's turn to grin. "I wouldn't dream of it."

Master Himmal returned and escorted them toward one side of the workyard where ten of the cargo-slots stood, all doors facing the same way. She didn't see their activation points, however.

Tala noted groups of workers standing next to nearby warehouses, seemingly awaiting the completion of her task.

As she drew closer, her magesight highlighted the inactive scripts, and the activations points became obvious on the side of each wooden device. They were oriented lower than she thought optimal, and she was shorter than the average Mage. Aside from the odd placement, everything seemed in order, and as she looked, Tala was able to decipher the descriptive scripts. "These are equal to my second to last test." Her tone bore a bit of accusation.

Master Himmal grinned. "That is true. It is the most complex set we keep on hand for regular use. I can assure you that we will be making a set with greater capacity than these for the next time you venture forth from our fair city."

Lyn spoke softly, trusting to Tala's enhanced hearing to allow her to pick up the words. "When they can be used, that will earn both you and the Wainwright's Guild a bonus for each trip. Not every trip will need such capacity, so it wouldn't earn the bonus, then, but it will help in other ways."

Tala smiled and nodded towards Master Himmal. "I thank you. May we both benefit from their use." *I didn't consider that the Caravan Guild would effectively be renting these...* The Wainwrights must charge more for the use of their own Mages for transport than even Tala, herself, was offered. *Huh... worth thinking about.* She was sure that such would necessarily include fees for the Wainwright's Guild, so she doubted her pay would have been better, either way.

Millennial Mage 1 - Mageling

Without waiting, she walked up to the first and placed her hand against the smooth, well-treated wood. *There's a slight impression, here. I wonder how many hundreds of hands have been exactly where mine is, now.*

She opened her gate further by activating her keystone and drew deeply on her power.

Instead of simply dumping the magic through her hand, she remembered what Master Himmal said. She tried to envision exactly what her power was going to do and channeled the magic through that mental construct before it exited her hand to enter the golden channels in the wood.

Whether the tests were, indeed, much harder; her mental structure had worked; or a combination of both, she was able to fully empower all three symbols of the first script before she'd reached a slow count of ten.

As Tala stepped back, she felt a satisfied smile pulling at her lips. *Nice job, Tala. Just nine more to go.*

She continued using the mental construction as a conduit for her power, and it did seem to help. In addition, every successful empowerment, using that model, made it stronger and firmer in her mind, causing the following efforts to be more efficient. At least, it seemed that way to her. In addition, she was no longer having to pull power from her body to enact the empowering. That had to be a good sign.

By the time she got to the end, she felt tired but not nearly so much as after the equivalent test. As an added bonus, it wasn't the feeling of power exhaustion but simple mental strain. *Like learning a new type of math or delving deeper into the sciences.*

"Well done, Mistress Tala. Thank you." Master Himmal waved to the workers, and they began carrying large crates out towards them, even as his two Mage underlings were finalizing their inspection of her work.

They, too, congratulated her and indicated success.

"I suppose we will see you tomorrow, then?"

"Bright and early, yes. These will be here?"

"Just as you see them."

"Thank you." She bowed once more to each of the Mages and bid them farewell.

Lyn, similarly, made her goodbyes and departed with Tala. "Not bad. Don't let them poach you." She had an obvious smile in her tone. "We will *always* pay better."

Tala smiled in turn. "See that you do, and you'll never have to worry.

The two chuckled and, together, decided it was well past time for brunch.

Chapter: 11
Mysteries and Chowder

As it turned out, Lyn had to go in to do some paperwork and thought it would be instructive for Tala to accompany her to the guild's main office.

Lyn promised coffee, so Tala agreed.

In retrospect, that was an early sign that Tala had failed: Coffee was becoming integral.

As they walked back through the city, Lyn seemed to be mulling over an idea. Finally, she turned to Tala as they continued. "Would you consider wearing gloves when around other Mages? We might want to find a way to reduce the… cloud around you."

Tala glanced at the other woman and then briefly down at their feet. The older woman was walking just out of arm's reach. "Is it that bad?"

Lyn hesitated, then finally sighed. "Yes."

Tala waited for more, but when nothing more was said, her eyebrows rose. "Oh… Ummm… I'm sorry?"

Lyn smiled. "It seemed that honesty would be best."

"Well, thank you." Tala contemplated for just a moment. "I don't have any money for gloves—" She stopped speaking as Lyn's arm extended her way, proffering a set of thin, black, leather gloves. "You… already bought me a pair."

"I did." Lyn smiled apologetically. "I wasn't quite sure how to approach you about it…" As Tala took the gloves and began putting them on, Lyn continued, "They are treated and sealed inside and out, so they *shouldn't* be able to pick up any iron, but I'll leave that to you to verify."

"I... Thank you. This is a kind gift." If she was being honest, it hurt a bit that something about her offended her friend so much that she'd preemptively sought ways to hide it. Tala took a deep breath and let it out. *I'm being touchy. She is looking out for me, as well as how I am, and will be, perceived by other Mages.*

Did she care what other Mages thought?

If Ashin's reaction to her was indicative of how non-Mages would view her, she likely couldn't have many friends if she drove all Mages away. Tala finally nodded, as they continued their trek through the city. "Truly, thank you."

Lyn seemed to relax. "With those, we only need to find a way of dealing with your... lack of aura."

Tala frowned. "What?"

"In my magesight, you basically don't exist..." There was a long pause, during which Lyn began to frown. "No... that's not right. You are like a human-shaped mirror to my magesight, walking around." After a moment, she nodded. "The result can't really be described any other way. In some situations, you are virtually invisible. In others, you stand out like a human-shaped oddity." Her eyes flicked to Tala's face, then away. "Except your eyes." She shivered slightly. "Honestly, the combination is a bit..."

Tala quirked a smile, remembering her own view in Lyn's washroom mirror. "Terrifying?"

Lyn laughed. "Just a bit. And even without my magesight, you feel a bit strange, like a piece of paper lightly brushing across my skin. I'd guess it is something with the iron reflecting my own power back my way." She shrugged. "But really, I've no idea."

Tala didn't really have a response. She remembered her classmates' awkwardness and hesitancy around her. *Were they just feeling a weaker version of what Lyn is?* What would that do to the already socially hesitant Mages-to-be? Her years of near-isolation took on a new cast. *Did I do that all to myself?* She felt a deep seed of sadness and loneliness blossom within her. *No, don't focus on that. I have a task to complete.*

Tala remained silent on their trek back toward the Caravanners Guildhall, even while Lyn pointed out interesting shops, restaurants, and features of the city.

"That shop sells the best hats."

"This gate is named after…"

"The spinach soup, there, is to die for!"

Finally, a last comment brought her from her silence. Indicating a door tucked back between the two neighboring buildings, Lyn said, "He buys and sells artifacts and arcane goods."

Tala's head snapped up, and she noticed the look of smug satisfaction on Lyn's lips.

"I thought that might interest you."

Tala took a step towards the door. *Artifacts, magical items that have no visible inscriptions and only need power, every so often, to continue functioning.* She'd never seen one and had only heard of them through hearsay, so she'd no idea if that was actually true, but it was enticing. What would it be like to not require metal to keep items functional? *I need to study some.*

Lyn stopped her. "You can come back later… when you have money to buy something."

Tala groaned. *Right… fundless.* "Fine. How much should I have?"

"If you want a trinket, something that works similarly to an empowered item? Ten to fifty ounces of gold. An item of real power, though?" Her smile turned wicked. "You should have a soul or two to trade."

Millennial Mage 1 - Mageling

Tala laughed but trailed off when Lyn didn't join in. "You aren't serious... Right?"

Lyn shrugged. "I've never heard of someone buying one of the truly rare ones, and every Mage I've known to sell one retired shortly after."

Tala swallowed. *So... not cheap.* She wasn't sure what she'd expected, but she still felt disappointed. "Maybe... he'd let me study them?"

Lyn laughed, then, and turned to keep walking. "He keeps a large book, which describes the items for customers to peruse. The items, themselves, are kept under tight security somewhere in the city. To be clear, the book describes the trinkets. He keeps knowledge of the truly powerful ones in his own head, supposedly."

"Somewhere?" Tala fell in beside her friend.

"I certainly don't know where, and while many have fun guessing, I don't know of anyone who actually knows." Her eyes were twinkling. "I do know of several *very* skilled trackers, Mages all, who worked together to tail him after several sales. According to them, he never left the shop."

Tala rolled her eyes. "He obviously has some artifact teleportation item or an expanded space."

Lyn cocked an eyebrow. "Of course! How could we all be so foolish as to not consider the obvious."

Tala sighed. "Fine. So, he never leaves, and the items just... what? Disappear?"

"That's the mystery."

Tala turned back, allowing her eyes to rest on the shop front and focus on it more intently. It was still an odd, new experience, but she *thought* she was allowing her magesight to sweep through the store. She certainly got a good look at the inside of the buildings on either side, both family homes, both empty for the day. The view was mainly just the impression of the various types of magical connections present in mundane objects, but it was enough to get a general idea. Even so, she couldn't see anything beyond the front of the building she was interested in, and that looked... strange, but also strangely familiar.

Tala blinked rapidly, trying to clear her vision of the odd effects associated with the building. She made an incoherent sound of distaste and wiped at her eyes absently. "Mleh... What is that?"

Lyn sighed. "Too bad. I'd hoped your sight could penetrate it. He has iron plates up on the inside of his walls."

Tala glared. "You could have warned me."

"That's what it feels like to look at you. Or to stand near you, for that matter. Consider it educational." A small smile was tugging at the older woman's lips.

"I've seen myself, thank you."

"Ahh, then a reinforcement of the notion?"

"You're..."

"So helpful?" Lyn offered.

"Yes." Tala nodded, adding in a monotone, "So, so very helpful."

"I aim to be of assistance."

The silence broken, the two chatted amiably for the rest of the walk to the guildhall.

When they arrived, Lyn led Tala through a chorus of greetings, almost universally directed at Lyn. Lyn introduced Tala in passing, but no one stuck in the younger Mage's mind.

Together, they passed through a large set of beautifully crafted doors into a lushly appointed side room. Her magesight immediately overwhelmed her with information as it apprised her that every single occupant, except the occasional tray-bearing server, was a Mage. There were at least thirty people that she could see. The influx caused her eyes to go out of focus for a moment and her balance to become unsteady for an instant before it passed.

Millennial Mage 1 - Mageling

Even so, she found that she could easily recall the auras surrounding each—if she wished to. She did not.

The sounds of cooking and the clink of plates and cutlery came from an adjoining space, and the low buzz of conversation rested comfortably throughout the room.

A restaurant?

"This, Tala, is the guild's Mage lounge. You can't afford the food right now, and I'd recommend against it, even if you have the money." She leaned in and faked a whisper. "They charge *much* more than they should."

An occupant of a nearby table laughed at the comment, which he was obviously meant to have heard. "The prices *are* high, but the company is second to none." The young man, perhaps around Lyn's age, stood and walked over to them. "Did I hear right? Your name is Tala?" He offered a hand.

Tala took it hesitantly. "Yes, and you are…?"

But he was looking down at her hand. "Gloves? What an interesting fashion choice. And no robes?" He glanced at Lyn. "Is your friend trying to shame us all into purchasing better wardrobes?" He turned back to Tala, smiling with evident humor. "I'm entranced, but you can call me Cran." He shook her hand once more, firmly but not in an 'I want to prove how strong I am' sort of way, and released her.

"Master Cran, then. Nice to meet you… I suppose?"

Lyn grinned. "Master Cran, you really shouldn't overwhelm the poor dear. She's new to…" Lyn hesitated, then sighed. "I was going to say, 'Mage society,' but that makes us sound like the sort of club that, honestly, we'd avoid."

His smile, somehow, seemed to widen. "New, eh? A mageling, then?" He glanced between the two women. "Mistress Lyn? Have you finally taken on a mageling? I thought you'd sworn off the idea."

Lyn shook her head. "No, not a mageling..." She glanced to Tala. "She can tell her own story, if she wants to, but she isn't used to all of this."

Cran turned to regard Tala, looking truly excited. "No... You aren't an outland Mage, are you?"

Lyn groaned, placing a hand over her face.

Tala frowned. "An outland Mage?"

Lyn sighed. "Master Cran has a pet theory that there are human Mages beyond the cities. He guesses that they'd have to be much more powerful, and use different methods to cope with the greater amounts of magic and the more powerful entities out there."

"It's not *my* theory, Mistress Lyn. Many Mages believe some variation on the same." He gave Tala a conspiratorial smile and shifted into a half-whisper. "It doesn't help that so many of our most gifted associates seem to vanish for long stints, then refuse to tell us where they've been."

"They aren't going outside, Cran."

"You don't know that."

Lyn sighed, but Tala shook her head and interjected. "No. I'm from the cities. I even trained at the academy."

Cran looked vaguely disappointed but recovered. After a pause, his smile shifted to one of friendly interest. "May I look?"

Tala frowned. "...What?"

Lyn leaned over to whisper, truly this time, though Tala thought Cran might still be able to hear. "He's asking to use his magesight on you. It is usually rude to gaze upon another Mage without permission. Yet another way that Mistress Holly's decisions were... unusual."

Cran seemed to misunderstand the whispering. "You can look at me as well, of course."

Oh, he couldn't hear. Now that she thought about it, Lyn had spoken so quietly, she might not have even known the woman was speaking before Holly's work on her inscriptions. *She adapted incredibly fast to what I can perceive...* She might have to ask about that.

In the meantime, however, Cran was looking expectant.

"Oh! Of course, but I think you might..." She trailed off as she saw the inscriptions lacing around his eyes ripple with power.

Cran frowned, staring down at her feet. "Huh... Is it working or—" He had swept his gaze upward, and his words cut off abruptly as his eyes met hers. He seemed to visibly restrain himself for an instant, his hands twitching so subtly that Tala knew she would not have noticed it even a few days earlier. "Oh... I don't quite understand but..." He leaned forward, seemingly despite himself. "Well, chrome my ba—"

Lyn cut him off. "Cran! Language."

He cleared his throat, his eyes flicking to her briefly. "My apologies, Mistress Lyn. Mistress Tala, what...?" His gaze swept across their surroundings, seeming to note a few curious stares. He lowered his voice and continued, "What are you?"

Tala quirked a smile. "*Very* hungry. Are you buying?" She glanced to Lyn. "*You* promised me coffee, and don't you have work to do?"

Cran opened his mouth, then closed it before his smile returned in full force, bringing with it a soft laugh. "I suppose I *should* buy you dinner before—" His eyes ticked to Lyn again before he sighed. "You aren't much fun sometimes, Mistress Lyn."

"I didn't say anything."

"But you were thinking it." He gestured for them to follow him back towards his table.

Lyn waved down a server and ordered coffee for Tala, paying as she did so. "As Mistress Tala so kindly pointed out, I have work to be about." She gave Cran a flat stare. "You treat her well, yes? If possible, try to introduce her to those leaving with her in a few days." She handed over a card.

Cran took it and nodded. "I will. Mistress Tala?"

Tala gave Lyn a small wave in goodbye, then turned and followed him. The table was large enough for four and with enough chairs, though he'd been sitting there alone.

The book resting on it immediately gave Tala the impression that he was seeking solitude, simply enjoying a quiet evening. She frowned slightly as she sat down. *Solitude at the table closest to the entrance?* A front then? *Or a show.* He wanted to see everyone who came and went, but wasn't interested in having anyone join him. *Until us.*

It was also possible that it had been the only available table when he'd arrived, and she was just overthinking things. *That would be typical.*

Cran's voice cut across her thoughts as he held out a menu towards her. "What will you have?"

Tala took the menu and glanced at the prices. Lyn had *not* been exaggerating. "I can't order anything from here!" She felt mortified.

He just smiled. "Tell you what: Order any one meal, and repay me with all your darkest secrets."

Tala gave him a flat look.

"Fine, fine. Tell me your quadrant, if that even applies, and we can go from there?"

She smiled widely. "Deal."

Tala ordered a sweet potato and yam chowder served in a wheat-sourdough bread bowl.

She did *not* think about how much it cost. *Three silver, and the coffee Lyn ordered for me was twenty copper!* She most certainly did *not* feel guilty at the expense.

As the server departed, Tala flicked back through her memory to what her magesight had shown of Cran when she'd first entered.

Millennial Mage 1 - Mageling

Immaterial Creator, specializing in kinetic energy. He has a series of gold-powered, silver-activated spell-forms designed to drive any incoming threat away. Her analysis hadn't been detailed enough to determine exactly how it detected incoming attacks, nor exactly how the magic would respond, but if Cran was true to his word, she could look more closely if she wanted.

In addition, he had several concentrations of earth energy scattered throughout his body. If she had to guess, she'd say they were now-healed breaks to his bones, but it would have been just a guess. *Am I seeing earth because it is, or is that simply the closest thing I can recognize?* She would not be surprised if bones had a magic all their own, somehow.

By his spell-lines, his magesight was very basic, in that it would likely just highlight sources of power around him, likely color coding for the type of power. It didn't seem nearly detailed enough to provide any analysis.

How is mine doing that? I haven't studied spell-lines as an inscriber, but the knowledge of what spell-lines do seems ready at hand... Another 'Holly addition' most likely.

Cran cleared his throat. "So... do we need to wait for the food to arrive or...?"

"Hmmm? Oh! I apologize, my mind was elsewhere."

"I could see that." But he smiled, removing some of the sting from the rejoinder.

"To answer your question: I am of the Immaterial Guide quadrant."

He nodded. "I thought your lines had a familiar feel to them." He squinted, even though there was plenty of light. "Though, the tone of your skin makes it difficult to see them very clearly... Why do you have a gray cast? And why can't my magesight see you properly?" He lightly rubbed at his arms for a moment before pausing and glancing down. He looked back up, eyes narrowing. "This feeling is you, too, right?"

"How many dinners are you planning on buying me?" She smiled mischievously, trying to hide her own nervousness.

He smiled in return. "At least confirm that I am right, even if not the method?"

After a moment's hesitation, she realized that answering was a triviality. He would know when she left that she was the source of the feeling. She gave a tentative nod. "I am the source of what you're feeling, if I understand you correctly." After a moment, she felt concern paint her features in a sort of frown. "Is it terrible? I can leave…"

He shook his head, his smile growing. "Honestly, it isn't. It feels almost like a light pressure against me." He let out a low chuckle. "Sort of like having a blanket thrown over me on the side facing you."

"That… doesn't sound too bad." *Pressure? Is that because his magics tend towards kinetic energy?* Was every Mage around her feeling something unique to their own emphasis? *Probably only those within a pace or two.*

"It isn't." He smiled again. "Now, you leave in a few days. Where are you going?"

Tala opened her mouth to answer and found that she didn't know; she closed it again. She frowned.

"Oh, come now. I'm not paying for information like that," he teased.

She quirked a smile. "I'd not ask you to, but I actually don't know. I didn't ask."

"You didn't…" He seemed stunned.

"I needed to leave and return on a tight, specific timeline, and Lyn found the best set of routes for that aim."

Cran nodded, seeming somewhat mollified. "I see. A bit odd, but to each their own, I suppose. How long will you be gone?"

Again, she was stumped. Even so, she did have a semblance of an answer. "Just a couple weeks."

"A couple weeks to get there and back, eh? With a tight turnaround in the middle…" He seemed to be contemplating. "You're likely going to either Alefast or Marliweather."

Tala stiffened, slightly. "I hope it's Alefast."

"Oh? Don't like Marliweather?"

She shrugged. "I know some people there…"

"Might be nice to visit them, then?" He'd cocked his head just slightly, clearly puzzled.

"I don't know, yet." She took a deep breath and let it out, pulling a smile back in place. "What do you know of those cities?"

His puzzlement was replaced with a knowing smile. "Well! I've got to tell you, I've been to both, and neither hold a shine to here." He nodded. "Bandfast is the place to be." He hesitated before adding, "Though, Alefast *is* worth a visit—if a short one. Waning cities are always fascinating."

"Well, I'm glad I'll be back so quickly, then." *I've never been to a waning city.* She almost laughed at herself. *I've never been anywhere, really.*

He shook a finger her way. "But I know your type. The guild will have you running hither and yon, and you'll soon have no time for your old friend, Cran."

She cocked an eyebrow, allowing a small smile. "Old friend?" She looked around. "I believe we've just met." The server returned then with her coffee. She thanked the man, and he bowed slightly before leaving.

"Yes! And with a habit like that"—he pointed at her coffee—"you'll need many friends, deep pockets, or both." He winked.

She laughed. "True enough." She took a careful sip of her new dark necessity and exhaled in contentment. "So, *old friend,* do you intend to tell me about my possible destinations?"

He did, in fact, have many stories about his times in each city, and she soon had a bevy of recommendations should she find herself in either place. There were also several warnings among the good news: a leatherworker whose products never held up to rain, somehow; a tailor whose stitching was never *quite* right, and even though the clothes fit, they pulled and pinched in ways that shouldn't be possible; and many more. Most were about Marliweather, in truth, as he'd only been to Alefast once, and that had been years earlier.

Tala's food came, and she ate while listening as each recommendation or warning came with a tale, some short and some long. She was easily able to hear conversations at the surrounding tables, and while she processed them, seeking any mention of her, or anything else of interest, she didn't actually listen closely. *I suppose I can remember later if I so desire.* She doubted she would.

All told, Tala found herself whisked through the morning and into early afternoon in a rather pleasant fashion. The cadence changed, however, when Cran's eyes flicked to the door, and he abruptly stopped his current tale. "Oi! Renix, Master Trent, get over here!"

Chapter: 12
One Has to Dream

Tala turned to see that two Mages had just entered the lounge. Both were Materialists, one Creator and one Guide, and both seemed to specialize in ice and lightning. *Interesting combination.*

The two turned at Cran's voice and smiled when they saw him. The younger's smile morphed into a wide grin as he called back, "Oi, yourself!" They walked over, and Cran stood to greet them.

Tala followed his lead, and he introduced her. "Renix, Master Trent, this is Mistress Tala." He turned to her. "Mistress Tala, Renix and Master Trent."

She nodded her head in a slight bow and took their hands as they offered them, each in turn. Renix, it seemed, was the Creator and Trent the Guide. They were both taller than she was, with Renix being the taller by half a head at least. They had brown hair cut close to their heads, though Trent's was slightly longer, darker, and curly. They both had the lean, careful physique of Mages and faces with well-used smile lines.

Despite their similarities, Trent was clearly older, likely ten years her senior, while Renix seemed barely older than she was. *Might just be the attitude?*

"Pleasure to meet you, Mistress Tala."

"Glad to meet you." Renix glanced down. "Nice gloves."

Cran grinned and motioned for everyone to sit. "She's starting a new trend."

As they all sat, Tala felt her cheeks redden. "I am not." But when she glanced around the table, she saw they were all smiling amiably.

Cran waved to the group, bringing their focus back to him. "You three seem to be destined to meet."

Trent rolled his eyes. "You are not destiny, Master Cran, no matter what your mother told you—in or out of the womb."

Cran snorted a laugh. "I *mean*, you will be traveling together."

"Oh?" Trent glanced towards Tala. "You're going to Alefast?"

Tala felt a small knot of tension evaporate. *Not Marliweather.* "Seems so." She glanced at Cran and saw a twinkle in his eye, but he didn't comment.

Renix looked eager. "Do you work alone? Are you the other defender of the caravan, or will you be our baggage handler? Where is your master, or do you have your own mageling?"

Trent held up his hand. "Easy there, Renix. Let her speak." He then turned back to Tala, his smile still obvious. "I am curious, though."

They haven't seen *me, then. They don't know what quadrant I'm of.*

"Careful, boys, she makes you pay for answers with food."

Trent's smile widened. "Well, why didn't you say so?" He glanced at the now-empty space before her. "Let's get you something to eat and my mageling some answers, yes?"

Tala held up a hand. "No need for that, Master Trent. I am an Immaterial Guide, and I suppose 'baggage handler' is as good a term as any."

"Dimensional magic." The older man shook his head. "Never could understand it, but I guess I wasn't meant to." He smiled again. "I'm a Material Guide."

"And I'm a Material Creator."

Trent gave Renix an amused glance but continued. "We'll be working, as a set, to help safeguard the caravan. I believe we have another Mage to collaborate with for that duty, but I don't know if they have a mageling."

Renix shivered. "Is it just me, or is it colder in here than usual?"

Cran glanced to Tala with a knowing smile and made a 'you should say something' gesture.

Tala sighed. Like with Cran, they would soon realize it was her. "It's actually me."

Trent turned his full focus on her, and his smile was gone. "Are you leaking that much magic? What idiot inscribed you? You shouldn't go to back-alley inscribers, or you'll die of magic poisoning before thirty."

She held up her hands. "No, no. Nothing like that."

Cran sighed. "Mistress Tala, just let him look."

Trent glanced to Cran, then back to her. "Would that explain it, then? Do you approve?"

After a moment's hesitation, she nodded. Then, she looked to Renix. "You can, too."

She saw power ripple across both of their faces, and their eyes glowed faintly. Their magesight inscriptions were identical in function, being much more complex than Cran's, but they each had to be laid out slightly differently, due to the unique contours and size of the two men's faces.

Their reactions could not have been more opposite, without one resorting to violence or fleeing the room.

Renix leaned forward, a look of awe blossoming across his features. "Amazing! How are you doing that?"

Trent pushed himself backward, seeming to barely restrain himself from jumping to his feet. "How are you doing that? What...?" He looked around, seeming to see the many eyes now turned their way. Carefully, he pulled himself forward again, and he lowered his voice. "What are you, Mistress Tala? I've never seen anything like that, save..." His eyes widened. "Did you find a set of invisible armor?"

Cran snapped his fingers. "That's it! It's like she's wearing an iron suit."

Tala found herself nervously laughing. "No, I don't have invisible... Wait. Such things exist?"

Trent waved a hand dismissively. "In theory. I've seen stranger things. Now, what *are* you doing? Do you have an active shield against magic, constantly empowered? That seems needlessly wasteful, though the inscriptions must be flawless to achieve such results. I've never seen anything exactly like *that*..." He seemed to hesitate. "Well, no, that's not true. It looks a bit like Master Grediv, but there are quite a few differences..." He frowned, seeming to contemplate.

"It isn't an inscription." She hesitated, unsure of how much she wanted to share with three men who were still basically strangers. *And any in the lounge with enhanced hearing.* She couldn't be the only person with such abilities. "For ease's sake, let's assume I have a very high iron content in my skin."

Trent didn't look satisfied, but he didn't press on that issue. "And your eyes?"

"I need to keep some mysteries."

The older Guide seemed even less happy at that answer, but he let the matter drop. "Very well, then. We did come to eat an early dinner." He glanced at Renix and noted the younger man's clear ardor. He sighed. "May we join you, here? We're going to be spending quite some time together in the near future, after all."

Cran looked to her, but Tala was already nodding. "It would be my pleasure."

Tala spent the rest of the afternoon with Cran, Renix, and Trent. Lyn joined them in the early evening, and they chatted until well after dark about trivial things.

In the end, Tala was the first to leave as she had an early morning at the workyard the following day, and Lyn opted to go with her. They were, after all, staying in the same house.

Tala, again, slept in her bedroll, though she did seriously consider the bed. *It is mine, now, after all*—assuming she took Lyn up on her offer.

* * *

Tala woke early, her own mind rousing her well before dawn.

She stretched, exercised, bathed, and added to her iron salve, finishing just as the sky began to lighten.

Lyn was gone before Tala came out into the main area, and a note simply stated that Lyn had a lot of work to catch up on.

A small pouch of coins held the note down and was described therein as: 'Food money for my new housemate. Pay me back when you can.'

Tala sighed. The pouch contained a mix of mostly copper coins with a little bit of silver. The total value of the pouch was two silver ounces. *And my debt grows…*

Still, she took the pouch gratefully. There was no interest implied, and she *did* need to be able to eat during her last day in the city. Thankfully, her food would be taken care of on the trip, itself, and she would receive her pay on the far end, with which to cover her costs for the two days in Alefast before her return.

With nothing further to do in the home, Tala gathered what she thought she'd need for the day into her satchel and departed.

She'd also found an iron key in the money pouch, as the note had indicated she would, and she used that to lock Lyn's front door on her way out. *Mine too, unless I find a better rate...*

She did find the iron amusing, however. From what she knew, and what she'd gleaned, most Mages avoided iron as much as possible, which was why Lyn's own key had been brass. *She must have had it specially cast for me... for some reason.* It seemed an odd gesture, but Tala found that she appreciated it, nonetheless.

She had a warmth in her heart and a spring in her step as she moved towards the workyard.

To her surprise, without someone walking beside her, setting the pace, she moved *much* faster than she thought usual. Her motions felt natural as if it were still her regular pace, but the world moved by at a brisk pace. She caught and passed other early risers with surprising ease, and each step seemed to carry her farther than expected.

It appeared that her quicker reactions were causing her to push the boundaries of walking at a regular pace. *I likely look pretty odd. 'Come on, woman, just run if you're in that much of a hurry!'* She grinned to herself. Then, with a mild effort of will, she slowed her pace until the passing of the surrounding city, if not the movement of her limbs, felt right.

This... is... so... slow... She sighed internally. *I should buy a book or two.* Hesitantly, she pulled out a notebook and pencil and began writing her musings. Surprisingly, she found it trivially easy to both write out her thoughts and keep track of her own movements. As an added bonus, it made the slower pace seem less grinding.

Thus, she amused herself by doing quick sketches of things she passed; writing out her thought processes, and working through some of her more esoteric ideas; and adding to the letter for Holly that she'd begun earlier.

She stopped through a café to pick up a breakfast of eggs and coffee for half an ounce of silver. Only after she'd departed, with a full stomach, did she realize that she'd never stopped her work in her notebook.

I read the menu, ordered, paid, and ate, all while continuing to sketch, write, and contemplate. She'd never been terrible at multitasking, but this seemed more extreme than that. *I'll have to ask Holly.*

She arrived at the workyard as she finished adding a brief explanation and inquiry about just that to her missive to the inscriber.

The cargo-slots were exactly as they had been, and workmen were working on each, seemingly taking great care to arrange everything within. *This seems like a process that would have been standardized and made as efficient as possible...*

Even as she had that thought, however, she realized that, given there weren't daily deliveries to each other city, the exact cargo going would likely be expanding until they departed, maybe even hourly. Thus, they might have to do some rearranging if new items came in.

Why not stage it in a warehouse and move it over the day before? Or the morning of departure? They could even take exact measurements...

She didn't know, but it didn't really seem that relevant. *This is the job; I don't suppose I need to know exactly why they need it of me.*

As she approached, she noted that only one symbol on each script was still active, demonstrating their need for recharging. *Why not just add more capacity and have Mages charge them on each end?* Yet another question she couldn't answer herself. Still, she added both the questions and her musings to the notebook she'd designated for ongoing questions for future inquiry. *Probably due to higher concentrations of magic dissipating more quickly…*

She charged all ten scripts quickly. As before, she worked to envision exactly what her power was going to do and channeled the magic through that mental construct before it exited her hand to enter the inscriptions in the wood. Also as before, each such empowering seemed to get easier as her mind settled into the truth of her mental model and even adjusted it, ever so slightly, to match small variations from her expectations.

In the end, it took her about five minutes to charge all ten. It had taken longer than the day before, but she'd also felt as if the open doors, and the actively entering and exiting workers, had slowed her down.

In retrospect, it had likely been unwise to allow them to continue working while she was actively dumping power into dimensional distortion magic. She might have… *Nope, not going to think about that.*

What was done was done. *In the future, I'll ask them to hold off on the one I'm actively charging.* This was likely another thing a master would have taught her if she'd done a stint as a mageling. *Or maybe not? The workers seem to know what they're about, and they didn't hesitate to continue to work…* A master might also have alleviated her concerns. *I'd have known, one way or another.*

She left the workyard without fanfare, though she did smile and wave to the various workmen who acknowledged her.

In fact, more such smiled her direction as she got farther from the cargo-slots, and she had a realization. *With the iron salve, at any distance, it would be hard to tell that I was a Mage at all.* She cocked a humored smile at that. *I wonder why they think I'm here.*

She did *not* write that question in her re-opened notebook, though she did sketch out what she could remember of the inscriptions on the cargo-slots. To her decreasing surprise, she was able to create a full sketch. *I'll have to check it against the real thing tomorrow.*

To accurately render the depth, she'd used various pressures with her pencil to create darker and lighter lines, also breaking up some of the lines to help emphasize their depth within the wood.

As the lines were magical in nature, her magesight had allowed her to see them, easily, even through the wood.

She had two realizations as she studied her finished work. First, she'd never had the fine motor control to sketch so precisely before. Even earlier this morning, her lines had been more hesitant and less practiced, but in a no-longer-surprisingly short amount of time, her movements had adjusted to her mind's intent. *My body and mind are better connected, making the refining of skills much faster.* Or that was her best guess.

The second thing she realized was that the Wainwrights Guild would likely be less than pleased that she was able to copy out every layer of their spell-forms. *I'll just keep that to myself, I suppose.* That might make verifying the accuracy of her copy more difficult, but she'd manage. *Somehow.*

Tala spent much of the rest of her morning combing the city for rooms to rent, either temporary or long-term.

In short: Lyn was offering her a *very* good deal, if not so inexpensive as to be obviously charity. *Even though it is...*

Money. Tala's woes were almost entirely money-related. *They'll be a little* better, *after I return, but with my ideas for Holly, on top of all the debt I need to pay off...* She was likely to have money problems for quite some time.

Millennial Mage 1 - Mageling

Instead of going by a restaurant for her lunch, as she desperately wanted to, she found the local food market and used the last of her borrowed funds to buy dried fruit and meat, a quarter pound of butter to fill a small wooden box she'd already purchased for the purpose, and biscuits. The latter she found in a little bakery, which seemed to specialize in portable food for workers.

As such, the biscuits were dense, delicious, and filling. She still had to eat lunch, after all, and the butter she'd bought didn't *quite* fit into the container. So, she ate one of the biscuits with butter and found herself satisfied.

The purchase of traveling food had been somewhat of an internal debate with her, as she was supposed to have her food provided for her on the trip.

That said, she had no way of knowing the quality or quantity of what would be offered. *Another thing a master could have easily told me.* And she was not willing to be at the mercy of whatever cook or quartermaster happened to be on the journey with her.

There was also always the possibility of some sort of disaster. Thus, she'd eventually decided that buying a few days' worth of such food was wise.

Her lack of funds had changed her mind until Lyn's generosity. *Spend the money you have, Tala, and you'll always be poor.*

That wasn't entirely fair, as she could also eat this food in Alefast if she didn't need it on the journey, thus reducing her expenses overall, but she still felt fairly irritated.

Today was her last day in Bandfast, as the caravan would depart just after dawn the next morning. With that in mind, she wandered the city, taking in the sights and sketching many of them.

The shorter days and softer autumn light cast an almost dreamy aesthetic to the city, and she found herself enjoying each feature she passed—from the imposing, spell-lined city walls to the small homes. She passed large block buildings that appeared to be apartment complexes and some that seemed to be factories—by the sounds coming from within. She passed people of every description and age going about their business throughout the city.

Honestly? It was exhausting.

The academy hadn't been vacant, not by any means, but it spanned tens of thousands of acres and had a population that maxed out in the ten thousands. Thus, there was never want for room.

This city, and every city, was teeming with people, and with her newly heightened senses, it was… a lot.

In the end, she sought refuge atop an outer wall.

The farmland stretched out beyond that wall, defensive towers flaring with power every so often to deter, or bring down, arcanous creatures that drew too close. Some people came and went through a nearby gate, and soldiers patrolled the walls at regular intervals, but overall? It was quiet.

What would it be like to leave the cities behind forever?

She laughed at the thought. Even as a Mage, she couldn't survive in the wilds for very long. Her magics were finite, and once they expired, so would she.

Still… If she were free of debt and able to earn enough, she could spend most of her time *away*.

One has to dream, right?

She ate some of her trail food and drank from a waterskin as the sun sank below the horizon to the southwest. *And thus, my last day here is done.* She'd be back, but it still had a sad, sweet quality to it.

I've only been here a week or so—and only conscious for half that. Still, she felt like she was becoming attached.

Tala laughed at herself, then. *I want to go into the Wilds, forever! I cannot believe I'm leaving this city I somehow love so much...* She snorted. *Get it together, Tala. You've work to do.*

Chapter: 13
Late-Night Meetings

As the light of the setting sun was still fading, painting the sky in vivid hues, Tala descended from the wall and set her path towards home. She didn't bother to be efficient about it, though. Instead, she took her time and enjoyed the walk.

Even after the sunlight faded completely, she continued alternating writing and sketching by the light of the night's sky and the occasional streetlight. In truth, the latter was more a hindrance than a help. With that in mind, she chose less-illuminated paths.

That, in retrospect, was likely a mistake.

As she walked through the darkness, flickers of magic light would occasionally illuminate her, side-effects of the city's magical defenses dealing with an incoming threat.

She was almost back to the residential circle when the quiet sound of following footsteps came to her attention. Scanning back in her memory, she realized that a group had been following her for close to five minutes.

The streets were quiet, most businesses closed and most citizens were already back to the residential district.

She flicked through the snatches of whispered words she'd been hearing since they'd been tailing her and sighed.

Great... I'm going to be robbed.

Stopping, she tucked her book and pencil away, turning to face her would-be muggers.

She cleared her throat, and the three men stopped close to twenty feet from her. They all looked to be workmen, in rough, home-sewn clothing. They carried thick wooden sticks, each about as long as their wielder's forearm. *Would those qualify as truncheons?* They each also had a knife at their belt, but that wasn't unusual. Almost everyone carried a knife at their belt.

She smiled, making sure to show teeth, so they would be able to see the expression in the dim light.

"To answer your questions"—she alternated pointing between the three men as she continued— "yes, I am a woman. No, I am not an idiot. No, I don't have any money. No, this is not a good idea. Yes, I am a Mage. Yes, your device?" She frowned, taking a more purposeful look at the odd, carved stick that one was holding before she continued. *That seems to be for detecting if their target is a Mage.* "Pardon, yes, your device is failing you. And yes, I know there are two more of you waiting around the next bend." She pointed behind herself, in the direction she'd been going. "Did that about cover it?"

The men had paled further at each of her statements, clearly horrified that she had not only heard their whispers but could easily identify exactly what each of them had asked.

Neat trick, that. I didn't know I could do it. She smiled.

One of them stepped forward. He was bigger than the others and looked to weigh close to three times what she did, though it seemed evenly divided between muscle and paunch. "No. How can you be a Mage and have no money? You're just trying to scare us off! You're no Mage." He lifted the stick, not the carved one, and shook it at her. "And you've likely got gold in the bag."

Tala sighed. "If only that were true. My life would be better with a bit of gold in my satchel." *Well, no, it wouldn't be. I'd just have to give it to someone else as repayment…*

"Give us the *satchel*, and we'll let you go." His voice hesitated on the word that was unusual to him, and she almost laughed. *Seems I'm not the only one failed by the education system.*

Instead, Tala cocked an eyebrow, though she realized they probably couldn't see it. "I need this, and I doubt, very much, that you would be satisfied with just my satchel."

One of the others whispered for his companions, but she heard him clearly and easily. "She sounds pretty."

Well, this is going nowhere good. Could she call for the guards? *No, I can't hear any, and that means they are out of calling range.* Similarly, she couldn't hear any other people nearby, save those attempting to waylay her. "You know I can hear you, right?"

The man blushed. He *blushed*! "Are you pretty?"

"What sort of question is that?"

He huffed. "A reasonable one."

"Look, gentlemen. I'm a Mage, and I don't really have very good non-lethal options. My inscriber stuck me without a lot of choice here. Are you really going to make me kill one or more of you?" She thought for a moment. "In this light, you likely wouldn't even see your friend die, so I'd have to kill you all." She nodded. "Let's part as unlikely strangers and pretend this never happened." She had a twinge of guilt as these men would likely accost someone else if they let her go, but she *really* didn't want to kill them. *I can call the guard, after I'm away.*

"You'll just call the guard, once you're away."

She was momentarily stymied by the uncanny statement. Then, the full weight of what he said clicked into place. "You won't let me go, no matter what."

I could just disable them, here, and run for the guard? Yes. That was the wise course. It wasn't a perfect solution, though she'd not tested Holly's modifications... *No time like the present, I suppose.*

Without further thought, she lifted her right hand, first two fingers extended upward, her ring finger and pinky tucked down, all four pressed together, palm pointed towards the three men and her thumb tucked in tight. She channeled magic into the activation and focused.

She held the features of the front-most man in her mind, along with the knowledge that he was a potential danger to herself and others. *They are fools.*

The larger man lit blue to her eyes, and she shifted to focus on the next, firmly fixing him in her mind before he, too, lit in her sight. The larger man remained blue.

The three men were arguing with each other, but she was past listening. Once all three were highlighted, she spun, her hand out, and found the other two men who were still waiting in ignorance to ambush her.

"She's running!"

The three men behind her had seen her turn and mistaken the motion. Even so, their call was heard by those ahead, and five men were suddenly sprinting towards her from two sides.

Come on, Tala! She focused on the first ambusher, locking her view of him into place, and he began to glow. She focused on the final man, and as she did so, she jumped right, avoiding the club she'd only vaguely been aware of swinging for her head.

The jump broke her focus, but her lock on the four others held. She quickly refocused on the final man and was able to click her magic into place. All five now had a blue glow to them in her view.

She kept her outer two fingers firmly down and internally commanded: *restrain.* Her power rippled through her.

Deep-set spell-lines ran through a thousand calculations that Tala understood but could not have hoped to complete that quickly. They noted the current elevation and latitude, as well as a dozen other factors before moving the power into a single activation for each target.

In that instant, five golden rings blazed with power on the back of her hand, visible to her normal vision even through her glove, and faded. Though she couldn't see her skin, she knew that those rings were gone, their metal used up. As an interesting side-effect, the Mage-detecting device, now hanging from one of the mugger's belts, suddenly blazed with a harsh warning glare. *Huh, so it does detect magic.*

The five men stopped moving, all kinetic energy stolen in an instant. That energy was immediately reapplied, picking them ever so slightly off the ground.

Then, gravity changed.

To be clear, gravity, as a whole, did not shift. Every other Immaterial Guide she'd ever heard of who used gravity manipulation created pockets of differing gravity. They targeted a volume, within the world, and changed how gravity worked within it. This was useful because any number of enemies could be trapped by the same effect, and it could create zones of safety or help fortify positions. It, however, had many weaknesses.

True, in this case, none of them would have applied, and she likely could have gotten a similar outcome with less power, but this was not the situation her magics were tailored to.

She sighed, regretting the massive expense of the casting, even as her power made a fundamental exception and alteration to the gravitational constant for each of the five.

Each change was precisely calculated per target based on their center of mass, among other things. As a result, each of the five men were now effectively in a perfectly stable orbit around the world, in their precise position.

Millennial Mage 1 - Mageling

That was surprisingly effective. Thank you, Holly. Her old version hadn't been quite so precise, so they would have maintained the ability to move, if with awkward bounces. *Not anymore.* She grinned. *Non-lethal option, perfected.* She was quite pleased.

They began flailing about, trying to find purchase on the ground that they couldn't reach, but that did little good.

Tala was panting. She'd never been able to target so many at once, before, and she mentally thanked Holly for the augmentations she'd given. "You might not want to move. If you manage to reach the ground and push off too hard, you will drift upward... and, well, nothing will stop you."

The men paled and stopped moving. Even so, one of them began drifting up ever so slightly, having already brushed against the ground with his truncheon.

"Good choice." Tala smiled.

"See! She is a Mage."

"Please! Let us go. We're sorry we tried to rob you."

Tala sighed, striding towards the self-doomed man. "Don't fight me." He stiffened, and she grabbed him, dragging him back down, and leaving him stably around a foot off the ground. "Better." She took his knife and cudgel and tossed them to the side. Then, she walked to each of the others, disarmed them, and easily moved them away from anything they might accidentally push off. "There. Now, I am going for the guard. You can wait patiently and spend some time behind bars, or you can try to escape and likely end up killing yourselves." She shrugged, but once again, she wasn't sure if they could see the gesture. "Up to you."

Well, that was expensive. Even so, she'd safeguarded herself and likely taken some dangerous people off the street. *For the low, low price of three-quarter ounces of gold.*

Justice, as it turned out, was expensive.

One of the men nodded vigorously. "Yes, Mistress. We were foolish to cross you."

Huh, maybe that one isn't so— Even as the thought swept through her head, she realized her mistake. *I thought of them as idiots when I targeted them.*

The one who'd spoken suddenly dropped to the ground. Her view of him had changed, and so he was no longer a valid target for her spell-working.

He laughed, feeling himself and giving a little hop, seeming to revel in the feeling of coming back to the ground.

Tala quickly took control of herself, straightening and facing him, attempting an air of command. "You may not be as much a fool as the others. Go, get the guards. If you do not return in five minutes, I will hunt you down." She extended her hand towards the man in the same manner as earlier, and she focused upon him, making sure she didn't make the same mistake.

He lit blue to her eyes, once more.

It was a loathsome expense, as she'd be burning silver until she released the lock, but she'd needed to test her effective range so… *I've got to test it sometime.*

The man bowed and ran.

She was able to track him easily as he remained a blazing blue beacon to her sight, even through the intervening buildings.

To her surprise, and relief, after a few minutes, he did seem to be making his way back.

Sure enough, in less than five minutes, the man returned with a small patrol of guards. They were, understandably, shocked to see the four men slowly drifting just off the ground.

Millennial Mage 1 - Mageling

One guard stepped forward, and he was seemingly in charge of the patrol. "Miss. I think we need an explanation."

*   *   *

It didn't take long for Tala to tell the guards what had happened. In the light of their lanterns, her spell-lines were easily visible, as were the still-floating men, confirming her identity as a Mage.

The man who had grabbed the guards was surprisingly cooperative and confirmed her story utterly.

He was still arrested, of course.

As each man had manacles affixed to his wrists, the exception for him was broken, and gravity returned to normal. *No longer a potential threat.*

The man leading this patrol told Tala that he thought there was a reward for these particular men.

Thus, after the guards had gathered up the criminals, and their weaponry, Tala followed them all back to the nearest guardhouse.

She did not turn over the Mage detector, which she'd taken from one of the men. *I need to figure out how they powered it, and if I can sell it.* Many magic items were powered by bits of arcane beast, usually ones with powers either similar to what the item was meant to do or directly opposite.

More common items were powered by more common beasts, as the bits were used up at a steady rate, and it was uncommon for rarer arcanous creatures to have been harvested enough for items based on their powers to be perfected.

She had never heard of a magic detection device. *Though, to be fair, I really haven't gone hunting for magic items...* No money. She sighed.

The men were each checked in, and the Justice Archive confirmed that, yes, these five men were wanted for many confirmed, and even more suspected, robberies and assaults.

Total reward: one ounce gold.

Tala blinked at the pouch now in her hand. It held a half-ounce, a quarter-ounce, and two-tenth ounces in gold coinage along with five silver.

I... made a profit? Who knew? Justice *does* pay. *Maybe... Should I be a bounty hunter?* It was a silly notion, but it still made her smile. *Tala, hunter of criminals! Mage for the managing of Justice.* What an idea.

With a small smile on her face, and a stern admonition from the guard that she should keep to lit streets more often, Tala headed home.

As she walked, she did not take a notebook out. Instead, she studied the Mage stick. *Terrible name.* Magic detector? *Better.*

She examined the magic detector. The base was a simple wooden rod, six inches long. *White oak?* It was as thick as her thumb at one end and tapered to the size of a pencil at the other. The smaller end had a hole, which she couldn't see the bottom of. The outside was wrapped with copper inlay, set deep enough that the metal would never contact the holder's skin. That left the surface feeling quite unusual in her hand.

As she pointed it at various objects, she noticed that, to her eye, it almost always had a subtle glow. In a moment of insight, she realized that its glow, to her normal vision, almost perfectly matched the glow of the object she pointed it at when she viewed the target with her magesight.

Fascinating. It's like a blind man's stick, but for magic. She stopped walking, then. Tala smiled. *Wow, that was a great analogy. Nice work, Tala.* Her smile widened to a happy grin, and she began walking again.

Millennial Mage 1 - Mageling

Her analysis had provided an obvious answer to the device's power source. There wasn't one. It simply absorbed the radiant magic coming off whatever it was pointed at and manifested that as light.

I do wonder how often the copper has to be refreshed. She clucked to herself in thought. *I should get a cap fitted with a piece of iron to block it off when I don't need it. That should extend the life a bit.* She actually had the materials for such in her travel gear back at the house. *It's late. I should just use that as a distraction for the road.*

She frowned. *Every minute it's uncapped costs copper.* True, copper wasn't expensive, but it would be expensive to get wire joined in the proper network and inlaid back into this device when it stopped working. *Or to pay a Material Guide to do the same.* That would probably be required, given the complexity and interconnectivity of the spell-form.

With a sigh, she placed the tip against her belt buckle and noted that it went completely dark. *That should hold it. I can do something temporary, tonight, and make a proper solution as I travel.*

With that decided, she picked up her pace, reaching her house shortly.

Lyn greeted her just inside the door once Tala had unlocked and opened it.

"There you are! Don't you know that it's nearly midnight?"

Tala was taken aback. "You waited up for me?"

"Of course. Do you know how I'd feel if you were lying dead in the streets somewhere?"

She cocked her head. "No? I imagine you'd be sad."

"Yes, Mistress Tala, I'd be sad." Lyn huffed. "Well, come in, come in. No need to stand there like a solicitor."

Tala came in and wiped her feet on a mat, waiting off to the side. "This new?"

"Well, yes. If you're going to stay here, I had to find a better solution for your shoelessness than requiring you to wash your feet every time you came in."

Tala was strangely touched. "But... it's going to get covered in iron."

"Good thing it's only for you, then." Lyn smiled. "What were you doing?"

"Just seeing the city."

"Oh... alright then." Lyn seemed mollified.

Tala quirked a mischievous smile. "And getting mugged, stopping the thieves, and collecting a reward."

Lyn had started to turn away but froze. "What."

"Oh!" Tala grabbed the quarter-ounce gold coin from her pouch and tossed it to Lyn. "For the food money and my room for a month. You were right. I'm not going to find a better place or a better deal."

Lyn caught the coin, examining it. She didn't look up as she spoke. "You engaged and captured a criminal with a bounty of a quarter-ounce gold? That seems... dangerous."

"Hmmm? No, not really, and the total reward was a gold." She hesitated. "Though I suppose each reward was only two-tenths of one."

Lyn's head came up. "You fought *five* criminals? By yourself? Mistress Tala!" Her mouth worked as she tried to decide what else to say.

Tala grinned. "Fought is being overly generous to them, I'd wager."

"That is not the point! You are an Immaterial Mage. You aren't supposed to be a front-line fighter."

"I never really understood that. Especially with my enhancements, I should be *better* on the front lines than any Material Mage."

Lyn huffed. "*Maybe* in terms of survivability, but not in regard to stopping enemies! One on one? Sure, I suppose, but Mistress Tala, you fought *five!*"

Tala cocked her head. "Mistress Lyn? Are you alright?" The older woman was slightly flushed, and her breathing was a little rapid.

Instead of answering, Lyn turned and strode into the sitting room, flopping down on the chair.

Tala followed her in and heard the woman muttering under her breath.

"Worse than I feared. The silly girl is hunting bounties, now."

Tala raised her hands. "Hey, now. I didn't go searching for them. I just made the best of a bad situation."

Lyn's eyes flicked to her, showing mild surprise.

Wow, she must be really rattled to have forgotten about my hearing.

After a long moment, Lyn sighed. "I do know, Mistress Tala. I—" She hesitated. "I am just worried. Alright?"

"Alright. I apologize for worrying you."

Lyn smiled wearily. "It isn't your fault. I've no right to worry over you."

Tala barked a short laugh as she sat down in another chair. "No one else will. I don't mind."

Lyn eyed her. "You've not mentioned your family. Are they…?"

"Not dead." After a pause, Tala amended, "Well, they might be. I don't really know."

"Lost touch?"

"Lost implies an accident."

Lyn nodded. "Broke contact, then."

"Don't really want to discuss it."

She raised her hands in acquiescence. "Alright. Say no more." She glanced at the coin in her hand. "This is too much. I'll get you change." She stood and began rummaging around in a pouch at her side. She muttered through the simple math as she grabbed the needed coinage. She pulled out three coins, her voice returning to a normal volume. "Here. Three ounces silver in change."

Tala thanked her and took the money.

Lyn glanced at the stick that Tala was still holding in her other hand, tip against her belt buckle. "Do I want to know?"

Tala grinned. "Magic detector. Took it from one of the muggers."

Lyn hesitated, then nodded slowly. "They were verifying you weren't a Mage. But they still—" Lyn barked a laugh of her own. "Your iron! They didn't know you were a Mage." She was practically brimming with glee. "Oh, Mistress Tala, that's spectacular! They must have thought you were some helpless little thing." Her eyes were twinkling with mirth. "Did you obliterate them?"

Tala was understandably uncertain about Lyn's change of attitude. "I thought you didn't approve."

"Hmm? Oh! The way you described it, I thought five men waylaid you, knowing you were a Mage. *That* would have been colossally dangerous."

She blinked, processing that. "People do that?"

Lyn sighed, her mirth vanishing. "Yes, Mistress Tala. Mages, for the most part, are very wealthy, and if thieves are properly prepared, they can sometimes steal a great deal. It helps that most Mages are rather vulnerable when they are caught unawares, and even prepared, many are as helpless as those without magic when faced with iron-tipped arrows or bolts."

Tala had not considered that. "Huh. Your concern makes much more sense."

Lyn glanced back at the stick. "That does explain why Mages are rarely accosted by those unprepared for them." Her hand twitched towards Tala, but she restrained herself. "I would dearly like to study it."

"When I get back? I think it might be useful on the trip."

Lyn nodded. "That is likely wise. Speaking of which, it is quite late."

Tala nodded as well. "And I need to get some sleep." She stood, heading towards her room. She paused before reaching the hallway, turning back. "Mistress Lyn?"

"Yes?"

"Thank you."

"What for?"

"Everything."

Lyn quirked a smile. "Of course. Good night."

"Good night."

Chapter: 14
An Auspicious Start

Tala, once again, woke early.

She had not gotten enough sleep, partially because she had taken the time to rig up a small case for the magic detector. Even so, she didn't let that stop her. She rose quickly, stretched, exercised, cleansed, and verified the integrity of her iron skin.

The magic detector was invaluable for this. If she was uncertain about any location, she simply pointed the device at her skin, and if it glowed at all, she applied more salve to that location. *Huh... I should have gotten something like this earlier.* True, her own magesight could do something similar, but it was less acutely accurate and, even with a mirror, harder to be sure that she wasn't seeing magic reflected off the iron from her surroundings.

I do wonder why the magic detector doesn't seem to respond to reflections off iron. Another mystery for when she could get it examined more closely.

She finished packing up her pack and satchel, hanging her bedroll below the pack, and strode out into the common space.

Lyn was waiting for her with coffee and a breakfast pasty. "Eggs and sausage."

Tala gratefully took the food and quickly ate it, washing it down with the coffee. "Thank you, Lyn. That was very kind."

"I had to do some sort of sendoff. You'll be safe, yes?"

"I'll do my best."

Lyn looked like she wanted to respond to that, but instead, she simply nodded.

"Oh!" Tala pulled out the letter she'd written to Holly, detailing some requests, and handed it to Lyn. "Could you get this to Mistress Holly?"

Lyn cocked an eyebrow as she took the letter. "Sure? What is it?"

"A few ideas and scripting requests. Nothing too major." Tala shrugged. "You're welcome to read it if you'd like."

"Alright, sure."

She smiled. "Take care, Mistress Lyn. I'll see you in just about two weeks."

"I'll see you, then." Lyn, then, stepped forward and gave her a quick hug, being exceedingly careful to avoid skin contact. "I'll miss you."

Tala accepted the hug and returned it to the best of her ability, trying to keep her own skin away from Lyn's clothing. "I'll miss you, too." To her surprise, Tala felt like it was actually true.

"Now, get! You shouldn't be the last one at the workyard, and the sun is almost up as it is."

Tala grinned. "Bye, then!" With a wave, but no further words, Tala departed, walking briskly towards the workyard, near the outside of the city proper.

As she was moving quickly, and heading directly for her destination, it was a much faster trip out to the outer wall than it had been from the outer wall back to her house. *I have a house.* She did not camp on the thought, but it still made a smile tug at her lips. She had a home, again.

And I'm leaving it.

But, just for a time. She could do this.

I can do this.

She arrived at the workyard to find a very different scene than she had on other days.

Firstly, all the cargo-slots had been loaded onto a single wagon on the far side of the yard. They were fully encased within the wagon, save holes for each of the places she needed to contact for recharging of the scripts. The back was also open, to grant access to the door into one of the cargo-slots. *That likely holds the supplies for the voyage itself as part of the contents.* She'd find out either way, soon enough.

Aside from carrying the cargo-slots, this wagon was different from her test wagons in several ways. First, the wheels were of an overlapping segmented design, with each piece held outward with a sort of leaf spring, allowing it to collapse inward, somewhat, if the wheel went over particularly rough terrain. The plates' overlapping was oriented so that no metal edge would ever come down onto the ground, so long as the wagon moved forward.

Secondly, the wagon had what looked to be a very robust suspension system, to further steady the load and smooth out rough terrain.

Finally, a pair of mundane oxen were hooked to the front, being tended by the driver, and all three beings were nearly ready to depart.

Beyond her own charge, there was a string of seven other wagons, each nearly twenty feet long and pulled by their own pair of oxen. As she walked past each, towards her charge, she got a good look at them. By the activity around them, and the brief look inside given by her magesight as she got within range, there were four types: two wagons were for the other Mages, with a driver and servant each bustling about, preparing for departure; three were for passengers; one looked like nothing so much as a bunkhouse on wheels, likely for the mundane guards; and

Millennial Mage 1 - Mageling

the final was clearly a traveling kitchen. *At least the food will be good... I hope.*

The Mages' wagons were each set up differently. She immediately identified Trent and Renix's wagon because there were three beds. One plush bed was fully separated in a front compartment, one equally plush bed was behind a curtain, and the third was nice enough, near the rear of the wagon, clearly for the servant. The other wagon only had two beds, one vastly nicer than the other, confirming that the other Mage did not have a mageling. It was still odd, intuiting the physical nature of things from their magical imprint.

I suppose the driver sleeps across the driver's seat at night? It made sense, as it seemed that great care had been taken to make those a comfortable place to be throughout a long day's travel. *And through a night's sleep.*

Of the passenger wagons, it looked like two were for more wealthy patrons, as there were only two or three occupants in the large wagons, not including the driver and servants. They were actually similar to the Mages' wagons but seemed to be more generic, whereas the Mage wagons appeared to have been customized for their passengers. The other passenger wagon appeared to be for poorer travelers, as her magesight detected a full five people in that wagon, again not including the driver and servant. Even with the five people, it didn't look too cramped. There was a stack of five beds against the front of the wagon, and what looked like reasonable seating within.

I guess passengers tend to stay in their wagons during the day. Seemed like it would be boring.

Neither she, nor anyone she'd known as a child, had ever traveled between cities, so it was all new to her. *Except for magical transport to and from the academy, but that is altogether different.*

The bunk wagon looked to be outfitted with ten beds and a small area for ten more people to rest. *Three shifts, then?* If she had to guess, there would be ten guards out and about, ten sleeping, and ten resting each in rotation. Indeed, it did seem that eight were already asleep within.

The culinary wagon had three occupants and no apparent driver. *I suppose one of them drives?* They seemed to be doing final preparations, locking down things within the wagon. *I wonder if they will be able to cook as we travel or if we'll have to stop for meals?* It was a sign of her ignorance that she didn't even consider that lunch might be made ahead of time in the morning, though her own preparations should have planted the idea. There was a bit of odd obscuring on this wagon, which reminded her of looking at Holly, but she couldn't determine the source. *All the metal implements?* That was as good a guess as any.

Every wagon had what looked like a flat, padded seat on the top, higher even than the driver seat, near the center of the wagon. *A lookout post?* She'd have to wait and see how they were used. Additionally, each wagon had specialized steel and spring wheels, along with what appeared to be highly articulating suspension systems. *I suppose that makes sense. There isn't a road we can take, and standard wagons don't do so well on rough terrain.*

Around the wagons, she could see many people moving to and fro. Twenty guards were in evidence, including Ashin, who waved to her when their eyes met. She waved back.

She easily picked out the three other Mages, each busy with their own tasks. *And each with a horse.* As she noted those, she saw at least fifteen other horses as well. *Back-ups for the Mages, and mounts for the guards?* She really had no idea, as she'd never so much as touched a horse in her life. *My own two legs are good enough.*

As she thought about it, she realized that she wasn't sure how long each day's travels would actually be. *Maybe, I can ride beside one of the drivers, now and again?*

Lyn had never mentioned horses... *Though, she did initially offer me a wagon...* It seemed that Tala might have missed something critical. *Nothing for it, now.*

She *did* have a wide-brimmed hat, which she planned to pull out once they were on their way. *No reason to get burned by being in the sun all day.*

The third Mage, a woman, was obvious by her spell-lines even at a distance, but Tala didn't focus on her in order to analyze them, yet. *I'll wait until we're closer.* She also wanted to complete her task quickly. *I'd hate to be the hold-up.*

She finally reached the cargo wagon, and, noting that the outermost cargo-slot was shut, she decided to empower that one first. *No need to inconvenience someone by barring their entry, later.*

She placed her hand on the first, formed the mental construct, and poured her power through it, into the construction.

She was still marginally improving her speed, both at constructing the mental model and at attenuating the expression of her power.

It was complicated by the spell-lines in her right hand, as she had to forcibly direct the power around them.

Huh, I suppose I could use my left hand, but not on this first one. Her left was, as of yet, un-inscribed. So, in theory, there should be less interference, if any.

She quickly filled the first, waiting till all three symbols glowed with an inner light, and moved to the second. On this second one, she did decide to use her left.

She rested her left hand against the activation panel and formed the construct in her mind.

Her power refused to flow through it and out of her left hand. *Strange.* No matter how she twisted her mind, she couldn't make it work. After close to a minute, she gave up. *I'll have to ask someone—probably Holly—why that didn't work.*

In hindsight, she realized that it had been a bit foolish to experiment with an actively empowered construct. *Glad it didn't explode...*

She quickly finished her work and stepped back, double-checking that all thirty symbols glowed brightly. *Done.* Even with her ill-advised experiment, it had taken her roughly five minutes. *Having the doors closed really does speed up the process.* In addition, just like the day before, wearing her gloves had not slowed the process at all. She noted both things for later.

Once she'd placed her notebook back in her satchel, she walked to her driver, placing a smile on her face. "Hello!" She waved, and he started, turning to bow in her direction.

"Greetings, Mistress. How can I serve?"

Tala waved a hand. "First, my name is Tala. Second, what can I call you?"

He glanced up at her, seeming uncertain. "You may call me 'Driver,' if you so wish."

"Driver? May I know your name, instead?"

He seemed at a loss before finally shrugging. "I see no harm. I am Den."

"Well met, Den." She extended her hand.

He started back but quickly mastered himself. When no magic seemed in evidence, he slowly took her hand in his and shook. "Good to meet you, Mistress."

"Please, call me Tala."

"Mistress Tala." He smiled, seeming to gain a bit of confidence.

"Now, Den, would you have a space up near your seat that I could stow my pack?" She pointed her thumb over her shoulder and down behind her, indicating the pack on her back.

Den's eyes widened. "Oh! Is your wagon not sufficient?"

She smiled. "No, no. I don't have a wagon."

He blinked, clearly confused. "But… how can you not have a wagon?"

"I don't want one. That said, I *also* don't want to carry my pack, if I don't have to. Do you have a place?"

Den nodded quickly. "Of course, Mistress Tala." He patted the ox he'd been working with and led her back to the wagon. Below the seat, opening on either side, were large wooden boxes. "On longer trips, we often have two drivers per wagon, and so we each get one of these." He pointed under the seat to an identical one on the other side. "That one is mine." He hesitated. "But you can have that one if—"

She held up a hand. "This will do perfectly." She opened the well-made box, noting several clasps meant to secure it for the road without impeding its use. *Cleverly done.* It was roughly four times the size of her pack inside, being much longer than it was deep or tall, oriented along the length of the wagon. The lid hinged from the bottom of the outward face, so it seemed like she *should* be able to access it from the ground, from the driver seat, or from the ladder, just behind the driver seat on this side of the wagon. She stuck her pack inside, keeping her satchel to carry a few necessities. "Thank you, Den." She then pointed to the top of the wagon. "Would you mind if I rode up there, on occasion?"

"Ahh, to give yourself a rest from the saddle?" He smiled, kindly. "Of course!"

Tala scratched the back of her head. "Well, I won't be riding, so it will mainly be to rest my feet, or just to allow me to change things up."

Den's eyes widened, again.
I'm going to stress this man into an early grave.

"No horse? You're going to walk!" He closed his eyes and muttered something under his breath, clearly not intending Tala to hear. "Never question the decisions or ways of Mages, Den. You know better than this." He pasted a smile on his face, opening his eyes once more. "I'm sorry, Mistress Tala, of course you can ride whenever you wish."

Tala sighed. "Den, thank you. I'm not going to be upset if you ask me questions, don't obey, or anything like that."

After a moment's hesitation, Den seemed to come to a decision, and his smile became more genuine. "In that case, Mistress Tala: thank you, and welcome." He extended his hand again, and Tala took it once more.

She left him to finish with the oxen, and now that her pack was secured, she felt light and ready to go. She now wore her wide-brimmed hat, taken out of her pack, and she thought she looked rather nice, all things considered. *Who knows what a week of trail dust will do, but right now? I'm quite alright.*

While the hat mainly protected her from the sun, it also had the benefit of further obscuring her spell-lines. That, along with her gloves and lack of Mage's robes, caused her to look positively mundane to the casual glance.

In that regard, she realized she had to forgive the guard who walked up to her, hand on his sword. "Miss, this is no place for civilians, unless you've purchased a ticket."

They both knew that all passengers were already in their assigned wagons. Tala smiled and turned to the man. He was a good head taller than her and clad in leather and mail. A round shield hung from his back, and an iron cap sat on his head. He was armed both with a long sword and what appeared to be a short chopping blade. In addition, she saw loops on his belt for both a quiver and a crossbow to hang, though he wasn't wearing them at the moment. In that first look, her magesight also swept over him and saw through the holes in his mail. He had quite a few old injuries that seemed to be causing mild discomfort, though she wasn't sure exactly how she knew that. As a final bit of information, she knew that if she jumped right, he was likely to have a harder time following her than if she moved left, due to something that hadn't healed quite right in that ankle.

She took all this in in less than a moment, and her smile grew just a hair. She was feeling playful. *And why not? I'm supposed to be here.* "I'm sorry, I didn't catch your name."

"Miss, that isn't relevant—"

She pulled off her hat casually and stretched her neck to each side. His hesitation confirmed that he'd been able to see her spell-lines.

The big man, to his credit, immediately changed tack. "Apologies, Mistress. I am Sergeant Holdman, second in command of the third squad for this caravan. Are you, by chance, Mistress Tala, our third Mage?"

Third? Interesting, Renix doesn't count as a full Mage to mundanes, I suppose. She, herself, wouldn't have counted if she'd followed standard practices. "I am Tala, yes." She extended her hand.

Sergeant Holdman hesitated, just as Den had, but he took her hand and shook it carefully. "A pleasure, Mistress."

"Please, call me Tala."

He gave a half bow. "As you wish, Mistress Tala."

Tala struggled not to roll her eyes.

He glanced over his shoulder. "The master sergeant is eager to get us underway. If you would, could you empower our cargo-slots and then join us near the bunk wagon?"

She pointed before he could. "That one, right?"

"Ummm... Yes."

"Are you heading there, now?"

"Yes."

"Then, I will accompany you."

"Please, if you don't mind—"

She held up a hand. "I've already empowered the cargo-slots, sergeant. We're ready."

He took that in stride, not even glancing towards her charge. "Very well then. After you, ma'am."

"Tala."

"After you, Mistress Tala."

Despite what he said, they walked side-by-side around the kitchen wagon to the other side and down the caravan to beside the bunk wagon, where a group of some eight people waited for them. Five were guards, by their insignia, two were of like rank to Holdman, and three outranked him. The other three were her fellow Mages. *Renix is as much a Mage as I am.* She refused to let that imply she had a lackluster claim to the position.

She was introduced around but decided that she was making people uncomfortable with her handshakes, so she simply nodded at each in turn.

The first to catch her eye and give a shallow nod of greeting was the final Mage, a Material Guide named Atrexia. *She specializes in the manipulation of rock, earth, and their derivatives, though she avoids metals.* Tala briefly wondered how she would feel to the woman. *I hope nothing like sand rubbing against her skin.* That would make interacting... difficult.

Trent and Renix greeted Tala with smiles and nods of their own, while the sergeants and first sergeants bowed more deeply.

One of those who outranked Holdman was a master sergeant, and he oversaw all the guards for this caravan.

"A pleasure to meet you, Master Sergeant Divner."

He was the last to be introduced to her, and his bow was the least of those given by the sergeants. "Mistress Tala. I assume that the cargo-slots are ready to go?"

"They are."

"Then, we may depart." After a brief pause, he added, "I trust that you will inform us if any deviation requires our attention?"

He means with the cargo-slots. "I will keep an eye on them, yes. If I notice anything unusual, I'll let you know."

With that, he nodded and turned, calling for the wagons to begin moving.

Four of the sergeants jogged off to the bunk wagon, climbing in, while Divner and Holdman moved to direct the drivers and remaining guards.

Renix waved as he turned and climbed on his horse, and so she walked over towards him.

"Hi!"

She smiled at his enthusiasm. "Hello, Renix."

"Where is your horse?"

"I plan on walking or riding on my wagon."

That seemed to catch Atrexia's attention as she nudged her own horse in their direction. "You are going to walk?"

Tala turned to her and tried to direct her smile up at the woman. "That's the idea."

"You will throw off the defensive lines of the caravan. Get in your wagon and stay out of the way." Atrexia's eyes swept the caravan before a frown creased her face. "Where is your wagon?"

"I don't use one. Or do you mean where will I ride when I do so? That would be the cargo wagon."

"You don't—"

Renix grinned. "Oh! Mistress Tala, will you allow Atrexia to look at you?"

Atrexia turned her eyes to Renix. "You will address me as *Mistress* Atrexia, mageling, and it is rude to ask that on behalf of another. I'd thought Master Trent would have taught you better."

Trent, who had just mounted his own horse nearby, laughed. "He's fine, Mistress Atrexia. Look at the girl." He glanced at Tala. "Assuming that is acceptable?"

Tala sighed. *Might as well.* "Fine by me."

The spell-lines around Atrexia's face rippled, and her eyes widened in shock. "What—" She cut off as Tala lifted her gaze to meet the older Mage's.

"I'm certain you are very good at your job, Mistress Atrexia, and I wouldn't dream of telling you how to do it. I ask for the same courtesy in return. My actions are my own."

Atrexia visibly swallowed. "You can't be an arcane, but how…?"

Tala grinned. "I'm a bit odd. Even so, I'm sure we'll get along swimmingly if you're willing."

Atrexia leaned forward, and by the still pulsing spell-lines across her face, she was attempting to study Tala more closely. "Yes… I'd… I think I would like that." She nodded, and her spell-lines lost their power. "I apologize for any abruptness. I look forward to speaking with you on this trip."

Tala smiled and nodded. "That sounds wonderful."

By that time, the wagons had begun rolling forward at a pace that would have matched Tala's brisk walk only a week ago but now seemed quite leisurely to her. The other Mages were mounted and turning their horses in the same direction as the caravan.

Well, we're off! With no further discussion or thought, Tala set a pace to match the wagons and began walking.

Chapter: 15
The Journey Begins

Tala walked out through city gates for the first time that morning. The stone just outside felt about the same as that within to her feet, physically, but at a deeper level, it was utterly unique.

Growing up, her father had always maintained: 'If you don't need to leave the city, why would you?' Consequently, she'd never even been to the farms surrounding her home city.

She didn't feel any change, nor should she have. The outer wall was nowhere close to the outer defenses, at least not in one of this phase. Consequently, they were still well within what was considered the city. Even so, it was new.

The farms looked the same in person as from afar, just nearer. Workers toiled in the fields, using animals and machines, both mechanical and magical, to finish the fall harvests. A few looked to be tending autumn crops, as well. *Is Bandfast temperate enough to bring those to harvest?* It likely wasn't assured or every field would be planted thus. *I hope it works out for them.*

As the caravan slowly worked its way down the main road, through the farmland on this side of the city, they fell into a comfortable order. Two guards rode ahead, beginning the job of scouting for the wagons. Three rode behind, to protect from, and warn of, any dangers that might come up from the rear.

Millennial Mage 1 - Mageling

An additional five guards were stationed on various wagon rooftops, each of those armed with heavy crossbows. Besides the crossbows, each had a large shield, which seemed to be affixed to the roof on a hinge somehow. *I'll be curious to see how those work, and what they're for.*

Trent and Renix rode on one side, near the middle, and were mirrored by Atrexia on the other. Even still within city limits, their eyes were sweeping their surroundings. *Good habits, I suppose.*

The wagons, themselves, were in tight formation, with just enough room between the oxen's noses and the back of the next wagon to ensure the driver could stop in case of emergency. *Close and tight. Better protection? Or better to go unnoticed.*

She had a fleeting thought. *What if I could only have empowered the cargo wagons? We'd have an additional nine vehicles, just for goods transport. Would they have had to hire more guards, more bunk wagons, more Mages, more Mage wagons, and at that rate, another kitchen wagon?* It was a bit daunting. *And with that many more people, we'd likely need another wagon just for travel supplies.* No wonder the Caravanners Guild prized Immaterial Guides with dimensional distortion experience. *I'm saving them a fortune!*

She might need to apply a little pressure to Lyn when she returned.

Tala, herself, had climbed up to sit atop the foremost wagon, her charge, the cargo-slot wagon. There was a semi-padded square in the very center of the wagon's roof, reasonably comfortable for one person to sit upon. A free-spinning ring surrounded the seat, and Tala realized that the guard's large shields were likely affixed to that on their own wagon tops. *It gives them the ability to have cover from any direction, with the weight of their wagon lending support.* Clever.

Her hat was not providing much shade in the early morning light, but thankfully, they were heading south, first. *Alefast is almost due east of us, but I believe I heard that the route chosen is utilizing easier ground to the south.* Good thing, too, or the rising sun would be impossible.

She, of course, had a notebook out and was sketching a random assortment of things that they passed. It was more something to do than because she truly enjoyed it. *Or because I need it.* She was finding that she had virtually perfect recall. When she'd compared her sketch from memory to the cargo-slots, they had been a perfect match. *That has to be useful for something.* She'd find a use, eventually.

An hour later, they reached the edge of the farmland, and Tala stared out at the lines of regularly spaced towers that stretched out to either side, encircling the city. *The outermost, active defenses.*

Beyond this were the mines, but they had been abandoned in this city as it had moved to the next phase, contracting inward as the truly outermost defenses wound down.

As they neared, Tala took the time to focus on the closest defensive towers and sweep them with her magesight.

Each was three stories, with a contingent of ten guards manning the position. She also saw a Mage in each tower, ready to repair, re-empower, or bolster the defenses at need. After all, every arcanous creature brought down temporarily disabled the tower until the Mage in residence could empower the newly cast spell-lines.

She frowned at that thought. *No, I think some defenses have more than one casting before they are spent.* She'd never studied emplacements, and she decided that it wasn't something that interested her too much at the moment.

The spell-lines in the tower to the east were useless to her, as they were for a Material Creator, made to spawn stone before and above any detected threat. She copied them, nonetheless.

Those in the tower closest to the west, however, were clearly Immaterial Guide lines, and the spell was quite fascinating. It was clearly meant as a fallback if the surrounding towers had spent their castings and had yet to be re-empowered. As such, that tower held spell-work for a simple series of kinetic thievery workings. If she read the lines correctly, and her magesight had yet to disappoint her, each of the twenty-five scripts would steal all kinetic energy from a target for up to half an hour—or until the maximum capacity of the spell was reached. Then, the spell would dump all the stored energy back into the target, crushing them into the ground.

I don't see why the last part is necessary. After all, locking a creature's blood in place for half an hour would be fairly lethal, as would preventing their breathing. *Maybe some arcanous beasts can endure that?* That was a terrifying thought.

She copied these spell-lines as well, and as with those to the east, she noted what each part of each set seemed to do. *It seems reasonable to gain some knowledge of inscription and spell-lines, in general.*

She had begun sketching when the towers first came into sight, and thus, she finished just as they came abreast with the line of towers.

An unnecessary call went up to, "Keep sharp!" as they entered the Wilds.

As if cued by the shout, a large, lizard-like creature shot out from the surrounding forest, sprinting at a pace that would put a horse to shame.

Thankfully, it was not running at them.

It was a massive creature, which positively blazed to her magesight. Clearly a predator, it ran on its back legs, its forelegs stretched before it, ten-inch claws extended. All told, the beast was probably twelve feet tall.

Thankfully, it was half a mile away, running towards the line of towers.

As Tala watched, one of those towers activated, and a thick stone block materialized directly in front of the charging creature's head.

The impact was sickening even at this distance, likely due to her enhanced perception.

There had been no time for the creature to stop, and the rock was clearly quite heavy.

The creature's forward momentum broke its neck, and the stone fell with the collapsing body, crushing the torso as it slammed into the ground.

Thorough. It was a bit grisly, even so.

No one else seemed to be reacting to the sight. *Not close enough to be our concern, and not notable.* She'd known that arcanous creatures regularly tried to breach city defenses, but as she'd never left the walls, she'd never seen such up close. *Though, I have seen quite a few flying ones taken from the sky.*

There were probably *far* more land creatures than those in the air. *Huh. This might get... interesting.*

Before the caravan, a wide-open, grassy plain stretched towards the horizon, broken only by rolling hills and the occasional tree or mountain in the distance. There was no road.

In fact, there were *no* roads in the Wilds at all. Such would make it obvious where human caravans would be traveling, and thus any arcanous or magical creature could easily wait in ambush. Instead, each caravan took a unique route between cities, and though some components of each trip between two given cities were occasionally the same, it was always random, at least to the best of the Caravanners Guild's ability.

Don't let them know where you'll be.

There was also the fact that building and maintaining roads would be an *enormous* undertaking. Apparently, some would-be-emperor, about a thousand years ago, tried to build protected roadways, with towering defenses along the whole length, just as cities had.

The migrating arcanous beasts had not appreciated the blockage.

The road, connecting just two cities, was open for one glorious year before it was breached. Tens of thousands had died.

Apparently, the road had drawn the attention of a higher order of creature. Her teachers had called it a paragon or honored magical being, but hadn't elaborated. She'd suspected they, themselves, were ignorant.

Happy thoughts, Tala. This is an adventure!

It was not, in fact, adventurous. As if to belabor the point, nothing more of note happened or was passed by them until lunch. The oxen never stopped moving, and Tala guessed they covered nearly ten miles before noon.

As they traveled away from the city, the stone of the road became hard-packed dirt and then finally thick grass, which felt oddly uneven, yet pleasant, on her bare feet.

Aside from the change of footing, she did notice one thing. There was a growing sense of magical power from the world around her, the grass, the ground, and even in the air. It was a subtle thing, and would likely have been unnoticed, except that her magesight highlighted any change. Thus, the constant increase was a bit of an annoyance, as it filled her vision with hundreds of flickering motes and magical signatures. Thankfully, it leveled off just before lunch.

Unfortunately, the zeme, the flow of power through and between everything around her, caused ripples in her magesight even when the average ambient magic had leveled off.

I'm just going to have to get used to seeing magic, aren't I?

Tala had walked for a good portion of the time. Sometimes, she walked beside Renix, talking about small things. Sometimes, she walked or sat beside Den, and she learned about his family; his wife worked as a baker in Bandfast, and they had four children. Sometimes, she sat and wrote out her thoughts.

Sometimes? She was bored out of her mind.

Walking, at least, occupied much of her thoughts, but the caravan was progressing so slowly, she found herself easily walking up and down the length of the wagon train, even as it kept moving.

This is maddening.

Finally—*finally!*—just before high noon, a guard called out a warning from the front. "Beasts ahead!"

Tala sprinted up from near the back of the wagons and scrambled up to the perch atop her cargo wagon.

There, nearly a mile ahead of them across the open plains, was a herd of truly *massive* creatures.

Each was larger than any one of the wagons in their train and covered in long, blueish-black fur. Short, curving horns stood out prominently to either side of the creatures' heads, creating an almost helmet-like look to them.

What in zeme?

As she watched, two of the giant, cattle-like creatures faced each other, strutting and posturing. That seemed insufficient to establish dominance, however, as the two braced themselves and charged.

Their hooves tore up the turf as their gait ate up the distance in a breath.

Millennial Mage 1 - Mageling

Their heads slammed into each other with a concussion that was easily audible even at this distance.

The additional rippling of distant thunder from the group ahead let Tala know that those two were not, in fact, unique in their posturing within the herd.

It was with great wisdom that the caravan turned almost due east, aiming to skirt the notice of the numerous large, arcanous bovine.

Well, that isn't boring, at least.

It was a mixed blessing that the remainder of the day was anything but dull.

*   *   *

Tala had many questions answered she hadn't thought to ask.

First, shortly after they diverted to avoid the magic cows—*I am not giving them a silly name just to feel more secure*—the workers from the kitchen wagon began distributing food, with the help of the servants from the various wagons.

Second, it was called a chuckwagon, not a kitchen wagon. *That's what Master Himmal meant.* His metaphor made *so* much more sense, in retrospect.

Third, while Master Sergeant Divner seemed to direct the movements of the caravan, Trent and Atrexia had great sway over specifics, and the three of them closely consulted.

Fourth, by their many glances her way, where she sat on the lead wagon, she clearly had a right to weigh in, should she decide to join them.

She did not.

The food was a simple meat and vegetable pasty, and Tala found herself curious as to how they safely maintained an oven on the moving wagon, for the food was deliciously hot. Their travels were smooth, after a fashion, but she knew that she wouldn't want to wield a knife while on a wagon, let alone manage an active fire.

The chuckwagon might have better stabilization. Maybe some magics to aid it? She'd have to investigate.

The caravan kept moving even while most people ate and while the three debated the path ahead.

Renix guided his horse up beside her wagon, where she was licking her fingers clean of her third pasty, and she waved lazily. "Not much happening."

He shrugged. "The thunder cattle are interesting. I don't know that I've seen a full herd this close to a city before. Small families, yes, but those are usually only two to ten beasts. That?" He nodded his head towards the south and the source of frequently-sounding, concussive impacts. "That is something new. I'm surprised it hasn't drawn down larger predators." He grinned. "I wish we could get closer."

Maybe, I shouldn't be flattered by his interest in my... oddities. He seemed far too fascinated by things that could get him killed.

The mageling finished a pasty of his own and sighed. "I do wish we'd be attacked or something."

Tala snorted a laugh. "Oh? What's so bad about what you're doing?"

Renix held up a book. "We only really get paid if we actively defend the caravan, and Master Trent has me studying." He said the last with a scowl. "I got enough of that at the academy. At least if we fight, I can leave the books in my bag."

Tala sat up straighter at the sight of the book. "Does that say 'Inscriptions?'"

Renix glanced at it. "It does. Master Trent thinks a Mage should have a good understanding of inscriptions for all four quadrants. I have a matching set of four volumes."

Millennial Mage 1 - Mageling

Fascinating. So, I'm not alone in that thought? It was a bit reassuring that her own studies were aligning with what at least one master was teaching his mageling. Tala leaned forward. "I don't suppose I could borrow the Immaterial Guide one?" When he cocked his head to one side, she quickly added, "I'd like to review some of the basics."

He nodded. "That makes some sense, I suppose, though I don't know why you'd choose to." He made a disgruntled face. "I'll have to check with Master Trent, but it shouldn't be an issue." He smiled. "Hey! You can join us this evening for discussions on theory. It would make it much less boring if you were there?" He left the last as a question.

Couldn't hurt. "Sure. I'd like that. Thank you."

Her mind returning to the books, she smiled. *This is perfect!* Tala had always avoided classes on inscription theory or much deep understanding of spell-lines. As she understood it, she didn't need to know the intricacies of spell-line craft to use her own spell-lines. She just needed to know what the whole did, together. *After all, an alchemist doesn't need to know the chemistry of oxidation to burn a crucible to refine an elixir. He just needs to know it will help him in his work.*

That was *close* to how it worked for Mages. A Mage simply needed to know what effect a given set of spell-lines would create when she powered them. That way, her power would mold into that. She couldn't make the lines do something else if she had a misunderstanding, and the specifics were handled by the spell-lines themselves. The worst-case scenario would occur if a Mage didn't know what spell he was casting when he empowered his inscriptions. In that case, raw, unshaped power would pour through the lines and likely obliterate them, as well as the surrounding flesh.

Though, as Tala thought about it, the inscribed spell would probably still be enacted.

That was why a Mage had to trust their inscriber absolutely. If there was a miscommunication or faulty inscriptions, the best case would be the spell failing to work. Death was a very real possibility in any misapplication of magic.

Even though her new magesight let her know the function of most inscribed spell-lines, it didn't let her know if certain combinations were possible, or if un-empowered spell-forms were valid. *I've got time. I should put it to good use.*

While Tala had been pondering, Renix had returned to his wagon, snagging the desired book. He'd made a move towards Trent but noticed that the Mage was still debating with Divner and Atrexia. With that observation, he'd simply returned to Tala, offering her the book. "I'm sure it's fine." He smiled up at her.

Tala strained, reaching down, and took the leather-bound volume with a smile. "Thank you, Renix. I appreciate this."

Renix smiled back, then seemed to hesitate. "Thank you, Mistress Tala."

"Hmm?"

"You don't treat me like a hanger-on." He glanced away. "The best Mages talk to me and don't treat me badly, but I've not met a full Mage who treated me… like me." He shrugged. "Like an equal, I guess. Thank you for not looking down on me."

Tala grinned down at him, straightening her back to stretch just a bit higher, and cocked an eyebrow.

Renix laughed. "I meant metaphorically."

"Well, you're welcome, I guess." She settled back in. "You are you, after all. It would be silly to treat you as anyone else."

Millennial Mage 1 - Mageling

She was about to open the book and dig in, but she noticed that Renix was still riding beside the wagon. *Huh... He's still here.* Most people didn't stay around...

"So..." She closed the book. "How many of these have you gone on?"

Renix started, seeming to come out of his own thoughts. "Me? Oh... We don't do these very often. Let's see." He frowned in concentration, scratching above his right eyebrow. "Well, I've been with Master Trent close to two years, and we guard a caravan every couple of months, so... twelve? Twelve, give or take." He shrugged. "They start running together after a time."

Twelve. *This mageling has gone on* twelve *caravans.* She was out of her depth. "Wow. That's impressive."

He shrugged again. "The pay's not bad, even for a mageling." He glanced towards her. "Nothing like what you're making, if rumors hold true."

She stiffened. "Rumors? What rumors?"

Renix didn't seem to notice her tension. "Oh, you know, 'Baggage Mages get all the money. They barely have to do anything, while we spend our metal fighting and killing for scraps.' That sort of thing."

Oh! Generally speaking, not me in specific. "I see. I'd never thought to ask what Mage guards would make."

He drew himself up with a fake haughtiness. "It's Mage Protectors, and I'll thank you to remember that." He grinned.

Tala snorted a laugh. "Very well."

Renix shrugged. "We don't make much, though half of our inscribing costs are covered in the contract. No, the real money is in building and fabrication."

Tala cocked her head. "Building and fabrication?"

"Yeah! Demolishing buildings and helping to erect new ones. Helping artisans, making factories more efficient.

There are *loads* of jobs for Material Mages." He glanced to her. "I'm sure there are for Immaterials as well, but…"

"You've never really looked."

He shrugged, again. "Yeah, why scope out jobs you can't do?" He smiled. "I've tried to convince Master Trent to let me get some Material Guide inscriptions, to help augment my own, but he's convinced I don't have the 'right thinking' to make them work, yet." He sighed. "He's probably right. Not worth paying for inscriptions you can't empower, right?"

Tala nodded. Many Mages did cross quadrant lines here and there to lend their magics more power and versatility, but it was risky. To use magic, you had to understand what it did. Her own restraining spell, for example: she didn't have to know exactly what values were being plugged into the gravimetric equations, nor exactly what values each target's interactions with gravity were being set to, but she *did* have to understand what gravity was and how changing the gravitational constant for an object would affect every aspect of it. If she just understood the spell as 'it stops your target, makes the target float, and keeps them there,' the spell would fail, likely catastrophically.

"I can understand that. I've never been able to wrap my head around the creation of matter."

Renix grinned. "Oh, that's easy. Mainly, it's just imagining that there is *more* where once there was less."

"Huh?"

"More. You know. Rocks are heavier than air, and all that."

"You specialize in ice and lightning."

"Exactly! Lightning is the easier of the two, for me. My father was a builder, and I helped him install hundreds of lightning rods. Fascinating things, those."

"I don't follow."

"It's like petting a sheep with a cloth glove. When you're done, there's *more*. There's lightning… Well, just a bit, anyways."

Tala shook her head. "I suppose I just don't quite understand." She smiled. "But, we are diametrically opposing quadrants, so…"

He barked a short laugh. "Fair enough." He glanced at her, then down at the book. "Well, um… I suppose I'll leave you to—"

A deep bellow rattled the wagons, emanating from ahead and off to the left, the opposite direction from the herd.

"Oh, good!" Renix smiled, tension seeming to bleed from him. "We have unwanted guests."

Tala stood, looking towards the sound, and saw a group of four thunder cattle—*stupid name*—come over a nearby rise, walking slowly towards them. The sound had come when the lead animal, a bull, had seen the caravan, and their oxen, and had issued a challenge. *Isn't that the sound they make just before charging?*

She turned to ask Renix, but he was already spurring his horse forward.

Trent called to him. "Stay there. We're to guard the flank, while Mistress Atrexia handles these."

Renix slumped but reined in his horse. "Yes, sir."

As his horse slowed to a walk, the lead arcanous bull bellowed again, lowering its head to charge.

Chapter: 16
Arcanous Beasts

Tala stared in mute fascination as the arcanous bull rushed across the ground between his small herd and the caravan.

He's close to half a mile away! Nonetheless, he was covering the distance at a rapid pace.

Tala focused on him, willing her magesight to engage at a much further-than-normal range.

The bull was full of power.

She could see twisting, intricately flowing spell-lines woven through the beast's flesh, bone, hide, and hair. The long, curving horns were practically throbbing with power, though she couldn't quite tell what any of it did. The structure and design were eerily familiar, but the whole was still unintelligible.

In less than twenty seconds, the bull had covered the majority of the distance between him and the lead wagon, upon which Tala sat.

Atrexia, the Mage tasked with handling the threat, sat straight-backed on her horse.

As Tala watched, Atrexia extended a hand and made a series of quick gestures.

To Tala's magesight, power shot out from the woman's right shoulder, soaking into the ground just ahead of the charging bull. A small portion of the fringe of that working passed through the edge of Atrexia's clothing, and that minute portion was fractionally diminished. Even so, the end effect was impressive.

In that instant, two lances of stone erupted from the ground in unison, their points driving into each shoulder of the animal. The bull's charge was used up against the spikes, as its own momentum drove it far onto the hardened stone. The charge was halted barely one hundred yards from the oxen pulling Tala's wagon.

Atrexia swayed slightly, and Tala saw magic practically dripping from the woman. *That must have taken a great deal of power.* Tala frowned. *Why?*

She scanned the ground, willing her magesight to inspect it, and she had her answer.

There was no rock in the ground, at least not much. Atrexia had been forced to: first, tear the soil away from the roots of the deep, wild grasses; then, compact an immense amount of it into a dense enough form to be able to pierce the bull's hide; and finally, drive it upward quickly enough to effectively catch the bull off-guard.

There were now wide swaths of cavitation, deep beneath the ground. *She pulled from deep enough the wagons won't be at risk of causing a cave-in.* Yet another way in which the Mage had strained herself.

When looked at in that light, the attack had been an amazing feat of strength.

She would be a terror in mountainous regions or anywhere with any substantial amount of rock ready to hand.

The bull was shuddering as it rested, impaled upon the two earthen spikes, its blood slowly leaking out.

As Tala turned her attention back to the bull, she saw its power flowing through it in horrifyingly familiar patterns. *That's how my skin looks when it's pulling back together.* Healing magic. The bull was healing itself.

With a bellow of rage, the bull jerked upward. The crack of stone shattering filled the air as the spikes splintered, sending a cascade of gravel down towards the bull's hooves.

Atrexia yelled a challenge in return and kicked her horse into a forward walk.

Brave horse.

The bull shook itself, the last vestiges of the spikes falling from the fast-closing wounds.

Atrexia yelled again, raising her hand.

She doesn't have the strength to do that again. Tala leaned forward. *What is she doing?*

The bull took a step backward, flailing its horns in a warding gesture, a vain attempt to show strength.

Atrexia raised her other hand, and Tala saw power run across the woman's bare stomach in a completely different pattern than before.

What is she doing? That's not an earth magic working... is it? Tala was *not* a Material expert.

To Tala's surprise, she saw flickers of power around the bull's eyes, and the creature reacted as if it could see Atrexia's power coming to bear. It turned and ran back the way it had come.

They can perceive magic? That was news to her. *Can all arcanous creatures see power?*

Atrexia held herself stiff and straight but reined in her horse, bringing her advance to a halt. Soon, the bull had returned to its small group, and all of them had retreated, back down the far hill and out of sight. As soon as the thunder cattle were no longer in view, Atrexia slumped in her saddle.

One of the guards ran up to her, offering her water and talking quietly enough that, along with the distance, Tala couldn't catch what was said. Even so, she got the gist.

Atrexia would be retiring to her wagon for a few hours to recover. *I don't blame her.*

As the other woman turned her horse back, riding towards her rest, Tala raised a hand in acknowledgment and smiled. Atrexia gave her a strange look, but then she nodded, a small smile tugging at her lips as well.

On his horse, beside Tala's wagon, Renix groused. "That was a waste of power. We could have struck the whole group down and had magic to spare."

Tala turned to him, eyebrow cocked. "Oh?" She saw Trent riding nearby, but he didn't say anything, yet.

"Of course! Creating shards of ice is much easier than pulling rock from who knows how deep."

He doesn't know how she did it. That made sense, in retrospect. He'd likely not used his magesight, and it likely wouldn't have told him much if he had. "So, then why did she volunteer, and why did Master Trent allow it? Are they both fools?"

Master Trent was still riding where Renix couldn't quite see him, and Tala saw a smile pull at the older man's lips. Renix shook his head. "They aren't fools; they just don't want me in the fray."

Tala barked a laugh. "Charitable of Mistress Atrexia to expend so much power just to keep you a bit safer."

Renix frowned. "That doesn't make much sense, does it."

"No. So...?"

Renix sighed, seeming to take a moment to think. "Well, I suppose it makes sense for her to handle a threat she knows she can and leave the unknown to us, given we have more flexibility and capability in the current terrain and environment."

Trent took that moment to kick his horse forward and draw up beside Renix. "And there, you show that you are listening to your lessons after all. We'll get your quick mind educated soon enough, but at least your slow mind knows how to put the pieces together."

Tala frowned. "Quick mind? Slow?"

Renix grunted. "It's a metaphor Master Trent favors."

The older Mage interjected. "What you do on instinct, and without effort, is your quick mind. That is your assumptions and your reflexes. Your slow mind is how you act, what you say, and what you think when you take the time to contemplate before speaking or acting." He shrugged. "It always made sense to me."

"Huh." Tala thought about it. "Seems reasonable."

Trent then turned back to Renix. "Though, even your slow mind missed a bit. If we'd killed the bull on his test charge, the whole family would have attacked. In total, that would have taken much more energy. We can kill them more easily than she can, here, but her stopping power was able to do the trick, nonlethally, thus reducing our total use of magic."

Renix was nodding. "And our total use of metal in our inscriptions." After a moment, he added, "How much?"

Trent broke into a grin. "I only had to pay her one silver ounce. Apparently, that working is much heavier on power expenditure than on metallic consumption for her."

Tala didn't quite follow, but she decided it wasn't worth redirecting the conversation.

Renix nodded. "Probably worth it."

"Definitely worth it." Trent reined his horse around before adding, "I'll take the far side. We've got both fronts to guard until she's recovered."

Renix nodded. "Eyes sharp."

"Magic ready." Trent's reply came back readily, making clear that it was a familiar exchange.

Tala turned back to the book that Renix had lent her and began to read.

Millennial Mage 1 - Mageling

She was no more than two dozen pages in when one of the guards called out, "Above! Air hammer bolts, mark!"

Tala's eyes flicked up just in time to see a falcon diving towards her. *That's odd.*

It took a moment for her eye to properly focus before she realized, *Oh... that's big.*

The bird's wings were tucked in tight as it dove down towards them, but if they were spread wide, she'd have guessed their span at close to thirty feet. Even at this distance, rapidly decreasing though it was, she could see power rippling around the wings, and magic clearly augmented its flight. *No bird could be that big, naturally, and hope to fly.*

It had a look close to that of a peregrine falcon, hence her initial confusion.

It seems odd to encounter this creature so soon after the thunder cattle... unless it was hunting the bovine, noticed us, and decided we were easier prey? It was a possibility. That said, as the great arcanous avian streaked towards her, she realized that it was, indeed, diving for *her*, specifically.

Her eyes widened, and her hand began to come up.

In that moment, she heard the distinct '*twang, chunk*' of five different crossbows firing, and their bolts streaked through the air, guided by practiced aim.

As they flew, Tala got the impression of metal glinting along their shafts in irregular patterns.

In less than a blink, all five missiles had struck true, and the avian screeched in rage and pain.

Then, Tala's magesight blossomed with a story of power.

Each of the bolts, now firmly embedded in the great bird, flared to life, the irregular metallic gleam being revealed as non-empowered spell-lines.

They are using the bird as the source of power! It was genius, really. Magic items often used pieces of arcanous creatures to power them for a time, so it made sense that weapons could be crafted to take advantage of the same principle.

Each of the five bolts was inscribed with the same spell-form, and they all flared to life in near-perfect unison.

They were Material Guide spell-forms, and Tala didn't need her magesight to see what they did.

From five places on the creature's body, a working reached out and swept the air from beneath its wings.

The change in airflow radically altered the beast's flight path, and not even the last-minute flare of giant wings could slow it. After all, there was no air in place below the wings to catch on to.

The bird slammed into the ground at high speed, just off to the caravan's right.

Surprisingly, the body wasn't obliterated as Tala would have assumed.

Even more shockingly, the bird jerked and stuttered upright, coming to its feet to let out an ear-splitting shriek.

How is it still alive? There was a depression, nearly six feet deep, in which Tala could clearly see well-entrenched grass roots. *Yet, it acts almost unharmed.*

That wasn't quite correct; its wings did seem to have some new kinks in them. So, it would likely never fly again. *Without healing...*

The guards had not been idle, and even as the bird rose, two of the mounted guards rode past, jamming spears deep into the creature's neck.

Moments later, a bright flash of power told Tala that the spears had been inscribed too.

Well, that and the fact that each spear blossomed outward with a ring of cutting wind.

The bird's head fell free, and the great body toppled backward with an almost delicate *whoosh*.

Millennial Mage 1 - Mageling

And now, I know how the guards are useful. In truth, they likely had many tasks, but their ability to protect against such threats was noteworthy. *I wonder if those weapons are specific to arcanous birds? I suppose they would work against other creatures that used wind and air magic.*

Because the creature wasn't actively trying to activate the spells, the spell-forms had to be able to utilize magic already within the creature itself.

She shuddered at the thought, realizing that the beast likely could have sent great wheels of cutting wind into them if the guards hadn't been fast enough. The spears had simply tapped into the power first.

The guards, and the chuckwagon workers, were already swarming over the body, beginning to strip it down, and Tala grinned, an idea coming to her.

She set the book carefully aside and climbed down, walking over to the working men. The wagons still had not stopped their inexorable movement forward.

One of the guards looked up as she approached and saluted hesitantly. "Mistress? Can we help you?"

She pointed to the bird. "Will you be taking all of it?"

The man shook his head. "There isn't time to harvest everything." He pointed to the chuckwagon workers. "They will harvest the parts best known to be edible to supplement our supplies." He gestured to himself and the other guards. Those other guards had already retrieved the five bolts and two spears, their copper inscriptions still mostly intact. "We will harvest the wing bones. Those are known to be potent power sources for the making of wind and air constructs."

Tala nodded. "Any objection to me taking something?"

The guard looked nervous. "Pardon, Mistress, but the bones will be a great bonus to the men when they're sold in Alefast—"

She held up a hand, stopping him. "I won't take anything you've already mentioned."

The man brightened visibly. "Oh! Of course, then. Take whatever you wish, Mistress."

"Tala. My name is Tala."

He bowed. "A pleasure, Mistress Tala. I am Guardsman Adam."

"Good to meet you as well, Guardsman."

That out of the way, she bent to her task.

Fifteen minutes later, she was jogging to catch up to her cargo wagon. Blood was dripping down her arms, over her gloves, and speckling her face and clothing. She felt lightly strained from all the jerking and twisting she'd done to get parts free, and she was *very* pleased with her new knife, which had performed perfectly. *I'll have to thank Ashin, again, for taking me to that smith.*

Her harvest?

Guided by her magesight, which could still see the lingering power slowly bleeding from the newly dead beast, she'd taken all four talons from each foot and all three bones from each of the legs. She'd left the feet behind, mainly because she'd run out of time to work through the tough skin and sinew. And they were surprisingly heavy.

These do not feel like they came from a bird capable of flight. Magic allowed for wonderful incongruities, such as allowing for a beast to fly when it weighed more than her wagon, oxen team included.

The talons each resembled nothing so much as black, hooked blades, and to her best guess and understanding, they held a strange, arcanous version of power directed towards one thing: integrity of the talon itself, most strongly focused in preserving the beyond-razor-sharp edge on the interior curve. Consequently, she had tied a short length of rope around the base of each, below the sharpened portion, tying them together in a tight bundle.

The leg bones were as white as any mundane bone, and she'd lashed those together separately from the talons. The power in them seemed bent solely towards maintaining the strength and integrity of the bone, itself. *No wonder the impact with the ground didn't turn it to paste.*

Those fourteen pieces were all she'd had time to grab, and they were by no means clean. Bits of flesh, sinew, skin, and muscle clung all over them, making it a rather macabre prize.

She ignored the stares that the drivers, guards, and even Trent and Renix directed her way as she hauled her harvest up onto the roof of the wagon. Once settled in, she began to clean each item as thoroughly as possible.

In talking with the guards, while working on the body, she'd learned that they kept iron-plated chests in which to keep any trophies so that they wouldn't lose too much power before they could be sold and turned into the power sources of constructs.

Tala didn't have iron boxes, but she did have her iron salve.

Thus, she had retrieved one of the bars from her pack, stored in the box beneath Den's driver seat, and as she finished cleaning and drying each piece, she applied the salve thoroughly across the surfaces. *If it works to lock my power in, and others' power out, it should be sufficient for this.* It should also protect the bones and talons from rot if they lasted long enough for that to matter.

Honestly, she had no idea how it would actually work, but her best guess was that the bones would hold onto the power that was currently in them, and if anything put stress on them, such as an impact that would otherwise have caused a break or distortion, some of the power would be used to resist. Once all the power was expended, they would just be normal bones and talons again, since they didn't have any active source for new power.

I hope that's how they work. She might also be able to tap into their power for inscripted items, but that was a *whole* different area of study. *I'll bet Holly would have some thoughts.*

Worst-case scenario, she should be able to sell them. *And that's not a bad case at all.*

As she worked with the pieces, she noticed that the middle bone from each leg fit rather nicely in her hand. There was a comfortable place for her to grip, sinched against one end, and they were just over two feet in length. *These would be pretty nice weapons.* If she knew how to use such. Still, she'd seen students at the Academy doing a form of stick fighting for exercise and ostensibly for fun. *It would be easier than learning to fight with a blade.*

It was a relatively silly thought. After all, she had magic; why would she need to learn how to fight with a weapon? *Still, the guards brought down the bird with weapons... and magic* is *expensive to use in all cases.* It might just be wise to learn how to use mundane weaponry.

...I wonder if any of the guards know stick fighting. If they did, hopefully, she could convince them to teach her.

The task of cleaning the harvests and applying her salve complete, and close to half the afternoon gone, she turned back to her borrowed book.

Thankfully, they had no further arcanous encounters that afternoon.

Chapter: 17
The Evening Encampment

Sunset seemed only half an hour off or so when a halt was called, and the wagons trundled into a circle.

Tala climbed down, tucking her various odds and ends back into the box that Den was letting her use on the side of the cargo wagon.

Several large tables and benches were brought out of the back of her cargo wagon's backmost cargo-slot, and they were set up within the circle.

Tala also saw a group of guards digging a latrine pit a short walk downslope of the wagon circle.

During the day, Tala had walked just over a nearby rise to answer the call of nature, always being careful to sweep both land and sky with her magesight before going. She also suspected that she'd seen evidence of latrines within the wagons, which simply dropped the waste down onto the ground as they traveled. That obviously wouldn't be tenable overnight unless the latrines had a way of being closed up until the next day's traveling had begun.

She did not focus on any of the wagons to verify her theory.

Now that I think about it, there were a few times that Den asked a guard to take the reins, and he went into the bunk wagon... Had other drivers similarly left their posts for sporadic breaks?

Millennial Mage 1 - Mageling

Come on, Tala, this is ridiculous. Why, under the stars, would you care about the caravan's habits of defecation? She shook her head as she looked around.

One thing that her contemplations on what might have fallen from the bottom of wagons did do was to ensure that she would not be sleeping under any wagon, except maybe the cargo wagon.

She bent down to look underneath and was pleasantly surprised. Not only was the platform some four feet off the ground, making a rather nice space, but there appeared to be a rather thicker-than-average growth of grass, almost centered in the sheltered space.

That should be extra comfy.

But bed was later. Now, now was time for food.

Den had led the wagons into a circle, which left the right side of each wagon facing inwards, allowing for all the ladders to the top of the wagons to similarly be facing inward. *Defensible. Nice.* The man, himself, was unhitching the oxen and tending to their needs. Tala offered to help, but he declined.

With nothing better to do, she headed towards the chuckwagon.

Now that the caravan had stopped, the passengers were climbing from their wagons and stretching. Those in the two less-crowded wagons did seem to be dressed a bit nicer than the five from the other passenger carrier, though they were all dressed *much* more nicely than Tala, herself.

With the sun going down, she'd left her hat in the cargo wagon's box, and she felt a bit exposed.

The passengers seemed to be avoiding looking in her direction, and she frowned at that. *Did they not expect Mages on the trip?* No one would be that stupid.

Ashin walked up to her; he'd been in the second shift, so he was nearing the end of his time on duty.

She turned and smiled. "Ashin, did you have an easy afternoon?"

He smiled back. "Mostly. I was stationed on one of the passenger wagons, so I had to listen to those two bickering." He nodded his head towards two of the wealthier passengers, who had had a wagon to themselves.

"Oh? What about?"

"I couldn't tell." He frowned. "I don't generally try to listen in on other people's conversations."

Tala waved that away. "Once you start shouting, you lose the right to privacy." She sighed. "But if you didn't hear, you didn't hear."

He shrugged. Then, he glanced around, seeming a bit embarrassed. "So... can I help you find a washbasin?"

She blinked at him, confused. "What?"

"A basin filled with water, so you can get cleaned up."

She just stared at him. "What?"

Finally, he rolled his eyes and gestured at her. "You look like you came out of a butcher's shop."

Tala glanced down. Her sleeves were encrusted and stained deep red, almost black, with the arcanous bird's blood, and as she shifted her face, she realized that she likely still had some of the stuff stuck there, as well.

The front of her shirt was speckled in a rather pleasing pattern that would have been stylish, save for the source of the coloration.

She grinned, looking back to Ashin. "Don't like the look?"

He grunted. "Don't be difficult, Mistress Tala. You are scaring some of the passengers."

She glanced towards those whom she was apparently scaring and noted several of them look away as she turned. "Huh." She flicked her eyes back to Ashin. "And, what? You drew the short straw?"

"Master Sergeant Divner thought it would sound best coming from someone you knew."

"Meaning he was too much of a coward to ask a Mage to clean up himself."

Ashin raised a shushing hand and glanced around again. "I volunteered."

She frowned. "I thought he'd be asleep."

"He was resting, not on bunk rotation. He'll go down after dinner."

She grunted. "Fine, but I'm not going to be able to get the blood out of this shirt."

"Don't you have others?"

"I like this one."

He gave her a flat look.

"Fine." She sighed. "You've gotten some backbone."

"I'm used to the Wilds. Things make sense here." He looked at her, again. "And you're making it harder by scaring the passengers."

She rolled her eyes. "Fine. Where can I find a washbasin?"

He led her around to the far side of the cargo wagon and showed her where a tightly worked wood crate could fold open, making a passible basin. It also had a drop canvas, which blocked the view from under the wagon and provided a clean place to stand, regardless of the ground. *Clever.*

He also showed her a tap in a small cistern of water, embedded in the front of the wagon.

"It only holds about thirty gallons. Master Renix can refill it if we have to."

She nodded. "With ice, that makes sense."

Ashin nodded as well. "Yes, but it isn't ideal. We also have water barrels, but we don't want to have to transfer it to this."

"So, don't waste water, right?"

"Right."

"Understood."

He waved goodbye and left her to it.

Tala took a moment to go around the wagon and grab a change of clothes before returning to the washing station. She let some water out into the small basin and removed her gloves first, hanging them to the side. She'd cleaned them earlier, while stripping the bones of the remnants of flesh, and had ensured they were both dry and spotless before she touched Renix's book or her own notebooks.

That done, she cleaned her face and any other exposed skin of dried blood. Then, checking for any witnesses—there were none—she stripped off the blood-stained clothing and pulled on the new. It was only a quick moment, but it still felt odd to be naked in the middle of nowhere, beneath a darkening sky. *I suppose I'll get used to it...*

The water was warm, having been heated through the wagon's wood in the sun all day, but it wasn't hot. Still, it was a pleasant thing, washing off the road dust... and blood.

When she was done, she emptied the basin—she'd only used about two cups of water—and hung up the drop canvas so it was up off the ground.

She re-entered the circle of the wagons to find dinner service well underway.

She joined the back of the short line as everyone walked up to the chuckwagon and was served a heavy, hot soup with thick slices of buttered bread. *I would have guessed chicken soup, but given today's events...* She focused on the meat, and indeed, there was still lingering power swirling through the poultry in the deliciously savory-smelling soup.

Huh... I wonder what that does to a person when they eat it.

Looking around, she saw the three other trained Mages sitting at a table on the far side of the ring.

She walked over and set her bowl and bread down beside them on the provided tray, stepping over the bench to sit on it. There were already pitchers of water and wooden mugs for their use.

"So, what kind of effect does eating magic-infused meat actually have on people long term?"

All three stopped eating and turned to her.

Atrexia was the first to respond. "What?"

"This." Tala pointed at the soup. "The meat is from the arcanous avian that attacked us... Oh! Right, you were in your wagon."

"No, I heard about it." Atrexia looked at the soup. "Why do you think this is from that?"

Tala frowned. "Just look at it. It's practically dripping with power." She shrugged. "And I was there when the cooks harvested the meat from the beast earlier today." She took a bite, feeling an interesting pulse of energy as the bit of meat touched her tongue. "It does taste pretty good." Tala smiled.

The others didn't smile. Trent actually pushed his bowl away from himself.

Tala frowned. "Come on. You had to know. You've gone on dozens of these trips. This can't be unique." She took another bite. "You can *taste* the magic in it."

Atrexia cocked her head. "You can?"

"Of course! It's obvious..." She trailed off.

"Obvious to you. You also said you can *see* the power in it, but I haven't felt you activate your magesight... though I'm not sure I could sense that from you, even if I tried." She sighed. "No, Mistress Tala, we did not know they were feeding us arcanous meat. We knew they harvested from the creatures when they were killed, and we knew that they sold parts upon arrival. I, for one, never watched them harvest, so I never knew meat was taken."

"Never watched them? Are you serious? Arcanous creature parts are incredibly valuable!"

"And the guards get a good return on their work, harvesting. I don't really feel it is right to interfere."

Trent was nodding. "It's not really done." He hesitated. "Well, some Mages do harvest as they go, but when they do, they generally claim the entire creature." He shrugged. "I've never heard of a Mage sharing with the caravan. They either take it all or ignore the process."

"So, you're telling me no one knows they're eating magic meat?"

"I'm sure many know, but why would we?"

"Have you never asked what you're eating?"

"It's good, it's filling, no need to ask further."

Tala rolled her eyes. "You all are a strange lot."

"Says the demon girl."

Tala glared at Atrexia before she realized that the other woman had spoken so quietly that even Trent, who was sitting directly next to her, should not have even known she'd spoken. Atrexia met her glare, eyes widening. *Oh... rusted pyrite.*

"What are you?"

Tala looked away, taking another bite. "I'm a Mage, Mistress Atrexia. Leave it at that."

"A human Mage, right?"

Tala turned back to her, a questioning frown forming across her face. "Are there other kinds?"

Atrexia glanced towards Trent, who was giving her a hard look, then away. "Never mind. It was a silly question."

Tala kept eating, steadily. As she did so, she noticed that Renix was unusually quiet.

Finally, he muttered something to himself, and Tala caught it easily. "I just thought it was spicy."

Millennial Mage 1 - Mageling

She quirked a smile, and he seemed to notice because he glanced towards her and blushed. Tala pointed her spoon at Renix and swallowed her mouthful. "You've a good mageling, Master Trent. He's sensitive and perceptive, maybe more than either of you realize."

Renix's color deepened, and he looked away. Trent turned to study his student. "Huh. Might be worth testing him on it." The Mage looked around, then sighed. "But not in the Wilds." He looked back at his soup. "How often do you think they've been feeding us this?"

Tala shrugged, picking up her empty bowl. She'd been hungry. "I'll ask." She took her last bite of bread after mopping up the remnants of the soup and carried her plate back to the chuckwagon, where there was an obvious place to process her own dirty dishes. *No seconds, I guess.*

After cleaning her items and leaving them in the pile to dry, she walked around to the smaller door at the back of the chuckwagon. She knocked.

After a moment, a smaller man opened the back door and smiled at her. "Mistress Tala, yes?"

"That's right."

"You may call me Brand. What can I do for you?"

"Brand." Tala nodded formally in greeting. "What was the meat in tonight's dinner?"

His face didn't even twitch, but his eyes flicked to the left, just briefly. "Chicken, Mistress."

Tala cocked an eyebrow. "Oh?"

One of the other culinary workers stepped up behind Brand and whispered in his ear. Tala heard it clearly. "Brand, she was there when we harvested the meat."

Brand's face froze. After a long moment, he bowed slightly. "One moment, please."

And just that quickly, he stepped backward and closed the door.

The conversation was quick, quiet, and terse, but Tala heard every word.

"You let a Mage watch you harvest?"

"You wanted us to deny a Mage?"

"Of course not! If she wanted the body, you should have given it to her!"

"She didn't want the body, though. She just wanted pieces we weren't interested in. And you said get the meat if we could."

Brand growled.

The door opened briefly, and he stuck his head out. "One more moment, please." The door closed.

Tala found herself smiling.

"What are we going to do?"

"I'm not going to talk to her. She already knows *your* name."

It sounded like Brand took a deep breath and then let it out slowly. "Fine. I am head chef, I will take responsibility."

"Crack me over the head you are! You're just in charge of ingredient acquisition."

"You really want to argue with me, now?"

There was a long pause, then the other man responded, even more quietly, "No, Head Chef."

"I thought not."

The door opened once more, and Brand stepped out, closing it behind him. "Mistress Tala?"

"Hmmm?" She couldn't speak for fear of laughing.

"Please, follow me. I don't wish our discussion to be overheard by the passengers." There was a tremble to his voice, which hadn't been there before.

Nervous? Clearly, but that didn't seem quite right. Tala followed him away from the wagon circle, even while Brand darted looks left and right as if fearful of being seen.

It was fully dark, now, and they were deep in shadows within a half-dozen feet.

Brand turned to face her, a slight tremble obvious through his whole body at that point. "Now, what can I do for you?"

She cocked her head. "I just want to know what the meat in the soup was."

"Blade Wing Falcon, Mistress. Specifically, it was breast meat." He took a deep breath and let it out slowly, seemingly in an attempt to calm himself as if steeling himself for what was to come.

Tala nodded. "See? That wasn't so hard. Now, why—"

While she spoke, Brand had leaned to one side, looking past her, away from the wagon circle. He frowned and interrupted her to ask, "What is that?"

Tala turned her head to look, but when she scanned the countryside, she saw nothing. Turning back, she said as much. "I don't see any—"

Her words were cut off as a knife plunged down, into her chest.

No. That wasn't quite accurate. *Well… rust me to slag.*

Brand brought the knife downward in a forceful stab, driving the point through her shirt and into the top of her chest, but it did not break the skin.

At the moment of contact, her silver inscriptions had detected it, and a *flick* of power had activated the intercellular and intracellular bond strength enhancements.

Both she and Brand looked down at the knife, piercing through her shirt, dimpling her skin, and pushing her left breast towards the side. In a tight circle, directly around the tip of the knife, and extending out in a radius of roughly an inch, her skin glowed with a soft, grey-tinged, golden light. "Ow? I guess?"

Brand stepped back, horror written on his face as he dropped the knife, tripping and falling onto his backside.

"Oh... what have I done?" His voice was a harsh whisper as if he truly didn't know what was happening.

Tala was quite curious about that herself. *I'm knife-proof?* That was something she could have gone a lifetime without learning, but she supposed it was better than the alternative.

She knelt in front of Brand as he began incoherently babbling, begging for forgiveness, explaining that he had a family and that he needed to live.

After a long moment, Tala held up a hand, and he stopped instantly.

"Why did you do that?"

He swallowed. "We were told by Mages to never, under any circumstances, eat or feed others arcanous meat."

She quirked an eyebrow, and she was reasonably certain that he could see it in the reflected firelight that managed to reach them.

He swallowed. "A cook on one of these trading routes, years and years ago, probably a few decades, was running out of rations and used what he had on hand, meat from an arcanous beast killed that day." He glanced to the side, then continued. "To his surprise, he found that the men who ate it were stronger the next day and even seemed to heal faster than expected. One guard, who had been bedridden by the fight the day before, was able to stand and move about under his own power. It was a miracle."

The cook seemed to be calming down as he told his story.

"This head cook told other cooks, and together they tested the theory. After they had a solid body of evidence, they approached the Mages but were only able to state that they had a theory about eating arcanous meat. The Mages cut them off and simply stated: 'Never eat or feed anyone arcanous meat, and never mention it again.'"

Tala waited for a long moment before Brand continued.

Millennial Mage 1 - Mageling

"But it was helping the men. Fewer of us mundane folk were dying on the voyages, and those who were injured healed more quickly and completely. We couldn't stop…"

"So, you continued despite the Mages' instructions?"

He nodded, looking away from her.

"How have the guards not noticed?"

"Oh, they know, Mistress, at least the sergeants. They also know not to mention it to the Mages."

"Huh… Well, I hope I didn't just ruin it all for you."

Brand looked at her with obvious confusion. "What?"

I'm hearing that a lot, tonight. "It seems to be working and helping a lot of people. I'd hate to think I've taken that from you."

"I just tried to kill you…" He seemed quite hesitant about reminding her of the fact.

"If a child hits you with a twig, do you get angry? No matter his intention?"

Brand blinked at her. "So… I'm a child?"

She waved it away. "You couldn't have killed me." She hesitated, knowing full well that he *would* have killed most other Mages, had any one of them been in her place. "Maybe… don't do that again? I'll have to be watching the caravans you are a part of, going forward, and if any Mages die mysteriously, I'll come for you." She tried to look intimidating as she spoke the last. *There is no way I'm actually going to keep tabs on this guy…*

She apparently did it right because he paled, nodding vigorously. "Yes, of course, Mistress. I wouldn't dream of it."

She hesitated, thinking about all that she'd just learned. "You all wanted Mage involvement in the past, yes?"

He, likewise, seemed to hesitate before answering. "Yes?"

She nodded. "I want in. Get me all the information that you have and some way to indicate to future chefs that I'm in the loop. I saw your people harvesting, and they were very particular about what they took. I assume you have notes on what portions of the arcanous beasts create what effects, what portions aren't safe, and so on?"

The pause was longer, but finally, Brand seemed to make up his mind. "You'll help us? You won't cut us out or turn us in?"

She grinned widely. "I wouldn't dream of it. It sounds like you may have just saved me a *lot* of tedious work, and I'd love to help you in return." *They seem a bit on edge, but I suppose trying to hide something like this for more than a decade will do that... Hopefully, my involvement will ease that tension a bit.* She pointedly did *not* consider the fact that this unauthorized group might have killed to keep the secret before. It was, after all, unlikely; Holly had been insistent that Tala's form of magesight was unique, and only her magesight really clued her in.

Brand nodded, slumping with obvious relief. "I'll get you what you need."

"Good." She looked back towards the circled wagons. "Now, I just have to figure out what to tell the other Mages...

Chapter: 18
The Wilds Are My Workout

Tala walked back into the circle of wagons, possibilities whipping through her head.

She passingly noticed Brand re-entering the chuckwagon and quirked a smile. *He's going to have a fun time explaining what just happened.*

She returned her mind to the present task.

Do I lie?

No, there wasn't really anything convincing she could say.

Do I tell the whole truth?

That was folly. Besides, there was likely no surer way of preventing herself from learning the secrets that the cooks had uncovered.

Decades... She shook her head. That kind of time researching had to have yielded truly fantastic results. *I'll have to see if their methods were sound, else it might all be useless to me, anyways.*

Focus, Tala. Mages ahead. What are you going to say?

The question was taken from her as she approached the table.

All three of the occupants were staring at her chest.

Tala frowned, shifting a bit uncomfortably. "Um... Hi? Did I drop something on...?" She trailed off as she looked downward and saw that soft light was still visible, shining through the small slit in her tunic. *You know? I don't know if Brand grabbed his knife...*

Trent cleared his throat, looking up to meet her gaze. "Mistress Tala. Your breast is glowing."

She blushed deeply and couldn't think of a response.

Atrexia, taking Trent's comment as having breached the silence, stood and strode to her. The other woman stuck two fingers forward, towards the slit in Tala's shirt.

Tala slapped the encroaching hands away. "Hey, now! Hands to yourself, please."

Atrexia stopped, glancing around.

Several guards and passengers had turned, but when they saw the Mages looking back at them, they returned to their own business.

"Let me see, girl."

Tala glared. "I am your peer, *Mistress* Atrexia. You will address me as such."

Atrexia straightened. "Mistress Tala, please show me that spell-script."

Tala narrowed her eyes, then sighed, pulling the collar of her shirt down to expose the still-glowing, golden spell-lines.

Atrexia squinted, and Tala saw power ripple around the woman's eyes. *So much for asking for permission...* "It increases... something. Why does it look like that? The golden color is... off, like I'm seeing through tinted glass. Are you using a different metal than gold? An alloy? You know, that's incredibly dangerous."

You can use alloys? What would that even do? Tala had a notebook out and was making notes to herself before she truly realized that she was. She'd stepped back to give herself room to remove her notebook from her satchel and absently waved her pencil at Atrexia. "It's gold; it's just under a different layer of protection. You are correct, though, it enhances the interconnection between the cells in my skin."

Renix cleared his throat, and Tala saw that he was still staring at the glowing script. "Translation?"

Trent turned to his student and physically turned the boy's head. "It makes her skin tougher. Now, stop staring." He turned back to Tala, not mentioning that she was still taking notes on her thoughts and contemplating the ramifications. "What did you have to defend against? I'd say that almost anything that hit there could have killed you."

Tala briefly stopped writing. *Oh... right.* She finished the sentence she was working on, closed her book, and tucked it and the pencil away. *Never decided what to say, did I...*

Atrexia had crossed her arms and was waiting impatiently. "Well?"

Tala sighed. "Please sit down." She sat and waved to Atrexia and Trent's half-eaten food. "That's not going to hurt you." Tala began monitoring those around them, modulating her volume and tone to a pitch that she *believed* wouldn't be discernible by even the closest bystander, and the others must have picked up on it because they shifted their own voices to match.

Trent gave a suspicious glance to the bowl, then looked back to Tala. "How do you know?"

"Well, I suppose I don't *know*, but you've likely eaten this stuff, or the like, on every trade expedition you've ever gone on, and you're fine."

Trent grimaced. "Great..."

Atrexia sat, again, her magesight still active as she prodded her soup.

Tala sighed. "How about this? You eat a bite, and I'll watch what happens to the power within your system, okay?"

Trent, Renix, and Atrexia all stared, wide-eyed at her, as one.

It was Tala's turn to frown. "What?"

Renix swallowed, then leaned forward. "You can see the flows of magic *inside* people?"

Oh... right. She was putting her foot in all sorts of wonderful mistakes, wasn't she.

Atrexia held up a hand to forestall Renix's continued questions. "While that is a good question, mageling, I think the answer is rather obvious." She pondered for a moment. "Master Trent, you first, then me."

Trent turned to her. "Wait, what?"

"I have inscriptions that should reject any foreign power, no matter how it first affects me. I doubt I'd be a useful test, but I am willing to be a secondary perspective." She glanced to Tala. "Assuming you are willing?"

Tala shrugged. "Sure."

Trent looked back to the bowl, then sighed.

Tala watched him pick up a piece of meat, and she focused on it. The bite lit up to her magesight, highlighting the latent power within.

Trent glanced at her, and she nodded, assuming that he was asking if she was ready.

Without further delay, he ate the bite.

Immediately, power began to be drawn away from meat, even as he chewed. It flowed outward, through his spell-lines and towards his keystone and from there outward into his body.

"Fascinating." Tala leaned forward.

Trent stopped chewing. "What?" The question came out slightly garbled, around the food in his mouth.

"Power is leaving the meat and flowing backward along your inscriptions to your keystone."

Atrexia nodded. "So, it's wearing away at his spell-lines." She frowned. "An expensive—"

Tala held up her hand. "No, it isn't. The power isn't being shaped by the spell-lines, it is just following the same channels..." She leaned even closer. "It is entering your keystone, and... Huh."

Tala stood and walked around to stand behind Trent. The older man didn't turn, though he did twitch just slightly.

"It is entering your blood and... fading."

Atrexia stood, her own magesight still active. "What do you mean fading?" She seemed frustrated as she looked but obviously couldn't see what Tala saw.

"Like water on sand." Tala shrugged. "If I had to guess, your body is taking the energy and using it. No lingering magical signature."

Atrexia returned to her seat. "Now me."

Tala watched as the woman took a bite. The result was almost identical to that of Trent. The only difference was that the power took different paths to her keystone as her spell-lines were different.

"Basically the same result. Different paths, though, because you are inscribed differently."

Renix cleared his throat. "Were there commonalities in the types of spell-lines the power followed?"

All three Mages turned to look at him, and he hunched just slightly.

After a long moment, Trent nodded. "Good question, but that seems a bit specific for Mistress Tala to be able to determine."

Tala shook her head. "True, but not relevant. In each of you, the power followed the largest through-lines through each of your spell-forms, ignoring any ancillary lines."

Renix brightened. "Like lightning!"

Trent was already nodding. "Our spell-lines are acting to funnel the power throughout our bodies. Fascinating."

After another almost uncomfortable silence, Trent and Atrexia shared a look, then sighed and began eating in almost perfect sync.

Tala grinned. "Decided it wasn't dangerous?"

Trent glowered. "Decided it wasn't worth starving…" He sighed, looking at Atrexia. "What do we do about it, when we reach Alefast?"

Atrexia looked at Tala, then back to Trent. "This would kick up a mother of a storm…"

Trent grunted. "Best-case scenario?"

"We get poisoned on our next expedition." She pointed at Tala's breast again. It still had a subtly glowing circle. "I'm guessing we're right?"

Tala grimaced. "Yeah. Seems the cooks don't like seeing their friends die, and they are convinced that the meat makes themselves, and the guards, stronger." After a moment, she added, "They claim that they've seen it increase the speed of healing as well."

Trent grunted. "You're going to look into it?"

Tala hesitated, then nodded. "I hope to. It is in line with… several other avenues I'm already taking."

Atrexia cocked an eyebrow above another spoonful of soup. "Your glass-covered skin?"

Tala sighed. "It isn't glass. It's—" She stopped herself, then found herself grinning. "Did you think I'd give you the answer in order to correct you?"

Atrexia shrugged, continuing to eat. "Worth a shot."

Tala kept smiling. "My inscriber said she wouldn't wish my process on her worst enemy. Still curious?"

Atrexia smiled in turn. "Just because you haven't found an easy way to do it, doesn't mean it doesn't exist." She shrugged. "Assuming it's anything worth replicating."

Trent interjected. "Mistress Atrexia, all Mages have secrets."

She huffed. "And we're all worse for it."

Trent smiled ruefully. "Care to share yours?"

"Nope."

"So, what you meant was that *you* were worse for it."

"Can you guard this caravan without me?"

Trent hesitated. "I'd not like to try…"

Atrexia grinned. "Then, *we're* worse for it." She winked.

Trent rolled his eyes and turned to eating in earnest.

Tala sat back down beside Renix and leaned close. "Are they always like that?"

He shrugged, clearly trying not to stare at the glowing spot on her skin. "When we are in the same caravan, yeah. Master Trent tries to build good relations with any Mage he travels with. If that isn't possible, he learns how best to interact for the least friction." He quirked a smile. "If that isn't possible, he learns how far he can needle them as revenge for messing with his attempts to get along."

"Probably a good idea… Though the last is a bit odd."

It was well and truly dark, and the passengers and guards had moved back to their wagons, or posts, leaving the Mages to themselves.

With nothing really remaining to discuss, Tala bade them all goodnight.

She walked beneath the stars back to her wagon. As she approached, she could hear Den, lightly snoring from the driver's seat, up on the wagon. The oxen were staked out on leads and hobbled so they could graze and sleep at their leisure. *I don't see a water basin for them. I wonder how it's provided.*

She gave that a moment's thought, then shrugged. *Den knows what he's about.*

She glanced around, and though she could see perfectly, she realized that the darkness was enough to hide her from any observer or at least obscure the details.

With that in mind, she stripped off the stabbed shirt and pulled on another. She took her bedroll and unfurled it under the wagon, atop the thicker puff of grass.

Millennial Mage 1 - Mageling

She still marveled at how much magic wove through the ground and plants out here in the Wilds.

Shortly after she lay down, she heard a guard walk by some fifteen feet out, and she settled in, feeling safe.

*   *   *

Tala woke to the soft light of pre-dawn, the feeling of pins and needles all over her body, and the subtle, but pervasive, flash of power igniting spell-lines across her flesh.

Her eyes shot fully open, and she was suddenly aware of thorny vines constricting down upon her. In that frozen instant, she assessed her situation.

If she had to guess, the softer patch of plant she'd taken as a gift had turned out to be some sort of carnivorous plant. It seemed to have wormed vines up and across her entire body through the night. With the first light of dawn, it had uncovered thorns, spaced every one to two inches, and constricted in an obvious attempt to shred its victim apart and cover itself in her blood.

Her inscriptions had objected… strongly.

Golden light, with a slight grey tint, washed outward from her, even as her clothes were utterly shredded.

The vines began almost slithering across her, and she realized that if they had pierced her, they would now be sawing through her muscle and bone.

By all that shines. She flailed despite her bound limbs. Thankfully, she hadn't been bound to hold her down. No, the plant's aim seemed to have been to get its wicked weapons into position over her main arteries and open them to the sun.

She blessed Holly and her inscriptions, again.

Tala's hand found her belt knife, which she'd laid beside her head the night before.

Tala whipped the blade free and hacked.

In most circumstances, hacking at something so close to her own flesh would have been unwise, but her active inscriptions turned aside her own blade as easily as the thorns, though she still felt the impacts.

She tore herself free and rolled out from under her wagon.

Her shirt was simply gone. *Another one? Seriously?* She stood in just her smallclothes, which were miraculously mostly intact.

She had apparently been yelling because several guards were already running towards her, blades drawn, and Den was staring at her in mute horror.

She felt thick, sticky ichor slowly dribbling down her exposed skin. Apparently, the plant had something like blood, and she was coated in it.

Tala looked under the wagon and saw her bedroll, somehow entirely untouched, writhing atop the floundering plant. *It oriented all the spines and thorns towards me.* She was *not* going to pay for a new bedroll.

With a bellow of rage, she dove back under the wagon, grabbing her bedroll, whipping it off the plant creature, and tossing the gear out from under the wagon. She remained, slashing any vine she could hold onto long enough to cut.

She vaguely saw the guards skid to a stop and draw back as the now fully uncovered plant lashed out with half a hundred more tentacle-like vines.

With so many vines, she couldn't get close, not in the confined, four-foot-high space.

Tala had had enough. "Toss me your sword!" She glared over her shoulder at one of the guards, and he blanched.

Another tried to shuffle closer, but the vines were moving too quickly.

Millennial Mage 1 - Mageling

The vines struck Tala, herself, in a steady rhythm, but they lacked the mass to do any damage without the aid of their thorns.

"Don't bring it to me. *Toss it!*"

The guard flinched, then pitched his short sword to her, underhanded. Considering he was some ten feet back and aiming to toss it under a wagon *and* near someone in the middle of a maelstrom, he did a good job.

The tip struck her squarely in the side, causing another section of her inscriptions to blaze with light. How that one section had avoided activation up until then, she had no idea.

She picked up the blade from the ground and found herself grinning. "Now, you rusting patch of grass, you die."

She drove inward, hunched, yet cutting in great sweeping arcs, leaving dozens of tendrils twitching on the surrounding ground. After each swing, she was able to take a shuffling, crouching step forward.

Finally, she got close enough to the center to drive the blade straight down, into the core of the thing, buried in the ground.

The entire mass seemed to freeze in the instant, then fell limp.

Tala whooped in victory, ripped the blade free, and staggered out from under the wagon.

She was glowing like a small fire, and she would have been surprised if any part of her spell-forms hadn't been activated. *I'm glad they aren't one-shots...* What had Holly said? Each area should be able to activate at least a half-dozen times? *It was something like that.* She'd have to check her notes. At the moment, she was much too distracted.

Atrexia, Trent, Renix, and a half-dozen guards were standing in a ring around the wagon, staring at her in mute horror.

Den was still atop his driver's seat.

Tala looked around at all of them, saw the man who'd given her the sword, and tossed it back at his feet. "Sorry, I've nothing to clean it with. Thank you, though."

The man mutely bent down and retrieved it, holding it as if he were unsure if the weapon was safe.

Trent opened his mouth to speak, and by the smile tugging at the edges of his lips, Tala could guess it would be something about her chest glowing again.

She pointed the knife in her off hand at him and glared. "Now is *not* the time, Master Trent."

Trent closed his mouth, but the small smile remained. He seemed to be laughing at his own joke.

She looked down at herself. The glow wasn't strong enough to obscure the details of her figure, though the streaks of black ichor, which speckled her from head to toe, made it so she didn't *feel* mostly naked. She did feel gross, though. *And sticky...*

Her eyes flicked to Atrexia. The woman wore barely more than Tala currently was. *So, why are they staring at me?* She grunted. *Right... glowing.*

Tala sighed and growled. "It's done, now. I've work to do." When no one moved, she raised her voice. "Off with you!"

The watchers turned reluctantly, slowly scattering back to their morning tasks. Atrexia lingered for a moment to shake her head and mutter under her breath. "If we get a salad as part of breakfast, someone dies."

Tala almost laughed, and when she looked after the woman and their gazes met, she saw a twinkle in the other Mage's eyes. *Ahh, that was meant for me to hear.*

Tala walked around the wagon and opened the wash station. She had a building headache, and it was beginning to make her feel grumpy. After she scraped herself mostly clean, she used almost a gallon of water to get off the last bits.

As she got herself clean, she noticed her hands shaking. *That was… That was close.*

If she was like most Mages, she'd be dead.

More than ever before, she blessed the stars that she'd oriented most of her magic towards defense. That was the only reason she was still alive instead of being cut to bloody ribbons below the cargo wagon.

She dunked her head again, trying to ignore the few tears that leaked out, only to be washed away. *I'm fine. I'll be fine. My magic will keep me safe and see me through. I can do this.*

When she looked up from that final dunk, she saw Den's hand sticking out above her, his head nowhere in sight.

Grasped in that hand was her last, undamaged shirt, tightly folded so it wouldn't drop into the water. *How long has he been holding that there?* From the way he was positioned, he couldn't see any part of her, and it didn't look like he'd even tried to spy.

She scraped what water she could off herself and took the shirt. "Thank you, Den."

His voice came from the driver's seat. "I didn't want you to have to come back into the wagon circle just to get that." After a long moment, he added, "Are you okay?"

Tala thought about that as she pulled on the shirt. Finally, she sighed. "Yeah. I think I might have nightmares about grass, but yeah." She shivered. "I'll be sleeping on the roof from now on…" As she thought about that, she added, "Maybe I can get the guards to lend me one of those shields. Being snatched by some arcanous owl would be an unfortunate way to go…"

Den chuckled. "True enough. Most people sleep inside on these expeditions…" He didn't say more.

Tala sighed, closing the wash station and stretching up and back. This was *not* how she liked to wake up, but she could make the most of it.

She moved through her morning stretches but decided to forgo the workout. She felt a bit sore from her work harvesting arcanous parts the day before, and the morning's scuffle had added new aches. *Great. The Wilds are my workout…*

Chapter: 19
Not Soon Enough

Tala felt utterly amped despite her soreness and slowly growing headache. She was sure that a portion of that was lingering adrenaline from the attack, but a large part was also likely from her still glowing spell-lines stirring up the power within her system.

Her stretching done, she pulled on her shirt. Thankfully, it hung down nearly to her knees, so she was reasonably covered when she re-entered the wagon circle, grabbing a new pair of pants, her magic detector, and an iron salve bar.

She went back around the wagon and used the magic detector to quickly scan herself, applying salve to any areas that caused the inscribed device to show even a trace of a glow. *No reason to get complacent.*

That done, she pulled on her pants, up under her shirt, before fastening the ties. *There, dressed for the day.* She returned to the other side of the wagon and placed the magic detector and iron salve back in her box. She paused, glancing at her gloves, laying where she'd set them in the box. *No need for those, and not worth risking them.* She picked them up and tucked them into her bag.

Someone had gathered up her bedroll, folding it and placing it to one side. She looked about but couldn't find who to thank.

She opened it up and found it was blessedly free of ichor, somehow. *Miracles never cease.* That fear averted, she folded and rolled up the bedding, placing it back in the box. *Now, to my job.*

With quick efficiency, she empowered the cargo-slots in her wagon.

Soon, thirty symbols glowed happily, and she was done. *Not too bad.* She, herself, was also still glowing. The circle of activated script on her breast had glowed until after she fell asleep the night before, so she would likely stay alight for at least a couple of hours this morning. *Joy.*

She still felt the need to run around the wagons a couple of hundred times, but she schooled herself into calm, deciding there were other tasks she should attend to. Tala turned towards the chuckwagon and breakfast.

Several passengers were up and eating, but dawn was just beginning to break, so she suspected most had yet to arise. *All that fit in between first light and the first sliver of the sun becoming visible.* She shook her head.

The night shift of guards was eating, many casting furtive looks her way.

She easily heard several snatches of conversation about her, mainly composed of ignorant queries as to whether she was glowing because of the dawn's light. Even so, a few of the guards had seen at least a portion of her scuffle, and they were quietly entertaining their tablemates with the tale.

"I swear, I've never seen a Mage so covered in blood."

"She was a terror! I'd not want to wake her in the morning."

"She didn't even use magic to kill it! It was like she had a personal grudge against the thing."

There was a lot more in that vein, but after understanding the gist of things, Tala chose to ignore the retellings.

As she walked up to the chuckwagon, she saw Brand staring at her. She smiled at the man and took the bowl of thick, creamed oats. He swallowed unconsciously. "Are... are you glowing?"

She waited a moment to demonstrate her irritation at having to answer such an obvious question. When he didn't say anything further, she sighed. "Yes."

"But... last night when I—" He glanced around quickly. He'd clearly been about to say 'when I stabbed you' but thought better of it. "Last night, only a tiny ring lit up."

"That's right."

His eyes widened further. "What happened?"

"Carnivorous plant with *lots* of vines and thorns... Can I eat my breakfast now?"

Brand nodded, eyes still wide, and grabbed something from under the counter.

Tala almost flinched, but when she looked down, she saw he was pulling out a book and a small medallion.

"Here." He passed the two items to her.

She took them, glancing down. The book was a notebook, and a quick glance inside told her it was a hand-copied text. "Don't you need this?"

Brand shook his head. "We each have a copy. That is the one with the most legible handwriting." He glanced away.

She grinned. "Yours?"

He cleared his throat, then seemed to ignore the question. "The medallion will identify you as one who knows."

The iron coin bore the deeply inset relief of a scythe. "Oh?"

"We call ourselves the Order of the Harvest." He blushed slightly at that, and her grin widened. "I'm sure it sounds silly to you."

"It sounds fitting." She picked up her bowl as well. "Iron because Mages avoid the metal, right?"

He stiffened. "I'm sorry, Mistress, I didn't think. I—"

She waved his concern away. "I'm fine with iron, Brand. Thank you." He turned to regard her, frowning slightly. He looked skeptical, so she added, "I mean it. Thank you."

He nodded uncertainly, but she saw an easing of tension. "Glad to have your help."

She took her bowl and the two items to the table she'd eaten at the night before. Several guards were already sitting there, but she greeted them and sat, nonetheless.

They gave her hesitant greetings, but that was the extent of their interactions.

Tala was already poring through the new book, devouring it and her food with equal abandon.

All it would take to recover the morning was coffee… but sadly, the likelihood of that being available was minimal. *Maybe I should ask?* No. Her head was pounding, and she didn't want to go back to the chuckwagon.

Tomorrow. I'll ask tomorrow.

* * *

The caravan departed less than an hour after dawn. Tala's wagon, driven by Den, led the way once more.

The morning began in a blessedly boring fashion. Tala read the books she'd been given, both the one on Immaterial Guide spell-forms and the cook's guide to arcanous harvests.

Each was fascinating in its own way, but neither was particularly useful in the moment. *Though, when we get attacked again…*

The principles for harvesting and consumption seemed to align with those of powering created items. Don't feed people parts of the animal empowered with magic of types they can't handle.

No arcanous bone broth from a blade wing... She shuddered, thinking about the havoc such energy would cause if a person tried to absorb it.

Less than two hours into the day's travels, Tala's magesight flared a warning at her, alerting her to nearby power. Her head whipped up from the book she'd been reading just as her wagon crested a hill.

In the valley below, she saw a small herd of deer with lightning dancing between their antlers. They were smaller than horses with fur of a thundercloud-gray color with white streaks woven through in beautiful, seemingly random highlights. The antlers, themselves, had a silvery, golden sheen, and as the myriad flicks of lightning danced among the deer, the bolts almost seemed to have a playful quality. The energy would break apart into smaller sparks, flitting from beast to beast, then portions would come back together for grander jumps, across open spaces among the herd. No deer remained untouched for longer than a heartbeat, but the strikes didn't seem to be following any sort of pattern that Tala could quickly recognize.

Blessedly, there was no accompanying thunder.

The lightning never stopped moving, and it never struck anywhere but from antler to antler. *What purpose does that serve? Does each animal add their own power to the storm, so that it can be harnessed for collective defense?* She wasn't close enough for her magesight to pick up the details, let alone the internal form of the magics, and without that, the only real way to test the theory would be to attack or to see the herd attacked. *Yeah... that doesn't seem wise.*

The lightning fractured outward, and the deer, almost as one, turned to regard the oxen and one wagon currently visible to them, all seeming to freeze.

Millennial Mage 1 - Mageling

Den didn't stop the wagon's progress, and soon it was meandering down the slope, toward the herd, the other wagons close behind.

After the momentary pause, the lightning flashed towards one side of the herd, and the entire group turned, unified in purpose, and dashed away at surprising speed, seeming to follow the direction that the lightning had indicated. As they ran, sparks flickered around their flashing hooves, and the lead animal let out a trumpeting bellow that sounded like an odd cross between a cow's moo and a squeaky hinge. In less than a minute, every one of the creatures was lost to sight in the varied landscape of hills, valleys, and dells.

Huh… They moved as one, seeming to follow the lightning… Could they be one consciousness in multiple bodies, and the lightning is just the firing of the various portions of its mind? That was impossible for her to test. While at the academy, Tala had come across a theory that you could treat all of humanity as if it were one giant organism, and that better explained human behavior than the idea that every human was an individual. She shook her head. *Too much. Too theoretical. Isn't actionable.*

She returned to her books and notes.

She wasn't reading long before she sensed an approaching, building power from the direction opposite of that which the deer had run.

Her interest piqued, Tala looked around, scanning the hills to that side, and she thought she could catch flickers of fire magic and the flash of fur-covered bodies, low to the ground.

A few minutes later, she was certain enough to call out that a wolf pack was trailing them off to that side. *They might have been stalking the deer, but we appeared to be easier prey?*

Atrexia rode up beside her. "Where do you see them?"

Tala pointed the beasts out, described what she saw, and the other woman nodded. "Burn wolves. They've been known to stalk both caravans and the cloud hind we passed back there. They have even been occasionally observed to take down small thunder cattle families."

The other Mage rode over to the sergeant on duty, and they had a quick discussion but did nothing else that Tala could see.

Another quarter-hour passed before the wolves came into easy sight.

They were no bigger than large dogs, but were leaner in appearance. Their eyes glowed an ember red, and the tips of their fur were each a soft, luminescent yellow. Each hair was black, despite the tip, and had an almost charcoal quality to their appearance, though they still moved as fur would on a dog. The last thing that jumped out to Tala, upon quick inspection, was the trails of smoke rising from each lolling, fang-filled maw.

Ahh, burn wolves… I can see why they got the name. After a moment's consideration, she found herself smiling. *If we kill any, they would make perfect fuel for my fire starter.* In addition, such obvious uses meant that the parts would be eminently salable.

It was a large pack, not that Tala knew much about the average size of such things, but nearly thirty arcanous canines certainly *seemed* like a large number.

They padded along silently through the grass, some hundred yards from the caravan.

To the credit of both the drivers and the oxen, the wagons' pace never changed, and there were no sounds of panic or fear.

As the wolves began closing the final distance, Atrexia rode out towards them and gestured across herself, pointing at the ground.

Millennial Mage 1 - Mageling

Tala saw power flash from the woman's keystone, down her left leg, activating a spell-form on that calf, ankle, and foot. The working then flowed out, through Atrexia's bare sole, and into the ground.

Immediately, a trench, ten feet deep and twice as wide, opened between the wolves and the caravan.

As the ground shifted, compacting outward to create the defensive bulwark, five guards loosed into the pack. Each arrow struck true, and five wolves yelped in pain.

There was no accompanying bloom of power. *Mundane arrows? Do they not have any of the fire variety, or was the use of mundane ammunition purposeful?*

The pack stopped then, the largest wolf ambling up to the deep trench.

The matriarchal wolf looked down into the pit, then up to Atrexia. After a long moment, in which the two locked gazes, the wolf dipped her head, then turned, leading her pack away.

Tala had a moment's hope that there would be five bodies to harvest, but as the wolves left, she saw five bolts, coated in smoldering blood, laying in the grass behind the departing canines.

Atrexia motioned again, and the ground seemed to flow like water, rushing to return to its original shape.

Unlike with the thunder cattle the day before, the effort did not seem to strain her.

I suppose creating the spikes so quickly yesterday was much more straining than making a trench and refilling it? She really didn't understand Material magic well enough to fully comprehend why that might be the case, but the evidence was obvious.

No burn wolf parts for me. She then felt a moment's guilt that she wished the animals harm. *They'd been about to attack us. If some died as a result of our defense, it makes sense to make their deaths worth something.* Even so, she felt conflicted; they were in the Wilds, and this was the wolves' home, not hers.

An hour after the departure of the wolves, Tala began to notice small animals hiding or scurrying about in the grass as the wagons passed.

None were easily visible to the eye, those farther away seeming to go to great effort to hide. While the myriad rabbits and other small creatures fled from the approaching wagons, they didn't usually go far, seeming to simply wish to wait for the humans to pass. A few were of note because instead of bounding or scampering away, they simply vanished. Some, she assumed, simply became invisible, even to her magesight, which was a fascinating possibility as it seemed to closely mirror her own iron skin. Others, however, instantly appeared elsewhere, farther away. *Dimensional variants.* Creatures with teleportation magic, and possibly other dimensional powers, woven into their being.

She contemplated capturing one of the invisible type, then had to laugh at herself. *How could I find one to capture?* True, if she had hours to hunt, lay traps, or analyze the terrain, she could likely begin finding them easily, but by then the caravan would be miles away, and they would not be pleased if she tried to stay behind just to hunt. *I do wonder how they do it, though. Do they somehow wrap power back in on themselves to hide any leakage that would give them away? Do they do the same with light?* It was worth studying, but she didn't have the time, at least not at the moment.

The dimensional variants were much more tempting. *The right parts from them could power a dimensional storage bag with a great deal of efficiency.* That, of course, meant that they'd be valuable to sell as power sources for constructed items. She almost hopped down to try to capture some, but then she imagined herself running all around the meadows, trying to catch a creature that could instantly teleport away.

I could kill it? Or ask a guard to shoot one with their crossbow... That wouldn't work. Even if the guard could see the animal, and she was sure at least some of the creatures were visible to the guards, there was no way one would stay in place long enough for a bolt to strike home. *Trent or Renix could strike one down with lightning?* But if that were feasible and profitable, she had no doubt they'd already be doing it...

She sighed. *No dimensional parts for me...* Though, with regard to item power sources, she had no real use for them. *I can empower such myself... Huh.* That sent her flipping through the spell-form book, and in the end, she came to the realization that the power source didn't matter for the form of spells or magic. Any power source of a given type could power any spell of that type. The most the variation would affect was efficiency.

I could buy dimensional storage and power it myself? It was an interesting idea. The only thing she saw pertaining to power sources, or items for that matter, was a brief comment: 'Spell-forms powered directly by human Mages tend to consume more precious metals during enactment than those empowered by arcanous harvests or points of natural power in the world. Whether this is due to flawed mental constructs on the part of the Mage or some other factor is unknown, but no item has successfully been powered by any portion of a Mage's remains. For more details see...' And there, the author referenced another book, which she had written on the construction and conception of magical items.

All in all, the book was frustratingly vague. *Directly powered? How do I indirectly power something?*

True, it gave many detailed diagrams and had fascinating discussions on inscription theory, but most of the spell-forms were depicted and described in two dimensions. As the book said, 'Any discussion of inscribing is too complicated to fit within this tome, as no part of any human is perfectly flat, and every variance away from perfectly flat alters how the spell-form will function.'

In short: humans are irregular in shape, and that must be accounted for. The End.

It didn't mention *how* to do this.

This really is the most basic book on the subject. She sighed.

Tala had just recently stopped glowing—*That lasted much longer than I'd expected*—and she was beginning to feel hungry. *I wonder exactly how long it is until lunch?* She glanced at the sky. *Not soon enough.*

She climbed down, grabbed some of her trail food, and ate it while walking beside the wagons. As she walked, she noted the huge variety in plants that surrounded them. They each had subtly different magical flavors, and she began to realize that an herbalist could spend a dozen lifetimes experimenting with the properties of all these plants. At first glance, none seemed particularly useful to humans, as most magics she could see were variations of growth, fibrous strength, or photosynthesis-enhancing effects.

Even so, as the morning wore on, the wide array of arcanous creatures and plants that they passed began blending together.

If everything is unique… nothing is. She sighed. It was nearly noon before that thought was put to lie.

Chapter: 20
Around the 'Death' Tree

Tala looked up as her wagon took a somewhat abrupt turn, pulling away from her to the left as she walked. From the look of things, Den was guiding the caravan in a wide arc around a lone tree, which was swaying gently despite the lack of strong wind.

Tala tilted her head back, taking in the nearly perfectly clear sky. *That's strange. There's no storm to explain odd wind patterns.* She thought back over the trip so far. They'd passed countless bushes and were constantly around the all-covering grass, but Tala didn't think she'd seen a tree since early the previous day.

The bark of this one was almost bone white and looked as smooth as polished marble, at least at this distance. The leaves were green and full, and there were what looked like red berries scattered throughout the canopy.

As she looked closer, she could see that the plant positively *blazed* with magic, and Tala was tempted to try to go harvest a branch or something, but her better reasoning warred with that first temptation. Additionally, the aura of the power in the tree somehow tasted like a graveyard—an *old* graveyard at that. *How can a living thing radiate a feeling of death?* She had no idea. Even so, she somehow knew that 'death' wasn't *quite* right.

Millennial Mage 1 - Mageling

They were almost halfway through their circuitous arc, and Tala was just pulling her attention away from the tree when a bird landed in one of the upper branches.

Huh… Maybe I was—

Even as she was contemplating, the bird simply fell apart. It turned to a fine powder, raining down upon the tree, which seemed to sway just a bit more. *It likes it?* She might have been anthropomorphizing just a bit, but even so… *A tree that makes its own fertilizer… wonderful.*

Had the bird eaten a berry, or had just touching the tree been enough to kill it? Maybe both? *Maybe it didn't eat a berry quickly enough?* That could make sense. If the berries contained a counteracting magic to that of the tree, the tree's seeds could be spread, else they likely wouldn't move very far, and the berries would be pretty useless.

She didn't understand why any animal would ever come near until she realized that there was no *smell* of death, no bones, nothing to indicate that animals died here. *Ooooo… that's evil.* Well, not actually evil, but it was devious.

Tala found herself wanting a stick even more.

She'd hoped to harvest the burn wolves, but they'd gotten away. The cloud hind had retreated before she'd really been able to contemplate plans for them, but the possibilities for their parts were numerous, and finally, the dimensional and invisible arcanous critters had been eluding her. She wanted *something* from today's encounters.

You know? I bet I can get close enough… the iron should protect me. The question was: how would she harvest a limb? She didn't trust herself to throw a rope over one, and she wasn't sure a rope would survive contact anyways. The more she thought about it, the more she was sure. *I want a death stick.*

The tree was at least three hundred yards away.

She glanced at the grass, living happily beneath the tree. *No effect on plant matter, then?* That was good. Her clothes were linen and should be fine. *Either that, or it takes direct contact...* In either case, her clothes should be fine. She'd never thought of herself as wardrobe obsessed, but this was, after all, her last set of unstained, undamaged clothing.

She stuck her hat and satchel in the box of her wagon. Den gave her a questioning look but didn't slow the oxen or comment.

She grabbed one of her sticks with iron salve from her box and strode towards the tree.

Trent rode up to her before she'd made it ten feet from the wagon. "Mistress Tala... that tree..."

"Death magic, right?"

He stared down at her. "Death magic... No? I mean, I suppose you could call it that, but it really is more like dissolution."

"Huh. Good to know." She turned back to the tree.

Trent cleared his throat. "*Mistress* Tala. What are you going to do?"

"I want a death stick."

"You want... a death stick..." He sighed. "Firstly, as I said, it would be a dissolution stick. Secondly, are you sure that's wise?"

She shrugged. "Is *dissolution* magic blocked by iron?"

Millennial Mage 1 - Mageling

He frowned. "Yes, as far as I know, but to get it in an iron box, you will have to get close. That magic is very powerful, and from a tree that old, it could shatter most defenses in moments. Please reconsider, Mistress Tala." He glanced back towards the caravan. "You are somewhat imperative for this mission, and I believe that Mistress Atrexia, Renix, and I would be blamed if harm were to come to you."

Tala hadn't considered that. She growled in frustration. Then, a thought occurred to her. "Could you shoot off one of the smaller branches? Such as sending an ice spike into it, or strike it with lightning, or something?"

Trent blinked at her for a long moment. "I don't see how..." He groaned and scratched his forehead. "Were you planning on *climbing* the tree to get a branch before I came to talk to you?"

When he put it like that, it did sound foolish. *After all, there is no way I could have kept my clothes out of contact with the trunk.* "No?"

He sighed, shaking his head. "You are something else, Mage Tala." He glanced at the tree. "Yes, I can, but it wouldn't be free, and you'd still have a stick, full of lethal magic, that you couldn't actually touch."

"Leave that to me."

He cocked an eyebrow. "Oh? You have a plan better than 'climb the *death* tree' for dealing with the branch?"

She ignored his obvious jab and nodded. "I do."

"Care to share?"

"Not particularly."

Trent groused for a moment, then sighed. "Two silver ounces, for the inscriptions this will cost, and if the tree reacts to defend the fallen piece, you swear to pull back. I get paid either way."

Tala frowned. "Can I pay you in Alefast?"

He waved a hand. "Fine, fine. Deal?"

After a moment, she nodded. "Deal."

Trent turned and focused on the tree. "How big?"

"No larger than a walking stick, please." After a moment, she added, "If possible, I'd love a couple of leaves and berries?"

He nodded and lifted his right hand, pointing the first two fingers, muttering quietly. "Small it is, then." Then, he spoke without sound, and Tala saw a brief flicker of power on the man's throat. *Verbal caster?* Those weren't very common.

The brief flicker zipped down his arm to his fingers, then back to his throat, where it was diverted to his right knee. There, it became a flash, too fast for her to follow.

An instant later, lightning struck up from the ground and neatly sheared off one of the smaller, ancillary branches close to their side.

The boom of thunder came not a heartbeat later.

"Thank you."

Trent grunted.

Tala strode forward confidently, her magesight sweeping the ground for any other arcanous plants that might be a threat.

She found none, though she did see the tree's roots extending almost all the way to the wagons. *That's crazy! The root system's circumference is nearly ten times that of the branches.*

Millennial Mage 1 - Mageling

That couldn't be normal. Thankfully, the roots were deep as well, the closest to the surface being at least fifteen feet down at this radius. *That should be safe.*

After a moment, she continued pondering, *I wonder what the life cycle of a tree like this even is?* Would it kill any little trees that grew up near it? Did the tips of the roots grow upward, after they were far enough away, to make new trunks?

She glanced around, noting, again, that there were no other trees in sight. *How would this even get here?* So many questions. She promised herself to add the questions to her notes for later. *If later ever comes.* With her growing list of questions, it just might not.

When she reached the fallen branch, she eyed the tree critically. It didn't seem to be reacting to her presence. The limb was just over one foot long, barely curving. *A little small, don't you think, Trent?* But she couldn't really complain; it would be easier to deal with at this length. A cluster of four leaves and some ten berries hung from one end.

This close, she could easily see that the spell-forms in the berries, while still unintelligible to her, *felt* opposed to that within the leaves and branch, itself.

She *almost* reached for it with her hand, but she remembered that her palms were not protected by her iron salve. Instead, she extended the iron salve bar, on its stick, and began rubbing it across the limb.

To her surprise, the salve came off easily, clearly at least tangentially affected by the magic of the hefty twig. The salve melted easily and resolidified quickly atop the bark. Her magesight told her that it was effectively blocking the power within.

Interestingly, the grass beneath the limb only began to crumble after she'd coated the top with the iron salve. *Concentrating the power? And directing downward enough to cause it to affect vegetation when it wasn't meant to?* It seemed plausible, but she was just guessing. *Interesting.*

She gingerly flipped the stick over and coated the other side, along with the leaves, using her magesight to verify that she left no holes in the coating. She did not coat the berries.

After double, triple, and quadruple checking, she took a breath and picked up the stick.

Nothing happened.

Nothing continued to happen.

Hah! It worked. She'd never been in doubt… not really… It would have been a foolish risk if she wasn't sure, beforehand.

Tala turned and strode for her wagon, which had completed another quarter of its trip around the radius of the tree. She could see many of the drivers, several guards, Trent, and Renix all watching her as she walked back.

The mundane folks returned to their tasks as she returned, but Renix and Trent awaited her, just outside of the tree's root radius. *Can they sense it, or does folk wisdom regarding plants like this simply cover the outside cases?* Probably not worth asking.

Trent was looking at the dissolution stick. *Stupid name.* His eyes then went to the stick holding the remains of her bar of salve. "Iron dust in the soap?"

Millennial Mage 1 - Mageling

She shrugged. "Not soap, more of a salve-like medium to facilitate spread and cohesion, but yeah, something like that."

He was nodding. "Clever, I suppose, if you are careful."

Renix grinned at her, pointing to the dissolution stick in her hand. "Do you want to get me a few? I'll pay."

"I don't want to sell you death sticks." Her eyes flicked to Trent, who was shaking his head in bemusement.

Renix frowned. "Fine, then."

"Renix, this is dangerous. If it broke, the exposed ends might dissolve anything they touch."

Trent looked around sharply, scanning the caravan. It didn't look like anyone was close enough to overhear, but even so, his voice was a harsh whisper when he spoke. "Mistress Tala. Such things should *not* be said where they can be overheard. That is a dangerous item, and I will be *very* cross if I learn that it has been taken. Do we understand each other?"

Tala swallowed involuntarily. She responded with a soft voice of her own. "Sure, but I don't see the problem. It really isn't that hard to kill a person."

Trent scratched above his right eye. "Not for a Mage, no. And you are technically right that anyone can stab a knife into someone's back, but that takes some skill and strength and leaves evidence. *That*." He pointed at the stick in her hand. "That could kill with a touch and would likely leave no evidence save a missing person."

Oh... She hadn't thought of it in that way.

"Do you want me to hold onto it? I have a lockbox in my wagon…"

Tala almost grew angry at the implication, as well as the patronizing tone, but she calmed herself. "No. I'll be careful."

Trent narrowed his eyes, then relaxed, just slightly. Power rippled around his eyes, and he began digging in a pouch. "I can still see power coming off the berries. Do you want a small iron box for those?" He pulled out a box that was just a bit larger than a stereotypical ring box. "Those should fit in here without trouble." After a moment, he saw her hesitation and smiled. "No charge."

She accepted the little box with a nod of thanks and closed it over the berries, using the box, itself, to snip them free. That exposed a small bit of the branch to air, and it blazed with power to her sight. She quickly pressed the iron salve bar to the stub, sealing it once more.

Trent nodded, seeming appeased. "What do you want it for, anyways?" By his look, he seemed to be regretting that he hadn't asked that question before helping her get it.

She tucked the little box under her belt and opened her mouth to respond but realized that she actually had no idea. In truth, what the branch did, breaking down cells to their base components, was the exact opposite of what her own inscriptions accomplished. In theory, that meant that it should be able to power constructs like her own defenses, just like fire magic could be used to spread fires or suppress them. But was that really why she'd wanted a sample?

Why did I want this? The answer was both simple and trite. She was loath to pass on *anything*, and she'd been frustrated by missing the chance to harvest arcanous components so far that morning.

Millennial Mage 1 - Mageling

Trent turned to face her more fully, and his tone was more probing. "Mistress Tala. Why did you want that?"

She cleared her throat. "Mages have their secrets."

He just stared at her for a long moment, then let out a long, long sigh, scratching furiously between his eyebrows. He spoke very quietly, so quietly that Renix likely didn't hear, but Tala could. "Rust and ruin, Mistress Atrexia is right. You're a child." He looked back up. "What is wrong with you?" He swung off his horse and tossed the reins to Renix, who fumbled them but managed to grab them at the last moment. Trent stalked closer to her. "Do you want a pack full of poisons, too? I can create a lightning crystal for you that will obliterate a couple of wagons if you drop it. Would you like six or seven of those?"

Tala was backing up, but not as quickly as he was advancing. *What is going on?* She had flashes of her teachers advancing on her in rage after one of her many… unusual solutions, and she felt her pulse quicken.

"What, by all that shines, possessed you, girl?" He wasn't shouting, but his voice was reaching the upper end of what could be called a whisper.

Tala stopped retreating and stood her ground. *No. I am a Mage, and he is* not *my teacher.* She glared up at him, truly realizing for the first time that he was, indeed, much larger than she was. Her magesight told her that his keystone was holding his gate wide open, likely in response to his own emotions. He was keyed up for magic, though he made no move to cast.

Trent halted his advance just out of arm's reach. His eyes flicked to the stick but returned to meet her gaze an instant later. He seemed to be fighting within himself, but after a long moment of silence, he asked, in a level tone, "Well?"

"I am collecting all I can. I am learning all I can. I..." *I'm short on money, and need to sell anything I can...*

Trent's eyes narrowed, and he raised a finger to point at her. "Tell me that you didn't consider selling it. *That* would be very rusting foolish. As Mages, we are supposed to *protect* people from powers such as that." His finger now stabbed at the stick still in her hand. "And you would give it into the hands of a stranger to use for who knows what sort of slag?"

Tala looked away. "I want to study it, alright? Its effect is almost directly opposed to some of my own defenses. Why, by all that shines, would I sell it?" *Okay, not going to sell it. That was a bad idea...*

Trent grunted. "If you truly don't intend on selling it, and you will be careful..."

Tala held up a hand. "You've made your point, and while you aren't precisely wrong, you are *not* correct. Now, I don't have the correct book to properly research this. I'm done with the basic book on Immaterial Guide spell-forms. Do you have the whole set of tomes, or will I have to carry this dangerous item for the remainder of the trip and seek the book in Alefast?"

He threw up his hands. "You can have any book you want, girl. I'm trying to help you, not keep things from you. I want you, and everyone else, to be as safe as reasonable."

"Fine, fine. I'd promise not to do anything with it before consulting you..."

"But you'd be lying."

Millennial Mage 1 - Mageling

She grinned.

She saw Trent's cheek twitch, though she couldn't have said whether it was threatening a smile or a sign of deep frustration and stress. "Would another perspective really be so bad? Even just to run your thoughts by?"

Renix piped up. "I'm happy to bounce ideas around, too!"

Trent paused. "That would probably be good for him." He glanced back at her. "And for you."

"Fine. I'll talk with both of you before I do anything major."

He grunted. "Probably as much as I can hope for." He gave her a long look. "You know, there is more to the Master-Mageling relationship than obligation. The academy does *not* prepare a Mage for the realities of the world; it isn't intended to."

Tala knew he'd guessed she'd never had a master, but she chose not to acknowledge that. "And Renix has a good one. I hope to learn some from you, myself, during this trip."

He pointed back to the stick. "Throw it back?"

She chuffed a laugh. "No, but when I'm done with it, if any part is left, I'll let you burn it."

He hesitated. "Far from anyone or anything?"

She thought about it for a moment, then nodded. "That sounds wise."

They both nodded their assent. "Very well, Mistress Tala. Thank you." After a moment, he smiled slightly. "In case you care, that is called an ending tree."

With the name, everything clicked into place. *Oh! That makes sense.* Before humanity left the wilds for good, ending trees were used for disposing of waste, the creation of fertilizers, and... for ritual suicides. They supposedly couldn't survive within cities. *Wonder why...*

Trent glanced to Renix. "Can you show her where the books are?"

Renix seemed to relax, handing Trent back his reins. "Of course."

Together, Renix and Tala went to Trent's wagon, and Trent went back to riding as flanking guard for the column of wagons, still winding through the open grasslands.

The strange, isolated tree silently shrank into the distance behind them.

Chapter: 21
Berries and Jerky

When lunch was ready, Tala was *very* excited. Research, as it turned out, was exhausting work.

She tucked her borrowed book, along with her own notebook, into her satchel, made sure her hat was secure, and went to meet the chuckwagon worker on his way to her.

It was Brand.

"Hello, Brand. How is the day treating you?"

He smiled hesitantly. "Well, Mistress." He offered her the cloth-wrapped pasty.

"Anything special in today's meal?" She could already see the power flickering within the meat, inside the pasty.

He started to shake his head, then stopped, sighed, and nodded. He glanced around, ensuring that no one was within easy listening distance. "Another portion of the blade-wing, Mistress. The remainder is being made into jerky."

Her eyebrows rose. "Oh? Would it be reasonable for me to ask for some?"

He looked mildly uncomfortable, even as he fell into step beside her. "We do try to keep it for the guards as its benefits to them are more..." He cleared his throat, then continued in a rush. "They need the help more than Mages generally do."

She nodded. "That's fair, I suppose. If you have any extra or are willing to part with some, let me know. Yeah?"

Millennial Mage 1 - Mageling

Brand stopped walking, and Tala came to a stop herself, a step or two later. They'd been walking off to one side, so their lack of movement didn't affect anyone else's progress forward.

Tala turned back towards him, head tilted in question. "Brand?"

"You... You aren't going to demand any?" He seemed completely unsure of himself, once again.

"Why would I do that?"

He began walking again, and Tala fell into step once he caught up.

They walked in silence for long enough that Tala decided to begin eating her lunch.

It was delicious and filling. Coupled with the walk, it was exactly what she'd needed.

"This is great! Thank you, Brand."

He nodded in acknowledgment but didn't say anything.

Finally, Tala decided to change the subject. "I want your thoughts on something." She licked the remnants off her fingers. "Are arcanous berries usually safe to eat? I haven't had a chance to hunt down that information in your book."

Brand shrugged. "About as often as mundane berries. Though, truth be told, even most arcanous plants don't spend any power on their berries." He frowned. "Why? Did you find some?"

"Harvested, but yes."

He was nodding. "Saw a bit of magic and snatched the berries? Might be interesting to see what you found."

She grunted. "They're from an ending tree."

Brand turned to her, eyes wide and mouth open. "What?"

"They are from the ending tree we circumnavigated an hour or so ago." She cocked her head to one side again. "Why?"

"You must be pulling my leg. *Everyone* knows about ending trees."

She shrugged. "Yeah, I know that in our ancient past they were used for creating fertilizers, disposing of waste, and... other things before we moved into the cities."

He shook his head. "Haven't you heard the stories of ancient warriors shrugging off blows in battles and taking on arcanous beasts barehanded?" He cocked an eyebrow at her, clearly referencing her own escapade.

"Yeah, of course. It is actually one reason I've pursued the avenues that I have. I love those old tales: Galadria, Akmaneous, Heleculies, Krator, Manastous, Synathia..." She smiled happily to herself before she remembered that it had been her father who'd told and read those stories to her. The smile faded.

"So, you do know."

She sighed, feeling the weight of sadness settling in. "No, Brand, and this conversation is becoming exhausting. Can you just tell me?"

He grunted. "Endingberries confer resistance to physical damage that usually lasts around an hour after they are eaten. One berry is sufficient for a fully grown man to receive this effect." He was becoming animated. "Moreover, legend says that the effect built, and the effects lasted slightly longer each time a berry was used. The greatest of warriors only needed to eat a berry once a day to be considered nearly invincible." He then gave her a sheepish look. "If I hadn't seen your spell-lines, myself, I might have assumed that such were the source of your resistance to... blades." He looked away. "That would, of course, have been foolish."

Tala cocked an eyebrow, then looked back over her shoulder. "Then, why didn't we pick that tree bare as we passed it?"

Millennial Mage 1 - Mageling

"Two reasons that I am aware of: First, the art of harvesting the berries without dying from exposure to the tree has been lost. All I know of those who've tried recently is that they were forced to consume all that they picked, just to counteract the tree's magic against them, and most still ended up with missing fingers, if not more."

Tala nodded. That made some sense. Even the stems of the berries had radiated the power of dissolution. Then, she frowned. "Iron tongs would solve that, and so would heavy gloves. I think I remember seeing a type of berry picker that should work, too."

"In theory, yes, but the trees move unpredictably and become more and more agitated the more berries that are picked."

"Cut down the tree?"

Brand paled. "The chips and sawdust carry the magic even more effectively than the unharmed tree. Cutting it down would fill the air with death. The same goes for burning the wood."

"I'm sure Mages could find a way if they knew the berries were so valuable."

He nodded. "And some do, but as the effects even extend to breaking down spell workings in unpredictable ways, it proves dangerous, on top of the cost of using their magics in the first place. I think I've seen a total of a dozen pounds of the berries sold across various markets since I joined the Order of the Harvest."

"You seem awfully knowledgeable about this specific fruit, Brand."

He sighed. "It is one of the core examples we, of the Order of the Harvest, learn of. It is a harvestable piece, which humans can eat and get obvious benefits from. If we could safely harvest them, not only would that help pay for our cause, but it would also greatly aid our cause, in myriad ways."

She was nodding. "So, these berries *aren't* common knowledge?" She gave him a bit of a reproachful glance.

He shrugged, not seeing, or ignoring, her implication. "I'd assumed that they were, among Mages, but I could understand if they didn't want guards finding out. Learning that a thing is, in theory, worth double its weight in gold causes men to take... risks."

"Ahh... I think I understand." She hesitated. "What's the second reason?"

"Hmm?"

"The second reason. You said there were two."

"Oh! Right. Each berry has a seed inside, and while naturally dormant, anything that tries to harm it will cause it to activate with a blaze of power like that of the tree."

"Anything?"

He nodded.

"Including biting or digestion..." She gave a low whistle.

"In addition, the seeds are *incredibly* virile. They will grow in *anything*, even open air, once they are outside of their berry. Most people don't want lots of little ending trees sprouting." He thought for a moment. "I do think that they need sunlight to grow, though, but not much. The first activation of their power powders anything above them, letting light in, even it if is diffuse."

Tala frowned. "Except within cities, right?"

"Hmm?"

"Ending trees can't grow within cities?"

"Oh, yeah." Brand frowned. "I'd forgotten that." He shrugged. "Probably a part of cities' defensive magics. You know, 'no hostile magics shall, herein, endure,' and all that."

"Maybe, I suppose." She thought for a long moment before continuing. "So... I do actually have some, but they are still on their stems."

Brand looked at her as if trying to assess if she was joking. After a long moment, he spoke. "I cannot pay for such, nor do I know of any who could buy them despite their value. You might have luck in Alefast, but be careful."

"Would you trade some jerky for a berry or two?"

He hesitated, giving her another odd look. "We don't have enough jerky to equal the value of one berry, let alone two, and they'd be of limited use to us... though, I will admit that we do have a few tasks we could use them for." He frowned. "I think two would be helpful, but again, we don't have nearly enough jerky to actually be worth the trade, for you."

She shrugged, lowering her voice. "A pound of arcanous jerky per berry seems reasonable to me."

He gave her a skeptical look. "Making it jerky doesn't give it extra power." He nodded to indicate her mostly finished meat pie. "It would be, in essence, like the meat within that."

"Does it fade beyond that?"

He hesitated. "Not when properly prepared."

"In the book?"

"Yes, described in the book."

I need to find that section... "Very well. Do we have a deal?"

"If you remove the stems and seeds?"

She nodded. I can probably do that, safely.

"Deal." He held out his hand, and Tala took it.

Brand went to fetch two pounds of jerky, along with a small dish for her to put the berries into. Tala jogged back to her wagon, quickly climbing the ladder, and settling into a stable seated position upon the padded square in the center of the rooftop.

When she felt ready, she pulled out the small iron box that she'd gotten for the berries and opened it. The conflicting magics radiated outward to her magesight, and she felt herself smiling. *Eleven berries.* She'd miscounted earlier and was now *very* happy that there were more than the ten she'd thought she'd seen.

The first thing she did was pick up the small bunch by the berries and rub the stem across her iron salve. As before, the salve liquified and resolidified *very* quickly, clinging to the stem. Then, using her magesight to guide her so that she only grabbed the treated portion, she began pulling off the berries closest to her new point of grip.

It was slow going, and she had to continually work up the stems, coating any part she revealed with iron.

When she was done, she had the stem in four roughly equal pieces, entirely coated in iron salve, and tucked into a very small pouch.

The berries sat, alone, in the small iron box.

Brand came to her wagon shortly after that and climbed up to join her. He carried a small wooden bowl in one hand.

The man handed her the bowl, then sat down a good five feet back, watching with interest. He had a small bundle of what she assumed was the jerky tucked under one arm.

"I assume you don't want berries that come out of my mouth?"

He snorted. "No. No, I do not."

Each berry resembled a cherry, more than any other berry, though they'd grown in bunches like grapes. She frowned. "You know, if it only has the one seed inside, it really isn't a berry."

Brand shrugged. "It's called an endingberry. I guess that doesn't actually make it one, but…" He shrugged again. "Not much we can do about a silly name."

She sighed. "Fair." *It seems like a lot of things have ridiculous names.*

Being very careful, she gripped the two halves of the 'berry' and twisted.

They came apart with surprising ease, and she carefully placed one half in Brand's bowl.

The seed was, then, sticking out, white and slick with black juice. *Interesting. Red berries, black juice, white seed.* She delicately removed the seed and placed the second half in the bowl.

She could see magic in the seed, slowly beginning to awaken. If she was right, she had just about twenty seconds before something happened.

She also saw power in the juice, coating the seed.

Without taking time to consider, she popped the seed into her mouth, sucking off the juice.

A pleasant power buzzed through her, and she felt her enhancing and regenerative spell-lines tingle with an odd resonance. Thankfully, they didn't activate.

Tala took out the seed, carefully dried it off, then rubbed it against the salve bar, quickly coating it. The magic hadn't triggered before she finished the process. *Good. No issues.* She smiled triumphantly.

"One done!" She looked up to see Brand much farther back. "Brand?"

"What…? Why? Are you mad? You put the seed *in your mouth*?"

Tala thought she saw Den glance over his shoulder, but the driver didn't interject. "There was juice on it. I didn't want that power to go to waste."

"I told you that it activated with a pulse of power, and your first reaction is to put it in *inside your head*."

"My mouth."

He gave her a look.

She sighed. "It was perfectly fine. I could see the magic building, and there wasn't any danger of it activating before I finished." *Unless it nicked a tooth or was otherwise damaged, I suppose.*

He seemed somewhat mollified. "I guess you are the expert in things of magic…"

She did not correct him. *Yes, good. Believe I am an all-knowing Mage.* She smiled slightly.

After a long moment, he seemed to relax. "Very well… Are you going to do the second one?"

She smiled. "Of course!" The second berry was no more difficult than the first, though its power began building much more quickly, and she guessed that she was only barely fast enough in getting it coated in salve. *Different paces for different seeds. Good to know.*

She offered the bowl back to Brand, the tingle of the berries' magic causing an interesting feeling of rippling tension within her. Brand hesitantly took the bowl. After examining the meat of the berries, he nodded. "Alright, then." He held out the small package. "Just came out of the smoker an hour or so ago."

Tala frowned. "I definitely didn't see any smoke."

Brand waved the objection away. "Of course not. We capture it all to ensure we can use it towards properly smoking the meat."

She was pretty sure that wasn't how that worked but didn't press him on it. "Fine." She took the package. It felt light, but two pounds wasn't actually *that* much. "A pleasure doing business with you."

Brand grunted. "Same to you." As he climbed down to return to his own wagon, Tala clearly heard him muttering to himself. "She'll put grey in my hair, sure as the sun'll rise, tomorrow." Then, he sighed. "I hope this doesn't rusting kill me."

With no further audible complaints, Brand was gone.

Tala tucked the seeds into the pouch with the stems, closed the iron box on the berries, and sighed. "There we go. All in all, a profitable morning."

<u>Millennial Mage 1 - Mageling</u>

*   *   *

Tala quickly began flipping through Brand's book after he departed. With her enhanced senses and perception, she was able to find the section on jerkies quite quickly, even though it was *very* small.

> 'Cure the jerky within an iron box. The smaller the box in relation to the meat and the smaller and fewer holes in the box, the less loss in power will be experienced. This isn't a recipe book, so learn how to make jerky somewhere else.'

Tala snorted. It matched the tone of most of the rest of the text, which often seemed to relish belaboring the fact that it was staying on topic.

That found, she began flipping through to find the section on berries. When she did, it was similarly to the point.

> 'Berries, roots, fruits, leaves, etc. taken from arcanous plants are no more or less poisonous than their nearest mundane kin. Thus, if you can identify the core species of plant, which is now filled with power, you will have a good idea of the edibility of the item. That said, the magic in question might, itself, be unhealthy or even lethal if incorporated into the human body, thus analysis of that must be accomplished separately.
>
> 'The only known universally healthful produce from an arcanous plant is the endingberry, though extreme caution is advised as any damage to the pit will cause either nullification of the beneficial effects or death. No consistently viable means of harvesting the endingberry is known. Benefits: One berry will confer

> nigh invulnerability towards mundane damage to the consumer, lasting roughly one hour. Nothing short of magic, or a concussion, has been known to harm a man when under the influence of an endingberry, though things that should have caused great injury seem to reduce the length of time the effect lasts. Legend indicates the long-term consumption of these berries causes each subsequent berry's effect to last longer, but such has not been tested, reliably, by the Order of the Harvest.'

That settles it. I need to find a means of harvesting these. The way their use is described is almost identical to my own enhancements. In truth, that wasn't by accident. Tala had grown up hearing of the warriors of old and had sought to mimic them as a Mage. Though she hadn't known about the berries.

She did *not* contemplate that it might have been a subconscious means of reaching out to those who had abandoned her to debt, a search for happier times.

'Other plants are healthful under specific circumstances.'

The book went on to detail quite a few varieties of fruits, berries, vegetables, and herbs. One leaf could be chewed to dull extreme pain but would cause permanently mind-altering hallucinations if there were no significant pain to dull. A root would heal a broken bone if eaten in *exactly* matching weight to the bone to be healed, otherwise, it would not fully work or would fuse an amount of cartilage equivalent to the excess. In this case, aiming low was the recommended path.

There were more, but as only the name of the origin species was mentioned, along with a brief description of how the arcanous version differed in appearance, the book was not useful to her in identifying the plants in question.

As the book said: *'This is not an herbiary, nor a picture book. Find your herbology and plant lore elsewhere.'*

Unfortunately, her work under her father, in the apothecary, had not included foraging for herbs or parts of plants. They'd had a small garden with well-labeled varieties and purchased the remainder of what they'd needed from the local market. She likely would have learned the specifics of identification and prime harvesting, but that opportunity had vanished.

She turned her mind back towards the book and realized that she was starting to like the author, though she knew it was more the universal tone of the Order of the Harvest, as the particular voice of the writing varied widely throughout the book.

A side realization came from that breadth of authors. *This has taken more than a few decades to compile.* The Order was older than Brand had implied. *Or maybe older than he knows?*

Those two specific sections found and read, she decided to stretch her legs once more.

Hat atop her head and satchel at her side, she climbed down, greeting Den as she passed, and strode towards the back of the caravan.

Various guards inclined their heads to her, and Guardsman Adam waved. She responded in kind to each. There was no sign of Ashin.

Atrexia smiled and nodded but didn't otherwise acknowledge her, and it seemed that Trent and Renix were on the other side of the wagons at the moment.

Tala still felt the buzz of power from sucking the juice off the ending seeds. *That's odd. It's been, what… twenty minutes?* She knew that she hadn't consumed a third of a berry's worth of juice. *Not that I really understand how it works…*

Perhaps her iron skin was preventing the power from dissipating, or maybe her spell-forms were somehow helping the power be more efficient. Or the amount consumed only affected the power of the defense, not the duration. She really had no way of knowing. *Not yet.*

It was a curiosity, though, and she was quite focused on the question as she strode past the last wagon and began to turn back to continue her pacing.

Her inward focus likely explained why she didn't register the flare of power until it was almost too late.

Dimensional magic blossomed less than five feet from her as *something* flickered into being in that space.

Chapter: 22
A Frustratingly Fitting Name

Tala's eyes focused on the pulse of dimensional magic, and her mind registered the newly appeared creature, scanning it from talon to beak.

It looked like nothing so much as an oversized hawk, if the bird had trained for long-distance sprinting instead of flying. It was taller than she was, and its legs were *much* larger than its wings.

The three forward talons on each of its feet looked to be useful as much for gaining traction on the ground as tearing into their prey. The legs were covered in thick, grey, ridged hide up well past the back-bending knees, and above that, feathers coated the beast.

The feathers were a mottled grey and black in patterns that made it difficult to pick out the exact shape, even against the greenish-brown background of the grasslands. Nonetheless, her magesight saw detail where her eyes failed her. There were two thin, minuscule wings, which were clearly meant for balance rather than flight. A short, stabilizing tail sprouted from the rear.

The neck was long and curving but proportioned more like a horse than a swan.

Finally, the head. The beak was iron-grey but flecked with glinting accents of what looked to be gold, silver, and copper. It was hooked, clearly designed for biting and tearing prey into pieces small enough to swallow. The face was highlighted with twisting lines of deep blue and blood red, and the eyes were an absolutely stunning golden yellow.

There was a terrifying intelligence in those eyes.

Underlying it all was a truly chilling depth of *power*. The sight of it almost overwhelmed her before she forced her magesight to disengage from the beast.

Tala didn't even have a chance to finish her gasp of shock before the talons of one foot were whipping at her. The great bird had planted the other foot firmly, gripping the earth, and seemed to be aiming to slice her open in the first attack.

In mute horror, she fell backward, raising her arms in a vain attempt at defense as the razor-sharp weapons came in.

The pain of impact tore down her left arm, splitting open the sleeve of her shirt more easily than a tailor's scissors. She felt the minute traces of the endingberries' power used up in an instant. It wasn't enough.

Her gate was open, the keystone funneling power to her enhancements, and her arm pulsed with a soft, golden glow.

Her arm was not torn open.

The bones *did* break with a nauseatingly wet *crack*.

She was still falling backward.

Tala was able to vaguely register what might have been surprise in the beast's eyes before dimensional power warped around it. It vanished, appearing behind her in the same instant.

Three lines of fire blazed across her back as the talons caught her again, stopping her backward movement and throwing her forward.

Her spell-lines activated for that portion of her flesh and saved her from the shearing strike. Thankfully, the hit to her back was less focused, and therefore, it did not break bone. *Stars be praised for small miracles.*

The bird let out a piercing cry of frustration, which sounded like nothing so much as a hawk's call that had been deepened and given a volume to rival a basso trumpet's blare.

The beast's power pulsed again, even as Tala heard guards beginning to call out.

It was beside her this time, and its head snapped forward, beak chopping into her temple.

The world went black.

* * *

A pulse of power exploded from the base of Tala's skull, and she returned to consciousness, violently.

She was falling in a spinning twist. The bird's three quick strikes had completely tangled her body. Even so, she was able to flop in a semblance of a roll and come up to one knee; one foot and her right hand granted her greater stability.

Thus, an instant after the bird's beak struck, she was glaring up at it from the ground.

A shiver ran through her from head to toe, and a sense akin to her magesight picked up the signature of what had awoken her. It was the inscription set to watch for any loss of consciousness not due to falling asleep.

Once again, a sound, almost like a bell, hummed through her thoughts. Despite herself, she still found the note calming. Then, a mockery of her own voice came to her once again.

-Consciousness lost for 0.10 seconds due to a sharp blow to the head. Skull fracture and severe concussion were imminent.-

-Cranial inscriptions activated to prevent skull fracture and cushion dura-mater.-

Millennial Mage 1 - Mageling

-Additional threat to consciousness detected, dual forearm fracture. No bone inscriptions available to repair the damage. Temporary neurotransmitter solution available.-

-Mild, targeted, electrical shock and hormone cocktail utilized for near-instant resuscitation and defense against immediate return to unconsciousness.-

-No lasting effects detected or predicted.-

-Log complete.-

The bird took a step back, eyes widening.

Tala cracked her neck as she stood. She tucked her left arm close against her stomach, feeling the pain and knowing that only a *ludicrous* amount of adrenaline was keeping her from collapsing from that pain, alone.

There was a *ka-chuck* of crossbow fire from the nearest wagon, and the bird flickered without moving.

The bolt passed straight through the beast without slowing or harming it, and only Tala's magesight let her know why. *It altered its own dimensionality so quickly and precisely?*

This was… not good. From what she could see, this beast was *old*, and the power coursing through it was a blazing inferno that made the blade-wing falcon look like a candle beside the sun. She didn't have time to let her magesight adjust to the intensity, so she could get more information. *What is this thing?*

Even terrified, she knew she had to act.

Her right hand came up, palm out as she extended her arm. Her first two fingers were extended towards the sky, the second two bent down. All four fingers and thumb were tucked close together.

One target this time. She held the features of the predator in her mind, and the bird was highlighted blue almost instantly. *Crush it?* There was easy justification for lethal force… *If I do that, there might be nothing but paste...* She still wanted to harvest. *Really? That's your priority?* Even with her injuries... Yeah... yeah, it was.

The bird, sensing the magic building within her, lunged forward. In the last instant, when a Mage like Trent or Atrexia would have attacked, the bird vanished, appearing behind her once again. Despite not moving, Tala did not lose her lock on the target.

Restrain!

A golden circle blazed with light on the back of her hand as power leapt from her gate down her arm and into her hand, spinning through the needed, deeply-scripted calculations and stealing kinetic energy from the bird at the same time. That energy was repurposed to move the beast off the ground, even as the spell-form calculations finished their work, and her power created an exception, precisely altering the gravitational constant for this creature in particular.

The bird stopped mid-attack, lifting off of the ground and hovering in place, now in a stable orbit just over a foot above the ground.

Just like the men that she'd restrained in Bandfast, the bird did not stop moving. It flailed, beginning to spin and twist in chaotic circles, each movement adding to the confusion.

When the bird realizes it can teleport around as easily as before, it will attack me again. She should have used lethal force.

The predator screeched in frustration once more.

Tala felt an incoming pulse of power and sighed in relief.

Lightning lashed up from the ground in a torrent and ripped through... empty air.

At the last instant, the bird had vanished, a slight ripple of power all that remained in its wake.

Millennial Mage 1 - Mageling

The thunderous *boom* from the lightning rattled Tala's skull, but she managed to maintain her feet. Even so, she felt inscriptions around her ears draw a bit more deeply on her power as they deadened the sound to protect both her eardrums and her hearing.

She spun, gritting her teeth against the pain in her arm, which the motion magnified.

Neither her magesight nor her eyes could find the bird.

Renix rode up to her less than ten seconds later, the clear source of the lightning.

"Mistress Tala! Are you alright?"

She stared up at him. "What the rust was that thing!?"

"I didn't get a look at the magic it held, but it was a terror bird, for sure."

Tala blinked back at him. *What a frustratingly fitting name...* "Dimensional."

Renix nodded. "That would have been my guess, but I've heard of lightning, air, or earth varieties which might have escaped my attack as well." He was scanning the surrounding landscape. "Is it gone?"

Tala nodded and found that the motion made her head spin. "From what I can tell, yes." After a moment, she added, "To be fair, though, I didn't detect it until it attacked the first time. So…"

Renix kept scanning. "We'll be more vigilant. They rarely travel alone. They usually have a pack; three or four strong is the smallest I've heard of. They can get as large as twenty."

More of them? Great…

Trent rode up and demanded an explanation. Renix gave it.

Shortly thereafter, the duty sergeant for the guards arrived and asked for the same. Renix happily complied.

The wagon train did not stop its slow march forward.

Tala, for her part, bent down to pick up her satchel. The shoulder strap was neatly severed, and she had two short strips of strapping cut cleanly free as well. She sighed, decided it wasn't worth fixing immediately, and began eating jerky. After a moment's chewing, she realized that she should go to the chuckwagon.

Trent tried to stop her, but when she indicated her arm and reminded him that the chuckwagon workers were also the medics for non-lethal injuries, he relented.

Less than a minute later, she was knocking on the back door of the wagon.

It was not Brand who opened the door, but the young man's eyes widened when he saw her clearly broken arm, and he motioned her inside.

Brand was working on dinner, but he stopped to come and assist when he saw her.

She told him a brief, flavorless version of events. "Giant, slag-begotten chicken attacked me. We drove it off."

He was unsatisfied but agreed to set her arm before pressing for details.

The two cooks, who were trained as medics, worked together to pull her arm straight and reset the bones, Brand, himself checking their alignment before splinting her forearm.

She did not lose consciousness when they set the arm, but it was a near thing. To distract herself, she began talking. "What, no 'bone-be-fixed' meat?"

Brand rolled his eyes. "If we had harvested something that would speed healing, sure. But we haven't."

Her eyebrows went up. "You don't keep any stock?"

"That would be prohibitively expensive and unreliable. The older the harvest, the more it loses power. Jerking the meat will contain the effects, but meat doesn't contain bone-healing magics. That would be… odd."

Tala grunted.

Brand shrugged. "Besides, Mistress Atrexia should be able to heal this with ease."

Material Guide. Right. And her emphasis on earth and rock would more easily align with bone than Trent's ice and lightning.

As if on cue, a knock came at the door, and Brand's assistant opened it to reveal Atrexia.

The assistant bowed and backed away before the Mage as she stepped inside.

"You're alive. And not bleeding out. Wonder of wonders."

"You already knew that I'm not easily cut, Mistress Atrexia."

"Ahh, yes, the plant." She tsked. "You're making this into a habit, Mistress Tala."

Tala held out her splinted left arm. "Can you just fix this, please?"

Atrexia cocked an eyebrow. "How? I can't see through your skin with magesight, so why should I be able to affect you?"

Brand's eyes moved to stare first at Atrexia then Tala, but he held his tongue.

Tala groaned. This had been a problem before, but she hadn't considered it in this instance. After a moment's thought, she used her right hand to point at her left palm. "Can you work through here?"

Atrexia frowned, stepping forward. She took Tala's hand with surprising gentleness. The spell-lines around the woman's eyes pulsed with power as she examined Tala's palm. "Is all your skin naturally this color?" She indicated Tala's palms.

"I suppose?"

Atrexia blinked at her for a moment. "Wow. You're really light-skinned, aren't you?"

Tala glowered but otherwise didn't respond.

The other Mage returned her attention to the examination of Tala's palm. "Ah! Yes. I can see now that… What the rust!" Her mouth stayed open as she stared at Tala's palm. "How many spell-forms do you have active at the moment, ch—" She had almost said 'child,' but her eyes flicked to Brand, and she cut off.

"Just the ones reinforcing the skin of my forearm, back, and head." She hesitated. "Well, and reinforcing my head in general." *And those enhancing my nervous system. And those watching for the need of further enhancement effects. And my magesight.* She contemplated. *Yeah, that's it.* She, of course, was not going to give that full list to Atrexia, but it was wise for Tala, herself, to know.

Atrexia nodded, slowly, in the silence. "That shouldn't be enough to explain the level of magic I'm detecting." She glanced up to Tala's eyes and then away. "But I suppose that's standard for you… isn't it?"

Tala didn't respond.

"Well, I'll see what I can do." Power flexed outward from Atrexia, driving into Tala's palm. An instant later, there was a weird *click*, and most of the pain in Tala's arm vanished, leaving only a lingering ache. "Huh… That was surprisingly easy… Were you able to suppress your magical defenses that perfectly?"

"Hmm? Oh! Well… no."

Atrexia waited for a moment before cocking an eyebrow. "So… your magical defenses are that weak?"

"They don't exist, at least not for my palms."

Atrexia's magesight was still active, and the woman looked back down at Tala's palm. "Then these spell forms are"—she started nodding—"only for the enhancement of your skin. Whatever you've done to the rest of your body to protect you from magic, you've left off of here. Why?"

Tala opened her mouth to respond, but the other Mage was already waving a hand to silence her.

"Because it's too perfect. If you completely sealed yourself, you couldn't affect the outside world…" Her eyes widened, and her gaze, once again, flicked to Brand before returning to Tala. "We will discuss this, later. Yes?"

Tala sighed. "I suppose so." She flexed her arm and hand, removing the temporary splint. "Thank you, by the way."

"Hmm? Oh, think nothing of it. It is part of my contract to provide such services." Atrexia turned and opened the door, already departing.

"Thank you, nonetheless."

At that, the Mage paused, looking back towards Tala. After a short silence, she nodded. "You are most welcome, Mistress Tala. We will speak tonight."

Without further delay, Atrexia stepped out, closing the door behind her.

*   *   *

Tala rested atop her wagon, her shirt flapping in the steady breeze.

The wagon wasn't really moving fast enough to create a breeze, so she was grateful that the weather aligned to bring the pleasant wind.

The only irritant was the small hole in the front of her shirt, causing the garment to move unpredictably, snapping in the breeze. This, unfortunately, was her least damaged shirt, even with the hole courtesy of Brand's knife.

Four shirts should have been plenty…

She was working to stitch the leather strap of her satchel back together, using the two pieces that had been cut loose as bracing on either side of the butt-jointed leather pieces of the strap. All in all, she'd lost less than a foot of the strap, and she blessed her luck that she'd not cut the strap down to a perfect fit. Instead, she'd had the excess dangling beyond the buckle, which had let her adjust it to fit her most comfortably after the repair.

I won't even have to punch new holes to keep using this. Altogether, it wasn't more than a mild inconvenience.

She felt a flash of dimensional magic and jerked to the side, her eyes sweeping her surroundings. She nearly dropped the satchel in her moment of panic, and her heart was racing when she caught sight of a ground-squirrel blinking away from a much larger rival some hundred feet to the caravan's right.

Dimensional rodent... The feeling had not been any stronger or weaker than that of the terror bird. She shuddered. *Apparently, the magic for such teleportation doesn't care about size.* As she thought about it, the bird could have grabbed her and jumped away, leaving her at its mercy. *Well, if I didn't have the iron salve to block such magic from affecting me.*

It was also possible the magic couldn't take another living being. *At least not an unwilling one?* She did not have a good understanding of teleportation magic despite her intensive studies before her naked transport attempt.

She shook her head and returned her attention to the stitching. She blessed her foresight when she'd purchased the heavy needles and waxed thread. A bit of delicate knife work was all it took to make the needed holes for stitching, her precision augmented by her enhancements.

Start to finish, it took her less than ten minutes to finish the repair.

During that time, she fearfully responded to no less than five instances of dimensional magic, all of which turned out to be benign sources—at least, relatively.

Millennial Mage 1 - Mageling

This... might be untenable. She had no remaining injuries, per se, but her head, back, and arm all had deep-rooted, softly throbbing aches. *I need a bath...*

At that thought, she considered the berries. *Brand said that the berries would mitigate and might even reverse damage in some cases...* It was likely worth one berry, as a test.

She readied her iron salve bar and pulled out a whole berry.

Instead of twisting it open, as she'd done for Brand, she popped the whole thing in her mouth and crushed it against the roof of her mouth with her tongue.

Power blossomed behind her lips, and she almost gasped at the sensation.

Working quickly, she picked the seed out from the berry's meat and expelled it into her hand. Its power was building towards activation, and she quickly coated it in iron salve before placing it in the pouch with the other ending tree bits.

As she did that, she relished the sweet flavor of the endingberry. The juice, before, had not been sufficient to truly give her a taste for the treat, and a treat it was.

I'd take this over a donut any day. And that wasn't factoring in the power.

She felt the energy flowing outward, seeming to cling to her spell-lines like water to an aqueduct as if her lines were made for such power. *I suppose they were, in a sense.*

She felt the rush fade, just slightly, as her aches were soothed away, and she let out a breath of silent pleasure at the sudden relief. It wasn't a healing, per se, more like her body knew it wasn't in danger of further damage, so it didn't need to scream at her so loudly.

Aside from the brief, initial dip, the torrent did not lessen as it suffused her. It didn't fill her with the nondescript restlessness of undirected power but instead with a sense of wholeness, completeness, and togetherness.

She understood immediately. *The magic is meant to keep the consumer whole and healthy, and my magesight is picking that up and presenting it to me as a general feel for the power within myself.*

She felt a familiar comfort and was strongly reminded of her time at the academy.

On rainy days, when she hadn't had classes to attend, she would curl up in her rooms, beside a low-burning fire, and read as the gentle murmur of water filled the air outside. She'd missed many meals—and if she was being truthful, quite a few classes—whiling away the hours in any number of good books.

I could get used to this.

She contemplated eating a second but dismissed it as one of the reasons she ate one now was to see how long it lasted. Eating a second would throw off the test. She had no idea if the berries were standardly cumulative or multiplicative. *Assuming more would add to the duration at all.*

Still enjoying the taste that lingered in her mouth, she found herself contemplating. *Could I make wine out of this? Or just juice? Or jam?* She gave a short, soft laugh. *I wonder if cooking it down would concentrate the power or disperse it...* She needed *vastly* more berries with which to experiment.

With that in mind, she found herself mentally jumping at every bush that peeked over a hill or looked like it *could* be a tree. It was an added, sporadic, irritating interruption. They did not see any more trees of any kind that day.

Tala spent her time reading, walking, taking notes, and sketching. Additionally, she continued to find herself flinching at any spark of power she felt, which had even a flavor of dimensional magic to it. It made for a less-than-pleasant afternoon.

Chapter: 23
Around the Dinner Table

As before, when sunset was close, Den found a relatively flat stretch of ground and led the wagons in a great circle.

As they rolled to a stop, the guardsmen and servants immediately began setting up camp, and the drivers tended their oxen.

Since Tala didn't have blood to clean off this evening, she used the opportunity to do some standing stretches. The wagons were incredibly stable, but she did not trust herself to balance atop them; at least, she hadn't yet. *Maybe tomorrow.* It would probably be good for her stability to try.

Newly limbered, she strode towards the chuckwagon.

To her joy, she could still feel the comfortable energy of the berry within herself. It seemed to have diminished slightly but certainly not by more than a quarter, even though she'd eaten the fruit at least two hours earlier. *This is even better than I'd hoped!*

As she walked across the wagon circle, more guards were sizing her up than ever before, but Tala ignored their stares.

She greeted Brand and the other cooks cheerily and took the offered bowl of…

"What is tonight's meal, exactly?"

Millennial Mage 1 - Mageling

Brand cracked a half smile. "Stewed barley, root vegetables, and *chicken*." He emphasized the last, and Tala understood.

So, they didn't jerk all the blade-wing meat, just what they weren't using for tonight. "It looks wonderful." And it did. It had a thick, porridge-like consistency, but orange vegetables and green spices gave it a pleasing aesthetic.

As she looked about, a waving Renix drew her over to the table where the other Mages were sitting. Once again, it was set a bit apart, which gave some privacy, along with a sense of 'other-ness.' *Like at the academy, but this time I'm segregated* with *the other magic users.* She almost smirked at the irony.

Trent smiled up at her. "Care to join us?"

Renix grinned. "We haven't gotten a chance to hear your side of the terror bird's attack."

Atrexia sighed and grudgingly motioned for Tala to join them as well. "Go ahead."

She stepped over the bench and settled on Atrexia's right. "Thank you, don't mind if I do, but the story will have to wait until I eat a bit."

Renix nodded in concession, taking another bite of his own dinner.

Atrexia grunted.

Tala settled in, took a bite, and blinked down at the bowl. *This is fantastic.* She looked back towards the chuckwagon. *Maybe they are culinary Mages of some kind...* That was unlikely.

This seemed to be the perfect way to end the day.

Tala continued eating at a dedicatedly steady pace, making sure she did not rush and enjoying every bite.

After a few moments of silence, Trent cleared his throat. "So, before we hear the story, we have to discuss the fee."

Tala sighed. "Master Trent, I do not see how it is reasonable to expect me to pay you and Renix for his aid or Mistress Atrexia for her healing."

Trent's forehead crinkled in a frown. "No, Mistress Tala. Our fee to you."

Tala returned her attention fully to him. "What?"

"You are not employed to defend the caravan or engage arcanous beasts. We are."

"I was just defending myself."

Trent sighed. "Do you know how we are paid?" He gestured to himself and Atrexia.

"No, I can't say that I do."

He nodded. "We are paid per arcanous threat the caravan survives." He hesitated, then added, "In addition to our wagon and half of our inscribing costs."

Tala pondered that. "No base rate?"

"None."

Renix piped up. "Master Trent pays me a straight amount and covers half of the remaining cost for my inscriptions."

Trent gave Renix a look, and the younger man returned to eating. The older Mage then turned back to Tala. "You did most of the work driving off the terror bird, and the guard will *definitely* report it as a threat driven off. Your inscriptions won't be reimbursed, and you were in considerable danger." He glanced at Atrexia. "We don't want you to interfere, so don't see this as an ongoing arrangement." He returned his gaze to Tala. "But we do want you to feel inclined to help if the need arises."

Tala, while listening, was enjoying another mouthful of the food. *Is Brand married? No, Tala, you shouldn't marry a man for his cooking...* He had stabbed her in the chest, trying to kill her to hide his own secrets. *So... he's not afraid to stand up for himself?* It was still a bad idea. *Didn't he say something about a family? Might have just been lies to gain pity…* She sighed, her mind returning to what Trent had said. "I think I understand. What do you propose?"

"Half an ounce of gold."

Tala blinked at him. "What."

"We will be paid one ounce of gold for a threat the caravan survives of that bird's magnitude. We then split it among ourselves as we see fit. My mageling did deliver the final attack, but you did the bulk of the work and will bear the greater cost in inscriptions. That said—"

Tala held up her hand. "I understand. You don't want me throwing myself in harm's way, trying to 'earn' more."

Trent was nodding, but it was Atrexia who answered. "If you die or are unable to maintain the cargo, the caravan is considered a loss, and we are paid a meager percentage of the passengers' fees."

Renix made a face. "Never happened to us, but I've heard it isn't even an ounce of gold to split."

Atrexia continued as if Renix hadn't spoken. "It would also be a mark against us and make it *much* harder for us to get further contracts. You are our charge, Mistress Tala, and your safety is part of our responsibility." After a moment, she added, "No matter how little *any* of us like that fact."

Tala nodded. "Understood. Thank you, I suppose." After a moment, she cocked her head. "Could I take payment in the form of favors?"

Trent's eyes narrowed in suspicion. "What kind of favor?"

"Well, you see, I'd like to harvest some more materials from any ending tree we might pass."

Atrexia's face had paled. "Master Trent… what does she mean: 'more?'"

Trent put his forehead in his palm and rubbed vigorously. "She…" He sighed. "She has a short stick and several berries."

Atrexia turned horrified eyes on Tala. "Were all your teachers *rusting morons*!" She *almost* shouted the last but managed to keep it to an intensely loud whisper.

"It is safely contained."

"Mistress Tala—" Atrexia looked to the darkening sky for a long moment, seeming to be trying to gather herself. Her hands were clenching and unclenching under the table. Finally, she looked back at the younger Mage. "Mistress Tala. You have gambled against the arcane king and won. Do not take that for evidence that the game is *fair*."

Tala sighed. "Yes, I am familiar with the fable, Mistress Atrexia. I know that just because a thing was easy once, that does not mean it always will be."

"That is *not* the point of the fable, Mistress Tala." Atrexia was drumming the fingers of her left hand on the table in an anxious rhythm.

"Oh? Then, enlighten me."

"The arcane king *often* let his opponent win the first round, so they became complacent. If he read them to be a true fool, he would let them win more than once. Then, he seduced them into *one more* bet, in which they lost everything."

"Ending trees are not intelligent, nor are they linked."

"It. Is. A. Metaphor." Atrexia seemed to be under a great deal of stress as she was rubbing her sternum, unconsciously, with the heel of her right palm. "Mistress Tala. You are a *Guide*! You should be able to understand these things."

"Mistress Atrexia, I am not a child. I know it is a metaphor. It is also a tale meant to inspire consistent caution, no matter how things have gone in the past. I am not asking for help to burn an ending tree or pluck its berries by hand. I am *not* a fool."

"Then prove it. Take the money and leave the golden cage alone."

"A golden cage would be entirely ineffective."

Atrexia returned a look of *pure* condescension. "Our ancestors ceased harvesting endingberries for a reason, Mistress Tala. Foolish are those who neglect the lessons of history."

"And do you know the reason?"

Atrexia hesitated. "Well… no…"

"I do."

Trent and Renix had turned to their meals when the two women had begun arguing, but both perked up at Tala's words.

Trent leaned forward. "I'd be curious to know, Mistress Tala."

Atrexia glared at Trent. "Don't humor her, Master Trent. How could she possibly know?" She turned back to Tala. "Are you a scholar of the deep histories? Are you informed beyond the sages of the academy?"

"No and probably?" She shrugged. "I have different insights."

Trent cleared his throat. "To be fair, Mistress Tala, you didn't know it was an ending tree before you asked me for help."

Atrexia let out an exasperated breath.

"You are right, I did not, but I *did* know that the power it radiated was identical to my own enhancements, just utilized in reverse."

Atrexia stiffened at that, turning to examine Tala.

Tala continued. "With the name, I was able to research my hypothesis and confirm that the berries are of the same power but act as my inscriptions do."

"So, why aren't they harvested?" Renix was leaning forward as well.

"First, the trees are exceedingly dangerous." She held up a hand, forestalling comment. "I have no intention of collecting any more from the trees, themselves. I just want the berries." She lowered her hand. "The danger of the trees is magnified in that they move erratically and without warning. The only known salvation, if a harvester accidentally touches a branch, is to eat a berry. From what I can tell, and from looking at the relative power of each, eating a single berry would save a person from a single solid touch with the tree, maybe two if they had some resistance to magic. The window for eating the berry after a touch is mere seconds, so if you don't already have one…" She shrugged.

"That's all well and good, but that could be overcome."

"Exactly, Mistress Atrexia, I believe we can overcome that."

Trent sighed. "What is the second reason?"

"The pit, at the center, contains the same effect as the tree, though implemented more like an explosive reaction."

"Explain."

"Once the seed is removed, or damaged in any way, it concentrates its power and releases it all in a pulse. Eating a single berry is not sufficient to allow you to survive exposure to that pulse."

Trent was nodding. "That's how it spreads. A bird swallows the berry, allowing it to survive having landed on the tree. Then, as it is flying away, the seed is either exposed or damaged, and it activates."

Tala nodded. "Within a short time, it triggers, obliterating the bird, and dropping the seed in a new location, ideally surrounded by a fresh pile of fertilizer."

Renix's eyes were wide. "That's… devious."

She quirked a smile. "My thoughts exactly, though, obviously, the tree isn't sapient, so devious doesn't apply." She gave a pointed look to Atrexia.

The other woman rolled her eyes. "So, you stated the problem. The berry is both useful and valuable but not sufficiently so to justify the risk. It's like a dragon's hoard.

Sure, *if* you manage to kill the dragon, you get some money, but the chances for death are numerous."

Trent was shaking his head. "No, it's like an infinite den of vipers, where each viper has a silk ribbon around its neck. Sure, you can probably kill a snake and take the silk, but you also might damage the silk, making the effort useless. It is unlikely that you would get rich before you got bit." Trent saw the look on Tala's face and rolled his eyes. "And for the metaphor, you *don't* have access to defensive or healing magic to remove that risk."

Atrexia was nodding. "That is a better metaphor. It isn't one big risk for massive gain; it is a thousand possibilities of death each for minor gain. Not worth it."

To the other's obvious surprise, Tala nodded in turn. "Exactly. That is why they are no longer harvested."

Atrexia grunted. "Oh. I see."

Trent grinned. "She got you there, Mistress Atrexia."

Atrexia rolled her eyes again. "Nonetheless. That problem still holds true for… us…" She looked back to Tala, examining her more closely. "You say your spell-forms counter the tree's magic?"

Tala grinned. "If the magic can get to me at all."

"That would remove the first hurdle." After a moment, Atrexia amended. "Well, it would mitigate it." She frowned. "Mistress Tala, that is the harvesting. The part you requested us to assist with. That seems to be the hurdle that you can actively overcome."

Trent pointed to Atrexia. "She's got a point."

Tala sighed. "No. I said that I would like to harvest more. I hadn't actually told you what favor I would ask."

Trent nodded. "True. True."

Atrexia sighed in exasperation, and Renix grinned.

Tala continued. "As I was saying: I would like your help spotting the trees, as well as the use of a larger iron box." She hesitated. "Well, an iron flask would be better…" She nodded. "Yeah, an iron flask. And I need time to actually harvest."

After a moment, Atrexia shook her head. "No."

"What?" Tala frowned. "What do you mean 'no?'"

"You are asking us to risk this entire contract to repay you for half an ounce of gold. No. That is foolishness."

Tala felt her anger rising, but Trent held up his hand before she could respond. "Mistress Tala, we cannot stop you." He gave Atrexia a silencing look when she opened her mouth to object, then continued, "While we cannot stop you, we will not help you. In fact, we will do anything we reasonably can to discourage you."

Tala opened her mouth to object in turn, but Trent wiggled his still-aloft hand. "However. I am willing to try to help you after we arrive in Alefast. There are some known groves of ending trees within a couple hours' walk of the city, and you could easily go out and get back before nightfall."

Tala closed her mouth. *I'll need to be charging these cargo-slots for unloading, and the new set for my return trip, but if I do that in the morning...* She found herself nodding. "You would offer guidance and protection?"

Trent paused. "Well… no. I would buy you a map and make sure you could read it and follow it to the grove. Half an ounce of gold is *not* worth the inscriptions it would take for me to make such a journey safely."

Renix straightened. "I could—" He cut off as Trent turned on him, eyebrow raised. Renix deflated. "I could wish you the best and buy you an iron flask…"

Tala almost found herself smiling at the exchange. Finally, she sighed and nodded. "Fair, but that doesn't erase the debt. Half an ounce of gold. Yes?"

Trent paused for just an instant before nodding. "Fair enough. The grove is well known, and maps of the region around Alefast are cheap." He smiled. "I'd be happy to help a friend, especially if that friend refrained from dying until then?"

Tala snorted. "Fine. I'll try to exercise greater caution."

Atrexia took her last bite of food and straightened. "That *insanity* out of the way, Master Trent, didn't you want to review something with Renix?"

"Ahh! Yes, quite right." He glanced to Tala. "Mistress Tala, I was going to give Renix here a brief refresher on the use of magic, but he's heard it from me half a hundred times, and I've gotten Mistress Atrexia to give her take at least six times."

"Ten," Renix said with a glower. "She can make *magic* boring, Mistress Tala. Magic!"

Atrexia rolled her eyes. "It is only boring to those who do not properly understand, *mageling*. Watch your attitude when discussing those who take their time to enlighten you."

Renix ducked his head, but grimaced nonetheless.

Tala did her best to hide a smile. "I've had teachers that didn't teach how I learned best." She looked inquiringly at Trent. "Do I hear a question in there?"

"Would you provide the refresher?"

She blinked back at Trent. "On… the use of magic…"

"Yes."

"Are you sure you don't want me to enlighten him on 'what stuff is?'"

Trent grinned. "I find that a broad prompt allows a Mage to convey what they feel is important. It prevents too much repetition."

She shrugged, taking the last bite of her own, fantastically delicious dinner. She swallowed. "Sure, I suppose." Setting her bowl aside, she turned to face Renix more fully. "Any act of magic requires three things: First, power. Second, a shape. Third, a will. The less of any one of the three you have, the more of the other two are required, and vice versa." She held up a hand. "Spell-lines grant a spell its shape; we, through our gate and keystone, provide the power. The will comes through our understanding of what we are enacting. That is why a Mage cannot use magic they don't comprehend."

Renix was nodding. "Of course, this is basic."

Tala quirked a smile. "Am I giving an overview or not?"

Renix shrugged. "Fair enough."

"Now, the shape is 'used' by the consumption of our inscriptions, the metal slowly being eroded with subsequent uses. The power is obvious—our gates can only open so wide, and the power accumulation rate varies from Mage to Mage—but here is the point of note, where a Mage can truly influence things. If the power is sifted, controlled, and provided to the spell-form exactly as it needs to be used, then the burden on the inscription lightens, and they will last longer."

Trent was nodding, a small smile on his lips, but Renix was frowning. "We have filters on our keystone, right? That is how the type and quantity of power going to each spell-line is governed."

Thank you, Master Himmal, for filling in this gap in my education. "Well, yes, but that is like trusting your knife to perfectly purée an herb. The mortar and pestle will do a better, finer job. And as with herbs, your gate, as governed by your mind, can better modulate the type and quantity of power given to your spell-lines."

"And you do this?"

She shrugged. "Me? Not particularly."

Atrexia scoffed, taking a drink of water. "Of course, you don't."

Tala ignored the other woman. "I have chosen my spell-forms to take advantage of my… peculiarities. And thus, I have no need to feather the power. My spell-lines will use, efficiently, anything I give them."

Renix was frowning.

Tala sighed. "Most of my inscriptions are not… finessed. They simply act. You would not want to throw your full power behind a lightning strike because…?"

Renix started nodding. "Because I could blow a crater the size of a wagon in the ground. If I was too close, I could kill myself. It's imprecise, sloppy, and prone to collateral damage." He glanced to his smiling and nodding master.

Tala smiled, too. "Whereas if I dump too much power into my protection?"

"You are simply better protected."

"Exactly. Now, the final component, the mind, is where every Mage works and refines themselves over their lifetime. The clearer and more accurately you can perceive what your power should do, the better. The more closely you can make your mental construct to the effect that is to come, the less power, and the less inscription material, will be required to achieve the same result." She smiled. "In cases where you are using all the power you can, that simply means that the effect will be greater, instead of the power requirement dropping." She touched her two thumbs and two index fingers together, making a triangle. "Imagine this triangle, fixed at its midpoint; that midpoint is the spell-working, the output. The higher you raise each corner"—she rocked her hand around, tilting the triangle in demonstration—"the lower the other corners can get. You will always need all three corners to make a triangle, but you can alter their elevation."

Renix looked thoughtful. "Yeah, I think I knew that… I just hadn't thought of it that way before."

Trent inclined his head, briefly. "Thank you, Mistress Tala. I think that is sufficient, for now."

Tala actually felt a flicker of disappointment. She'd been starting to enjoy the monologue. Even so, she nodded in return. "As you say, Master Trent. Is there anything that you would correct?"

Trent seemed to think for a moment, then shook his head. "Not specifically. You spoke in generalities, so of course it wasn't perfectly accurate, but you weren't aiming for precision, nor did I request such." Trent nodded to Tala. "Thank you, again."

She smiled in return. "Of course."

Atrexia didn't comment as Tala stood, taking her bowl, cup, and spoon to the washing station. Every other dish either had been, or would be, washed by one of the caravan's servants, but Tala found she didn't mind the quick task.

Hah, I never had to tell my side of the terror bird attack. She decided to see that as an absolute win.

Chapter: 24
There Would Be a Next Time

Before heading back to her wagon, she stopped by the chuckwagon's still-propped-open side to tell Brand how much she'd liked the meal.

They talked briefly, and then Tala thought to ask him if he had an iron flask. He said he thought he might and went to dig in the back.

While she waited, she chatted with one of the other cooks, thanking him, again, for his help with her arm earlier.

Brand returned with a large flask and a few small vials. "This flask held a chili oil, but we've used all we needed. It's been cleaned thoroughly and doesn't smell like it's been flavored. Two-cup capacity." He then held up the vials, which also appeared to be iron. "These three held spices for the meals on the first day. They've also been cleaned."

"Why not use glass…?" She nodded in understanding. "Not worth the risk of breaking." *I thought they could make glass that was fairly resilient.* She supposed that, when considering hundreds of trading missions, the difference in durability between glass and iron would matter.

"Exactly." He hesitated. "Now, I can't just give these to you…"

"Two silver sound fair?"

He blinked at her in surprise. "No. That is much too much!"

"Well, I don't have it on me. You'll have to wait until Alefast."

Still, he shook his head. "I cannot sell caravan supplies at a profit."

"Huh… okay, then. How much?"

"For all four?"

"Yes."

"One silver, to be paid in Alefast."

"Agreed." She took the four vessels and turned… to find Atrexia standing behind her, glowering.

"You promised caution."

"And I'll give caution. I have materials I'd like to work with."

Atrexia's expression did not improve. "I'll be watching you."

Tala shrugged. "Fair enough." She turned and strode towards a sergeant, whom she'd seen in the distance.

She ended up having to crisscross the wagon-circle several times before she was able to catch a sergeant and grab their attention. "Sergeant?"

"Yes, ma'am?"

"Could I borrow a shield or two, to fasten to the top of my wagon?"

He frowned. "Mistress. We need those to—"

She held up a hand, cutting him off. "Just at night. I will return them in the morning."

He hesitated for just a moment before nodding. "I suppose that makes sense. You will be sleeping on the roof of your wagon, yes?"

She nodded.

"Then having a fixed shield to keep you safe as you sleep is wise. I'll send one to you right away."

That handled, Tala thanked the sergeant and headed back to her wagon for a much-needed night's sleep.

* * *

Tala slept deeply and well, her bedroll spread out comfortably, one of the large tower shields clipped into the defensive ring atop the wagon, laying overtop her. The wagon occasionally shifted as either Den moved down in his sleeping area, or a breeze rocked the wagon just a bit.

She did not know what she had been dreaming about, but she came slowly awake to an itch on her left ankle and a vague memory of the wagon shifting.

Groggily, she pulled her leg back in to scratch the itch and found the foot cold. *Guess it was outside the blankets...* She scratched absently.

A soft glow and a pull of power called to her sleepy thoughts, and she looked down in puzzlement. A linear series of spell-work was softly shedding light across her ankle, and as she focused, she realized that power was, indeed, flowing through her.

The magic of the berry she'd eaten earlier was gone, but she didn't know if that was due to time or something else.

Did I scratch that hard? Or were the activation forms that sensitive? *No... if I'd activated it, there would be a whole host of scratches, not one clear line.*

She was almost fully awake now, and she sat up... straight into the shield arching over her.

A loud *thump* accompanied her muffled exclamation. "Ow!" She rubbed at her forehead. "That rusting hurt..." She felt a flash of dimensional magic, and the wagon swayed, as if someone had just jumped onto, or off of, the top. She froze, eyes locking on the space where the dimensional magic had originated.

Her magesight penetrated the heavy wooden shield with ease, only being blocked by the intermittent iron banding... revealing nothing.

Millennial Mage 1 - Mageling

She stood in a rush, pushing the shield out of the way, and swept her gaze around her.

It was late in the night, and the caravan's fires were nothing but banked coals, only visible to her because of her enhanced perception and magesight.

Guards were patrolling regularly, and most everyone else was asleep.

Wind brushed her skin, tugged at her clothes and hair, and coated her with a beautiful, blessed coolness. She felt herself relax, even as she continued to scan. She loved the way the wind felt across her skin and longed to pull off the clothing she was wearing, just to enjoy the breeze more fully. She ignored the urge. *It is neither the time nor the place, Tala.* Even so, she took both comfort and joy in the sweeping caress of the air, tugging at her hair and clothing.

Finally, her magesight found another source of dimensional magic, though it was currently, largely inactive.

An avian head was just visible, eyes glowing in the low light, staring at her from under a large bush, some fifty feet away, down in a small dell. The bush's magic had hidden the creature from her initial sweeps as the bush seemed alive with power, just as most were in the Wilds. Sadly, the magic in the bushes she'd seen was almost entirely focused on the growth of the particular species of bush and a creation of unpleasantness in the digestive system of any who consumed it. Not useless, but hardly useful to Tala.

Tala ignored the useless bush and stared at the creature, knowing, beyond any doubt, that it was the same dimensional terror bird that had attacked her the day before.

She did not let herself shudder in trepidation. She did not break eye contact. Slowly, following some instinct she couldn't place, she lifted her left arm and waved. *This is the arm you broke, you rusting pile of slag. If you are at all intelligent, you will remember—*

There was a dimensional *blink*, and the bird was standing with her on top of the wagon, crouched low.

The wagon rocked subtly under the new weight, and Tala found herself crouching in response to both the motion of the planks underfoot and the suddenly all-too-close threat.

Do I call the guards? What could they do? *I could call for the other Mages...*

The terror bird didn't advance. Instead, it seemed to be studying her.

Tala glanced down at her ankle, a thin line of almost golden light obvious in the gloom. Her eyes lifted back up, briefly examining the bird's talons. She gestured to her ankle. "That was you. Wasn't it?"

The avian cocked its head to the side, then righted it, its feathers rippling in the wind. It let out a very soft, low squawk. Tala heard several of the caravan's oxen shift and make investigative noises following the sound, but no one else seemed to have noticed.

"Is that a 'yes?'"

It didn't answer. *Was it testing if I was puncture-proof while sleeping?* She did shudder, then. *What would it have done if I wasn't?* She imagined it clamping onto her foot and dragging her out into the night, blood gushing from her leg, screams filling her throat and... *Nope. Not thinking about that.*

The arcanous bird's eyes narrowed, likely responding to her shudder.

Don't show fear, Tala. She straightened. "What now? Are we to stare at each other until dawn? Fight to the death?"

Millennial Mage 1 - Mageling

The terror bird shook its head in a motion reminiscent of a dog shaking off water. The motion was accompanied by the soft rustle of feathers but nothing else.

Tala found herself smiling. "You don't like either idea, do you."

The avian *chuffed*, softly. Its eyes flicked around, clearly trying to watch for other threats.

She let herself glance around as well. "Where is your pack?" She suddenly felt an itch between her shoulder blades. *It's distracting me so that another one can kill me from behind.* She fought the urge to spin around and face the new threat. Her reason won out, and she kept her eyes on the terror bird before her. No dimensional magic flashed behind her, and she had a thought. *It wouldn't need others to flank an enemy. It does that quite well alone.*

The bird seemed to have lowered its crouch at her question, and its gaze was now entirely focusing on her once again.

"You're all alone." She felt a flicker of sadness at the thought. She knew what it was to be alone.

No response was forthcoming.

"Here." She bent, sticking her hand into her pack to grab a bit of jerky and pull it out.

At her sudden motion, the terror bird blinked out of existence. Before she had even brought the jerky forth, it was gone.

"Oh…" She sighed, taking a long moment to scan around herself, again. Even looking closely at nearby sources of magic, to see if it had hidden from her magesight there, she couldn't pinpoint the creature. *Doesn't mean it isn't still watching…* She sighed, again, and ate the small bite of jerky she'd grabbed. "What time is it?" She looked up at the sky. She was *not* good at telling time by the stars, but she saw no brightness on any horizon. *Somewhere in the middle of the night then.* Not precisely helpful but worth knowing. *I should sleep…*

She repositioned the shield and was about to slide back under it when a thought crossed her mind.

Shrugging to herself, she took out a larger section of jerky; the piece would be two good bites for her. The section selected, she set it on the roof, some five feet from her. *There.* She wasn't sure what she was hoping to accomplish, but she still felt a bit of sadness when she thought about the lone bird. *Even if it did try to gut me…*

That done, she slipped under the shield, under her blankets, and back towards sleep.

* * *

In the morning, she awoke with vague memories of flickering dimensional magic and a rocking of the wagon, but it could also have been a dream. She checked; the jerky was gone. A small smile tugged at her lips. She'd done at least some good, then. *Not that that is a fitting meal for a three-hundred-pound creature.*

At that thought, she froze. *It rocked the wagon.* Her alteration of the terror bird's interactions with gravity had broken. *I didn't put any conditions on that lock. Only death or some other equivalent physical alteration should have broken my restraining spell.* Unless the beast could counter her magic, directly? That was a terror-inducing thought.

She was suddenly less sure about her pity for the large predator. *I… may be in trouble…*

Tala was waking slowly, the light of pre-dawn tickling at the edges of her awareness. Despite the implications of the avian's release from her magics, she felt rested, refreshed, and relaxed. *The terror bird will not terrorize me.* She did, indeed, feel wonderful.

Millennial Mage 1 - Mageling

She slipped out from under the shield and quickly folded and rolled her bedroll. Most of the camp was still asleep despite the lightening sky, but she could see Brand and the other cooks working in the chuckwagon, through the upper half of one wall, which they propped open when the wagons were stopped. The click of metal on metal and the other low sounds of kitchen work floated to her as well, now that she'd turned her focus in that direction.

Guards still patrolled the outskirts of the caravan. Others sat atop some of the wagons, keeping a lookout. One of those caught her attention as he waved to her. *Ashin?* Had he been assigned night duty? *I didn't think that guards would rotate their assigned shift, but I suppose I never asked.*

She waved back. *Maybe I'll stop by, after my morning work.*

She climbed down as quietly as she could, attempting to let Den continue to sleep.

He slept on.

She stored her gear and went to find the privy. When she returned, she took out the magic detector and iron salve. With a glance around at the mostly silent wagons, she decided not to go to the other side of the wagon.

A minute later, she had swept herself with the inscripted stick and touched up her iron salve protection, erring on the side of over-applying.

When that was done, she returned those items to her box and moved through her stretches. This morning, she decided it was worth doing her exercises, and she moved through them quickly once she was limbered sufficiently. Thanks to the coolness of the morning, she didn't work up much of a sweat but quickly cleaned herself off afterward, nonetheless.

Her personal morning tasks complete, she turned her attention to the cargo-slots, one symbol cheerfully ablaze on each. *You know… those are glowing even to my normal sight. I wonder how much of the total energy is used just to have an easily visible beacon that doesn't require magesight?* She made a note to send a missive back to the Wainwrights' Guild to forgo that, when they made her specialized set of cargo-slots.

Musings aside, she moved down the line with quick efficiency. Her mini-lecture to Renix the night before came back to her, and she focused special attention on her mental construct for the empowering and found that the added attention, likely aided by her own mental enhancements, was continuing to pay dividends. *More efficient, indeed.*

Soon, thirty symbols glowed happily, and she was done. *I'm getting faster every day.* It had only taken her about four and a half minutes this morning, even with the added focus on perfecting her mental construct of the working. Those efforts had also removed most of the power requirement when compared to her first attempts.

She frowned at that. *All I'm doing is filling the spellforms' power reserves. How can I be reducing the amount of power that takes? That'd be like saying it no longer takes a gallon of water to fully fill a gallon jug… Unless…* Was she really spilling so much power, when she'd been trying to fill the forms, earlier? *More crucially, does it really take so little power to maintain a dimensional distortion?* She supposed that her concept of how much power a given working should take was based on how much power she, and those she'd observed, had needed in the past.

Are we really so inefficient, most of the time? It was an interesting thought.

Sighing, she walked over to the chuckwagon. Dawn had still not fully broken, the sun was still not visible, and most people were still in their respective wagons. *Am I efficient, or is everyone else lazy?* Tala resisted the urge to scan the wagons with her magesight as it felt too much like peeping for her taste.

As she approached the open side of the chuckwagon, Brand held out a steaming earthenware mug. "Fresh."

Tala frowned and took the drink. *It couldn't be...* She looked down at the dark brown liquid and caught a whiff of heaven. "This isn't…"

"Coffee? Yeah. I thought you'd like a cup, today. Especially since you skipped yours yesterday."

Tala's head came up, eyes narrowing. "I was due a cup of coffee yesterday?"

Brand shrugged, not catching her tone. "Of course. The caravans are one of the primary consumers of the stuff, outside of the intelligentsia. It's one of the perks of taking the trip: 'All the coffee you can drink.'"

Her eye twitched. *I could have had coffee yesterday...* She took a deep breath and steadied her mind. "Thank you, Brand. Could I have another cup?"

He eyed her still full, untouched mug. "Could you finish that one first?"

Tala looked down, then smiled wryly. "I'm going to take it to one of the guards."

"Oh! Of course." He quickly fetched another mug for her, and she accepted it gratefully.

She carefully navigated her way over to the wagon on which she'd seen Ashin. It was there that she was presented with a dilemma. *I can't climb the ladder, and I can't reach the roof...*

Thankfully, Ashin, who was still on duty, must have noticed her because he leaned over the side. "Mistress?"

She held the coffees up. "Can you take these?"

Looking puzzled, he leaned down and did so, freeing her hands.

Thus liberated, she clambered up the ladder quickly. Once she was atop the wagon, specifically the bunk wagon for the guards, she took one of the mugs back. "Thank you."

He offered her the second mug as well.

"Oh! No, that's for you."

Ashin frowned. "Oh?"

She shrugged. "I thought you'd like it. Are you just starting your shift or just ending it?" She settled down into a cross-legged, seated position.

Ashin looked from her to the coffee and back a couple of times before sighing and returning to stand in the center of the wagon, as he had been. "Just near the end. I'll be relieved when the sun is halfway over the horizon and be able to grab breakfast before climbing into the bunk wagon for the day." He tapped his foot lightly in an unneeded indication of the wagon he meant.

Tala took a long, slow drink of the smooth, dark coffee, and again, she contemplated marrying Brand. *He's already married, Tala, and you could hire a cook.* It was an odd thought, having enough money to hire a cook. She'd never do it, of course. Such a frivolous expenditure would have to await consideration till after her debts were expunged. *I could marry wealthy?* She sighed, ruefully, shaking her head. *No, Tala.* That was a bad idea. Truly terrible. Not worth considering further.

Ashin took a careful sip, and Tala saw his face twitch.

"Do you not drink coffee?" She suddenly felt foolish. *Why am I up here? I'm just bugging him and making him feel obligated...*

He smiled. "Not too much, no. It seemed a waste of money to me, and I didn't think it wise to pick up the habit while out on a job." He hesitated, looking down at the drink. "It isn't bad, and I suppose I am in a caravan more often than I'm not." He turned back towards her slightly and nodded, lifting the cup slightly. "Thank you, Mistress Tala."

She smiled. "You are welcome." She took another long drink from her own mug. *Delicious.* "We're, what, three days from Alefast?"

"Just about, yeah. We should arrive sometime before sunset on the final day. It's about one-hundred-twenty-five miles between Alefast and Bandfast, and we cover about…" He trailed off, seeming a bit embarrassed, then cleared his throat. "Anyways, yes. We should see the third sunset from now from the city walls."

Tala nodded, deciding not to comment on his initial ramble. "And you're heading back to Bandfast soon thereafter?"

He nodded. "I try to do out and back trips as much as possible." After a moment's hesitation, he spoke on, his eyes continuing to scan the surrounding landscape. "Each spring, I contract for a big loop that takes two or three months, but this late in the season, I want to be as sure as I can be to winter in Bandfast."

Tala nodded. "Makes sense. That's your home, right?"

He just nodded.

Tala found herself finishing off the last of her coffee, and she stared mournfully down into her cup. *I suppose Brand will give me more?*

She saw Ashin tense.

"What is it?"

"I keep thinking I see something out there, but whenever I look closer, or turn back to look, it's gone." He frowned. "It might be your friend from yesterday afternoon."

Tala scoffed. "Friend? The thing that tried to gut me?" *Oh, rust and slag, what have I done? Does he know I fed it? Does he know it tried to take off my foot last night? What have I done—*

He quirked a smile. "Yes, Mistress Tala. I'm aware. I meant it as a joke."

"Oh! Yes." She laughed awkwardly. "Of course."

He cocked his eyebrow at her, then shook his head and turned back to scanning their surroundings. "You continue to amaze, Mistress."

She almost asked him to explain but then realized that she didn't really want him to. "Well... I suppose I should get more coffee."

Ashin glanced back to her and raised his own mug in salute. "Thank you for this." After a moment's silence, he smiled. "And for the company."

She smiled and nodded in return before climbing down and heading towards more coffee. *Well, that went well.* She was halfway back to the chuckwagon when she realized that she'd neglected to tell Ashin that she was returning with the next available wagon train, as well. *Well, that's awkward of me...* She sighed. *I suppose it's an item for next time.*

And she was sure there *would* be a next time.

Chapter: 25
A Blood Star

Tala basked in the warm morning sunlight as the wagon rumbled beneath her. The soft breeze was a perfect counterpoint to that warmth, and she found herself deliciously comfortable. Adding to her delight, a large pitcher of coffee rode beside her, her mug already filled.

She'd convinced Brand to give her the extra that had been brewed, but not drunk, before they were underway.

As a final little joy, she'd eaten another endingberry as they set out. *Hopefully, today, I won't use up the energy by being attacked.* She did need to know how long the power from one would stay in her system.

She'd seen Den freshly greasing the axles and joints in the wagon's wheels before they left that morning, and they now trundled along with hardly a squeak or squeal.

They were moving slowly higher as they came closer to the mountains to the southeast. Additionally, the grasslands were interspersed more often with large outcroppings or formations of rock. *Well, Atrexia will be more effective at least.*

She didn't read. She didn't take notes or sketch.

She simply laid back, sipped her coffee, and enjoyed the morning.

The only thing to spoil her good mood was the occasional flicker of dimensional power trailing the caravan near the edge of her perception.

Millennial Mage 1 - Mageling

The terror bird was no real threat to her, and she'd demonstrated that to the creature. *Aside from broken bones...* In that light, it *should* leave her alone. *Then, why is it following, Tala?* She didn't have a good answer.

She would not let it affect her mood.

And it didn't.

Not one bit.

Tala sighed, sitting up straight and glaring back down the line of wagons. Her magesight tickled her perception, and she looked up to see a large bird of prey winging past, up above them.

Such creatures were common, but none had attacked their group since that first day. Apparently, those closer to human cities tended to be a bit more aggressive towards humans, while those farther out tended to avoid more often than attack.

Boring... and, she supposed, impoverishing to Trent and Atrexia. At least, none of the mundane folks were in danger of dying. *Huh, everything's a trade-off, I suppose.*

They'd also seen scattered groups of the thunder cattle over the past few days, and this morning, in particular. Den had informed her that there were often small groups of the beasts up to seventy or eighty miles from the main herd. She'd looked them up in the Order of the Harvest's book. Almost all of the animal could be harvested.

The meat gave good strength-enhancing effects, and bone-broth or bone-meal made from the bovines would rapidly restore broken or cracked bones. *Doesn't store well, though, even in iron containers.* The Order seemed baffled, and quite irritated, at that fact.

Den had also told her that the hides were highly prized, and that the guards always did their utmost to skin the creatures—if they had the opportunity.

How much meat would be on one of those things anyways? She *really* wanted to hunt for one. It wouldn't hurt to have some of the bone powder, either. *Broken bones seem to be my greatest danger, at the moment.* But the stuff was only good for a week or so. *I really hope I don't break anything else that soon.*

She found herself idly playing with one of the iron vials that Brand had sold her. It had an iron screw-on cap, lined with a leather gasket. The threading was on the outside of the vial so that the spices that had been held inside couldn't easily be caught in the thread. *This is fine work.*

The seal seemed intact, and the vessel had a delicate artistry to it. *I wonder what I'll use it for?* She was already planning on putting the remaining seven endingberries in the flask, but what was she to do with the vials? *I'll find a use for them.*

Two of the vials were of this refined make, but the third was much cruder. It had likely held coarser spices and so hadn't needed the same type of fine seal. *Salt crystals, maybe?* Regardless, it was secured by a small, tough cord, which wrapped around a smaller portion of the vial. The rougher vial also had a slightly larger inner diameter, just larger than her thumb, and it was shorter so that her thumb could easily touch the inside of the bottom.

As she was playing with one of the finer vials, she found her mind wandering.

She drank more coffee.

Atrexia doesn't seem to know what to make of me. I feel like she sees me as a child, but also as some sort of monster. Tala sighed, then quirked a smile. *I suppose that Holly and Lyn weren't much different when they saw my fully empowered blood.*

Tala's mind stopped on that thought and refused to move onward. *My blood was unusually powerful...* Her eyes rested on the fine iron vial. *I wonder...* She found herself grinning.

Millennial Mage 1 - Mageling

With precise care, she shifted her mind towards deactivating her protective scripts at one specific point on her left ring finger. As she did so, she threw her gate open wide.

It might have been the coffee in her system, or something else, but she felt the nervous energy much more strongly. As she thought about it, it seemed like a horrifically discordant mountain lion beside the calmly purring power of the endingberry within her.

She waited until she was practically ready to scream from the discordance of it. Her legs were trembling with nervous energy, almost causing the vial to shake free from where she held it between her knees, and the knife was shaking in her right hand.

She exerted her will and pulled all that nervous, raw power into her finger as she compressed it, pricking the place with deactivated magics quickly before compressing it and releasing a drop of blood.

The nervous energy left her in a rush, and the drop of blood seemed almost to vibrate as it fell.

Tala's magesight saw what resembled a falling bonfire as the blood dropped into the vial, and she fought a wave of dizziness in order to cap the vial and trap the power within.

Even through all that, she kept her control and prevented her inscriptions from activating to heal the minor cut.

The vial closed, she sheathed her knife, and took several long, slow breaths.

Coffee helped as well.

The prick to her finger was small enough that it wasn't actively bleeding if she didn't compress it, and she took a long few minutes to recover. Even though she'd tried to draw all the power within her into that one drop of blood, there was still a low level of saturation remaining—the power that hadn't easily been pulled free.

When she was able to turn her full focus inward once more, she happily found the endingberry's power still there, undiminished, undisturbed, and comfortably swirling through her. *Good, I didn't wash away one power with the other.*

The image of her blood, glowing like a beacon before her magesight, was powerful to her memory.

I didn't have a mental construct, just a maximum amount of power. She was ready to try again.

This time, as she built the power up within her, she forced it into a mental construct, just as she did when empowering the cargo-slots. In this case, however, she formed a star of swirling, intertwining power, her blood as the medium for that flow. Its sole purpose was to contain and maintain power. *It's a reservoir, a container for my power, that I can tap later. It is for me and tied to me.*

The image reminded her of some of the rope and knot games her family had played with in her childhood. *Almost like a monkey's fist knot, but not quite.* There would be no trailing ends to this spell-form.

She banished the memory.

She bent almost her entire will to the mental application of power, even as the power itself grew to a greater height than before.

This time, the energy didn't feel frantic. It didn't feel like she was a water skin, full to bursting. It felt like the flowing star she was imagining was blossoming into existence within the tip of her finger.

Following some deep instinct, she removed the cap to the metal vial once more. With the cap gone, her magesight could see the power of her first drop of blood shining forth.

Almost as soon as the cap came off the vial, Tala brought her finger above it and felt a strange tugging disconnect. It was almost like gently, but steadily, pulling a hair out by the root from an infected pore. It was relieving and painful at the same time, and she felt a rippling magical *pop* as the second drop of blood came free without the need for her to compress her finger to bring it forth.

The blood sang to her magesight as it fell into the vial, and she passingly realized that in that one drop of blood, there was more power than she'd put into all ten cargo-slots below her.

In rote motions, she capped the vial and twisted the cap down securely.

She felt exhausted. When she glanced inward, she found that no power, save that of the endingberry, remained within her. *Oh... huh...*

She yawned and poured the last of the coffee into her mug before draining it in one long pull. It didn't really help.

Her wide-open gate was dumping power back into her as fast as she was able, but it was a piddly flow against the tide of her exhaustion.

She stared at the metal vial for a long moment, without really seeing it. She jerked and shuddered, the vial coming back into focus. *Why am I so tired?* She yawned, again.

Tala tucked the vial into her satchel and curled down, using the bag as a pillow.

She was asleep before she realized that she was drifting away.

* * *

Tala started awake as someone climbed up onto the wagon behind her.

Her head was pillowed comfortably on her satchel, and a warm, fluffy something was curled in the crook of her arm, against her chest and stomach. She idly moved her hand across it and marveled at the softness.

Right, someone on the wagon. She pushed herself up and stretched. As she did so, she felt a flicker of magic but didn't register what kind.

She opened her eyes as she twisted around to find Brand setting a plate down for her. "You didn't need to wake, Mistress Tala. The food will be here when you are ready."

Tala smiled tiredly at him. "Thank you, Brand." She tucked her hair behind one ear. "You know, you don't have to bring me my meals, yourself."

He shrugged. "The other cooks…" He smiled. "They may be a bit scared of you." He shrugged, again. "It also lets me stretch my legs." He noticed the empty pitcher and mug and collected them without a word.

"Thank you for the coffee."

He nodded to her. "If I'd known you were so tired, I wouldn't have hesitated to give you the extra." He barked a laugh. "I'd have made you more!"

Her smile perked up a bit. "More?"

Brand sighed. "Would have. Not now, though."

She sagged just slightly, then hesitated. *What was I holding?* She looked around but found nothing. *A dream?*

"Did you lose something?"

"Hmm? No… I don't think so?" She turned back to face him, shaking her head in an attempt to clear it. "Still waking up, I suppose."

"Well, let me know if you need anything." She opened her mouth, but he spoke again before she could. "*Besides* coffee."

It was her turn to chuckle. "Fair enough. I will."

Without another word, he climbed down, leaving her to enjoy her lunch in peace.

As she pulled her plate over to rest in her lap, she noticed a small grey feather, trapped beneath her own leg. It was *far* too small to belong to any animal she'd seen up close, though it did have traces of magic on it—as most things did in the Wilds. *Did it fall from the sky and just happen to catch there?* She still remembered the soft fluffiness she'd been holding upon waking. It hadn't *felt* like a dream…

You're going crazy, Tala. Some random pigeon didn't fly down to cuddle with you, then vanish when you woke up. That would be ridiculous.

Without giving it more thought, she focused on devouring her lunch, finding herself as ravenously in need of food as she'd apparently been for sleep.

* * *

Tala stared down at her third empty plate.

She was still hungry. *What did I do?* She pulled out the iron vial that held her blood. She felt a strange connection to the blood within the vial, which wasn't hampered by the iron in the least. It felt like an old friend was there for her, just inside the vial, waiting to greet her. *That is really odd…*

She still felt a strange form of exhaustion. *I've never done a working that left me so hungry and tired.* Though, her several-hour nap had mostly rectified the tired portion.

If she thought about it, she could see a bit of a correlation in her past between high amounts of magic usage and increased appetite and fatigue.

I'm out of my depth. With a strange hesitation, she opened the vial and looked inside.

To her normal vision, a single, large drop of blood rested in the bottom of the vial. *Not two?* Strangely, she felt like she'd known there would only be one.

That single drop was a darker red than blood normally was, almost like a scab, but it was clearly still liquid. It was as close to a perfect sphere as she'd ever seen, and she couldn't see a single flaw in its shape. The last thing she noticed with her eyes was that it appeared to be spinning, very slowly, but the motion seemed to be just beneath the surface.

To her magesight, it was a spinning, twisting vortex of power.

It looked a bit more powerful than when she'd first created it. *Did it absorb the other drop?* That seemed likely. It did not seem to be leaking power despite the open vial lid.

She groaned. *I need to talk to Trent.*

She slung her satchel across her back and carried the now-closed vial, along with her empty plates, to the ground below.

She dropped the last foot or so from the moving wagon and steadied her hat.

After a quick detour past the chuckwagon to drop off her plates and thank the cooks, Tala walked towards where she'd last seen Trent, riding his horse on the left side of the caravan.

"Mistress Tala! Greetings and good afternoon." He grinned down at her. "I trust that you slept well?" She could see humor dancing in his eyes.

"Greetings, Master Trent. Would you walk with me?"

Something in her tone must have stood out to him because his mirth faded, and he nodded. Trent swung from his saddle with grace and walked to the nearest wagon to tie the reins to a hitch. The mount would now follow the wagon without the need of his minding the animal.

"Thank you."

He nodded. "What seems to be the issue?"

Tala cleared her throat, feeling suddenly self-conscious. After a moment, she lowered her voice to be barely loud enough for him to hear. "I would guess that you've figured this out, but I never had a master."

He nodded but remained silent.

"In fact, I just graduated..." She hesitated, reckoning the days in her mind. "A week and a half?" She shrugged. "I graduated less than two weeks ago."

Trent's eyebrows shot up in clear surprise. "Then, did you deceive the Caravanner's Guild?"

She shook her head. "No, no, but I did manage to maintain most of my inscribing. That, coupled with my dimensional magic experience, was sufficient for them to indenture me as a full Mage." *No need to mention that I tried to deceive them.*

He frowned, clearly contemplating. "I suppose that makes some sense... Hmmm..."

She waved a hand. "But that isn't why I'm here."

"Oh?"

"No... I have a question that I would ask a master, but..."

"You don't have one."

"Yes." She bit her lip, not willing to meet his gaze. "Can I ask you?"

Trent smiled, and she saw his features soften out of the corner of her eyes. "Of course, Mistress Tala. I am honored to be asked."

She felt herself relax. "Thank you, Master Trent. Thank you."

"What seems to be the issue?"

"I... I did a working which left me utterly exhausted. Immediately afterward, I fell asleep and remained so for close to four hours. I'm not sure when I'd have awoken if Brand hadn't brought me lunch. As to lunch, I ate three very large portions and could likely eat more."

He was nodding. "Often magelings, and even some Mages, will experience such physical needs when they push their boundaries."

"So... I haven't hurt myself?"

He chuckled. "No, no. One way of thinking about it is that you were stretching your gate wider, opening yourself more fully to your magic. An increase in power is taxing on your physical self, and you will need time to adjust. It usually only results in true exhaustion, the kind you describe, if you also are low on power within your body, however."

She sighed in relief. "Oh… That is so good to hear." She remembered the difference in her power density after the two drops. *That does seem to line up.*

"So, what did you do? Charge the cargo-slots more quickly? If I read their scripts correctly, and if I have a good measure of your power, it should take you close to a minute to charge each. Did you breach that hurdle? Empowering those scripts at all is a remarkable achievement, but if you've already gotten that charging down to such a quick process…"

She blinked at him for a moment. *What? I'd thought he would have noticed how quickly I charged the scripts… Tala, the whole world doesn't revolve around you, and Mages don't stare in awe every time you do a working.* She shook her head. "No… that's not what happened."

He shrugged, clearly misunderstanding her. "Don't worry about that then, you'll get there."

She opened her mouth to correct him, but then shook her head. That wasn't the point of this conversation. "I did this." She held out the iron vial, still closed.

He took it, giving her a skeptical look. "I'm not your teacher, so a prank would be *highly* inappropriate."

"No! I'd never… Wait, you pranked your teachers?"

He waved her away, opening the vial. "No matter." He looked inside and frowned. "Is that a drop of blood? Why is it not adhering to the sides of…" His eyes widened. "No… it can't be." Tala saw power move through the inscriptions across his face, and his eyes widened further. "Tala. Who taught you how to make an Archon Star?"

"A what?"

He turned to face her, holding up the vial. "Who taught you how to do this?"

"No one? It just felt right, after something my inscriber had me do to test my body's power density."

Trent was frowning. "Did you keep it in this vial to bypass the stabilization requirements?" He was muttering to himself. "That shouldn't have been enough…" He looked to her. "You did this in less than two weeks?"

Tala was frowning. "Wait, back up, please. I don't understand; what is an Archon Star?"

Trent took a deep breath and nodded. "Yes, that would be a good place to start."

Chapter: 26
Please Don't Kill Us

Tala almost smiled as Trent let out a frustrated breath. *So, what is an Archon star, Trent? Teach me your secrets.*

After a moment, he nodded to himself. "Alright, from my understanding: as one step to being elevated from Mage to Archon, a Mage will dedicate themselves to pouring and concentrating power into a small item, usually a gem or something similar. They must maintain the steady influx of power for days, or even weeks, until it reaches a sufficient quantity to manipulate into this self-sustaining vortex. The entire time, they must maintain the flow of power and keep it moving perfectly…" He was frowning. "There is no way you maintained that level of focus when the terror bird attacked, or when you went to the ending tree." His frown was deepening. "And how would you have focused it into a drop of blood unless—" His frown shattered into a look of confused wonder, and he spun on her. "Did you build this *within* your own body?"

"Umm… yes?"

He looked down at it, then back to her. "How long did this take you? How much time did it take to build up the power necessary to cycle it in this manner?"

"Twenty minutes? Probably a lot less, but it felt like a long time."

Trent gaped at her. "It should take enough power to level a city to make an Archon star. There is *no* way you can divulge that amount of magic so quickly." He frowned down into the vial again. "But I've also never heard of a Blood Archon…"

She frowned. "A what?"

Trent sighed. "Your title as an Archon is derived from the material you used to create your first Archon Star. Gems are standard, but vary in difficulty. Diamond is the easiest, and ruby is the most difficult of the gems. A rare few use something other than a gem. As an example, to my knowledge, there are three Glass Archons. I've met one Oak Archon, who used a sphere of polished, black oak as her medium, and she is the most powerful Mage I've ever even heard of. I've *never* heard of someone using a liquid…"

Master Himmal said he was a Glass Archon. *That… that makes sense, now.* "So… would it be harder or easier?"

Trent scoffed. "Is it harder or easier to make a chair out of water when compared to emerald?"

"I've never seen a chair made out of either?"

He sighed. "You can't make one out of water, Mistress Tala. You could make it out of ice, encase the water in something, or manipulate it with magic, but then the chair wouldn't be out of water, it would be out of ice, out of whatever you encased the water in, or out of magic. Sure, the substance would be water, but the chair wouldn't be, not really."

"So…?"

"So, I've no idea." He frowned. "There honestly doesn't look to be enough power here to create a stable Archon Star at all. My magesight should be overwhelmed by the mere presence of such…" He sighed. "But, since I've never made one, myself, I am deeply out of my depth. Can I show this to Mistress Atrexia?"

Tala bristled. "Why her? Has she made one?"

"No, she has not, but she often carries constructs to measure quantities, and specific minutia of constructions, of magic, and if we could get an accurate reading on this…" He looked to her. "You don't even know what this could mean, do you?"

She frowned. "No. That's why I'm asking you."

A small smile quirked at his lips. "If two independent Mages verify an Archon Star, meaning that they can't have been the applicant's master or previous acquaintance, then the Mage who made the star is immediately placed in candidacy for being raised to Archon." Trent tsked. "You don't have the requisite years of experience for serious candidacy, and you'd need an Archon to sponsor you, as neither of us are Archons."

Tala grunted irritably. "Master Himmal said the same thing."

"You met the Glass Archon, Void Key?"

She blinked back at Trent. "You know of him?"

"Most Mages know of all the Archons…" He frowned. "No, that's not true. Most Mages know the Archons raised in their lifetime; it's widely publicized in Mage society. I suppose I could go back and look, to get a full roster…"

She snapped her fingers, bringing his attention back. "Focus, Master Trent. Yes, I know him. He proctored my test when we were determining which cargo wagons to use." She felt her irritation rise and glared at Trent, though her anger was directed elsewhere. "Why doesn't the academy teach us about the Archons? Or any of this?"

He smiled consolingly. "My understanding is that many students used to kill themselves attempting to create Archon Stars before they were ready, so the academy determined it wisest to let a master teach their mageling about such when the master deemed the mageling wise enough not to attempt it." He gave her a meaningful look.

She grunted. "They should still teach us about Archons."

"You learned about the Archons of old, yes?"

"Of course, as part of our history."

"There you go."

"We weren't told what made them Archons, just that they were powerful Mages."

Trent sighed. "I've already explained that to you."

"We weren't even told what the Archon titles meant, Trent. What rusted slag is my education useful for anyways?"

"They were teaching you how to learn."

She gave him a withering look.

He sighed. "Nonetheless, it is what it is. I should show this to Mistress Atrexia and get a measurement from it." He held up the vial, now sealed. "May I keep this for a time?"

Tala grunted. "Fine."

"Thank you." After a moment, he smiled. "You know, the guards are already talking about you. If you aren't careful, you might earn yourself a nickname."

She sighed. "Great. I'll be 'The Ambushed' or 'The One Who Was Stabbed.'"

Trent laughed. "I think I've heard variations on 'Iron Skin' or 'Armored Vengeance.'"

Tala was rendered speechless. *How do I respond to that?*

"The man whose sword you used?" When she didn't respond, he added, "On the blood fern?"

Who picks these names? Nonetheless, she nodded.

"He's already had half a dozen offers from other guards to buy that sword. Each far higher than the last."

She grunted. "And?"

"He's turned them down. Says it's a lucky sword, and he won't part with it."

"Helped me, I suppose."

"Not what he meant."

Tala threw up her hands. "What do you want me to say, Master Trent?"

He shrugged. "You're an odd one, Mistress Tala. People are noticing that." He snorted. "Though, I imagine 'Blood Archon' will wash away any other title." He grinned.

She grunted, again. "Great."

Trent held up the vial, briefly. "I'll talk to Mistress Atrexia and find you shortly, yes?"

"Fine."

With no further discussion, Tala went back to her wagon, and Trent re-mounted his horse, moving off to find Atrexia. As Tala moved away, and Trent did as well, Tala felt like she could still feel the drop of blood pulling at her. She couldn't have said *exactly* where it was, but she had no doubt that she could find it if she had to. *Like a string with one end tied to my finger...* It wasn't a perfect analogy, but it did seem to fit, at least slightly.

Tala sighed and thought she saw Trent have a quick conversation with Renix, likely telling the mageling that he was on his own for a bit, watching the left side of the wagon train.

With a sense of foreboding, Tala pulled herself back up to wait on the roof of her wagon.

* * *

Tala was left to her own devices for less than an hour before Trent rode up beside her wagon and swung onto the ladder from his horse. He paused briefly to tie the reins in place, then climbed up.

"May I join you?"

"You kind of already have."

He smiled. "Fair enough."

"So?"

Trent sat in front of her, just out of arm's reach. He held up the iron vial. "Mistress Atrexia agrees, it's an Archon Star."

Something in the way he said it made her hesitate. "...But?"

"But its power is lower than any we've heard of. It shouldn't be stable."

"Explain?"

Trent was nodding. "Normally, an Archon Star requires a *vast* quantity of power, equal to what an experienced Mage can produce over the course of days, if not weeks. The power fights itself and the medium, and the vast majority of the power is required just to force the remainder into a stable structure." He lifted the vial. "There is no way you expended that much magic in twenty minutes, and this isn't enough power, in any case. It is underpowered by at least a factor of fifty, if not a bit more."

"But this one is stable."

"But it's stable," he agreed. "No idea how or why." He glanced from her to the vial. "Just so you are aware, the amount of power in this is insanely impressive, if your guess on how long it took you to create is accurate. If we're correct in our measurements, you might be able to make a more conventional, if on the weaker end, Archon Star in less than a day. Either your power accumulation rate is insane, or you are somehow being incredibly efficient."

But an Archon is measured by the potency of their star, so...? "So, I'm a powerful Mage but the world's weakest Archon?"

He grinned. "They'll likely want to consider you for raising to Archon, but no? I doubt this will qualify you for the title." He handed her the vial. "You've cut down a tree with a paper sword, but that doesn't make you a master swordsmith."

Tala cocked her head. "If I track with your analogy, making a sword capable of cutting through a tree in one stroke would be a requirement for being a master craftsman?"

"Of course, but no one wants to buy a paper sword."

She blinked at him. "You lost me."

He sighed. "A paper sword that can cut through a tree is incredibly impressive, arguably more impressive than a steel sword that could do the same, but a smithing guild isn't going to certify you as a master swordsmith for accomplishing such a feat."

"Ahh... I think I understand. The Archon Star is supposed to be an achievement of power, not finesse. I broke the test because I didn't know I was taking it."

"An accurate way to look at it. You could do it, though."

"Do what?"

"Make a true Archon Star."

She held up the vial. "Didn't I?"

"I mean one of power, one that would give you a good chance for a positive evaluation."

"I could just add power to this one?"

Trent shook his head. "From my understanding, once an Archon Star is made, any power added isn't stable, so the star, itself, doesn't increase in potency."

But it absorbed my other blood—and the power within it... She decided it wasn't worth arguing. "So..." She looked down at the vial. "What good is this?"

"I've no idea." He snorted a laugh. "Ask an Archon?"

Tala sighed. "I suppose I'll have to." She looked at the vial, again. "But what can I use this for?"

"As I said, I have literally no idea." He looked around before nodding to himself. "I've got to get back to my post, but, Mistress Tala?"

"Hmm?"

"Thank you."

"What for?"

"For coming to me and asking my advice."

She smiled up at him as he stood. "Thank you for your answers."

He nodded, then climbed down the ladder without another word. A moment later, he rode away, maneuvering back to his position on the left side of the column.

Well, that's a lot to think on…

* * *

Tala did not, in fact, contemplate all that she'd learned.

Instead, she went and got more food, eating until she was stuffed full, then returned carrying a plate stacked high with food that didn't need to be warmed to eat.

That done, she examined her left ring finger. The spell-forms had activated as soon as she'd fallen asleep that morning, and the minuscule cut had closed without a trace.

"Den?"

Den's head poked up, looking back to her. "Mistress Tala?"

"Can you note where we are, and tell me how far we've traveled when I ask again?"

He shrugged. "Certainly."

"Thank you!"

Without another word, he smiled and turned back to his work.

Experiment number one! Well, she'd created the first one already, so maybe this was number two? *Doesn't matter. Let's do this.*

Again, she mentally pulled back from the inscriptions in her finger, even as she began dumping power into her system, pouring it into the mental construct of the spinning, twisting, flowing star of power. As with the cargo-slots, repeated use of a mental construct refined and strengthened her mental image of it, increasing efficiency.

As she wasn't working for a specific goal, simply attempting to force as much power as possible into the construct, the process didn't truly speed up, she was just able to put *more* in.

True to Trent's words, her gate did *feel* wider, but it could easily have been her imagination. *Expect a result, and that's what you'll see.*

She dismissed the thoughts and brought the full force of her mind back to the task at hand. *Hehe, at hand.*

She shook her head and focused.

When she felt like she was going to burst, she again pricked her finger over an open iron vial. It was a different iron vial and was currently empty. *If I'm going to sleep, I want them separate so that I don't miss anything.*

"Den."

"Roughly half a mile," he called back without turning around.

"Thank you." *Around fifteen minutes, then.* Very nice, indeed.

The spinning star of power *blipped* out of her finger and into the vial, seeming to draw all of her strength from her into itself. If anything, it felt like it pulled out *more* than before.

In mute exhaustion, she capped the vial and tucked it into her satchel. *Yeah… sleep sounds great.* As her eyes fluttered closed, she found herself grateful that she'd gathered the extra food ahead of time.

*   *   *

Tala woke much later and groggily tore through the food that she'd gathered ahead of time.

She came to near-full consciousness as she ate the last of the sustenance. She passingly noted that her finger was fully healed, once again. *I might have to use a different finger next time?* She didn't want to over-tax the healing inscriptions in that one finger, exclusively.

"Den?"

"Yes, Mistress Tala?" He glanced back at her, once again.

"How long until we stop for the night?"

"Another hour, at most."

She'd slept the day away. *Good use of time, Tala.* Well, it had been useful, at least she hoped so. "Thank you, Den."

"Of course." He turned back.

Trent seemed to notice her sitting up and rode up beside her wagon. "Still tired from this morning?"

She cleared her throat and felt her cheeks heat. "Yes… that's it."

Trent's eyes narrowed. "You made another one, didn't you."

"Well, I needed to test a couple of theories."

"Mistress Tala. You're going to kill yourself—or someone else."

"I'll aim for the former?"

"Please, please don't." He was shaking his head. "Mistress Tala, did you at least learn something interesting?"

She shrugged. "I was about to find out." She pulled open the new vial and opened it. It looked exactly like the first. Tala frowned. *Did I open the wrong vial?* She closed this one up and opened the other. *Virtually identical.* Her frown deepened.

"Is something wrong?" He'd seen her reaction and was clearly concerned.

"They are almost identical."

"That doesn't seem odd, right?"

She shook her head. "One was added in on top of another source of power, which it absorbed."

"Mistress Tala, Archon Stars can't—" She held up a hand to cut him off.

"I'm not going to argue with you, Master Trent." She looked between the two vials. *Maybe, I was able to put more in the second one? And they are just close enough in power I can't easily tell a difference?* That seemed likely. "So... what would normally happen if two Archon Stars were put together?"

Trent sighed. "The gems would rest against each other, and they would be easier to carry in one hand."

Right, Archon Stars are solid... "Huh, maybe the solid medium is why they can't absorb more power?" She carefully took off both caps, then grinned at Trent. "Care to witness something new?"

He seemed to fight within himself for a long moment, then he sighed. "Just a moment. I'll be right up."

True to his word, he got around the wagon and up onto the roof with surprising swiftness, leaving his horse, once again, tied to her wagon's ladder.

"Please don't kill us."

"You know I can't promise that." She grinned mischievously.

"*I* know that, but you seem bent on doing this anyways. I feel like *you* don't know that you aren't actually safe."

She shrugged. "Nothing ventured..."

"Nothing lost."

"That's not how it goes."

"But it could and be no less true."

She shook her head. "No; it would be a lie. If you venture nothing, you lose opportunities." She glanced to Trent. "Activate your magesight, if you wish."

Power wove across the spell-lines on his face, and Tala nodded.

Carefully, she overturned one vial into the other.

The tiny blood-sphere rolled out, almost like a tiny marble, and dropped into the lower vial, leaving no trace behind. There was a startlingly deep *plump*, presumably as the two drops met, and Tala saw a flicker of power jet out the top of the open vial. It was so minuscule she wasn't sure that Trent would have been able to detect it.

She looked down into the vial and saw one sphere of blood, just slightly bigger than the first. Maybe as much as twenty-five percent larger? It also radiated a power deeper than before, like she was looking into a well, and the bottom was farther below the surface of the water than she'd expected. The final thing she noted was that she felt more connected to the drop than before. It was as if two strings, tied to her finger, had been intertwined to make a larger cord.

"Well? What do you see?"

"They combined."

"What?"

"See for yourself." She held out the vial to him, and he took it hesitantly.

He looked in slowly, as if afraid something was going to lance out and hit him in the eye. "Fascinating." He looked back up at her. "My guess would be a near doubling in power." He frowned. "Can you add more power without adding blood?"

Tala briefly chewed on one side of her lip, thinking. "You mean like I do to the cargo-slots? Let's try." She grinned, holding her hand out.

Trent returned the vial to her and leaned forward, watching expectantly.

She stuck her right index finger into the vial, resting it just above the blood, and concentrated. She pictured the mental construct she'd used, opened her gate, and poured power out, just like she had for the cargo-slots the last few days.

Nothing happened. "Huh… Nothing." Well, that wasn't precisely true. Her power poured over the drop of blood, bouncing off the inside of the iron vial and flowing out, around her finger.

"Are you touching it?"

"No. I thought that would be a bad idea?"

"Hmmm… You aren't wrong, but it might be required?"

"Worth a try." She shifted her finger just slightly to touch the blood.

Nothing happened, again. She tried to push power into the star, but it seemed to just wash over it, reflecting off the iron and out, around her finger. The star didn't seem to react in the slightest.

"Well. That was anticlimactic."

"Did your defensive spells activate?"

"Hmm? No, and this is touching bare skin."

Trent sighed. "Well, as interesting as this is—" He hesitated. "And don't mistake me, it is interesting… I have a job to do, and I'm neglecting it." He swung down onto the ladder, pausing to look back to her one more time. "Talk tonight?"

She nodded. "That sounds like a plan. We're nearly to the end of the travel day."

Trent smiled, then disappeared from sight, the soft *clomp* of his horse's hooves on the turf slowly fading as he moved back to his position alongside the caravan.

She sighed, closed the vial, and stuck it back into her bag. *Might be worth adding the creation of one of these to my morning routine...* And render herself insensate with fatigue every morning? *Maybe after breakfast...* She hadn't slept as long the second time, and she'd woken feeling much better rested… *Maybe my body will improve its recovery time?* Or maybe she'd abuse herself into an early grave. *Maybe, I could keep it from drawing all the power out of me?* Might be worth trying…

She sighed. *No more than once every other day—until I can get back to Holly and ask her about it.* She hesitated. She'd have some funds in Alefast, so she could purchase an archive tablet and use that to communicate with Holly earlier.

It was an irregular form of communication as it was equivalent to checking a note into a library, which the recipient would have no knowledge of until they came to check out something else. Then, *if* they spoke to a librarian who knew about the note, it would be given to them.

Thankfully, Tala could give a note to the Caravanners' Guild, and they'd get it to Master Himmal so that he could take her information into account when making her custom cargo-slots. It shouldn't be too much to ask them to deliver a message to Holly as well.

As she was thinking, she was rummaging through her satchel. In one of the inner pockets, she found a book, Trent's book on item creation. *Oh! I completely forgot that I borrowed this.*

She grinned. *I know what I'm doing until dinner.*

Chapter: 27
That's... a Big Bull

An hour later, Tala had a headache.

Den was already tending to the oxen, and the wagons were comfortably circled for the night, but Tala was still trying to wrap her mind around the concepts in the *introduction* of the item creation book.

She threw her hands up. "This is maddening!"

She heard a throat clear and looked over the side of the wagon.

"Renix?"

The mageling looked up at her from beneath dirty blond hair. "Master Trent asked me to come check on you. Will you be joining us for dinner?"

Tala sighed. *He was afraid I'd made another star and was sleeping off the fatigue.* "Tell the old man I'm coming."

Renix frowned. "Mistress Tala, he is still younger than many magelings still beneath their masters. He is a prodigy! I expect he'll be an Archon by thirty—or just after."

Tala sighed again, swinging down onto the ladder, satchel and hat firmly in place. "I meant no disrespect, Renix. I was just meaning to tease."

"Oh…" He looked away, seeming slightly embarrassed.

"I apologize, and I think that it is admirable that you defended your master's good name, and a credit to him that you think so highly of his abilities." She tapped her lips with one finger, contemplating. "Though, I suppose having a high opinion of the man who is training you could be a form of narcissism... Are you vain, Renix?"

Renix started; he seemed to have been staring at her finger. "What? No! I mean... no? Wouldn't a vain person claim to be humble?"

"True, true." She shrugged. "Then, I guess we'll never know."

They stood for a moment, then Tala quirked a smile. "Dinner, right?" She gestured towards the chuckwagon, which was already serving people as quickly as they walked up. "After you."

Renix colored, for some reason, and spun to stride towards the open side of the wagon. Tala followed, her headache already fading.

They were able to walk directly up to get their food, and Brand gave her a concerned look as he handed her a plate that was mounded especially high.

Tala's eyes widened when she saw power flickering through the meat. She leaned forward to whisper her question. "Brand? What is this?"

Renix had already headed towards the table at which the Mages were already sitting. Brand leaned forward and spoke quickly, as others were coming up behind her. "A thunder bull was slain, today, and we were able to harvest some meat before a large pack of blaze wolves drove the harvesters off."

"How much did you get?"

"Only about forty pounds, raw." He sighed. "Just enough for tonight's meal."

"You use three-quarter pounds of meat per person?" *Well, including me, that's fifty-one people, but still...*

He pointed at the ground meat patty on bread. "It reduces by close to a quarter when cooked, and people are hungry on the road." He shrugged. "We might have some extra because no one else has been eating like you." He smiled cheerily.

Tala had to admit that her plate was the only one she could see with two sandwiches. "Fair enough. Thank you, Brand."

He bowed slightly. "You are too kind, Mistress Tala."

Tala's eyes flicked to the woman who had come up behind her. *One of the richer passengers… Traveling with her husband, if I remember correctly.* Tala nodded to Brand in turn and turned to go.

"Mistress Tala, is it?" The woman's voice was soft but carried a tone of authority.

Tala turned to face the woman. "Yes. May I help you?"

The woman wore a simple, elegant travel dress of deep green linen. It was clearly very clean, if not new. The neckline was low, but not indecent, and the toes of soft leather slippers peeked out from under the embroidered hem. Tala kept herself from glancing down at her own outfit, which consisted of clean pants and a shirt with a stab slit stitched shut over her upper left breast. Tala still wore no shoes, but that was by choice.

After a moment's silence, during which the woman seemed to be examining Tala in turn, Tala cleared her throat. "I'm sorry, can I help you? I really am quite hungry." She lifted her plate just slightly to emphasize the point.

The woman's eyes returned to Tala's face. "Yes, of course. Are you the one they're calling the Iron Vengeance, or some such thing?"

Tala felt her cheeks heat and blessed her iron salve for its added camouflage. "I've not heard that one, but it sounds like it might be meant for me…" After a moment, she continued. "So… can I help you?"

The woman sighed, then glanced around and noted that no one else had come up to get food behind her. "I want a thunder bull horn."

Tala took a moment to absorb that. To the side, now behind the woman's back, Brand was nodding and giving Tala an affirmative gesture. "Alright. I'll see what I can do." Brand smiled, and the woman seemed to relax. Even so, Tala found herself frowning. "What fee would you be willing to pay for this harvest?"

"Well…" She swallowed. "Two gold ounces?"

Tala's eyes widened, and she was about to accept enthusiastically, but Brand was shaking his head. Tala changed tact. "Two? Are you sure?"

"Well, I don't need a full horn…"

"And I have to fight a magical creature to get it. It's not like I can just rip off a piece of the beast's horn and run away." She might actually be able to do that, but it was unlikely to succeed long-term.

The as-of-yet-unnamed woman seemed to deflate, just slightly.

"Let's start over. I'm Tala. What is your name?"

"You may call me Janice."

"Janice." Tala nodded. "In order to get you a thunder bull horn, I must slay the beast and have time to harvest from it. As we cannot halt the caravan, that means that I cannot guarantee time to harvest other pieces for which I have use."

Janice sighed. "Fine, fine. That makes sense, I suppose. Five gold ounces?"

Tala didn't let her gaze move to Brand, but she could still see him as he shrugged. *A reasonable price.* "Could work. Do you need both horns?"

Janice shook her head. "No. One will be more than sufficient. Thank you."

Tala nodded. *I wonder what she wants it for.* "I will do what I can. We have an agreement?"

"We have an agreement."

Tala nodded to Janice before turning to walk to her table, cooling food held on the plate before her. *What a strange woman.*

Tala sat down beside Renix, across the table from Atrexia and Trent. "Evening."

Atrexia set a hand-sized, flat river rock on the table. It was covered in what looked to be copper wire, set into delicately carved grooves within the stone. The carving seemed to have been done so perfectly, or so long ago, that there were no longer any tooling marks visible. "Give me the vial."

Tala cocked an eyebrow. "Good evening, Mistress Atrexia. I hope you had a pleasant day." Tala turned to look at Renix. "Why yes, I did, Mistress Tala, thank you for asking. How was your day?" She turned to look back at Atrexia. "Oh, you know how it goes, sleep a little, perform mystically complex magic. All in a day's work."

Renix choked. "What!?"

Atrexia sighed. "Today was awful for many reasons. Thunder bulls are a *pain* to kill, and it took so long to manage it, we couldn't even properly harvest the beast." She made a face. "I *hate* leaving the thing to rot when it is one of *the* most harvestable animals."

Tala was taken aback. She actually felt the same as the other woman. *Maybe, I misjudged her?*

"In addition, I had to devote resources to analyzing a truly *heinous* piece of magic, which is nothing but a child's attempt at true art."

And... good feelings gone.

"Now, give me the newest abomination so we can test it and move on with our lives."

Millennial Mage 1 - Mageling

Tala opened her mouth to argue, but Trent shook his head once, then quirked an eyebrow, tilting his head towards Atrexia, clearly indicating that she should just follow instructions. Tala sighed and pulled out the vial, handing it over.

"There. Happy now?"

"Hardly."

Renix was looking around at each of them in turn. "Ummm… Mageling here… Can someone explain?"

Trent gave Tala a mildly irritated look, then simply said, "One step to being raised to Archon is to create a self-sustaining spell-form, called an Archon Star. Tala has accidentally stumbled upon a way of creating something similar, and we are investigating."

Renix's eyes widened, and he looked to Tala. "That's amazing!"

She grinned. "Got to pass the time somehow, right?"

In that short time, Atrexia had removed the cap from the vial and was now holding the rock over the opening. Power rippled across the copper to Tala's magesight, and a symbol that Tala didn't recognize flashed into view of her normal vision.

Atrexia's face registered shock. "Your guess was right, Master Trent." She looked at Tala, narrowing her eyes. "What did you do?"

"You tell me what you found, and I'll tell you how I did it."

Atrexia commented under her breath, "Child."

Tala did *not* vocalize her response. It would have been unprofessional.

Tala watched as Atrexia returned her attention to the iron vial.

Atrexia sighed, shaking herself free of some of her lingering irritation. She addressed Tala when she spoke.

"This... star is just almost twice as potent as the one I analyzed earlier today."

"Twice?" Tala found herself surprised as well. "Huh, that's strange."

Atrexia waited for a moment... but just a moment. "Well?"

"The first was a combination of two efforts of power, and I would have guessed the first was minuscule when compared to the second. Together, they made up the first star I showed Trent, which he took to you."

Atrexia didn't look like she believed Tala, but she remained silent.

"This afternoon, I made a second star and placed them into the same vial." Tala shrugged. "There was a flicker of power and an odd, resonant sound. When I looked, there was only that." She nodded her head to the vial, still in Atrexia's hand.

Atrexia looked to Trent, who nodded in affirmation. "That's what I saw, as well as my understanding of events." He smiled wryly. "Just as I've already told you."

Atrexia sighed. "Fine, fine. But are you telling me that you've somehow... What? Increased your output or efficiency on your second attempt?"

Tala shrugged. "It seems like you're telling me that."

Atrexia frowned but capped the vial and handed it back. "I'm not sure how I feel about this..." She glanced to Trent, then rolled her eyes. "But... it is a fully stable, manifested spell-form, which *resembles* an Archon Star. I will certify such in Alefast."

Tala nodded. "Thank you, I think? I'm still not really sure what that means."

Atrexia blinked a few times. "What do you mean?"

Trent put his forehead down on his palm, groaning quietly.

Tala realized that Trent had *not* told Atrexia about her own situation and recent graduation. She cleared her throat. "I mean that I've never known anyone who's gone through the process before." She shrugged. "I don't know what to expect."

Atrexia narrowed her eyes as she examined Tala's face for a moment, then sighed, shrugging. "I suppose I don't either. Most Mages that make it there reach Archon in their late fifties, and I've not socialized with the previous generations of Mages overmuch." Speaking to herself, under her breath, she added, "I am *not* okay with this fledgling girl becoming the first Archon I've met before their raising."

Tala grinned at her but took a large bite of her food as soon as Atrexia seemed to notice. *Oh my... This is fantastic.* She needed to see if Brand and his fellow cooks had a recipe book, or something. Everything of their make that she ate was beyond compare. *Or, Tala, you just like food, and you're hungry.* It could be that, she supposed.

Despite starting after the other three, and having more, Tala finished her food first and was sitting comfortably when she felt flickers of dimensional magic. She spun around, searching everywhere, but she couldn't find the source, even though it *felt* close by. As she was looking about, she saw Janice moving back towards her own wagon. *Right!*

"Oh! I forgot to ask: We only have about a day and a half of travel left, correct?"

Trent gave her a searching look. "Yes… why?"

Tala nodded. "Then, I need to kill a thunder bull tomorrow."

Atrexia leaned forward, placing her head in both her hands, and groaned. "Of course, she does…"

*   *   *

Tala slept very well that night, under her re-borrowed shield, atop the cargo wagon.

Before she'd turned in for the night, she'd secured Brand's assurance that if she brought down a thunder bull, with enough time to work, he would jerk as much of the meat for her as possible. She, in turn, promised to help in the harvesting of the bones and other parts.

Dealing with Atrexia had been surprisingly easy. *I suppose I've pushed her to the point that she's given up?* Trent had taken a bit of convincing, but as he'd said before, he couldn't actually stop her.

Thus, when she woke in the cool pre-dawn air and rose to find a single thunder bull staring back at her from the next hill over, she was overjoyed. It looked to be a lone, young bull, likely newly out on its own. It did look a little frazzled, or stressed? *Can cattle look stressed? Maybe harried...*

She shook her head, refocusing. *I cannot be this lucky.* Keeping her eye on the bull, she decided to charge the cargo-slots first, just in case something went terribly wrong.

It was hard to force herself to focus, but she did it, taking a little longer than the day before, due to her distraction and newly wakened state. She'd gotten used to having time to stretch and bring her thoughts under control before charging the cargo-slots, and the alteration of the pattern added to her mind's disgruntlement.

Finally, she had her gear stored, the shield leaning where she'd promised to leave it, and she realized: *I have no way to kill a thunder bull.*

She groaned, scratching the center of her forehead, a frown creasing her features.

I've a knife, but that won't kill it any quicker than a bee sting would me. What do I have?

To her joy and surprise, she could still feel the barest lingering of the endingberry's power, which she'd eaten the morning before. *Nearly twenty-four hours, eh?* That was good. Well, truth be told, she had no idea what that actually meant, but it wasn't bad... she hoped.

She refocused on the bull, peaceably chewing its cud less than a quarter-mile away. *Think, Tala. How can you end the beast?* Her eyes widened, and she found herself grinning. *The ending stick.*

She fished the short stick out, quickly looking it over to ensure that the iron salve containment hadn't been broken. It hadn't.

The power contained within the stick could easily kill a mundane human, and it should do the same to a thunder bull. It also *shouldn't* destroy more than a modest chunk of the magically reinforced creature, but she didn't have the formula to be sure. *I'll have to aim for the head, and if it takes out the horns, I'll find another method to kill the next one.*

In the other extreme, the stick only wounded the beast and it survived, the lingering endingberry power within her and defensive scripts should allow her to retreat from the exchange.

She examined the stick more closely. Now, h*ow do I make this an effective weapon?*

She could break it in half, but then she'd have two shorter sticks, and she'd be faced with the same problem, later. *If there is any magic left later.*

Then, she had a thought.

Grinning to herself, she pulled out the larger, rougher vial and opened it. *It fits!*

Using her knife, she carefully scraped the iron salve off of one end of the stick, and as soon as she saw the ending stick's power, clearly radiating through, she thrust it into the iron vial, using the vial's cord to hook on a nub of the little stick.

There. Contained.

It wasn't perfect, and she'd have to work out a more secure way to store it long-term, but for now? It was a good plan.

Humming happily to herself, she strode out of the camp, angling out to circle slightly to one side of the bull.

One of the guards had to have seen her depart, but no one spoke to her or tried to prevent her departure.

It took her less than five minutes to draw near to the massive animal, and she found herself pausing, little more than fifty feet away.

That's... a big bull.

The beast was easily twice the size of one of the caravan's oxen, and it was eyeing her, a look on its face of... not curiosity. Like a bird eyeing a stick that was resting beside a pile of seeds. *Oddly specific comparison.*

She shook her head, considering. *It can't see any magic about me. If their magesight, or whatever their equivalent is, is more sensitive than most humans, they might even use it to see what is or is not a creature or a threat. They could use that to determine the nature of anything they faced.* She almost laughed. *I might just look like some strange bit of mud that is flowing its way.*

It was now or never, and she wasn't sure how the beast would react if she turned her back on it.

She strode forward, the stick in her right hand, her left clutching the vial atop it, the cord no longer holding it in place.

Forty feet.

The bull bent down to take another mouthful of grass.

Thirty feet.

It looked up, eyeing her.

Twenty feet.

Millennial Mage 1 - Mageling

It shifted, orienting its head her way, its back end swinging around away from her.

Ten feet; it lowered its head and let out a low chuff of questioning inquiry.

Tala lunged forward, ripping the vial free.

Now, the bull could easily see the power radiating from the ending stick, and it released a tremendous bellow of challenge. The beast's head, lowering defensively, was just above her eye level.

Her magesight saw power tearing through the beast, quickly building towards an attack, directed at her.

The ending stick struck home as she thrust it into the top of the bull's skull.

In that instant, quite a few things happened at once.

First, the power in the ending stick exploded into the bull's skull. The ending stick's power was shaped to work as part of a larger tree, so it attempted to draw in more power to throw into the dissolution of the bull. It found none, and the iron salve prevented it from pulling from Tala, herself. In that instant, the stick eviscerated itself, draining itself entirely, even breaking apart the bonds within its cellular structure in a final desperate attempt to strike down its target.

Tala's hand closed on almost empty air, her fist filling with a puff of iron dust.

Yes! It didn't take out the horns.

Second, the bull's own, internal magics *strongly* objected to being dissolved, and waves of reinforcing power swelled to defend the great creature.

The result was both spectacular and horrifying.

The ending stick had spent its power, its very existence, to obliterate a circle of the bull's head roughly two feet wide and four inches deep. Just deep enough to fully expose that portion of the bovine's brain.

The bull's scalp and cranial cap had puffed to dust. The brain beneath was surprisingly large, fairly folded, and very much alive.

Rust... It's still alive. Endure and retreat was the name of the game, now.

It was then that the bull's counterattack manifested, and its species' name—thunder cattle—was proved applicable. As she saw the power flicker forward, Tala closed her eyes.

Lightning struck from the clear sky in a column four feet wide, utterly enveloping Tala in light and power.

Chapter: 28
Messy Work

Even through Tala's closed eyelids, the light from the thunder bull's counterattack was blinding. In that instant, her entire body felt hot, as if she'd been standing naked beneath the sun, slowly rotating to be evenly toasty, for hours.

Eyes closed or not, she could *see* the ten-thousand licks of lightning, which had combined into the column of power. Her magesight could not be closed.

The electricity danced across the iron on her skin, heating it in a blinding instant. The heat threatened to burn her flesh, which activated her defensive enhancements, along with using up the last drops of endingberry, defensive power. Though the iron salve didn't protect against the lightning, it did create an easy path for the power to flow across, thus shunting the lethal levels of power away from her internal organs.

Her palms had no iron salve to protect them from the magic, directly, or to redirect the flow away from her flesh. Consequently, the power that struck there burned through the flesh itself, on the way towards the iron salve on the surrounding tissue.

A horrifically clanging silence fell upon her, and she staggered.

The lightning had passed, and she caught herself on near-molten ground, a circle twenty feet wide blasted clear of grass, the earth beneath scooped out in a ring around her.

Millennial Mage 1 - Mageling

She thought she might have even seen the flicker of some lightning glass within the dirt, but she wasn't sure, given her eyes were *not* working properly. Everything was... wrong to her normal vision.

She felt power moving through the inscriptions across her ears, empowered and resonating, having dampened the booming thunder which otherwise had been enough to shatter her eardrums, at the very least, reducing it down to 'just' loud but not damaging.

The extra layers of defense on her feet, added so that she wouldn't need shoes and wouldn't exhaust her others, kept her flesh from melting on the still-glowing ground. Even so, those inscriptions were guzzling all the power her keystone could send their way, and the smell of cooking meat was a subtle undercurrent below the overwhelming tingle of ozone in the air.

The bull let out a groan of misery, and Tala's magesight saw licks of lightning dancing across the creature's brain. *Not used to using lightning without a skull, eh?*

Tala's eyes only saw dazzling brightness, overlaid with spots, though she could feel healing spell-forms activating to repair what damage had been done to them.

She tried to flex her hands, to reach for her knife, but instead, she let out a bellowing wail of agony.

Her palms were scorched, burned, and charred almost to the bone. *That would have been all of me.*

She could feel power rushing through her in a torrent as her regeneration spell-forms activated, and skin, muscle, and connective tissue began to reknit and return to function. Those inscriptions worked around the already ablaze lines of power, which held what remained in place. The metal in her palms had already had magic flowing through it, and thus, it had not been able to channel the lightning into the rest of her or, again, she'd be dead.

She was alive.

Even so, it *hurt*.

Yelling in rage more than pain this time, Tala kicked the side of the bull's head, or at least the blob of color that her eyes presented before her. The move was done out of frustration and emotion more than a thought that it would do damage. She needed to retreat, after all. *It'll be a good last distraction as I run.*

However, the damage had already been done. Tala had been premature in her assessment. The bull was dead on its feet; its brain fried by its own lightning magics.

Her kick triggered something within it, and the beast collapsed sideways.

As the thunder bull crashed to the ground with a very appropriate rumble, Tala felt further scripts activate across her scalp and was almost overcome by *incredible* itching.

Her hair had been incinerated, and Holly's work was now regrowing it.

A similar, but much more pointed, itching exploded on her palms, and though they were smaller, it was much more intense.

Grimacing against the pain, she brought her palms together and rubbed them furiously, sloughing off the remainder of the dead material, revealing whole, new-grown skin.

She sighed, smiling. *Not bad.* She brushed her hands off on her pants, removing the remaining ash… or she tried.

Her clothing, like her hair, had been obliterated.

She was utterly, stark naked.

The one bright spot was that she'd left her satchel, and most of her equipment, back at the caravan. She'd come with the ending stick and the vial, in just her shirt and a pair of pants.

She'd even forgotten to strap on a knife.

…*I was under-prepared…* But it had served her well. *This time.*

Millennial Mage 1 - Mageling

She'd have to go back to the caravan for new clothes. She looked down at the beast, now cooling against the ground. *How am I going to get one of these horns off?* Maybe she could borrow a saw?

There was no sign of her vial. It might have been flung into the surrounding countryside or buried in the upturned earth. She would likely never know. *Oh, the losses we suffer...* She chuckled at that, and then, the reality of how many ways she'd just come close to death began to crash over her, and she laughed harder.

She let her head fall backward, spread her arms wide in a stretch, and laughed and laughed.

Only the sound of horses' hooves crunching on broken earth brought her back, and she turned to see a group of guards approaching cautiously.

She pointed at the front-most guard. "You. Your cloak, now."

The man nearly jumped out of his saddle when she pointed at him and nearly fell again as he ripped the garment from his shoulders and tossed it to her.

She draped it around herself, holding it closed with one hand, and smiled at the guards, who did not seem sure about approaching her. She glanced over her shoulder at the downed bull. *Maybe it isn't me they're afraid of?*

"It's dead. Harvest away!" She grinned. "If you would be so kind as to free one horn for me, I'd be grateful. Either way, I'll be back."

The guards who'd been riding swung down, and they, along with those who'd been on foot, moved around her, to the great beast, never coming within arm's reach.

Behind them, Brand's two cooks approached tentatively. Tala smiled to them. "Will you have time to harvest the meat?"

They blinked at her, then glanced towards the horizon, where the barest hint of the sun's edge was beginning to show. "I think we can."

She glanced behind them where she saw that each of the two had a small, two-wheeled wagon. Her eyes narrowed as she looked closer. *Are those foldable?* It seemed likely.

"Hey!"

The two cooks jumped.

"My eyes are better." She grinned at the men. "All's well, eh?" Her mage sight still seemed a bit wonky, but it was recovering as well, if more slowly.

They laughed nervously and bowed as they went past her to join the guards already working to gut the great bovine.

I hope they're able to skin it, too; the guards deserve a bit of extra luck. She took a deep breath and let it out along with much of her tension. "I think," she spoke softly to herself, "I think it's time for breakfast." After a moment, her smile grew. "And coffee. Definitely time for coffee."

Without further delay, she strode back towards camp, clothes, and coffee. As the guards began to work in earnest, they'd started to speak to one another in low voices. Nonetheless, Tala caught snatches of it.

"It attacked her, but she just screamed at it, and the attack failed!"

"One kick. *One* kick and it has a hole blown in its head! How could a kick even do this?"

"She punched it first, the kick was just a finishing blow."

"Hah! It was dead on its feet from her punch! The kick was just to topple the thing."

"Speaking of kicks, did you see those legs?"

"Legs? Are you blind, man?! Didn't you see her—"

Tala stopped listening after that.

She could return after breakfast to harvest a bit for herself before the caravan departed. *I need to secure a horn, at the very least.*

Her to-dos settled, in her own mind at least, Tala strode determinedly into camp, keeping the guard's cloak carefully closed.

No one approached her as she went to her box on the side of her wagon and pulled out the clothes that she needed. *I'm going to be harvesting more, anyways.* She pulled on the blood-stained pants and shirt, pants first, working to keep herself covered by the cloak.

That done, she placed the cloak to the side, folding it in preparation to be returned to the guard who'd given it to her. She moved through her stretches, mindful of the eyes of the camp on her, furtive though they were.

No exercises this morning. I've a schedule to keep.

Stretching complete, she went to the chuckwagon and grabbed a large mug of coffee. She didn't move as she downed the whole thing. It had been a little hot but not enough to burn her.

This, she assured herself, *is the start of a wonderful day.*

*　　*　　*

Tala smiled as she sucked down the last drops of her second mug of coffee. "Ah! Thank you, Brand." She held out the mug, and he dutifully refilled it.

"Are you alright? I couldn't really see what happened from here, but a guard came to inform us that a thunder bull was available for harvest." He tilted his head inquisitively. "Got the horn already?"

She smiled back. "Assuming the guards get it for me." She shrugged. "I'll go back myself in a bit, to see what I can grab. Honestly, they're probably too busy to do that work for me."

"You look healthier today."

She paused at that. "What do you mean?"

"You…" He smiled, thinking. "You've got more color to you. Even your hair seems a lighter shade. Maybe, all the time outside is doing you good?"

She didn't really know what to say to that. "Umm… Thank you? I suppose."

He nodded to her and handed her a plate with three mini, egg-and-sausage pies.

She took the plate and lifted it in a gesture of salute. "Thank you for this."

Plate in one hand, coffee in the other, she strode to a table and plopped down, beginning to devour her breakfast immediately.

Trent wandered over; his own breakfast ostensibly finished. "So… that was a bit insane."

She grinned up at him, around her food. "Worked though, didn't it?"

He sighed and sat down across from her. "Just because a gamble pays off, it doesn't mean it was a wise gamble."

She gestured towards him with the remains of her last pie. "Wise words."

He looked at her curiously. "Something seems different about you…"

She shrugged. "Brand says I look healthier." She washed her mouth clear with coffee and grinned. "Maybe danger suits me?"

Trent frowned. "May I look?"

She instantly understood that he meant with his magesight. "By all means." She saw power weave across his face and then felt a tingle from her keystone. Someone was observing her with magic. She froze. *I shouldn't be able to feel that.*

Trent's eyes widened. "By all that shines. Mistress Tala, how many spell-forms do you have active?"

She looked down at her own hands and finally registered what had seemed odd.

Her iron salve had been burned, or blasted, away.

Oh, slag. "Ummm… a few?"

"A few? Tala, it looks like you have complete inscriptions individualized for each small patch of skin, and they are *all* active." He frowned, seeming to be trying to look deeper. "Do you have multiple layers of inscriptions?"

And, I need to leave. "That's a good question for another time." She stood, turning to take her plate and mug back to the chuckwagon, and came face to face with Atrexia.

"You."

"Me?"

"You! You—" She stopped, looking around at the other people present, who were conspicuously *not* looking at the yelling Mage. Atrexia took a deep breath and spoke levelly, through gritted teeth. "You were quite phenomenal, dispatching that thunder bull. Well done." Under her breath, the Mage added, "You are a fool of the highest order, *child*. I cannot *believe* that you assaulted a thunder bull on your own."

Tala grinned, understanding the position that Atrexia was in. She responded in a normal tone, not attempting to prevent others from overhearing. "Thank you, Mistress Atrexia. I am gratified that my strategy was successful." Tala gave a slight nod and stepped around the other woman.

Atrexia spoke under her breath, again. "This isn't over, *Mistress* Tala. I will not allow your folly to cost me this caravan."

Tala ignored her. As she walked away, though, she heard Trent whisper, too quiet for her to hear at this distance, but whatever he said caused Atrexia to spin, and a pulse of magic washed across what Tala presumed was her face. Without turning around, it was hard to tell.

Hey! I can sense behind me now, with some precision. She'd only had vague feelings before. Was the change a side effect of the loss of the iron salve or something else? She'd have to investigate further. Tala's keystone tingled again, letting her know that she was being observed with magic.

Atrexia let out a low, startled gasp, barely loud enough for Tala to hear, though it seemed unintentionally so.

She sensed the source of magic which was Atrexia's magesight sink lower, and the bench creaked just slightly.

I really need to salve up...

She quickly dealt with her dishes and returned to her wagon to fetch a bar of iron salve. With that in hand, she went outside the circle of wagons and quickly did her best to cover herself once again.

It was an imperfect job, but she could improve it later. After all, there was the harvest in progress, and time was wasting.

Tala, newly clothed and fully geared up, strode back across the rolling grass as camp began to be taken down behind her. If schedules held, she didn't have much time, maybe only half an hour. She'd asked Den, and he'd said their path would take them past the carcass, though she wasn't sure if that was because that was the best path or because Den was being kind.

She arrived to find the cook's pull-carts piled with carefully packaged meat. Apparently, one of the carts had held a folding table and a set of butcher's knives, because the two of them were working at a furious pace atop just such a table, processing the massive animal.

On the carcass itself, the guards were working together to try to roll the massive animal, now much lighter without the guts and large sections of its muscle. They were not having success.

Tala bit her lip, considering for just a moment before calling out to the men, "Step back!"

They obeyed instantly, jumping away from the body and allowing it to settle back to the ground.

Tala held out her hand, palm towards the beast. Her first two fingers were extended towards the sky, the second two bent down. All four fingers and thumb were tucked close together. To her sight, the body lit up with a blue light. She had been careful to target the body as a whole, not imagining the individual pieces. In this way, it could continue to be carved up and manipulated, but as each piece was taken away, that piece would fall outside the purview of her working. She *thought* it would hold until roughly half the beast had been harvested.

Restrain.

A golden circle blazed on the back of her hand, near the knife edge of her palm. *Seven castings used.*

Power flowed at her direction, flicking through the needed calculations. It was a blessing that gravity didn't care about the mass of a target; all things were equal before it.

Kinetic energy was redirected to lift it off of the ground.

As such, when her power created an exception, precisely altering the gravitational constant for this corpse, in particular, it hovered in place, now in a stable orbit just over a foot above the ground.

"Don't get under it. It should stay stable until roughly half of what's left is removed, but don't trust your life to that."

The men were gaping, but at her words they all uttered their understanding, quickly diving back in to work.

The corpse spun easily for them, though it still took quite a bit of effort to both overcome the inertia at the start and to stop it moving once they got it going. Even so, the alteration allowed them to strip the other half of the hide in mere moments.

I should have done this before I left...

She couldn't go back, now. *Time's wasting.* She pulled out a handsaw that Den had lent her and walked up to the head of the great beast. The guards had not gotten to the horns, yet.

Off to the side, two guards were stripping the now freed hide of the remaining strips of fat and flesh, which had clung to the inside. Several others were helping carry large slabs of meat to the cooks, who were eyeing the sky, clearly trying to decide whether it was time to start carting the meat they had back.

It seemed that they decided on a compromise, continuing to work while sending back the two carts, each maneuvered by two guards.

The final four guards were cutting away connections between bones to free those for salvage. Now that Tala was looking, she saw the gut pile a little down-slope of the great corpse, and as she saw that, she also saw something else.

The terror bird was ripping away at the great bull's heart, its eyes firmly locked on her as it ate.

The guards had noticed the animal and were keeping a wary eye, but there seemed to be an uneasy truce of sorts. The bird was content and clearly realized that there would be leftovers once the humans left. It had not needed to fight.

Still, it made Tala nervous.

Nope, I've got a job to do. She placed her saw against the great horn and began working. The bull was no longer free-spinning, and enough of the guards had grips on the animal that it didn't shift greatly as she sawed away. It was tedious work, not because it was hard but because the horn was massive, nearly a foot thick at the base, and she was cutting it as close to the skull as possible. The horns went straight out for a short span, then curved dramatically inward to point forward. *All the better to gore you with, dear Tala.*

She did *not* shudder at the idea of even more ways that she could have died. It was, after all, time to saw.

An interesting side-effect of her spell was that the horn never broke free. Up until the final stroke of the saw separated the horn from the skull, it remained perfectly in place despite large amounts of blood welling out around the cut. *You know? I never thought about it, but I bet the horns are more like fingernails than bone...* True to that thought, the centers did seem to be more tissue than hard material, though she was cutting close enough to the skull that a large part of what she cut through was the bone nub to which the horn was attached.

It was... messy work.

When the connection was finally broken between the horn and head, the horn dropped to the ground.

The horn probably weighed almost forty pounds, which actually surprised her. *I thought it would be heavier.* After a moment's thought, she realized that even having eighty pounds of horn on an animal's head would already be a strain, and, after all, the magics running through the piece were potent forms that hinted at bone stability, strength, and regrowth. *Also... bone destruction? Are these used to crush their enemies?*

I wonder what Janice wanted this for, anyways... As she contemplated, she began sawing off the other horn. *If one is valuable, then two are.* She had been mildly surprised that the thunder cattle didn't have lightning magics in their horns, but apparently, such powers were housed in the brain. *Somehow.* Interesting that the brain had still been vulnerable to those magics...

She didn't touch that.

Instead, once both horns were free, she coated one with her iron salve, and then she set them both aside. She didn't coat the one she'd gotten for Janice because she had no idea what purpose the woman needed the item for, and she was loath to do something that might make her reckless venture end as a failure.

Horns claimed, she turned her magesight back to the body as a whole, focusing on the points of greatest power, regardless of the type.

It wasn't surprising to her that, as she saw the final scraps of the beast's massive heart vanish down the terror bird's gullet, she noted that that had been the greatest point of power, aside from the brain. *Nope, not touching that.* For some reason, the idea of harvesting an animal's brain did not sit well with her. She clearly wasn't alone as no guard touched it, either.

The guards had returned with the empty pull-carts and were now helping the cooks load the rest of the butchered meat, along with as many of the remaining slabs as they could fit. Even so, they were going to leave a city banquet's volume of meat behind.

I suppose it's hard to butcher a literal ton of meat in close to an hour. Still, if she was right, they'd gotten as much meat as might be gathered from two or three mundane cattle.

I am going to have so, so much jerky. She grinned. *Worth it in every way.*

Back at the wagon circle, the oxen were being hitched up, and everyone not on duty was climbing back into their own wagons.

The guards working to harvest the great bull were clearly from the other shifts, as a full complement was moving through their assigned tasks around the wagons.

In the end, Tala's clothes had yet more blood drying on them, and she had secured for herself two horns.

Millennial Mage 1 - Mageling

Frustratingly, most other pieces which the Order of the Harvest's book had indicated had already been claimed by the cooks, but she couldn't really blame them for that. After all, she was stepping into their sphere. Thus, she'd mainly worked to help the other harvesters' efforts.

She gathered up her haul and trudged back towards the caravan. Den, driving the lead wagon, met her halfway.

He hooked his reins on a mount beside his seat and jumped down to help her with her burdens, even as the oxen continued apace. Together, they got her satchel, tools, and everything into her box, save the two horns—one because it wouldn't fit, and the other because she intended to visit Janice right away.

They were able to get the salved horn up onto the wagon's roof, and Den didn't even give her an exasperated look. Instead, he smiled and asked if there were any further ways in which he could help.

Bless the man. She said no, and he bowed and jogged to hop and pull himself back into the driver's seat.

Similar events were playing out up and down the caravan as guards helped unload the cook's harvests, along with their own, storing everything appropriately.

Tala hefted the weighty, naked horn and smiled, placing the inside of the curve across her shoulders.

"Time to collect."

Chapter: 29
You're a Mage, Figure It Out

Tala was walking behind one of the passenger wagons for wealthier patrons as she knocked.

There was a short pause before the wagon's servant opened the door.

"Yes? May I—*Gah!*" The poor man stumbled backward, clearly having not expected a blood-spattered Mage at his door.

Tala smiled, apologetically. "My apologies, good sir. I have something for…" She hesitated for just a moment. *What if the woman hadn't actually given her right name?* It didn't matter, really. Tala raised her voice and continued, "For Janice."

There was a soft squeak from inside, and Janice appeared, pausing for a moment to help steady the servant, who was recovering quite admirably.

Janice glanced at Tala before bowing. "Mistress Tala. Would you like to come in?"

Tala looked down at herself, even as she continued to walk, keeping pace just behind the wagon. "I don't think that would be kind to this good fellow." She gestured at the still-wet, red splatters across herself. "Blood is *not* easy to clean."

"Oh! Oh, of course. That was silly of me." Janice's eyes fell on the horn resting across Tala's shoulders, and her eyes widened. "It's true, then? That's a…"

"A thunder bull's horn, yes." Thankfully, most, if not all, of the blood had drained out of the horn since she'd cut it free.

Janice sank down against the door until she sat, still looking down at Tala. "I heard the thunder this morning, and everyone was talking about you bringing down a bull. I even thought I saw you working to harvest it, but still…" She smiled. "I didn't believe."

Tala smiled in return. "May I ask…?"

Janice nodded. "My husband… He was an explorer of the Wilds."

Tala's eyes widened, but she didn't interject.

"Some years ago, he wandered… somewhere he shouldn't have, and was changed." Janice shook her head. "No, that isn't right. Wild magics were worked upon him." She sighed. "We sought treatment, but no one could reverse it. Still, it didn't seem too severe. A little weakness, his bones seemed to break more easily, but not much." She scoffed. "It got worse. Finally, they were able to diagnose him with brittle bone syndrome. Somehow, magic had given him the disease as if from birth, and his body was working to catch up."

Tala was frowning in concern. "I think I understand. Some magics can strike humans with strange, inexplicable diseases, but what do you need the horn for?"

Janice brightened, clearly drawn from unpleasant musings. "We were able to purchase a construct, one that transferred power directly into him. If we hadn't, he'd likely have died months ago. Arcanous harvests that can power it are plentiful, but not potent enough to overcome the hostile magic completely. We only just recently learned that a thunder bull's horn should have sufficient power, of the right types, to empower the construct for complete healing." She smiled. "There were none for sale in

Bandfast, so we undertook this journey either to find one on the way or to acquire one in Alefast."

"Then why not just tell me?" *Why not use a bone? ...Because bones reinforce what's there? The horn is meant to alter the strength of bone if that were reversed...* She understood... *I think.*

Janice shrugged. "I approached one of the other Mages, but she said she could not kill a thunder bull unless provoked to it. Apparently, the small herds are *incredibly* vengeful." She sighed. "Even so, I was hopeful when I saw the thunder cattle on the first day, but nothing came of it. Then, one was killed the second day, but virtually nothing could be harvested from it." She grinned, once more. "Then you." Her eyes widened. "Oh! Your payment!"

Janice stood in a rush and vanished inside. She returned with a small, iron chest. "Four-and-a-half ounces gold, and fifty ounces silver—as agreed."

Tala was frowning to herself. After a long moment, she sighed, hefting the horn off and holding it out to the woman. "Here."

Janice set the iron box down, just outside the door, and took the horn from Tala. After a moment's pause, when Tala didn't take the money, she hesitated, starting to look nervous. "I... I can get more, if that is what you need, Mistress."

Tala started. "What? No! No. I... I just don't feel right taking—"

"Taking what you are owed?" Janice's hesitation had vanished, and she almost looked amused. "Mistress Tala. We've enough—more than enough. My husband's line of work was dangerous, and his earnings more than accounted for that. You've given us what we needed to restore him, and we are nothing but grateful. Please"—she tapped the box with her toe—"take the money."

Millennial Mage 1 - Mageling

Tala nodded, hefting the box. *This feels like close to seven or eight pounds! At least half the weight must be the box.* She flipped open the lid and saw five golden coins, four one-ounce and one half-ounce, resting atop a pile of silver.

"You are welcome to count it if—"

Tala shook her head, flipping the lid shut. "Everything looks in order." After a moment, she added, "If the single horn is insufficient, let me know. I harvested both."

Janice's smile widened further. "That is very kind of you. Thank you. I will send Mayhew if we need it." She bowed, turned, and retreated inside.

The servant, presumably Mayhew, studied her for a long moment before bowing as well. "Thank you, Mistress. Can I assist you further?"

Tala smiled slightly but shook her head. "No, thank you. Please do tell me if they need further assistance."

Mayhew bowed once more. "I will. Good day, Mistress."

"Good day."

He shut the door, and Tala trudged out to the side and back up the line of moving wagons, iron strong-box in hand.

She was sorely tempted to use her magesight to watch the goings on within the wagon but felt, more than ever, that that would be an invasion of privacy.

Still, when she heard a burst of startled, joyous, feminine laughter, followed by another laugh, this one from a much deeper, clearly masculine voice, she found herself grinning from ear to ear.

She had done good, this day. The iron chest felt light in her hands, and if anything, her smile widened. *I did good, and I was paid to do it.* She could get used to this. Things were definitely, irrevocably, looking up.

* * *

After placing her new iron box into the storage that Den had lent her on the lead wagon, Tala went back down the line to the chuckwagon. As she strolled up, the last of the small carts were being lifted into place against the outside wall, folded once more.

Brand was locking it in place, walking beside the continually moving wagon train, when he saw her. He smiled widely. "Mistress Tala! My friend. You delivered beyond all expectations. If it were not entirely inappropriate, I would kiss you."

"Yes. Inappropriate."

His smile hitched just slightly, but he recovered. "We got nearly a thousand pounds. A thousand pounds, Mistress Tala!" He laughed happily, raising his hands towards the heavens. "And we didn't even harvest the whole beast! We got most, true, but not all." He was still smiling. "I've never even heard of a caravan killing a thunder bull with enough time to do such a thorough harvest." He hesitated. "No, that's not true. I've heard of one or two who had to down a wayward beast in the dead of night, but in each case, they had to fend off scavengers or other predators through the dark hours as they worked. In the end, I doubt they got more than we did." He was nodding happily.

"You are most welcome?" She was a bit taken aback by his outpouring of words. *We didn't see any scavengers save the terror bird...* Had the avian been responsible for that?

"Ahh, your price, yes!"

She frowned. "I'm not always just after my price..."

He waved her away. "You did good work, and you deserve a reward. Yes?"

She thought a moment, then shrugged with a smile. "Yeah, I suppose so."

"Good, good. We are cutting strips for your jerky as we speak, see?" He pushed open the back door, and she could see one of the cooks doing just that, cutting strips of the red, bloody meat, and tossing them into a large cast-iron kettle. The lid to such rested off to one side. "We will marinate it overnight and should be able to complete the jerking process before we arrive at Alefast tomorrow afternoon."

"How much do you anticipate?"

"Weight, after the jerking is complete?" He pondered for a moment. "A hundred pounds?"

"What!"

He held up a hand. "I know we got close to a thousand, Tala, but we just don't have the resources to process that much. We'll be feeding the caravan with the other meat. Besides, jerky reduces quite a bit! To get you a hundred pounds, we'll be starting with almost half the meat we harvested, right around four hundred pounds. I will definitely be correcting the capacity issue on future trips, just in case."

Tala held up a hand. "No, you misunderstand. That seems like quite a substantial amount. I did not intend to complain..." She cleared her throat. "Honestly, I'm not actually sure I'll be able to carry all that." She thought about it further and realized that she had *many* things she really had no means of carrying. "I... I think I don't actually have a good place to store most of what I own while in Alefast."

"Oh!" Brand was nodding, excitedly. "Of course, of course. You are a young Mage, likely recently freed from her master and out on her own. What you need is a form of dimensional storage."

Tala did not expound upon the irony of *him* telling *her*, a Mage who'd been hired to facilitate dimensional storage, that that was what she needed... not the least because he was right.

"The vendor we sell excess harvests to, and the harvests we gather specifically for them? I'll introduce you. You can likely get a discounted rate."

"How much does such a thing even cost?" She was loath to admit it, but she'd known they were outside her budget, so she'd not even asked after them in Bandfast.

"For the most basic, inscripted item? Something with the storage of a small closet? I'd say the item itself would be around five ounces of gold."

Tala blinked. *That has to be wrong.* "There is no way they are that cheap." She still probably couldn't afford it, but...

Brand shrugged. "The main expense comes from ongoing impressing and the power sources. Dimensional creatures are a *rusting* pain to kill." He paled, glancing her way. "I'm sorry, Mistress. I wasn't watching my language."

Tala waved him off. "No matter." She thought. "So... the largest expense is the means to power it?"

He nodded. "And it costs almost as much as the item itself to have the inscriptions renewed. They usually have to have that done every three to six months." He shrugged. "I've never really understood why it varies."

"Quality of the power source, the mind behind that power, and the quality of the inscriptions themselves," she rattled off without much thought. Her eyes narrowed. "Will this vendor of yours carry quality goods?"

Brand seemed to be processing what she'd said but answered quickly nonetheless. "Of course! And she'll give you the best deal in the city after I introduce the two of you."

Tala nodded. "Then, I'd be grateful. Thank you."

Millennial Mage 1 - Mageling

"My pleasure." He glanced over his shoulder, to the other cooks who were clearly working dedicatedly within the wagon. "I should go."

"By all means. Thank you."

"You are most welcome." He bowed and closed the wagon door behind himself.

Brand had given her a lot to think about and a lot to look forward to. With that in mind, Tala began her daily walk, up and down the lumbering caravan, taking notes, making sketches, and thinking, always thinking.

*   *   *

An hour later, Tala was feverishly digging through the book on item creation, striving, in vain, to understand the theory behind using inscriptions on inanimate objects.

It should have been easy. After all, she understood her own inscriptions, so how hard could it be to place those same workings into an item?

The answer: very.

Apparently, spell-forms had to be altered depending on the medium in which they were set. Meaning, an item would have quite different lines if made out of differing materials: Wood differed from stone, which differed from glass, which differed from human skin. Human skin was also different from any other tissue or bone material, and those all differed from each other. That didn't even cover the variation within each of those broad categories of material. It made even the concepts behind inscriptions almost inscrutable. Apparently, inscribing animals was an art unto itself, and only a handful of humans had ever attempted it.

There'd been some mad emperor of ages past who'd wanted an army of magically enhanced war dogs, but that had gone… poorly.

Aside from a passing reference to the historic failure, magic in animals wasn't addressed in this book. *It would explain why I can't specifically understand exactly what an arcanous creature is capable of, unlike with most Mages.*

Within the pages, there also seemed to be indications that living, versus dead, also mattered. Meaning that she couldn't carve spell-forms for wood constructs into an arcanous tree and expect them to function properly.

Interestingly enough, it seemed that the spell-forms for items were, in general, less complicated than those for inscriptions. The brief explanation given was that human Mages required far more catch points, caveats, and safety to function properly, as the magics generated were directly linked to a living mind. Unfortunately, the book also explained that items that would be magic-bound, whatever that meant, had the same stringent requirements as skin inscriptions.

Unbound items simply followed prescribed, preset functions—nice and simple.

That provided hope but not answers. She was halfway through the book, and she'd yet to come across a single example that she could draw upon to begin expanding her practical knowledge.

There were two final flies in the ointment. First, the spell-lines for gold, silver, and copper each differed from each other as well, regardless of medium, adding another variable to the monstrous equation. Lastly, spell-forms were three-dimensionally sensitive, meaning a spell-form that functioned perfectly on a flat cloth would change radically when shifted, scrunched, rolled up, or otherwise not perfectly flat. That could be compensated for, as all human inscriptions had to, but it was yet more complexity.

Still, she persevered. *I am nothing if not stubborn.* She had determined to learn what she could about items, and slag anyone or anything that got in her way.

"Mistress Tala?"

Her head snapped up, and she *almost* glared as she took in someone poking their tousled, dirty-blond head over the side of her wagon's roof. "What?" She didn't snap at Renix, but it was a near thing.

He was clearly nervous, but he smiled, seemingly more to reassure himself than as a gesture towards her. "Are you busy?"

Yes, obviously. What kind of asinine question is that? "Somewhat." She sighed. "What can I do for you, Renix?" *Why am I so grumpy?*

"Well, I—" Renix started.

"Coffee!" She practically shouted it, completely overriding Renix. "I haven't had nearly enough coffee today." She quickly closed her books, tucking them away in her satchel as he tried to recover from her outburst. She finished before he did. "Walk with me and ask your question."

Without waiting for him to get off the ladder, she swung over the side and dangled down beside the wagon.

The wheels were rumbling to either side, and she realized that this might not be the wisest course. *Ah, well. What's done, and all that.* She kicked off the side of the wagon and dropped, landing outside the path of the wheels with a carefully exhaled breath, knees bending perfectly to absorb the impact on the soft turf.

Renix scrambled down the ladder to join her.

Where's his horse? She shrugged. *Doesn't matter.* Tala turned towards the chuckwagon, and Renix fell into step beside her. "So…?"

He cleared his throat. "Well…"

He seemed hesitant, but she didn't mind. Coffee was ahead.

They were almost to the chuckwagon when Renix coughed and rapidly mumbled out his question, "How did you become a Mage so fast? What's the secret? I feel like I'm going to be trapped as a mageling forever. I mean, I *could* advance any time, but I just don't feel ready. You know? Well… I guess you don't know. After all, you advanced and—"

Tala was so startled that she stopped walking, Renix stopping beside her. Thankfully, coffee was still drawing closer as the wagons continued to move past them. Tala stopped Renix's monologue with a raised hand. "Is Master Trent a good master?"

"What? Of course! Why would you ask that?"

She shrugged. "If you are learning from a good man, why would you want to leave? I can understand your wanting to stay. I can understand your feeling as though you have more to learn. Do you have any complaints?"

"Well, no, but he chooses our missions."

"Would you choose differently?"

"…No, but that's because he explains his reasoning each time, and of course, I agree."

"So…?"

Renix turned away. "I don't know… I… I hate being poor. I hate feeling like I'm owned by so many people, and I can't get ahead, but at the same time, I don't feel up to being out on my own just yet."

Tala blinked. *That's… that's close to home.* She cleared her throat. "Well, I'm indentured to the Caravan Guild. They own large chunks of my time until my contract is up."

Renix scoffed. "But you chose that, and you have so much freedom within that servitude."

Tala was shaking her head. "We are always beholden to others. Some by choice, like those we sell our service to, some by blood…" She hesitated, then shook her head and pressed on. "Some for labor, some for time, but in all cases, it is we who are responsible to fulfill those obligations. Even were you free and wealthy, you would be beholden to yourself. You'd have to eat, sleep, and exercise. If you wanted to work magic, you'd need to keep on good terms with an inscriber." She shook her head, again. "Renix, *life* is about needing other people and being beholden to them, and they to you."

Renix barked a laugh and turned back towards her. "That's easy for you to say. You are on a path to wealth, and I *know* you're younger than me."

Tala could see a bit of pain in Renix's eyes. *He's comparing himself to me and seeing failure.* "Renix, I…" She grunted out a sigh in frustration. "I am, and always have been, very odd. It has given me advantages, but I've hated most of it. I never wanted to be a Mage, but I was sold into this profession. Until my price is paid, I am owned, just like you."

Renix paled and glanced away.

Tala quirked a smile. "Ahh, you weren't sold into it. Let me guess, parents paid for your schooling?"

Renix didn't meet her eyes but nodded.

"No shame in that. Stars know I'd prefer that." She let out a long breath. "I was sold to pay my family's debts, Renix. I owe more than I'll make in *years*, at contract rates, and that's if I had no expenses." She touched his arm, and he turned to face her. "Life is about working with what you have, where you have it."

He was frowning. "Even so. You are so much further down the road than I… How can I catch up?"

The question was so genuine, that she paused to actually consider it before she answered. "One moment." She strode after the now-passed chuckwagon and knocked on the rear door.

Brand shoved it open. "What!" His expression shifted from anger to confusion when he saw her. "Mistress Tala?"

"Coffee?"

He hesitated for a moment, then laughed. "I'd thought you might want some." He stepped inside and returned with a large, earthenware jug, a simple cork sealing it shut. "Here you are. All that's left for today."

Tala eyed it warily. "Is it still good?"

"Mistress Tala, coffee doesn't spoil. It won't be hot, but you're a Mage. Figure it out."

Chapter: 30
A Morning to Decide

Tala snorted a laugh at Brand's words as he passed over the jug full of coffee. Brand then seemed to notice Renix for the first time. He straightened, brushed off his apron, and put on a diplomat's smile. "Mageling Renix." He bowed slightly. "How can I serve?"

Renix shook his head. "Nothing for me, thank you. I am simply walking with Mistress Tala."

"Very good. Mageling, Mistress." He bowed to each of them in turn, then shut the door.

As they walked back out from between the moving wagons, Renix gestured back towards the closed door. "Like that!"

Tala frowned. "What?"

"The cook! He anticipates your needs and works to meet them."

"We have… an understanding." *He tried to kill me and doesn't want me to seek vengeance…* Was that all it was? *No, we've come to an amicable understanding in truth.*

"Yes, but you seem to reach those with *everyone* you talk to. Your driver lets you spend most of the day on top of his wagon."

My wagon. But she didn't interrupt.

"The guards lend you shields whenever you want."

Well, only at night. I'd love one for shade… Maybe I should buy one in Alefast? Or a parasol? No, the hat is plenty.

"The cooks, I've already mentioned."

Stabbed, threatened, understanding reached, yes. She had uncorked the coffee and was beginning to drink. It was lukewarm and deliciously dark. Exactly what she needed.

"Master Trent and Mistress Atrexia let you do as you wish. They don't like it, but they don't stop you."

They'd have a hard time if they tried. Well, her iron salve was a bit haphazard, at the moment. *I should fix that.*

"And the passengers see you as a walking legend."

That was news to her. "Oh?"

"Of course! How could they not? You fought a terror bird, driving it away without any harm coming to the caravan. You harvested from an ending tree. You *punched out* a thunder bull; what do you expect them to think?"

Well, that last is a bit of a mischaracterization... She sighed. "I see your point. Do you want my answer, or do you wish to keep singing my virtues?"

Renix blushed deeply and cleared his throat. "Your answer, if you're willing… Mistress."

Tala's lips quirked up in a wry smile. "Be you."

He turned to her, frowning. "I can't really be anyone else."

She shook her head. "I mean, be true to what you want, how you want to act, what you want to do, who you want to be. That will require you to make sacrifices, as you can't expect the world to hand you anything, but every sacrifice to become more of who you are is easy to make, and you will *never* regret it." She paused, then her shoulders drooped just slightly, and she sighed. "It can be lonely, Renix, being who you wish to be. You won't make as many friends if you don't twist yourself into knots to please people, but those you do make will like you for *you*, not for who you are pretending to be." She smiled up at him, then took another long pull of coffee.

Renix didn't respond for a long while as they continued to walk alongside the caravan.

"Does that help?"

Renix laughed briefly. "Maybe? I don't know who I want to be, though... How do I figure that out?"

She smiled. "Find *one* thing that you want and figure out what you need to achieve that. That is who you want to be."

"What do you mean?"

She shrugged. "If you want to be a famous historian, you need to study history. Thus, even if you don't think that you want to read, you actually do because reading widely and retaining in great detail is what will allow you to become a famous historian. As an example. I mean, even if you go explore ruins, you will need to be able to read and articulate what you find there."

"Huh." He pondered, again, and Tala downed more of the coffee. "I think... I think I understand what you mean. I want to be strong, so even if I don't like exercising, I *do* want to exercise because it will make me stronger."

She pointed at him firmly, her gaze intense. "That! That is a better example."

He grinned back at her. "I do think I understand."

"Good. Let me know what you discover, yeah?"

He nodded. "I will. Thank you, Mistress Tala."

"You are most welcome."

He turned, striding back towards his own wagon, and she picked up her pace to return to the wagon at the front. *I hope that was the right thing to tell him...* It shouldn't hurt him, at the very least. *As long as he doesn't expect everyone to immediately accept him for who he wants to be, he should be fine. You can't force that.*

Sadly, the coffee didn't last for even the trip back to the cargo wagon, and she was left to shepherd an empty jug, at least until lunch.

Millennial Mage 1 - Mageling

* * *

Coffee gone but well imbibed, Tala felt much more awake, though slightly saddened by the loss.

It's just coffee, Tala. There will be more tomorrow. She didn't allow herself to dwell on it further.

Instead, she took out her magic detector and began sweeping herself to check how her iron salve was doing.

Not good.

She took the next hour to slowly, covertly, re-salve herself until the magic detector didn't register her at all.

She peeled the glue from her palms and tossed it aside, then contemplated how to spend the rest of the morning.

I could continue to study magic items? There was merit to that, as every bit of knowledge could help her in any negotiations for the creation or purchase of such items.

I could process the remaining endingberries and put them in the flask. Having endingberry juice ready to hand, pulp and all, might be quite useful. She didn't know the first thing about wine, and she suspected that the fermentation process could go *incredibly* awry, as the magic was more likely to act on the bacterium than be preserved in the final product. *Super wine is out, then.* Still, having the berries ready to hand could be useful…

The wagons were moving up through foothills, almost parallel to the range of mountains to their south. Early tomorrow, they'd go through a pass and come down upon Alefast from the north, but for now, the terrain was becoming rockier and much more starkly beautiful.

I could just enjoy the scenery and draw if the mood takes me. Just relax if not. She almost chose this, but she just couldn't bring herself to waste the time.

Make another star? That had merit. Not only was it potentially useful, as from what Trent had said it was training her body's ability to draw upon and use power. Her own experiments seemed to bear that out, as well. As Holly had designed her inscriptions, they would pull from every drop of power she gave them, so any increase she could facilitate to her own inflow of strength would directly benefit her, almost immediately. *Unlike other Mages, who would have to modify their inscriptions to take advantage of the increase.* Holly's way really was turning out to be a vast improvement upon what she'd been taught was the norm.

Is it actually Holly's way, though? From what she said, she'd decided it was viable only because *of my peculiar depth of power and the workings I wished to accomplish…* Worth considering, but not right now. Tala sighed, a slight smile tugging at her lips. *It's my way.*

How should I spend my remaining time? She glanced at the sky. *Two hours until lunch?* Her stomach growled, and she pulled out a bit of jerky, chewing and enjoying the comfortable influx of power.

A flicker of dimensional magic caused her to spin.

On the wagon top, directly behind where she'd been sitting, was a small bird, barely bigger than a crow but clearly flightless. *It looks exactly like a terror bird, but scaled down.* "How odd."

The bird tilted its head and screeched, eyes fixed on the remaining jerky in her hand.

"You want some of this?"

The bird looked her in the eye and bobbed a nod.

Tala's own eyes widened, and she took in a slow, deliberate breath. "So… you understand me."

It bobbed again, then returned its gaze to the jerky, which she still held.

She tossed it to the small bird, who easily caught it in its mouth and guzzled it down. "You're welcome, little guy."

The bird regarded her, then slightly tilted its head.

With two more pulses of dimensional power, the bird swelled to double its previous size, then vanished.

Tala stood, frantically scanning the surrounding landscape. *What in zeme? It changed size?* She was breathing faster. *Rust and ruin, slag and stagnation.* That hadn't just been *a* terror bird. That had been *the* terror bird, and it could change size.

No wonder my alteration to gravity didn't hold. Drastic changes in size would *certainly* free it of the working. That meant that she had no means of magically affecting it for any length of time. *Even my crushing attack would likely be shrugged off...*

It was far more dangerous than she'd guessed, and she'd fed it… again. *Oh, rust me to slag.*

After a long moment, she sat back down, having been unable to locate another dimensional signature or the bird itself.

She now knew what her morning would entail. She had a singular question to expand upon and delve into answering.

Now what?

* * *

Despite her lingering questions about the terror bird and what to do next, she did not, in fact, spend her morning simply contemplating them. After all, time was wasting, and an hour ignored was an hour lost.

Instead, she sought out one of the guards on duty. To her relief, the first one she came across was Adam. "Guardsman Adam!"

The man turned his gaze from the surrounding rolling hills and growing crags and towards her as she climbed up onto the roof of the wagon he stood upon. "Mistress Tala? How can I be of assistance?"

"I want to learn to fight." As his eyes widened in surprise, she decided that she should be clear from the outset. "I think that two sticks, or maces, or clubs, would be ideal for me, and I was hoping you might know of a guard who'd be willing to walk me through the basics?"

Adam seemed to rein himself in, and he glanced away. "There might be someone, but a true study of fighting would require hand-to-hand combat as well, along with groundwork and intimate understanding of the human form." He smiled slightly. "At least if you wish to be able to fight other humans. It is invaluable to know where to strike and how if you intend to end a fight quickly and efficiently. If you intend to fight non-humans, you'll want to study arcanous biology and extrapolate from there."

Tala was nodding. "That's fair. Who could give such instruction?"

Adam seemed to contemplate for a long moment. "Almost any guard could give you the basics." He shrugged. "These are highly sought-after posts, and no one is here who hasn't earned it." After a moment, he nodded to himself. "A few of us are better at teaching; I, for one, was an instructor for new recruits, full time, before transferring to more ranging assignments, and we've a couple others with similar backgrounds."

Tala's eyebrows rose at that. "Why would you leave a teaching position? Wouldn't that pay better or be more satisfying or… something?" She took a moment to really look at Guardsman Adam and realized that he was likely close to fifteen years older than she was, likely in his mid-thirties. He was heavily muscled but not in a bulky sort of way. He was barely taller than her, with grey-and-white-flecked, close-cropped hair and a beard.

She didn't focus on him long enough for her magesight to activate. *Not a Mage.*

She'd assumed that guarding a trade caravan would be an undesirable position, given to new recruits or those in disfavor, and she hadn't let her observations shake her initial assumptions.

Huh… That was pretty foolish of me.

Adam was smiling. "Fulfilling? Somewhat, I suppose. I do love teaching, but this pays so much better." He shrugged. "A bit more dangerous, but not overly so. My wife worries, but she also knows that I'm almost as likely to get seriously hurt in the city as out here, and out here, if anything does happen, Mages are ready to hand, so I might even have a better chance of surviving. The kids are getting older, and perhaps I'll move back to teaching once the eldest reaches ten or so." He shrugged.

And a family man… Was *everyone* in the caravan married? *People do get married pretty young, Tala. Mages are a bit of an exception but not over much.* Truthfully, she would likely be married by thirty as well. Most mundanes were married well before twenty-five.

"The danger is *why* the pay is better. I want to provide for my family, and spending the days outside, in the beauty of the Wilds? Well, that's not so bad."

She really didn't know what to say to that, so she just smiled in what she hoped was a companionable way.

"Anyways…" Adam's gaze swept the horizon, again, before returning to her. "Your training." He sighed. "I can't say I've seen many Mages interested in martial pursuits. Why hit a man when you can obliterate him at a hundred paces?"

"Killing is easy, but it is not always the best option."

Adam nodded. "Not everyone understands that. I'm glad that you do." He chuckled to himself. "Skies above, I hope all Mages understand that. Too many of us are at the mercy of your magical whims." He gave her a wink. "No disrespect intended, Mistress."

"None taken, Guardsman."

After another sweep of the terrain, Adam turned to face her fully. "I can teach you some, if you wish, but I'm not going to argue with you."

"That's fair."

"You do what I say, when I say it. No arguing."

She shrugged. "I suppose so."

"Shirt off."

She grabbed the base of her shirt and started to lift. Adam's eyes widened, and he spun around, clearly blushing deeply.

"Stop! Stop."

Tala started to laugh, letting her shirt fall back over her stomach. "That was a test, yes? You were trying to find an excuse to refuse?"

Adam scratched the back of his neck, still not looking at her. "Is your shirt on?"

"It is."

He turned back slowly, checking first. "Not precisely… We do something similar with new recruits, though for men it's 'drop your pants.' You'd be surprised how few follow instructions."

"So, you don't have to see pants-less men that often?"

"Or women. We do get some of those as recruits." He quirked a smile. "Strangely, they seem more willing to comply with random commands than the men. Maybe something about 'proving their worth' or justifying their being there. I should have remembered and expected you to act similarly."

"So… what's the point of the lesson? Or do you just like seeing who you can get pants-less?"

He reddened, again, but less so this time. "No, it's to drive home a notion: No one should be obeyed absolutely. Sometimes your commanders are *wrong*. Now, we also go out of our way to build trust in those commanders, but we don't want blind obedience. That gets people killed."

"Huh. Not what I'd have expected from the Guardsman Guild."

He shrugged. "We want our people to survive, same as any."

"Fair enough." She waited for a long moment as he continued to keep an eye on the surroundings. "So… you'll teach me?"

He smiled, again. "I said I would, didn't I?"

"How do we begin?"

"We fix how you walk."

Tala frowned. "What's wrong with how I walk?"

"You move like a Mage."

"…And?"

"And you don't want to fight like one, so you shouldn't move like one. I want you to walk up and down the caravan and keep your center of balance inside your planted foot at all times."

"Say again?"

He smiled. "You should be able to stop and be balanced almost instantly, no matter where in your stride you choose to stop." He thought for a moment, then nodded. "Imagine your center of balance as a dot on the ground and keep it inside the foot that is on the ground, at all times. When you step, it will obviously move between the feet, but that's fine, while they are both down. Understand?"

"Somewhat…" She nodded. "I'll see what I can do. What next?"

"Master that, then we'll talk."

She crossed her arms. "Walking. You want to teach me walking."

"Let's be clear. I gave you a direction, but *you* will be teaching you how to walk." He grinned.

Tala rolled her eyes. "Fine." She swung down onto the ladder and paused, looking back up towards Adam. "I'll be back shortly."

He snorted. "We'll see."

She climbed down quickly and began walking. As she did, she bent her focus towards her balance and began stopping herself at random intervals, noticing how unsteady she was much of the time. *I'm basically falling from one foot to the other, simply relying on my continued movement to catch me.* Adam had been right.

Well, let's do this. And the real work began.

As it turned out, changing how she walked was *hard*.

Her body was used to moving in certain ways, and it took active effort to change that. Worse, it didn't actually take all her effort. So, she was left having to focus, while not truly being distracted by what she was focusing on.

It...

Was...

Tedious...

In order to distract the petulant part of her mind, while she was kinesthetically focused on her walking, she created and focused upon the Archon Star spell-form.

Soon, she was walking, mind bent towards maintaining constant balance. She tested her progress by stopping and staying in place every so often, always aiming to be in a slightly different phase of her stride. In addition, she was locking the Archon Star spell-form into place and slowly running power through it.

As she had no intention of expending a monumental amount of energy and having to sleep for hours, she also wasn't planning on cutting her finger and expelling the drop of blood containing the star. Thus, she formed it in her center, just behind her sternum. Even so, she did *not* put it in her heart. She knew better than *that*.

Chapter: 31
The Foundation of Any Fighting Art

Over the next two hours, Tala split her mind across the two tasks and found she was able to maintain both, though it took all her concentration. *Perfect*. She wasn't bored.

At her halting pace, she only advanced up the wagon line slowly, and thus, when lunchtime came, Brand stepped out of the chuckwagon to find her barely one wagon away.

"Mistress Tala?"

His voice startled her, and she froze in place, perfectly balanced with her back foot an inch off the ground.

Her concentration on the Archon Star also broke, the power separating from her control, and she severed it before it could draw any more from her. She expected it to break free from the form and disperse back into her... It didn't.

She suddenly felt a horrific clenching in her throat, and she began to cough uncontrollably.

"Mistress Tala!" Brand set the food he'd been carrying back on the tail of his wagon and ran to her, even as she fell to her knees, coughing and heaving.

He brought out a handkerchief and offered it to her. She took it and pressed it over her mouth. Strangely, it helped.

The coughing slowed until, finally, one last colossal cough brought up *something* that had been caught inside her. It stuck in the handkerchief.

Tala pulled the cloth away, and both she and Brand gazed down at a small, spinning drop of blood.

"That… isn't normal, Mistress. Have you contracted some… hostile magic?" He began looking around, and before she could say anything, he was waving to someone. "Mistress Atrexia! Please, come quickly. I think Mistress Tala might be ill."

Tala groaned.

The sound of hooves on soft turf came to a stop nearby, and Atrexia dismounted. "What happened now, Mistress Tala?"

Tala coughed once more. "I was practicing the mental spell-forms for making a star, and unintentionally allowed power to fill it."

Atrexia was nodding. "In your lungs?"

"Esophagus, I think, but close enough."

"Let me see."

Tala held up the handkerchief, flecked with spittle and one, still spinning, drop of blood.

Atrexia frowned, power moving in waves around her eyes. "This looks like the first you created. I'll need to measure it, but I'd bet it is about that powerful. Master Trent told me how that effort exhausted you before. How are you feeling, now?"

She shrugged. "Fine? Except my throat hurts a bit. I concentrated on it longer, but didn't funnel my full power accumulation into it, and I prevented it from drawing from my reserves. If that makes sense."

Brand stood. "I'll get some honeyed tea."

"Thank you, Brand."

He nodded and jogged to catch the chuckwagon.

Tala stood and began walking. Atrexia fell in beside her, leading her horse by the reins. "How do you account for this?"

Tala shrugged. "I did it much slower. I was trying to occupy my mind, and so I think I was letting it build for... two hours? Give or take." She thought, then nodded. "Just about, yeah."

"And before?"

"It took about fifteen minutes. Again, give or take."

Atrexia grunted. "So, a much lower power input, over a much longer period, and likely with much less efficiency... That makes sense. Especially if it didn't scrape you empty in the end." She was nodding to herself. "You shouldn't have any negative effects, but you also won't experience any increase to your power accumulation rate." She gave Tala a firm look. "That is *not* a recommendation that you should push yourself as you did before, simply a statement of fact."

Tala nodded. "I'm not really interested in sleeping away hours of daylight, today."

Atrexia gave her a critical, searching look. Finally, she grunted again. "That was likely due to allowing the star to draw power out of your reserves, but very well. May I take that for testing?"

"Shouldn't I put it in a vial?"

"I have no idea. It's not like this is standard." She sighed. "At least you are moving towards a proper approach. Funneling the power gradually and letting it build within the spell-form is the right way to make an Archon Star." She frowned. "But please don't make it in anything so vital again? My understanding is that it isn't advisable to make it within yourself, at all. If you're going to kill yourself, please wait until after we reach Alefast?"

Tala rolled her eyes. "Fine, fine. It wasn't like I did it on purpose."

Atrexia huffed. "That is *precisely* my point, ignorant ch—" She took a deep breath, closing her eyes before exhaling in a rush. After a small, forced smile, as if to herself, Atrexia spoke on. "You continue to do reckless things, seemingly at random, and we are all startled by your miraculous survivals."

Tala thrust the handkerchief at Atrexia. "Here. Let me know what you find out."

The other Mage took the cloth without further chiding. "I will. Eat something and rest."

As Atrexia rode away, presumably towards her own wagon, Tala found herself filled with joy. She'd turned her focus back towards her stride and found that she was still using the altered version. *I did it!*

She wouldn't let her guard down,of course. She could always backslide if she wasn't careful, but she'd *done it*. She had altered her steps.

Now, what's next?

Lunch. Lunch was next. She felt her connection with the newly created star moving around as Atrexia went about her tests, but Tala didn't let it distract her.

Brand returned with her lunch and a large carafe of honeyed tea. He insisted on carrying both back to her wagon with her, and once he was satisfied that she was settled and resting, he took the empty coffee jug. "Let me know if you need anything else, please?"

"I will, Brand. Thank you."

He nodded once, emphatically, and climbed down, leaving her to her meal and the wonderful relief brought on by the tea.

*   *   *

Atrexia tossed her the handkerchief a few minutes after Tala had finished her lunch. "It's the same as the first, or near enough it doesn't matter." Without another word, she climbed back down the ladder. She seemed to hesitate, out of view, but then she rode away without saying anything else.

Tala had seen the light-colored cloth flick up into view, and she caught it, checking inside and verifying that the new little star was there. She'd known it would be because she could *feel* it like a light brush on her skin. She'd even known Atrexia was approaching with it well before the woman had arrived. *What now?*

She debated putting it into the vial with the larger one, hopefully to combine their power, but she didn't actually have a use for them yet. *Maybe more is better than stronger?* She had no idea. So, she put this new one in the other vial and stored that in her satchel.

The tea was gone, now, and her throat felt much better. There were no enhancement spell-lines to easily repair the modicum of damage she'd given herself there. So, she'd have to wait for it to heal like anyone else. It was frustrating that the endingberry's power had finally run dry. *Or, would it have kept the star trapped, unable to get free?* That was a horrifying thought…

They were nearing the pass, now, and she could see it just less than twenty miles ahead and to the south.

Two great peaks towered above the surrounding mountains, and the space between them dipped vastly lower than those same other peaks. *Not a usual formation.* At least she didn't think so. Geography hadn't ever been a passion of hers, let alone geology.

As she stared, she was able to pick out more detail, like the fact that the faces of the two mountains, nearest each other, were smooth, almost uniform slopes, giving the impression of a single mountain, split by one stroke of a titanic ax.

We are far from the land of arcanous gods. Humans had purposely moved to a greater distance from the magic-rich northern and eastern reaches of the continent, specifically to avoid those creatures.

If normal arcanous beasts could, on occasion, become two or three times the size of their non-magical equivalents, the arcanous gods often breached ten times that, if not greater. They were said to be ancient beyond the reckoning of man, and powerful beyond Mages' ability to measure. Though, her knowledge of such came from childhood tales, told around a dying fire, rather than her academy education. More and more, she was frustrated at what they *hadn't* taught her.

Did some arcanous god fight or die here, millennia ago?

She would likely never know.

Tala shook herself, bringing her thoughts back to the present. *I should check in with Adam, get my next task.*

Nodding to herself, she climbed down and walked back towards the wagon that Adam currently stood upon.

She was careful to walk as she'd been practicing, maintaining balance at all times. It was surprisingly effortful, and she was definitely feeling some soreness from her earlier walking.

Even so, she climbed the ladder and greeted Adam. "Now what?"

He glanced towards her. "I saw; you learned quickly." He was still armored as all the guard were, in iron chain and padded leather, an iron cap atop his head. He had one of the guard's large shields leaning against his side and a crossbow hanging from his belt. A quiver hung opposite, ready to hand, and a short sword was strapped inside the shield to complete his armament.

She waited for a long moment. "So…?" She noticed a two-and-a-half-foot-long, thick stick, carved and polished smooth, resting against the shield as well. "Are we going to start fighting, now?"

"Now"—Adam glanced towards her—"we are going to fix your breathing."

Tala groaned. "Adam. I just want to know how to fight! Can't we do the fast version?"

His mouth quirked, and he bent to pick up the stick. In a smooth motion, he tossed it to her.

She caught it. "Yes! Now, how do we start?"

"If you are threatened, hit the person or thing with that until you are no longer threatened. Quick version over. Have a wonderful day."

Tala blinked back at him. "What?"

"You wanted the quick version, right? That's it. It's not like you can cut yourself. Hit what's bothering you until it stops."

She grunted in irritation. "I sort of worked that out myself."

"I'd thought as much." He still didn't turn to face her.

"Adam. Teach me."

"Certainly, Mistress. Now, your breathing—"

She hit him in the back with the stick. He barely budged, and when she looked, she noticed that his knees were bent, and the shield that she'd thought was propped against him was, in fact, locked in place on the roof, holding him upright. She narrowed her eyes.

"Why did you hit me?" He turned his head to regard her.

"You were bothering me. I aim to follow instructions, *teacher*."

He snorted a laugh. "Fair enough."

"So…?"

"Your breathing."

She raised the stick as if to strike him again, and he quirked an eyebrow at her.

"Do you wish someone else to teach you?"

She grunted and lowered the simple weapon. "Fine. I'll hear you out."

"Good. Breath in slowly through your nose."

She did so, taking much longer to draw in the breath than it usually did.

"And out fast through your mouth."

She exhaled in a full-bodied, quick puff.

"Good. Now, breathe that way until it becomes natural."

Tala's own eyebrow twitched. "Seriously?"

"Yes. Proper balance and breathing are the foundation of any fighting art. If you just want to swing a stick, have at it." He gestured at her. "You can already do that just fine. However, if you want to learn how to *fight*, we will do it properly as if you were joining the Guardsmans' Guild in truth."

She grunted. *I suppose that each guild has to have something to offer, else they'd be replaced by freelancers. The Guardsmen's Guild must have some way to make their members more effective...* "Alright. I will do as you say."

She climbed back down the ladder, breathing as he'd instructed.

The stick, she left at his feet.

*   *   *

Tala breathed in, long and deliberately, through her nose.

She exhaled in a powerful pulse, through her mouth.

She read her books.

In through her nose.

Out through her mouth.

Sketch the increasingly mountainous scenery.

In nose.

Out mouth.

Walk, balance perfect.

In.

Out.

Balance.

Hours passed.

Tala didn't let herself be distracted as various people talked with her. She gave reasonable answers, explaining that she was focusing on something and could probably talk later… She did this on the exhale, of course.

She didn't stop her proper breathing when the guard drove off a flock of hornets, each the size of barn cats, though she did walk, maintaining balance, to the other side of the convoy. In, out, quick step away from acid-drenched stingers.

Horrifyingly, none of the hornets were actually killed, but after a few wings were lost to well-placed crossbow bolts, and lightning temporarily took one to the ground, they seemed to decide to search for easier targets.

Apparently, their armor scaled with them… Those hornets had been a startling realization for her as there had been thirty-three in the swarm. *Even if I was freshly inscribed, I could not have killed them all.* They would likely not have been able to kill her, either. After she used one *crush* on each of thirty of them, she would have been left with three *very* angry creatures that just might have harried her until her protections ran out.

In. Out. Balance. Even as she thought, she kept most of her mind on the changes Adam had instructed her to make.

I cannot assume that I am above the dangers out here, just because I've been lucky. My abilities help keep me alive and can crush powerful opponents in a pinch, but the Wilds are a place of attrition. The epiphany came with a renewed desire to hone her ability to fight. She could likely drive away the hornets with her bone clubs, once she knew what she was doing, and that prospect excited her. *Armor your weaknesses and hone your strengths.*

In, out, balance.

She found herself needing to yawn quite often, at first, but she stifled the urge with an effort—a *great* effort.

She felt flicks of magic as other creatures were dissuaded, but none were brought down, so she didn't pay particular attention. *No harvest means no need for my involvement.* She smiled at that, careful to not let it ruin her breathing.

Finally, after what *was* hours, Den led them over a particularly large, sloping foothill and into a circle atop it.

Framing their place of encampment, scarcely four miles distant, was the entrance to the pass that she'd noticed before.

A path ran almost straight towards it from the newly circled wagons, and she felt an involuntary shudder. *Caravans take random routes to prevent more powerful beasts from knowing where to lie in wait.* She continued to examine the deep cleft of the pass. *Clearly, this part of the route is used more often than others.*

If they were going to be attacked by something powerful, it would be tomorrow. This close, her magesight showed magical energy pouring through from the land beyond. That increased magic meant more, if not more powerful, arcanous creatures. If they were really unlucky, they might even cross paths with a magical beast.

I'll ask Trent tonight.

She froze, realizing that her mind had moved away from her breathing. *Am I?*

Long pull in, through her nose.

Short, full-bodied exhale through her mouth.

"*Victory!*" Several of the drivers turned to give her odd looks before returning to their work.

She'd done it. Still, she wouldn't let her guard down. *Or my Guard down.* She laughed inwardly at her own joke.

I am altering my basic patterns way too easily... She considered all the aspects that Holly had enhanced and came to the conclusion that altering innate, repeated patterns of action should be much easier with the enhanced connectivity and improved mental functions. *I'll likely learn to fight more easily, too.*

She didn't *quite* chide herself, even as she realized that Adam would say that she was already learning to fight, just by working on her stride and her breathing pattern.

Fine… I'll likely learn how to wield weapons more quickly, too.

Fair enough.

Adam walked over to her, having dismounted from his wagon. "So, you've corrected your breathing?"

She grinned back at him, answering on the exhale. "Yes. Next?"

He smiled. "You tell me."

She blinked at him, then brightened. "I pick? Basic combat, then!"

He smiled back. "Incorrect." He then turned and walked away, his stride perfectly balanced.

Tala stared after him. *What?*

He hadn't been asking her to pick. He'd be asking her to figure out what was next.

Tala groaned, then hesitated, watching him walk away. *What is he doing, that I'm not?*

As she looked, her magesight responded to the focus, highlighting the currents of power that moved through him, just as they moved through everything to one extent or another.

Each step showed shifting flows of power, clearly grounding him to the earth and giving him stability beyond what was normal. *Without spell-lines?* Somehow, his very movements seemed to invoke a sort of magic.

She could see his breath moving in and out of him as well, in the regular cadence he'd instructed her to use.

Finally, she noticed that he stood straight, shoulders back, posture controlled without being rigid.

She, herself, stood straight but in a different way.

As she shifted, she could feel the stiffness in her posture, hours of training to keep herself firmly upright had lent her an immovability like a boulder carried on the back of a cart. She was straight, strong, and inflexible.

Adam was a tree before the wind. His back and shoulders shifted with the rest of his body, allowing for a more flowing movement. The difference was subtle, but now that she noticed it, she couldn't *not* see it.

"Posture." She didn't shout, but Adam turned around, smiling.

"No, but yes."

She frowned, then rolled her eyes. "Observation, then posture."

He nodded. "I expect I'll give you the next step before we reach Alefast, tomorrow. Good luck." He turned half away, again, then paused, glancing back. "Please don't blow us up?"

She grinned. Mages often held their stiff postures to avoid crossing spell-lines. It was *incredibly* rare for there to be a reaction, and in every case that she knew of, it could be at least partially traced to poor quality inscriptions. Even so, no good Mage risked it. No one wanted to rip themselves apart. "I'll be careful."

Adam nodded one last time and continued walking away.

Because she'd been focused on him, her magesight active, she'd noticed that his breathing pattern had changed during their discussion. *That explains that.* She'd been attempting to discern how she was meant to effectively carry on a conversation with the long inhale and short exhale.

The answer was simple, as most were once found. She wasn't.

I'll have to practice breathing in that other pattern whenever I speak... Another thing to learn. She found herself smiling. *Another way I can improve.*

Chapter: 32
Terribly Wrong

Tala moved towards the chuckwagon, allowing her back and shoulders to move along with the rest of her, keeping balance.

It felt strange to relinquish the rigidity that she'd held for so long. The manner of movement didn't feel like something she did; it had become a part of her. Even so, she wasn't stiff, as her daily stretches and exercises had kept her limber despite her manner of movement.

Honestly, it felt like she was going to fall over, which was incredibly disconcerting given that she was focused on her balance, so she *knew* she was perfectly stable.

Like feeling starving on a full stomach... It made no sense.

Still, she rested in the feeling instead of fighting it and found a strange comfort in the flow of the movement, as her whole body seemed to harmonize with her balance and breath.

This is fantastic!

She easily got her food and made her way to the Mages' table, where the three people there were already gorging themselves.

Tala smiled at the three. "Rough day?"

Renix nodded emphatically, speaking around food. "Yeah, and tomorrow will be the hardest."

Tala found herself nodding. She'd noticed the slow increase in ambient magic as they progressed, and now having seen the power practically streaming through the pass, she understood. "Well, Alefast is a waning city, so…?"

All three stopped eating and turned to look at her.

Trent cleared his throat. "Mistress Tala. I know that your training was"—he glanced at Atrexia, then back to Tala—"unusual, but did you really not think to investigate what the implications were for the stage of our destination city?"

Tala shrugged. "Honestly? No. So, a city in its last stages, eh? Population in the tens of thousands, buttoning up and getting the last of the goods out." She smiled, sitting down with her food. "Magic coalescing about the walls like water in the ocean, luring in all manner of creatures, both the simply arcane and the truly magical."

Atrexia shook her head and continued eating. "Like a child with a bedtime story."

Trent ignored his fellow Mage protector. "Even the harvesting guilds will be beginning to pull out. Why do you think I wasn't willing to go with you to the ending tree grove?"

"You said it would be too expensive?"

He gave her a flat look. "And have we encountered so much lately that that made sense?"

"Oh." She nodded, digging into her food and talking around the mouthful. "I get it. The abandoned outer circles of the city, and the surrounding countryside, will be crawling with beasts."

Atrexia hesitated, then sighed. "That is close enough to true. You know, it would be better if you stayed in the city. You are taking the next caravan out, yes?"

Tala nodded. "I am, but I'm *very* interested in the endingberries, and I think it's worth the risk." Tala's eyes narrowed. "You didn't care if I risked myself the last time it was brought up."

Atrexia put on a false veneer of affront. "Mistress Tala! I never meant to imply I'd like to see you die. I only meant that your death would be a travesty to more than just you if you died before tomorrow morning."

Tala's eyes further narrowed. "You don't think there's another in the city who can empower cargo-slots." Atrexia took a hasty bite of food. Tala took the silence as a response and continued. "You're afraid of getting stuck in Alefast until a replacement can arrive if I die."

Renix was still shoveling food in his mouth, but he managed to give Atrexia a hurt look. "That's not very kind."

"I don't want her to die, okay? Why must you look for the reasons why? Isn't my desire enough?" She glanced Tala's way. "Besides, I won't be with the caravan coming back immediately anyways. My departure doesn't hinge on her."

That gave Tala pause. *Maybe, it's something else, then?* "Fair enough." She turned back to Trent. "So, what will tomorrow look like?"

"The pass will be the biggest gamble. Mistress Atrexia is uniquely suited to fight in that terrain, and that's largely why she was recruited for this particular venture."

"Strong-armed, more like," the woman muttered around her food.

"In either case, she should be able to drive back anything we encounter through the pass. Once we're out, the power in the area beyond the pass will have changed the local animals much more substantially than those we've seen so far, and there will likely be at least a few purely magical creatures."

"Trent? Why are you giving her the *most basic* lesson?" Atrexia had paused eating, once again, to regard him.

He shrugged. "I prefer to be thorough."

Atrexia grunted, seeming unsatisfied, but didn't press.

"Do you need me to be ready to help?"

Atrexia rolled her eyes but refrained from commenting.

Trent, though, was nodding. "Maybe. What sort of support could you offer?"

Tala hesitated, realizing that she didn't *really* want to explain her abilities. Finally, she settled on being accurate but vague. "I can remove single targets, largely without difficulty. There will be some magical creatures that can shrug off my attack for a time, but very few. I cannot easily affect a swarm, but I can remove up to…" She glanced at the back of her hand. "…twenty-three? I think I can remove any twenty-three opponents from the field, either one at a time or in groups. If there are particularly resilient opponents, treat them as more than one of that number, and it should still be accurate."

Renix whistled in appreciation around his food, somehow, but didn't comment further.

Trent nodded. "Big and focused. That might be useful. Renix and I are good at quickly removing lots of normal opponents, and the guards can handle a horde of weak, or a small number of normal enemies." He glanced to Atrexia and smiled. "She can obliterate almost anything arcane in the mountains, the few exceptions *should* be subject to Renix and me, but it's good to know we can call on you." He turned back to Tala. "Are you limited by what they are composed of?" He blinked, seeming to consider for himself, then shook his head. "Of course, you aren't; I apologize. You're an immaterial. The material that is around is irrelevant to you."

Tala smiled. "Reasonable question, nonetheless. If I can see or sense them, I can affect them."

"We'll keep that in mind. Thank you."

"Happy to help."

Small talk filled the remainder of the space around the consumption of their food, and the four parted ways for the night.

Tala felt somewhat strange as she made her way back to her wagon, requisitioning herself a shield along the way. She didn't feel sick, precisely, but she did feel *off.*

She dismissed it.

* * *

Tala woke, gasping for air and struggling to breathe, just as first light began to put the stars from the sky.

Something had gone *terribly* wrong.

She pulled in huge lungfuls of air through a gaping mouth, but it felt incorrect, *broken.* Like eating soup with a fork.

She pushed herself out from under the anchored shield and away from her bedroll, but she found herself stiff, and her movements stumbling. *Poisoned? Someone poisoned me?*

No, she didn't feel sick, she just couldn't seem to breathe right or move without tripping over herself…

Everything I focused on yesterday. Everything is wrong. Somehow, her body was fighting back against the changes she'd made to her breathing, posture, and balance.

It was *rusting* terrible.

She tried to draw in her breath through her nose, but it felt like breathing through a straw… which was actually pretty close to the truth. Even so, it was infuriating, and her lungs screamed at her for more air, faster.

She tried to focus on her movement, keeping her balance centered above her feet, and it felt like someone had broken her ankles.

Her whole back felt like it was a collection of tension, knots, and agony, the muscles bunching and twisting, fighting for control. It was as if someone had laced her back with rope from the abyss itself before cinching it taut.

She groaned, trying to stretch while fighting a growing sense of breathlessness.

What is going on?

She heard a man walk up to her wagon and begin to climb. She ignored it as she tried to force her body to *obey*. *You are my body! Come on, Tala, get it together.*

She heard a quizzical noise and turned to see Adam regarding her, his head just barely poking above the lip of the wagon. "What's wrong with you?"

She pulled in a quick breath through her mouth, despite how *wrong* that felt too, and cursed at him. "You rusting broke me! What's wrong with you, telling me to change all these"—she took in another gasping breath—"things about myself at once?"

Adam was frowning. "You should be experiencing some oddities, as well as difficulty in replicating what you did yesterday, but you seem to be having a somewhat extreme reaction. Are you sure you aren't overreacting?"

She glared at him as she panted, hating every inhaled breath, even as her lungs fought to keep her breathing *more*. "I learn much more quickly than most."

He nodded. "Your reaction makes sense then, I suppose. Your success yesterday was something we call beginners' competence, often known as beginners' luck. Most people are very good at most things, when they first attempt them, only falling into the traps of ignorance upon repeated attempts. Most of the time, that means that a student will feel like they are getting everything right on the first day. Then, they will feel that they are unable to take a single correct step for weeks after that."

Tala cursed again, then took in a great gasp and continued, "You mean, that I'll be this way for *weeks!?*"

He shook his head. "I would expect you to level out more quickly, but you won't return to the competence you experienced yesterday for quite a while."

She continued to glare.

"Take deep breaths. You know the pattern."

She opened her mouth to shout at him, but he held up a hand, climbing the rest of the way onto the roof.

"Try it."

She dropped into a cross-legged, seated position, focusing on her breathing and glaring.

"Close your eyes."

She obliged, turning all her focus onto fighting her body's certainty that she was drowning.

"Breathe."

She did. In through her nose, out through her mouth.

"Slowly, deeply."

She did so, feeling her panic begin to lessen, even while she still felt out of breath.

She heard Adam walking around her, seemingly examining her as she continued to breathe.

Tala didn't let that distract her from her ongoing, internal battle.

Suddenly, she felt Adam strike her back, right at one of the worst bunches of rebellious muscle. It was as if he severed the abyssal cord, and the taut rope of agony whipped through her back.

Instead of screaming, as she very much wanted to, she found herself utterly unable to breathe.

He'd struck her just at the end of an explosive exhale, and she was utterly without breath.

"In through your nose, Mistress Tala."

She obliged, if only to be able to scream at him.

Surprisingly, the immense flash of pain had passed, and her back felt incredible relief. She was by no means cured, as many muscular pain points still screamed at her, but her entire back was no longer a web of misery.

Tala grunted instead of screeching at him.

"Better?"

She grunted again, opening her eyes to glare. "You could have warned me."

"No, I couldn't have. Your unawareness is all that allowed me to break the core of your misalignment."

She grumbled, but she knew he was right. Her body was no longer screaming at her quite so loudly, and her lungs no longer felt like they were in open revolt.

"I've seen you stretching. It is a good set. Triple your time in it this morning, and do another set, just as long, at least twice more today. Try to focus on the things from yesterday, and don't be discouraged when you have more difficulty than before."

Tala grunted, then sighed. "Thank you." After a short pause, she added, "I think I still hate you, but thank you for not just abandoning me." After another pause, she continued, "You came because you knew I'd be off this morning?"

He quirked a smile. "That, and I could hear you gasping for air from the other side of the caravan."

She felt herself color. "Was it that loud?"

"I was waiting for some indication that you were awake, so I was paying *very* close attention."

She felt slightly mollified.

"I'll leave you to it, then." Without further comment from either of them, Adam departed.

After he was well out of earshot, Tala muttered to herself, "I hope some sort of masseuse is still in Alefast, because there is *no* way I'm getting all these knots out just by stretching…"

Breathing first, Tala. She calmed herself, centering her thoughts, and drawing her awareness inward, enforcing her breathing pattern. It wasn't perfect, but she was able to alleviate the feeling of drowning in perfectly good air.

That done, she clumsily gathered up her bedroll and tossed the shield down over the side. She'd normally have carried it but didn't want the added imbalance.

She returned the shield and stored her bedroll. Then, she went through her morning empowerment of the cargo-slots.

It was much more difficult today, as her body's aches and general feeling of being off-balance weakened her mental construct, thereby lowering efficiency.

Even so, it didn't take long for her to be finished with her work for the morning.

That done, she made her way to stand outside the wagon circle in the light of the rising sun and began to stretch, following Adam's advice and lingering deeply in each position when it was a static stretch, and increasing the repetitions for those that were dynamic.

Her body felt like a twisted cord being pulled. It was unwinding, but there were still spins in the line that caused strange pulling.

It was *deeply* uncomfortable.

Extended stretches complete, she moved through her exercises, then did another, normal set of stretches after. *More can't hurt.*

Through the body work, she'd been keeping a portion of her mind on her breathing, and it continued to settle into place.

All told, it was well after sunrise when she finished, and most people had finished their breakfasts by the time she grabbed hers. She found herself catching her feet on the uneven ground as she approached the chuckwagon but kept herself from falling, cursing, or making too much of a spectacle of herself.

Millennial Mage 1 - Mageling

Brand, bless the man, had a massive earthen jug of coffee to go with her food. It was at least a half-gallon in size. The meal itself was an omelet, containing a healthy helping of thunder bull meat along with cheeses, spices, peppers, and other vegetables.

She poured out her thanks, then took her breakfast back to her wagon, tripping several more times along the way. Thankfully, she was always able to recover herself before dropping anything.

As she ate, she stared at the pass they would traverse in the next few hours. The density of magic flowing through it was palpably higher than that in the surrounding hills. *What awaits us there?*

She'd find out soon enough, but she had more immediate concerns.

Her food eaten and coffee at the ready, Tala turned her focus inward and simply *breathed.*

Tala sat on top of her wagon in the shade of her wide-brimmed hat, eyes closed and thoughts directed inward.

Even so, she was able to hear the creak of the wagon beneath her and feel the growing warmth on her left side as the caravan moved towards the cleft that they would use as a pass.

As she directed her attention towards her breathing, it seemed to activate her magesight's deeper perception because she was suddenly able to see the air, lightly infused with magic, moving in and out with each cycling breath.

It was strange, as there seemed to be power relating to fire in each breath in, and her body was harvesting that, replacing it with something that appeared reminiscent of living plants—at least, that was the feeling she got. Strangely, the air she exhaled seemed to be denser with magic than that which she drew in.

Am I losing power with each breath? It was a strange thought but made a sort of sense. *Most Mages leak power all around themselves. I don't. I suppose losing some through breathing isn't unique to me, it is just more noticeable to me.*

It was more than sensing the contents of her lungs—though that was part of it, and that was strange enough.

Just as the thunder cattle, or terror bird, had been more than the animal they diverged from, so the air in her lungs was more than simply air.

Within most human cities, there was almost no magic free-floating, as all of it was harvested and directed towards the defenses of the city.

Here, in the Wilds, it was everywhere.

She could feel the slowly increasing quantity of magic in the air she drew in, steadily rising towards the density that she exhaled.

Experimentally, she held her breath and watched closely. Not only did the tint of the air in her lungs move away from a patron of fire and towards an aid to plant life, but it also became more and more magically dense, moving rapidly towards the levels of power observable throughout her body. *Could we make a device that measured a Mage's power via breath?*

She contemplated. *We'd have to have them hold their breath for a set amount of time...* As she continued to observe, she noticed that as the magic in the air she breathed increased, so did that in the air she exhaled. *We'd need to be in a magically sterile environment, too. So, it would only work in cities...*

Experimentally, as she continued to breathe, she reached out to the power in the air within her lungs. To her surprise, it moved easily, responding to her will.

In gleeful fervor, she concentrated the power, pushing it together as she exhaled.

Millennial Mage 1 - Mageling

A small *pop* caused her eyes to snap open. *What was that?* It hadn't truly been a sound, though a sound had accompanied the feeling.

Den turned his head around, barely able to see as he looked over the front edge of the wagon, a question in his eyes. She waved and smiled. After smiling and returning the gesture, he shrugged and turned back towards his work.

Den felt that? No, he likely heard the slight pop. It hadn't really sounded like anything natural. She couldn't think of a way to describe the sound as she took notes. *Pay more attention next time.*

Chapter: 33
Creature of Magic

Tala inhaled long and slow once more, focusing on the power coming in with the air, as well as the power leaking into her lungs.

Eyes open, she exhaled, while willing the power to come together, compressing it into as small a point as possible as it left her mouth.

As soon as the magic left the inside of her body, she lost sway over it, and it attempted to come to equilibrium with the air around her.

There was a *pop* and a minute flicker of light as the power dispersed.

Tala's breath caught. *That shouldn't be possible. Humans can't create magic without spell-lines. We can only...* She gasped. *Move power around within ourselves.* That's all that she had done. To be fair, only Immaterial Guides could manipulate power, freely, within themselves. Magic was, after all, Immaterial. *Though Immaterial Creators can't make it... Or can they? I'd bet it's like making gold, and it takes more power than it gives benefit.*

She returned her focus to what she'd just done. The power had left her because it was in the air she'd exhaled. She hadn't cast it forth as a spell.

She bent back over her notebook, recording what she had done and the result. Without a better way to describe the sound, she settled on: 'It creates a pop, which sounds

Millennial Mage 1 - Mageling

like a cork shooting from a bottle, but heard through your chest.' It was not a great description.

A world of *very* foolish ideas opened before her. *Could I direct the power within my lungs into a kinetic force amplification form?* The most likely outcome would be bursting her lungs from the inside, so she held off on that.

Tala had heard of Mages who treated their spells almost like breath weapons, breathing out their spells. Barbaric shamans of the past would cut themselves and fling out spells. She'd always thought of both as strange, but what if they were each doing what she had just done? Creating spell-forms within themselves and then finding a way to send them forth.

She let out a barking laugh, realizing that someone, at some point in history, had likely tried to urinate spells. *Assuming I'm right...*

She then felt a bit of embarrassment at having thought of the shamans as barbaric. *Spell-forms in blood is exactly how I've been making my Archon Star variant... And how everyone checks for identification and certification, though without the form.*

She needed to test this. *Gravity. I have the best grasp on that.*

She picked up a pencil and held it in front of her. Then, she took a deep breath, quickly bringing to mind a very basic gravity spell-form. It simply would deny gravity's effects on the solid object it hit first.

She moved to impose the simple spell-form onto the power within her lungs.

It was *much* trickier than she'd hoped.

The power fought her, seeming not to want to follow her guidance, and it didn't seem to want to flow as she expected, like trying to cut a hard, round herb with a dull knife. It kept slipping and sliding, and she could *feel* how dangerous it would be if it slipped fully from her grasp.

Her breath held, she bore down and forced it into shape, maintaining her mental construct both of the spell-form she was guiding the power through and the results the spell should accomplish.

She failed.

She let out a breath, the power popping violently within her mouth as she exhaled. It felt like someone had kicked her in the teeth... from the inside.

"Ow..."

She took a few calming breaths, focusing solely on using the correct pattern of inhalation and exhalation. To her surprise, she realized that the long, deep breath through her nose should be perfect for building the spell-form and adding power to it in a slow, controlled way, and the quick exhale would expel the magic quickly enough to make it useful for delivering concentrated spells.

This wouldn't work for a breath weapon. I'd need a long, steady exhale for that... How would that even work? I'm not going to experiment with heat forms. Not only were they not her expertise, thus not easy for her to picture and therefore enact, but she was also highly aware that generating magical heat in her own lungs was a recipe for disaster.

Anti-gravity, right? She was about to attempt it again when she heard a horse ride up beside her wagon.

"Mistress Tala! What are you doing?"

Tala turned and leaned to look over the side of the wagon, down on Trent. "Master Trent?"

"Are you trying to get us killed?" He seemed a bit flustered.

She frowned. "What do you mean?"

"Are you sending out magical pulses?"

She opened her mouth to say no, then stopped. *Oh...* "Um... Possibly?"

Trent closed his eyes, clearly steadying himself. "Mistress Tala, we are *trying* to thread this pass without garnering the attention of anything... unpleasant. Why, *by all that breathes,* would you be sending out magical pulses?!" His voice was barely contained below shout.

"I apologize, Master Trent. I did not think that what I was doing would be so obvious."

He pursed his lips. "It felt like you were poking me between the eyes, even without my magic-sight active. Whatever you were doing created ripples in all the magic in the area."

Oh... rust.

He took another calming breath. "Thankfully, it seems to have gone unnoticed. Please—"

A strange *chuff chuff* sound echoed out of the pass and across the caravan. It was as if a bear were sniffing at the wind—if the bear in question was the size of a mountain.

Tala turned to look back at the pass, and her magesight immediately highlighted two differences.

First, the magic coming out of the pass was even stronger than before, seeming to be rippling out like waves before a boat. Second, a blazing source of power was dropping down the sheer face of one of the mountains, deep in the pass, directly into their path.

She turned back to look at Trent as he stared down the pass. "Oh, child... what have you done?"

Tala stood, focusing down the pass once more, even while she was still unsteady on her feet. *Not the best time to have balance issues...*

She swallowed involuntarily at what she saw, concerns over her balance temporarily forgotten.

Where the arcanous creatures and plants she'd seen over the last few days had had magic in them, the beast striding their way *was* magic. Every fiber of its being inundated with power; a deep red aura underlay the magic she could see.

Though she'd never dug deeply into the study of magical creatures, even she knew of the kind coming their way.

A midnight fox.

As the name suggested, the basic appearance was that of a massive fox, its shoulder reaching higher than Tala's head, even standing on the wagon top. Its eyes were a gleaming silver with black slits, and its fur was a matte black that more closely resembled tar than the fur of animals, though it moved easily enough. Flicks of light glinted off the sliver of its claws, and there was the wrinkle of small gusts of wind in the surrounding grasses from each movement of its tail.

There were two main deviations from the vulpine form; the first was two horns, one on each side of the head, sprouting from just below the ear, curving inward, following the line of the upper jaw, and practically dripping with power. Her magesight gave her the impression of darkness, silence, and protection from those horns.

In addition to the horns, a pair of antlers sprouted up between the ears on top of the midnight fox's head. While the horns were an almost steel-grey color, banded with black, the antlers were as metallically silver as the midnight fox's eyes and claws. The power coming from each reminded her of an incoming thunderstorm. Each antler had eleven points, and if she remembered correctly, they grew a new prong for each decade they'd lived. *More than two hundred and twenty years old.*

There was a terrible beauty to the animal, even at their current distance. *It is young, for its kind.* Midnight foxes were said to live for centuries, if not millennia, continuing to accumulate power as they aged. And that ignored the theory that all such were originally ordinary foxes that became so infused with power that they transformed. *Do the antlers count their age from first birth or from transformation?* As she considered, she realized that it was hardly relevant.

"Master Trent… What now?"

Trent's eyes were locked on the pass. "We have to know what it is. I can't quite see it—"

"Midnight fox." She cut across him. "Eleven prongs, per side, if my count is correct."

He looked up at her sharply. "Are you sure?"

"As I can be. I've never seen one in person, but the standard markers are there. The horns and antlers, black fur that doesn't look quite right, silver eyes, et cetera."

Trent nodded. "Your magesight must be impressive to see it at this range. How did you get around the overstimulation—" He cut himself off. "This is hardly the time. I apologize. I must go speak with Mistress Atrexia." As he turned to ride away, in search of the other Mage, he paused, glancing back at her. "Were you serious, when you offered to eliminate singular, large threats?"

She nodded. "It is the least I could do, given…"

He held up a hand, shaking his head. "With where it came from, it likely would have noticed us either way. Now we can face it before going into the pass, where it would have had the advantage." He sighed. "I don't think we will be able to drive it off, but we can hope."

Tala frowned. *That's right.* Truly magical creatures couldn't be killed outright, not without incredible preparation. The best that could be hoped for was to kill this body and hope that there wasn't enough power in the area for it to come back.

Magical creatures were believed to be manifestations of the power in each region, which allowed ordinary animals to grow incredibly potent. Now that she thought about it, she'd never heard if the creature that came back was the same one, or if it was just usually the same kind. *How would you even test that? Unique markings? Even if they were different, that wouldn't prove that the intelligence inside was different...* Magical creatures acted as if they were unconcerned about death, as almost universally they would never retreat, even in the face of certain bodily defeat. There were exceptions, but they were rare. Supposedly, crippling one in a permanent way could get them to retreat, but that was difficult to do, often more difficult than simply killing them. All that considered, did it matter?

Not at the moment. Focus, Tala. "Is this one known?"

Trent was nodding. "It is one of those cataloged in the region, though I don't recall it being spotted in the last fifty years or so. It hasn't engaged caravans in the past." He was scratching his chin. "It is definitely better than some of the others noted nearby." He grunted. "I must go. Please be ready in case we need you."

He turned and rode away just as the wagon jostled her more than usual, and she lost her balance, sitting down hard. "Ow…"

Tala took a long pull from her coffee jug, thinking. *I could crush it, end the fight.* But she was having trouble focusing, and balancing, and with magic in general. Her teeth still hurt from her earlier experiment. *What's this, Tala, not confident?*

She let out an irritated grunt and drank more coffee. *I'll be ready if they need me.*

She deeply hoped that was the truth.

*   *   *

Less than an hour later, they were nearing the mouth of the pass, where the midnight fox waited, sitting back on its haunches, towering over the wagons.

The oxen were understandably skittish, but they were well-trained and well-handled. They wouldn't flee without good cause.

Looks like a good cause to me…

Tala sat near the front of the lead wagon, and Trent, Atrexia, and Renix walked well in front of the oxen, Renix in the middle and a little behind. They had all left their Mage's robes behind, and their spell-lines were fully uncovered. This would not be an easy fight, and they wanted every advantage.

The Mages were close to a hundred feet in front of Den's oxen, and when they stopped, Den pulled his animals to a halt as well, maintaining the distance.

There were irregular waves of power coming from the midnight fox, but Tala couldn't discern the exact source. To her magesight, the red aura of the beast made it look like it was bleeding out a fine mist, which swirled in the air around it. The fox didn't move, maintaining its position in the very center of the surprisingly wide, level pass entrance.

The pass itself stretched out behind the creature, nearly flat and wide enough for two wagons to easily pass with room to spare before the sides rose sharply up.

Yeah, that's definitely not natural.

The fox stood up, power moving up its antlers in waves, sparks jumping between the points.

With a yell, Atrexia countered, and power flowed from the spell-lines around her ankles, through the rock surrounding them.

Spears of stone shot from the ground beside the midnight fox, driving into its body and head and throwing it to the side just as lightning manifested from its antlers.

The spears of stone did not pierce the fox's fur, as power had surged in the fox's horns to counter the attack. Tala could see a sheen of magic, cracked and dissolving, which had sprung into place across the vulpine body.

Even so, the fox's lightning struck out in a cascading cavalcade of repetitive strikes, carving huge furrows in the earth as it skittered towards the Mages. Trent flicked his hand, and Tala thought she might have heard him utter something, but she wasn't sure. Power reached out from his left arm, and the lightning diverted in its leaping path, digging up rock and soil towards the east.

The conflict devolved from there, the fox rolling to its feet and lunging for the Mages, using the motion to throw out another attack.

The strikes, counterstrikes, blocks, and retreats of the four became almost a dance. They never closed the distance between them despite the fox's aggressive movements.

The three humans seemed to be barely holding their own against the massive creature, and Tala had to wonder why it didn't charge, simply tearing them to shreds via tooth, claw, horn, and antler.

Power flashed in the mouth of the pass for nearly a minute before Tala sensed an issue. She stood in a rush, even as the midnight fox must have sensed the same thing. There was a missing piece to the human warding, a gap.

A lance of lightning coalesced, threading through the complex net of defenses the three humans were wielding, striking Renix full in the bare chest.

The young man was thrown backward, tumbling feet over head, again and again, before coming to a rest near the oxen.

Tala quickly focused on him and determined that he'd prevented the power from penetrating his body, even though it had thrown him, and most of his injuries were due to the subsequent tumble across the rough ground. He was covered in scrapes and cuts, already welling with blood.

Millennial Mage 1 - Mageling

She looked back up in time to see the fox pounce atop Atrexia, its leap stopped by a dome of stone, which rose up in two halves to close over the Mage in a protective formation.

A spear of ice, as thick as Tala was tall, drove through the vulpine neck, courtesy of Trent, who had taken advantage of the animal's distraction, but it only seemed to slow the great creature marginally.

Trent called out. "Mistress Tala!"

The midnight fox's eyes turned to regard her, even as its antlers began the short process of charging for another raking lightning cascade.

There was no one between the fox and the caravan now, save the seemingly unconscious Renix.

Tala stared at the antlers, seeing the building power with all too much clarity.

"Tala!"

Her conscious mind frozen in horror, she acted on pure instinct, her right hand coming up as she extended her arm, palm out. Her first two fingers shook slightly as they extended towards the sky, the second two bending down. All four fingers and thumb were tucked close together.

She couldn't take her eyes from the antlers, and thus, as she locked onto her target, only the fox's antlers glowed blue to her sight.

No time to fix it. The lightning was about to be unleashed upon her.

Crush.

Unlike her restraining magic, there was no artistry here, no calculations, no light touch. Her power seized the gravitational constant for the target and dumped power into increasing it.

The fox, sensing the incoming attack, seemed to activate the defensive fields of its horns, causing a glittering field to manifest across its form.

It didn't matter.

One golden ring blazed to light on the back of Tala's outstretched hand, and the fox's head dipped slightly, the effective weight of the antlers quadrupling.

The lightning, it seemed, couldn't be released through the fox's own barrier, so the power still radiated in those metallic points.

Another golden ring blazed with power on the back of Tala's upraised hand before vanishing alongside the first.

The fox's head dropped to the ground as the antlers quadrupled in weight, again.

The animal let out a furious snarl.

A third golden ring flashed away in a blaze of power, and the fox began to try to scramble backward, causing the antlers to unbalance and slam into the ground to the side. It was dragging its head across the soil, the antlers digging trenches. They might have broken off, but the fox's magical defensive field seemed to be protecting them.

A fourth golden circle triggered, and the antlers, now two hundred and fifty-six times as heavy, cracked free from the fox's skull.

Power. Overwhelming, all-consuming power blossomed from the sharp tips, seeking to destroy. The fox's defenses were strong, however, and that power couldn't strike outward through its magical field. Instead, lightning tore through the creature in a brilliant blaze that briefly outshone the sun.

Tala turned away, stumbling as she twisted to shield her eyes, and she sat *hard,* bruising her backside with the awkward landing.

She groaned, rubbing her eyes to clear them before turning back towards the midnight fox.

There was no fox left to see.

Her magesight allowed her to perceive the remnants of the animal's protective shield, just then fading away, allowing a laughably small dusting of ash to fall to the ground.

The midnight fox had been obliterated, entirely, by its own magic.

Tala looked at the back of her hand. *Four. It took four rings, and even then, it only worked by happenstance.*

Her fear had locked her concentration on the antlers alone, instead of the fox as a whole. One ring should have been enough to slay the beast outright, as most creatures were not structured to keep blood flowing when the blood was four times as heavy, and they would usually drop into unconsciousness almost immediately due to shock, to die shortly thereafter.

Still, she'd had a failsafe built in so that when she came across a particularly resilient enemy, the magics would ramp up until death was inevitable. Today, that had both saved her and cost her. *Three castings... wasted.* Her inability to overcome her momentary panic had cost her not only the inscriptions, but the manner of victory had eliminated any possibility of harvesting.

It was the worst sort of victory; the only consolation was that it had been a victory.

She tried to pull herself out of her self-deprecating musings, and as she did so, she saw the earthen dome crumble away, Atrexia quickly taking in the remains of the battle.

Trent was already running towards Renix, and Tala found that Den was already beside the mageling, carefully shifting the man's body to a more natural, prone position.

Atrexia didn't run, but she did take up a quick pace as she returned to the caravan.

Tala unsteadily climbed down the wagon and met Trent beside Renix.

The Mage took in his mageling's state with a careful inspection and sighed. The young man was breathing, though clearly in a lot of pain, even while unconscious.

Trent looked up at Tala and smiled. "Thank you, Mistress Tala. That would have been..." He shook his head. "Thank you."

Tala tried to smile in return but felt sick. *I failed.* She felt like someone who had bludgeoned an attacker to death with a sword, still in its scabbard. Sure, the threat was gone, but she was a clumsy oaf, alive more from luck than anything else.

When she didn't reply, Trent stood from beside Renix and stepped around to her. "Hey? Are you alright?"

Atrexia arrived and immediately attended to Renix, not giving Tala a second glance. Even so, Tala turned away, so that the other woman wouldn't see the tear, which had escaped one eye. "I'll... I'll be fine."

Trent caught her up in a hug. "Thank you, Mistress Tala. No matter what, thank you. I might have been able to protect the caravan, but there was no easy endgame in that fight after it knocked Renix away. Thank you."

Tala hesitantly hugged him in return, silently nodding against his chest before he let her go.

"Go, see if the cooks will get you some food. We'll help Renix back to our wagon and be on the move again soon."

Tala nodded again and strode away in silence, Trent continuing to block her from Atrexia's sight.

Chapter: 34
Aftermath

Tala spoke as little as she reasonably could, both as she asked for something to eat and while requesting a larger-than-usual lunch for herself and the other magic users.

She took a platter back to her wagon, only slipping three times on the way up the ladder. Thankfully, she didn't drop her food. *Well, at least I'm finally readjusting…*

Den smiled back at her as she came up onto the roof. "I think we're ready to go, Mistress. Are you braced for me to start?"

She gave a forced smile in return. "Thank you, Den." She sat. "I'm ready."

Den flicked his reins, and the caravan moved across the broken landscape and into the pass, the wagons' articulated wheels handling the rough terrain with relative ease.

Three guards were riding to the front of the caravan, scouting the way, and she glanced back to see Atrexia standing on the middle-most wagon, eyes scanning their surroundings.

Trent said it would have found us either way.

Was that true?

Probably. It's not like it was far off the path, and a midnight fox, in this pass, would have been… difficult.

Tala had dealt with a truly magical creature and protected the caravan.

From a threat I brought down on us.

Trent had assured her it would have seen them, either way.

She couldn't escape the dual feelings of guilt and shame.

She'd instigated the attack, even if it would have happened either way, and she'd been sloppy in coming to the Mages' aid.

What happened back there, Tala?

She'd frozen. Her eyes had locked on the antlers, and their building magical power, and she hadn't been able to properly target the great beast. Trent had been calling to her for help. She'd offered to help, and she'd... succeeded?

This felt so different from the thunder bull. For that creature, she'd hunted it, going in with a plan, and executing the plan and the animal both. It hadn't been a great plan, but she'd followed through to victory.

This...

The midnight fox had been about to kill her.

Trent *might* have stopped it. Similarly, her iron salve *might* have protected her, but Den would have died, and the cargo wagon, her charge, would have been eliminated. She shuddered to think what would have happened if the cargo-slots were compromised. Violent dimensional realignment might have obliterated the whole caravan.

She snorted a mirthless laugh.

Might have killed the midnight fox, too. Though, its protections had been astoundingly powerful...

She took a bite of her food and reveled in the taste. The food did make her feel a bit better. Every meal, she felt like nothing could be so good again, and every meal, she was proven wrong. She devoured the remainder while continuing her contemplations.

Had fear been behind the hesitation and mistake? *No. At the time, I 'knew' I would survive. Thinking about it now, I realize that I probably wouldn't have, but I didn't know that, then.* She frowned. *I've never stared down an attack before.*

Training didn't really count. She knew her fellow students weren't a threat, and even if they had been, the training room defenses and on-call healers were ready to hand. No student at the academy had died in the course of their training in hundreds of years.

She'd checked.

Even the thunder bull's column of lightning hadn't truly been an attack that she'd had to face down. It had come after she was finished acting and was past before she really comprehended that it was coming.

That must be it. I've never looked upon a worthy opponent and known they were about to try their hardest to strike me down. She almost laughed at her own pretentious thoughts, but it did fit. She could still see the midnight fox's eyes, locked on her, calmly assured that it was about to snuff her from existence.

She shivered.

With the practice she'd recently had, she turned her magesight inward and examined herself.

Her body was flooded with the aftereffects of adrenaline, and she was still trembling with lingering... *Fear?*

Again, that didn't seem right.

Horror? That seemed closer to the mark. Fear was an emotion relating to what *might* happen, while horror was a response to what *was* happening.

She'd fought countless opponents in mock battles, all of whom had tried to best her. Even the thunder bull had struck her with a powerful blow, but the midnight fox... *It had* known *it would be victorious.* And Tala had picked up on that and almost made it true by her own reaction. *Or lack thereof.*

Millennial Mage 1 - Mageling

The terror bird had just been too fast an encounter for conscious thought. *Maybe, I'd have responded the same, there, if given the chance.*

Tala often put forward a confident air despite not usually being truly confident, but she'd never actually seen confidence wielded as a weapon. It was a lesson that she swore to learn.

Her plate clean, and her mind mostly settled, she returned her focus briefly to the world around them.

They were deep in the pass now, the sun not risen sufficiently to shine into the chasm that was the cleft. Thus, they were in deep, cool shade.

It felt wonderful.

She lay back on the roof of the wagon and basked in the cool dimness of it all, breathing regularly.

Long inhale through her nose. Short burst of an exhale through her mouth.

What should I do for the remainder of the morning? She had several books that she still had to read. *Trent will want his book on item crafting theory back...* Her eyes widened. *Oh... I'm an idiot.*

She pulled out the book and flipped back through it until she found the section, exactly as she remembered it.

Every medium has slight variations in the spell-forms required. She groaned. *Air is a new medium to me. Great...*

As she reread the section, she noticed a reference to methodology for discovering the means of inscribing new materials. The book, of course, didn't elaborate, but it was referenced. There was a warning that it was costly, due to the need to use precious metals for each test piece, and it was useless if the Mage only had a small sample of the material, but air was everywhere.

She grinned. *And I'm not using precious metals for the spell-forms.*

She blinked. *I didn't use precious metals for the spell-forms. That shouldn't be possible. Right?*

Tala thought back through her conversations with other Mages. *No, I made my Archon Star deviation in blood. No precious metals there. Archons also make their own stars in all sorts of materials, supposedly. Those spell-forms don't need precious metals. So… The precious metals are only a catalyst, forcing the power through prescribed pathways that are too complex for a human mind to reliably maintain.*

That was fair. *As good a guess as any.* She couldn't possibly maintain all her silver inscriptions in her mind, at all times, and she heavily relied on their monitoring of incoming damage, among other things.

So, the metal is a crutch, if a necessary one? The need for precious metals was a lie. She snorted, again. *Like our early math teachers insisting that we couldn't take a large number from a small number, removing negative numbers from the picture until later lessons.*

That seemed close but still not quite right. *The Archon Star has a form but no function. I've never pushed the power through a mental construct of what it is supposed to do…* The stars felt like a part of her. She sighed and added a book on the uses of Archon Stars to her shopping list.

She returned her thoughts to the main line of her musings: no arcane or magical beast that she knew of had inscriptions. *Do they maintain their spell-forms mentally?* No, that beggared the imagination. They somehow had their spell-forms imprinted on them naturally.

Magical creatures were even more extreme, seemingly completely created by magic. The midnight fox had seemed, somehow, to be *entirely* spell-forms, containing magic and forcing it into the animal's form. She opened one of her notebooks to the back and began copying out all the parts of the midnight fox's internal spell-forms that she could recall. There was a lot.

As she drew out the schemas, she continued her contemplations. The fact that magical creatures were mostly magic was hardly novel information, and it was the core reason why magical beast harvests were so much more valuable than arcane ones. While arcane harvests held vestiges of power, magical parts shaped any power that came into contact with them for an incredibly long time in comparison, in addition to being vastly greater reserves of magical energy. Though, Tala had a nagging feeling that she'd forgotten some caveat to their usefulness. *Can they only ever have one owner?* That might have been it, but it didn't quite fit.

I've still much to learn, and I'm getting all tangled up. There was no possible way that she was the first person to walk this path of thinking, so she needed to seek out books or a teacher if she could find one. *Master Trent has been trying to explain to me the benefits of the mageling-master relationship.*

She sighed.

That tincture's already off the fire.

Still, she could likely find someone to help connect some of the dots.

Plus, books. There are always books. Hopefully, she could find some general texts, along with a more specific one on how to test for inscribing methodology on new materials. *I'm not going to forget about that.*

Now, I just need to figure out how to test my theories on my breath, without becoming a magical beacon...

She spent the morning writing out, modifying, and rejecting hundreds of ideas. Even so, every flawed musing enlightened the overall methodology of her thinking, moving her ever closer towards reasonable possibilities. Around those brainstorming sessions, she continued to illustrate the midnight fox's spell-forms. Thankfully, she didn't have to recreate the whole creature, as most of the fox's magic had been duplicated. Thus, she was just sketching out the unique forms, along with her memory and interpretation of their purposes.

As to magic in her breath, the obvious solution was to practice inside cities, but as she fully intended to spend as much time as possible on trade caravans, that didn't help her much.

While she continued to contemplate that issue, her endingberries came to mind. Specifically, the seeds of destructive energy in their core.

She decided that keeping the endingberries as they were, when they got to the city, was a bad plan. She got a bar of her iron salve, her as-of-yet unused iron flask, and the berries.

With quick, now-practiced motions, she split the berries open and sucked the seeds clean, reveling in the buzz of power. That done, she coated the seeds in iron salve and added them to the others already so treated.

The meat of the berry, she dropped into the iron flask, making sure that all the juices got inside as well.

It was a quick process, and in less than five minutes, she'd processed the last seven berries.

There, now I'm not carrying potentially lethal snacks. She was still carrying the seeds, themselves, but she decided that was fine. *Incremental improvements for the win!*

She sighed, shaking her head at herself. Despite trying to focus her mind on other things, she still felt a seed of discomfort for her part in the morning's battle.

This isn't going away until I deal with it.

She stood up, swaying unsteadily with the movement of the wagon. *This is the rusting worst...* She focused on her balance, forcing her body to maintain her center of mass low and within her feet, and she felt muscles all through her thighs, hips, and legs cry out in protest. *I wasn't moving that differently... Was I?*

Her lower soreness, added to that still residing in her back, made her feel irritable. Well... more irritable.

She sighed, again.

With careful movements, she climbed down off the wagon and jumped out, clear of the wheels, keeping her footing with effort.

She swung by the chuckwagon to drop off her platter and thank the cooks on her way to Renix and Trent's wagon.

Once there, she stepped up onto the back step, took a long breath in through her nose, and exhaled in a near whistle through her mouth.

She knocked.

A man she'd seen on occasion opened the door. "Mistress Tala? Won't you please come in."

He was the servant for Trent's wagon. "Thank you, sir."

She followed his gesture in, allowing him to close the door and shut out what little dust there was.

Renix was resting on his bed, about halfway up the wagon, and Trent was just pulling on his boots. "Mistress Tala? What can we do for you?"

"May I have a seat?"

Trent gestured to the many available places to sit, and she took one. It was a surprisingly comfortable chair, considering it was bolted to the floor of the wagon and looked to have been made as lightly as possible.

"How are you, Renix?"

Renix had pushed himself up into a seated position. "Oh, I'll live. I was tossed quite a way and broke..." He glanced at Trent. "What did Mistress Atrexia say? Thirteen bones?"

"Fifteen, Renix."

Renix nodded. "Right. Fifteen. So, not too bad."

"Including a concussion."

Renix gestured at himself, still in bed. "Hence the bed rest."

Tala was frowning in concern. "She healed you up, right?"

"Oh yeah, of course! I'm right as rain." He leaned his head back against a pillow and sighed, contentedly.

Trent shook his head. "The bones are set right, but a concussion's no small thing. He'll be fine in a day or two though, even without healing. And we'll have the local flesh worker sort him out this evening. A shame Material Mages aren't great at preventing concussions, though."

Tala nodded, relaxing. "I'm glad you'll be alright."

"Oh, I'm hardly that."

She quirked an eyebrow. "I thought...?" She looked to Trent, who was rolling his eyes but didn't comment.

"I didn't get to see you put that mangy beast down!"

It wasn't mangy... Turn of phrase? "I guess, so... It wasn't that impressive."

"Not that...? Are you joking?" Renix looked from Tala to Trent, then back to her. "You turned its magic back on itself, obliterating it outright! I heard you even had it trying to flee before you were done. I've never even heard of a magical animal fleeing. You're incredible!"

Tala was frowning again as she turned to Trent. "Did you tell him this tale?"

The Mage shook his head. "I told the boy it was your story to tell. So, of course, when you weren't ready to hand, he got as many people as he could to tell him."

Tala winced. "I'm sorry, Renix. I really should have come to see how you were right away."

Renix waved her off. "No! It's fine. You have to think over a battle after it passes, analyze what worked, what didn't, and what you could have done better.

Contemplating self-improvement and meditating on what you discover is key to improving as a Mage." The young man beamed, looking to his master for affirmation.

Trent quirked a smile. "Renix is correct, Mistress Tala. The ways of honing one's craft are well known to us, and your delay is most understandable." His eyes were twinkling with hidden mirth.

Tala cleared her throat. *So, a book on Mage meditation and reflecting techniques too.* "Yes, well… I still wish I had come by sooner." She took in a deep breath, smelling the clean but lived-in interior of the wagon. "I froze up and almost got you killed."

Renix rolled his eyes. "Even if that's true, which I doubt, you finished the job."

Tala wanted to argue with him, to beat it into his head that she'd failed, but she realized that even if she succeeded in convincing him, it wouldn't be fair. He was concussed, not fully present. It would be like beating a cripple in a foot race. "Fine, but I still feel that I owe you an apology. Will you forgive me?"

"Absolutely! Done."

She looked to Trent, and he smiled, nodding. "I am grateful that you acted when you did, regardless of the surrounding details. Thank you."

Tala felt as if a great weight had lifted from her. A little voice in the back of her mind tried to tell her that she needed to apologize to Atrexia as well, but she snuffed that idea at its roots. "Thank you, both of you." She smiled, genuinely, as she stood up. "I'll leave you to your rest, Renix."

He smiled in return. "I think we're on the same caravan back, so don't think this is the last you'll see of me!"

She gave a short laugh. "I wouldn't dream of it."

Trent rose with her, his boots firmly in place. "I'll accompany you. I need to join Mistress Atrexia on duty for this last leg."

"Of course." After a short silence as they moved towards the door, she glanced at him. "If I can help…"

He smiled. "I will not hesitate to ask."

Tala and Trent stepped out of the wagon, one after another, and dropped to the ground, moving to the side so the closely following oxen of the wagon behind wouldn't have to slow or divert.

"Thank you, again, Master Trent."

He laughed. "I should be thanking you, honestly. I've fought through tougher spots, but it was about to get *expensive*."

She turned to look at him, questioningly.

"Another point that a master would have made sure you knew of."

She rolled her eyes and started walking along with the caravan, Trent fell into step beside her.

"I mean that to protect the caravan from a powerful attack, at such a distance, would have taken a heavy amount of power and would have eaten through several of my primary defensive inscriptions." He quirked a smile. "You're in a position to not need defensive inscriptions for anyone away from yourself."

She nodded, realizing what he was getting at. "I either disable my opponent, move out of the way, or trust myself to weather the attack. If it isn't directed at me, I can't really do much to stop it."

"Exactly."

She laughed. "I'd make a terrible caravan guard."

He shrugged. "Different skillset. For a larger caravan, or a harvesting expedition, I'd want you on as a striker: someone to take the fight to beasts, while others covered the non-combatants. For a smaller caravan, you should be paired with a shield specialist, or maybe a fast-moving Immaterial Creator?" He shrugged, again.

She felt an easy smile settle in place. "That might actually be some fun, assuming I finish getting my inscriptions."

Trent cocked his head frowning. "You aren't fully inscribed?"

Tala cleared her throat, glancing away a bit sheepishly. "Well, I sort of have money issues, and I got all I could afford." She scratched the side of her neck, absently. "My role in this caravan wasn't even supposed to require the ones I do have." She barked a mirthless laugh. "That didn't quite work out."

Trent snorted. "Too true. Even so, if you're working with half a deck, you're all the more impressive for pulling winning hands, again and again."

"Gambling metaphor? Really?"

"Are you saying what you've been doing is anything else?"

She grunted a laugh. "Fair, I suppose."

"So, with the payday this evening, will you be finishing out? Getting inscriptions in a waning city is expensive."

"I wish, even with the added expense. Mistress Holly's really the only one I trust to do it right, though." To her surprise, she realized that that was actually true. The inscriber was a bit inscrutable, but her work had proven itself.

"Wait, Mistress Holly, herself, actually did your work? *The* Mistress Holly?"

When Tala shrugged, then nodded, Trent whistled.

"Man. You really must be something special. She only bothers with one Mage in a thousand. Her apprentices do most of it, though even having her modifications and ideas implemented on you would set your work as a cut above. It's one reason I like being based out of Bandfast. Her work is second to none." He shook his head ruefully. "You are full of surprises, Mistress Tala."

Chapter: 35
Power Aplenty

Tala was frowning. *Holly can't be* that *special. I mean, she helped me a lot, but any inscriber would have done the same, right?* She knew that her own reticence to have another work on her proved that notion false, but she still didn't relent. "How does the inscriber matter that much?"

Trent shrugged. "Aside from the obvious need for a steady hand? It's the mind behind the inscriptions. It matters less for work on Mages than for item construction, because *our* minds come into play, but it still matters. A good inscriber has to mesh their thinking with the Mage they are working for and harmonize that Mage's capabilities, power, and ways of thinking with the inscriptions used. There's no one who works on Mages who's better than Holly." He smiled ruefully. "I've heard that there are a few inscribers that work exclusively with Archons, but you'll likely have better knowledge on that before I do."

"Huh. I had no idea." She briefly thought of the complex inscription on the back of her neck, ostensibly keeping record of much of what she did, and how. *So, Holly had more in mind for this, than simply keeping me from running off or some other such nonsense?*

"How did you connect with her?"

"A contact with the Caravan Guild, a friend, introduced me to her."

"Your handler, Mistress Lyn?"

Tala shrugged. "Started that way, yeah."

"Glad you're getting along with them. Bad blood, there, can really hurt you." He smiled, again. "It sounds like they're treating you well, too."

"Yeah, she really is." Tala looked up, past the caravan and towards the head of the pass. She could see sunlight on a few hills that peeked up high enough to be visible from her vantage. "I'm still trying to get a grasp on things." She glanced towards Trent. "Thank you for your kindness."

He shrugged. "Not hard to resist being a rust bucket."

Tala snorted, again. "Fair enough."

"We already discussed the commission we earn for protecting the caravan, remember?"

She cocked her head at the sudden change of topic, frowning slightly. "Yeah?"

"Magical creatures have a higher bounty—mainly because they generally cost so much more in inscriptions to deal with."

"Oh?"

"That one was a Bound, so the payout will be five gold."

Tala almost gasped. "For one attack?"

Trent sighed. "I'll need two of that to replace my inscriptions, even with the discount. If I guess right, Atrexia and Renix will each need between half and a full ounce for the same."

She grunted. "Even with how quick the fight was?"

He laughed. "Half the magics involved were negating each other. I doubt it looked like much."

Tala thought back to what her magesight had been showing her through the battle and realized that he was telling the truth. As she'd watched, it was as if the four combatants had been clashing with spell-forms rather than the effects that the spell-forms were meant to produce. Only the occasional magic was able to fully manifest its intended purpose. "I'd not thought of it in those terms before."

Trent shrugged. "It's a hard thing to convey if you haven't seen it."

"So, the whole bounty's spoken for, eh?"

He smiled. "Money trouble, right?"

"Fly's already in the ointment; no reason to deny it, now."

He laughed. "I think a half-ounce gold can be spared for your contributions. I'll have to verify with Atrexia, but I doubt she'll fight me too hard. It would have cost her a lot, too, if you hadn't intervened."

"Half an ounce, eh?" That would have been incredibly generous if she'd used her own magic correctly. As it was, that wouldn't even cover the cost of the inscriptions she had to replace. Still, it was something. "Thank you. That does help."

"Wish I could offer more."

She shrugged. "It's quite generous. My own bumbling isn't your fault."

He patted her shoulder comfortingly. "Want to talk about it?"

"Not now… Maybe on the trip back, in a few days?"

"Fair enough."

They'd been slowly outpacing the caravan, moving up the line as it continued forward, and were finally coming up beside the lead wagon.

"I've got to go check in with Atrexia. Take the day to rest. Recover and think about the fight. You did well for your first battle with a magical animal. Don't be too hard on yourself."

"I'll try. Thank you."

She pulled herself up onto the top of the wagon as Trent turned and walked back towards the center of the caravan. Atrexia was still up on the central wagon, scanning their surroundings with an ever-sweeping gaze. Tala could sense the woman's magesight from here.

She's a bit nervous. Tala couldn't blame her.

With a sigh, Tala sank into a comfortable seated position, looking forward.

Hey! I didn't trip. Thinking back, she could tell that she'd been mostly balanced as she moved, but she had fallen a little back towards her previous way of walking. Her aching legs and low back attested to the fact that she was moving in the right direction, but she swore to herself that she'd be more attentive going forward.

She'd check in with Adam after lunch, but she was fairly certain that his 'next step' would be to practice the foundational material he'd already given her.

Very well. I've much to improve, and time waits for no one.

Wait… Time is an immaterial thing. She gasped. *Are there time Mages?* She thought back through all the inscription theories and couldn't recall a single mention of such, which was a bit strange. Her teachers had gone out of their way to explain the few things that were definitively not possible through magic, the main one that had stood out to her being the 'from scratch' creation of a free-willed lifeform.

But she was getting off track. *Time magic… what would it even do?* She knew that some incredibly powerful gravity Mages could alter the flow of time minutely, but anything that would be affected was also destroyed under the astronomically amplified forces.

But can we modify the flow of time, directly?

It seems that she had yet another subject to research. *It's becoming quite the long list… Maybe, there's a book.*

She groaned. *Tala… focus. You don't really understand time, so you'd need to get a grasp on how it actually works before you could even consider altering it.* She snorted a laugh. *Maybe humans can't truly understand time. That would make time Mages impossible, even if the magic could exist, theoretically. No wonder our teachers never spoke about it. No reason to open a rancid fruit.*

She pulled her mind back to the present and returned to basics. *Breathe.*

After five minutes of breathing, Tala stood up and moved through her stretches atop the moving wagon. Allowing half of her mind to remain focused on her breathing, she tuned in her balance. To her surprise, the internal focus activated her magesight, and she was able to perceive her own body, the minute contraction of various muscles, the exact points of weakness and her center of balance.

It was especially odd as her iron salve kept her magesight from seeing beyond herself, containing the sight, and if anything, amplifying it.

She could move the focus back out, through her eyes, but that would make the internal awareness fade somewhat. *Another thing to practice.* She grinned.

With an exact map of how each muscle in her body responded to her desires, she was able to modify her movements to an incredible degree. She could perfectly stretch any muscle and isolate any fiber of any muscle for individual contraction… In theory, at least.

In practice? It wasn't perfect, as her mind wasn't used to sending such specified commands.

She'd been wielding her body like a hammer in the dark.

It's time to be a… She hesitated, holding a precariously balanced stretch, her leg muscles twitching in sequence to compensate for the sway of the wagon. She couldn't think of a good metaphor. *Well, rust.*

One of her stabilizing muscles, deep in the hip of her planted leg, seized up. Tala dropped to her knees, the knuckles of her left-hand driving into her hip, trying to relieve the pain. It was excruciating, her heightened focus making the pain much more acute than it would otherwise have been.

No. Focus, Tala! She narrowed her sight in on the spasmodically twitching muscle group, increasing her awareness of the pain many times over, as well.

She gritted her teeth and bent her mind towards the muscle fibers. *Release!*

They relaxed.

Oh... my... She let out a relieved breath. *That would have been—*

The muscles jerked in once more, contracting violently, responding to the build-up of bio-chemicals within.

Cursing to herself, under her breath, she bore down, turning her will upon the rebellious portion of her musculature, but as much as she desired, her muscles were not perfectly subject to her will.

Power, however, was.

Magic swept through her hip. It was relatively unfocused, but it responded to her directive, and the muscles of her hip were soothed, forcibly.

She flopped back onto her back, gasping, both hands clutching at her hip to guard against the lingering pain.

"Ow..."

She felt exhausted, fully spent: mind, body, will, and soul.

"Well... pain's gone... mostly." She groaned, not sitting up. "Maybe... maybe, I should take a little nap."

* * *

Tala woke from her short nap to the smell of food.

She sat up groggily, just in time to see Brand scale the last portion of the ladder with a platter of food.

"Lunch's here."

"Thank you!" She shook off the remnants of sleep and accepted the proffered meal. It was at least three times what she would normally eat, but it looked just about right. "Do you have—" She stopped with a laugh as he pulled a jug out from behind his back, where it had been hanging from a leather strap. "You brought coffee."

"Of course! I always felt bad pouring out the leftovers, but most people don't like it when it's not fresh." He shrugged. "Waste not, and all that."

"Well, thank you, regardless of the reasons."

Brand smiled as he climbed back down the ladder. "Of course! When we get into the city, come find me, and I'll make the promised introductions."

"Will do."

The sun was now easily reaching them. They were nearing the end of the pass, and it was nearly noon. Because it was late autumn, the sun looked to be ahead of her, out the mouth of the valley to the south. As such, it was a bit of a pain to look at what lay ahead, at least without her hat.

She pulled the hat a little lower as she dug into the food.

She'd heard someone else bring Den his lunch, while Brand was delivering to her, and she was glad to know that the driver was enjoying similar fare. *This is delicious.*

The coffee was cold, but she didn't really care. *I might have a problem.*

While she ate one of the beef pasties, she flipped through her various books, taking notes and consolidating her to-do list.

It was going to be a busy couple of days in Alefast. *Hopefully, the waning city will have the resources that I need.* She looked to the back of her hand, where only nineteen small golden circles remained. *Dare I wait for Holly?*

Things hadn't really been standard, and she'd used less than half her castings, but what if things were worse on the way back?

I'll take the first day to do the most dangerous stuff, and if I have to use more than another casting or two, I'll get a new set of rings inscribed.

She nodded to herself. It was a reasonable compromise.

Her first stop this evening would be a blacksmith, after meeting Brand's contact, of course.

And meeting with the Caravan Guild's representative for payment and to send messages.

But after that, a blacksmith. *My request shouldn't be too odd.* She snorted. *Except that it'll be a Mage requesting a farm implement. And out of as pure iron as they can manage.* She sighed. *I don't do subtle well, do I?*

True to his word, Adam swung by after lunch, and true to her guess, he simply emphasized focusing on the basics. He wanted her to let her body adjust and to strengthen the muscles that 'spoke' to her.

She agreed, and he confirmed that he would be on the caravan trip back. They'd continue her training, then, assuming she'd made good progress while in Alefast.

He was still on duty, so he left after their brief exchange of words, and Tala returned to her stretching and inner focus.

As she moved, she was careful to monitor the condition of her muscles, both ensuring that she pushed every part of herself and that she didn't go too far and strain anything else.

She still ached, deep in her hip. *Right, massage. I need to schedule… half a day is probably too long.* She sighed. *I'll see if anyone is available on short notice.*

Every so often, she shook the iron flask containing the paltry few endingberries she still had. *I want this filled.*

Trent had promised to point her to a grove of ending trees. If her visit to the blacksmith went well, she should be able to go to the grove and get back tomorrow, an easy harvest in hand.

She was just setting the flask aside once more when her wagon came over the top of the long rise of the pass, exiting at the same time.

Before her, a new world spread out, rolling hills basked in the sun, some grassy, others covered in trees.

A city was just more than a half-dozen miles distant, and she could already see how different it was from Bandfast, if only because of its nature as a waning city.

Only the innermost wall still stood.

There were no farms, no bustling industry, and no rings of towers protecting the outermost reaches.

The Wild had reclaimed everything once held by the city.

Small stands of trees that looked ancient grew right up near the white city walls. Deep shadows were easy to see, despite the hour, and the dark green of the leaves spoke of abundant life.

The air practically vibrated with magical power, and she could almost *feel* the plants growing around her.

The world is healing the wound of the human city, magic swelling to speed up the process even as our spell-lines and magics fade. This city had less than three decades remaining before the last walls fell. In that time, it would be the center of the most dangerous, and most profitable, harvesting expeditions.

There was magic to spare in the lands surrounding the city, and people were ready to collect on that, bringing power and utility back to the rest of humanity, for the betterment of all.

The cycle continues.

Millennial Mage 1 - Mageling

Aside from the trade caravan, she didn't see any other humans moving outside the city, and her magesight couldn't penetrate the defenses around the city.

Make no mistake, the defenses weren't blocking her sight so much as filling it with so much information anything from beyond it was unrecognizable.

She blinked rapidly and turned her focus away. She felt slightly nauseous. *Bandfast's defenses are nothing compared to these.* That made sense. Alefast now had to stand as a bastion against truly magical creatures, not just arcane, and midnight foxes weren't close to the most powerful among them.

Even aside from the plants that seemed to be growing so quickly that they almost moved as she watched them, she saw the ripples of magic from countless arcane animals bounding, hunting, and living within the landscape.

It was like finding a jungle after living in the desert.

This was the magical equivalent of verdant fields. She was used to highland, arid farming.

Amazing. Even the academy hadn't had this high a density of magic.

The arcane beasts kept their distance from the caravan, but she could sense them, even if she couldn't see them.

She could also occasionally still sense flickers of dimensional energy, near the edge of her range. *It's still out there... great.* She'd been hoping that it would stay on the other side of the pass.

As they trundled on down through the foothills, Tala caught glimpses of magical animals and beasts watching them.

Surprisingly, nothing made a move on the caravan, and after a bit of contemplation, she realized why. *There's nothing for them to gain. They live off power, and here, there is power aplenty.*

She glanced back towards Alefast and the beacon of magic that it was.

Human cities, in their early years, drained most of the power from the surrounding lands, providing protection by weakening the magic of anything that would come against it. As such, nothing powerful attacked them. The crazy would-be-emperor's road had been an exception because it completely cut off paths and routes, instead of simply being an irritating, prickly obstacle to move around.

As the city aged, the land would compensate, slowly increasing ambient magic in the region to balance it out until the rate of increase outpaced what the city could draw in. The result was a surge of power that coincided with the city's final years. Thus, allowing the enemies of mankind easy access to assault the walls.

After humans left the city, and the spell-lines lost the remnants of their functionality, magic in the region would level out, slowly returning to what it once had been.

A surprisingly mellow, cyclical war of attrition.

She returned from her musings, scanning their surroundings. Even though the creatures around them had no instinctive reason to attack, many magical creatures were sapient, and some might choose to attack on a whim or for some unknown purpose. For whatever reason, the more powerful magical creatures were, the more they seemed to dislike humanity. *Yet another thing my teachers couldn't, or wouldn't, explain...*

Given the potential for such powerful attackers, Trent and Atrexia were obvious in their diligence, allowing their defensive power to color the caravan to any with the magesight to see it.

In a land full of fruit, why dig through a thorn bush for berries, dried on the branch?

Maybe my venture won't be as dangerous as I'd feared? It was a bit of a fool's hope, and she wouldn't allow it to draw her into complacency, but she did allow it to lift her mood.

Two days in and around Alefast, then back on the road. Back home. She smiled. It was still new, but she was, indeed, making a home for herself in Bandfast.

I am still beholden to those I live with. It soured her thoughts, just slightly. She knew that Lyn genuinely liked her, but she had no illusions about the woman's first priority, which was to their indentured master. Like virtually everyone. Lyn bent to the whims of her contract even as Tala, herself, did.

Focus on the good. Work to change the bad. She did *not* think of her father's kind voice, speaking that truism.

If she'd judged the distance correctly, they had less than three hours left before reaching Alefast, and if patterns held, the workyard would be just inside the gates.

I could run ahead. She snorted a laugh. *I could walk ahead and arrive in half the time.* Still, she only considered it for a moment. While she was technically within her rights to do so, it would set a bad impression, and the wrong impression with the wrong people could severely hamper her contract opportunities, under her indenture, going forward.

Thus, she settled in to wait. She did, after all, have books to finish.

Chapter: 36
Through the Gatehouse

Tala closed the item creation primer and looked up just in time to see a group of caravan guards returning from the city gates, which were now only a few hundred yards away.

Adam was in the group, and while the others moved on to the wagons farther back, Adam paused to speak to Den, turning his horse to ride alongside their wagon.

Tala moved closer, and Adam smiled before speaking loudly enough to include her. "We're going to have to surrender to an inspection."

Den groaned. "Why? That is not the standard, Guardsman. You're delaying my delivery of goods."

Tala blinked in surprise. She'd never heard Den take that tone with anyone. Additionally, it conveyed to her that Adam was somehow subordinate to Den. *Wait... Den always chose the campsites. He directed our paths of travel...*

She found herself dumbstruck. *Den is in charge of the caravan. He just doesn't bother with minutia.*

She remembered the Mages looking her way when deciding how to change their path on the first day. *No, not my way. They were checking if Den was going to comment.*

That actually made a lot of sense.

She returned her mind to the conversation in time to hear Adam's calm, if deferring, response.

"I understand, First Driver, but it seems that a particularly mischievous magical entity attempted to breach the city in the last week by disguising itself as a caravan."

Den seemed taken aback at that as he took a moment to respond. "It disguised itself as a caravan wagon?"

Adam shook his head. "No, as an entire caravan. Wagons, oxen, drivers, even outriders."

"So… many working together."

Again, Adam shook his head. "Apparently, the Prime of this city's defenses verified it for herself. It was one entity."

"Huh…" Den scratched his head. "Well, I suppose that would make them a bit jumpy…" He grunted. "Fine, fine. What's the process?"

"Each wagon will need to stop within the gatehouse for a minute, while two Mages sweep it for deviation. Everyone not on a wagon will be separately inspected. It is encouraged that anyone who can, should go through the personal inspection, rather than being included in the general wagon scan."

Tala barked a laugh. "I'll pass, thank you."

Den glanced back at her and smiled. "You're welcome to stay with the wagon, Mistress."

Adam opened his mouth, likely to object, then seemed to think better of it, shrugging instead. "They didn't mandate it. You're lead wagon, so just stop within the gatehouse."

Den sighed. "So, if we're at all suspect, they can drop the portcullis on both sides, locking us in."

"It is what it is, First Driver."

"And it will be as it will be."

Adam grinned, bowed slightly to Den, then Tala, and wheeled his horse around to carry the information farther back.

Den eyed Tala. "You ever heard of something like that, Mistress? An entity taking multiple separate forms?"

She shook her head, then paused. "Well, I'm still rather... inexperienced, but I believe it is possible that such could be faked if each form were linked somehow that wasn't easily noticed... Shadows? Invisible tendrils?" She shrugged. "Just a shot in the dark, though." As she considered she smiled slightly. "Expect them to drop the portcullis."

He looked at her in alarm. "They'd only do that to trap us."

"Or, to put iron between us and the rest of the caravan."

He looked confused.

She sighed. "Iron can interfere with most types of magic. If we are of one being with the rest of the caravan, dropping iron between us could sever that connection, revealing a fake."

"Could?"

"I'm just guessing, but I thought I'd let you know, so you don't panic if the iron comes down."

He still looked nervous as they approached the gatehouse, but he didn't waver.

The gatehouse was a massive monument of strength and power. It had been crafted with skill and had been maintained with care. It didn't look like it had survived more than three hundred years. As she considered it, Tala realized that it had probably been built when this became the outer wall. *More efficient than maintaining gatehouses for every circle for the full life of the city, I suppose.*

The archway was wide enough for two of Den's wagons to pass side by side, reminding her of the pass they'd just gone through. As they entered the first arch, the wagon sliding into the building's shadowed interior, Tala looked up at the thick iron portcullis, held ready to descend.

Each iron strip in the basket weave was close to an inch thick, and the bottoms were wedged into spikes and blades.

Millennial Mage 1 - Mageling

They weren't razor-sharp, but with what must be at least two tons of iron behind it, they didn't need to be.

Den was eyeing the inside of the gatehouse as he slowed the oxen to a stop.

There were arrow slits to either side and murder holes above. They both knew that magically facilitated death could be poured out upon them in apocalyptic quantities through those openings—and likely through the solid stone of the walls, themselves.

The oxen came to a stop in very nearly the exact center of the darkened interior. Den had not allowed his trepidation to hamper his performance.

The wagon behind theirs had stopped just outside the gatehouse and was awaiting instruction. Tala could clearly hear a guard inside the second level of the gate, shouting down to the secondary wagon, but before she could focus in on that conversation, she felt magical senses sweep over them. There was a brief hesitation, then the portcullises dropped.

Tala saw them begin to fall and quickly clasped her hands over Den's ears, shielding them from the deafening racket.

The oxen were not so lucky, and Den had to fight them back into stillness after the sudden noise.

Tala, for her part, had trusted in the noise suppression inscriptions around her ears, and they had not failed her.

Any noise that came close to her ears was scaled down and suppressed until it was no longer of a harmful level. *Thank you, again, Holly.*

"Rust me to slag." Den glanced at Tala, even as her hands moved away. "Thank you. I couldn't let go of the reins, and that was *loud.*"

She smiled back. "Happy to help."

One of the murder holes opened, almost directly above them, and a Mage looked out.

Tala focused on him, and instantly, she could see him in his entirety, though only with her magesight. *Material Creator. He specializes in water? No...* She looked closer. It wasn't ice. *Acid? There are Mages who specialize in the creation of incredibly caustic acid?* She did *not* like the idea of that. Her iron salve would do nothing against acid created above and dropped on her head, and her protective inscriptions might be overwhelmed by a constant acid burn. She had no way to negate it, and that made her quite unhappy.

She met the man's gaze, knowing his magesight was active, and also knowing that she would look quite odd to him. "Well?"

He flinched back just slightly. "What are you?"

"I'm a *very* cranky Mage, whom you are keeping from her destination."

"How are you doing that? It's not like an Archon's veil at all..." He gestured through the hole, vaguely in her direction. Den glanced her way, cocking an eyebrow.

"How do I exist? How am I standing? How am I talking...? You really need to be more specific." *Really, Tala? Antagonizing the person who can kill you?*

"How are you invisible to my magesight, except your eyes... and palms?"

"Do Mages not have secrets in this city? We're clearly human, and you are delaying this shipment from entering. On what grounds are you delaying?"

The man narrowed his eyes. "Based on the fact that an unknown humanoid entity is on the lead wagon."

"You're joking."

A voice drifted from behind the man. "He's not."

Tala followed the second voice with her eyes, and her magesight showed her another Mage, waiting out of normal sight. *Material Creator, again...* She couldn't figure out what he focused on, though. It was some

Millennial Mage 1 - Mageling

complex biochemical, which was definitely not acid, but... *Venom? Poison?* Probably both. *Great. Yet another Mage whom I couldn't easily survive.* She frowned. Those were incredibly violent specialties, with virtually no use outside of overwhelmingly bringing death.

Well, mister acid could be on garbage disposal or some such...

"So... what now?"

"You tell me what you are."

"I already have."

"If you were a human Mage, your spell-lines would be glowing like the sun to my magesight. They just look like someone drew on you."

"Peeking is rude without permission."

"Then grant permission."

"I can't; I'm passively defended from magesight."

That truly seemed to stump the acid Mage. The sound of a shifting chair came from above, and the second voice murmured to the first, though loud enough for Tala to catch it. "Is the guy human?"

"Well, yes."

"And are the big things oxen?"

"Yes."

"And the wagon?"

"Checks out."

"So...?"

"She still doesn't look right."

"Rude!" Tala called out. The two men above stopped talking, and Den gave her an aghast look.

"Mistress Tala? What are you doing?" His voice came out as a harsh whisper.

The acid Mage's face reappeared. "So, superhuman hearing, eh? Not really giving credence to your claim."

Tala rubbed one hand across her face in frustrated irritation. "This is going nowhere. Listen to your friend, and let us through. If I'm not human, the city's defenses will fry me anyways, right?" She tilted her head to the side, showing her neck, free of any collar.

Again, poison man spoke quietly to acid. "She has a point."

"Shut up. She can probably still hear you. She might have found a collar that would work for her! Or something similar…" He sounded quite irritated.

"And a reasonable-sounding gentleman he is," Tala interjected. *You just can't shut up, can you…?*

There was a long pause as another person, non-Mage, came in to demand an explanation for the hold-up. Acid argued with the man, who turned out to be the gatehouse commander, but poison didn't back him up. So, it ended with acid being commanded to let them through.

Tala smiled, patting Den on the shoulder. "We're good."

Den looked uncertain but nodded his thanks. "I hope so…" He glanced her way. "Did you have to antagonize them?"

"They were being rude."

"They were doing their job."

After a moment, she grunted irritably. "Fine… you're right. Sorry about that."

The iron latticework lifted slowly back out of the way, both in front and behind them.

Acid spoke one last time. "Head on through to the workyard. It's to the right once you exit the gatehouse."

"Thank you!" Den called up, waving to the man as he flicked the reins, ushering the oxen into movement once more. As they came back out into sunlight, he glanced at her. "Next time, if there is a next time, would you mind doing the personalized inspection instead?" He seemed a bit hesitant as he said it.

She huffed a laugh and shook her head. "Fair's fair. I'll try not to be a source of your stress, again."

Millennial Mage 1 - Mageling

He snorted. "Don't make pretty, false promises, girl. You'll be a source of my stress for years. I can feel it."

He continued to watch her out of the corner of his eye, and she turned to fully face Den. "That is one of the nicest things anyone has ever said to me."

He barked a laugh. "You remind me of my brother's youngest daughter." He shook his head. "Too smart for her own good, that one, and she wants everyone to know it."

"That... is hurtfully accurate." She flopped down on the driver's bench beside him, even as he guided the oxen through the muster yard behind the gatehouse, and over to what was clearly the workyard, lined by stone warehouses. *A bit foolish to put the warehouses right up against the wall, but I suppose if anything could reach over the wall to harm the city, the defenses are as good as breached, so convenience takes precedence.*

The other wagons were not delayed nearly as long, and the portcullis stayed up.

Even so, it was almost an hour before all the wagons joined Den's in the workyard, and a contingent of city guards came out with a group of officials to greet them.

Den exchanged pleasantries with one of the men as Tala dropped off the wagon to store her things in the box and face the Mage who came to inspect the cargo-slots. *Immaterial Creator, dimensionally focused.*

The Mage ran her hand over each of the hand-shaped charging panels and looked closely at the indicators. She flicked at the wood of the cargo-slots themselves and poked around the edges of the wagon.

Tala, eventually, cleared her throat. "So... is everything in order?"

The Mage stuck out a stone slate in one hand. "Blood here."

Tala took the slate and read over it. It was a testament that she was Mage Tala and that the cargo had not been compromised on the trip; that she had kept the cargo-slots charged, would continue to do so for the next two days, and was now passing responsibility for the contents over to the waning city of Alefast.

Tala nodded along as she read the document. Finally, she pulled a small bit of power into her finger, while moving her defenses away, and pricked it on the sharpened nub of stone in one corner, moving to allow a drop of blood to fall onto the magical device.

The blood vanished on contact, and the stone flickered with light. After the flicker passed, new text at the bottom simply stated that her identity was confirmed, and the contract had been accepted.

Tala smiled, handing the slate back.

The Mage glanced at it, then nodded. "Very good. Would you like payment to be credited to your account, or would you like waning notes for the value of your payment?"

Tala frowned. "Not coins?"

"Oh no, dear." She glanced at Tala, again. "You've not been to a waning city before, I'd wager."

Tala shook her head.

"The precious metals are in much too high a demand to be used as coinage, here. They'd simply be melted down and sold as raw materials…" She hesitated. "I'd be happy to take any coins off your hands and place their value into your account, with a ten percent increase, of course."

Tala's eyes bulged. *I can make ten percent on my currency, just by bringing it here?*

Den cleared his throat as he finished his own conversation and moved to join Tala. "Ten percent? Is that really what you are offering?"

The Mage colored slightly. "It was meant as an opening offer."

Millennial Mage 1 - Mageling

Den laughed. "Mistress Tala. It is standard for gold, silver, and copper to be worth at least a quarter more than their stamped value in a waning city at this stage. As I understand it, that is one reason Mages *try* to avoid being inscribed in such cities, whenever possible. It is just too expensive."

That made a lot of sense. It also explained why Trent had estimated his expenses for inscription refreshment to be so high. *Well, that makes my decision easier. No reinscribing for me.* "It does make sense that metal would be at a premium in the last years of the city." She looked back to the Mage. "I think I'll keep my coinage and use it to trade for goods and services. My payment may be placed directly into my account." Every person in all the human cities had an account linked to their blood. Only Mages could use it easily, but it was effectively an unbreakable medium of exchange. Hers had many debts linked to it, but they wouldn't draw on her balance unless she fell drastically behind on her payments.

The Mage bowed. "As you will. The master moneychanger will see to it that you are paid." She gestured towards a table off to the side, where a line of caravan workers was already queuing up.

As Tala walked across the hard-packed earth of the workyard, she saw the last of the passengers departing, carrying their bags into the city or loading them onto waiting transport, which would do the same.

Workers were already wheeling out a great crane to pull the cargo-slots free of the wagon, and Tala found herself somewhat sad to see them actively disassembling the top of the vehicle to get access to the magically maintained cargo. *It's been a fun few days.* She had the trip back, which would come sooner than she likely realized, but it still felt like an ending. *I'll get over it.*

She walked with Den over to the payment line and took a position at the end.

Several of the servants and drivers who were waiting ahead of her looked back in confusion, seeming to expect her to have walked to the front. When she didn't move, they turned back towards their destination and their pay.

The line moved quickly, and it wasn't long before Tala approached the head of the line.

The only wrinkle came when Trent, Renix, and Atrexia had walked over, and Trent, along with Renix, joined Tala in waiting. Atrexia huffed a bit but didn't end up contesting the issue.

Renix, for his part, looked markedly better, seemingly mostly recovered from his concussion. *Rest does wonders, I suppose.*

Tala let the three go ahead of her and did her best not to listen in while they discussed things with the payment officer.

Her efforts were aided by Brand, who had already spoken to the man, and who came over to stand with her.

"Mistress Tala! We're here." He smiled as he walked up to her.

"Seems so." She returned the smile.

"I heard there was some issue in the gatehouse?"

She shrugged. "Nothing major."

After a moment's pause, Brand turned to regard her more fully. "Really? Not going to tell me any more than that?"

She gestured to Den, who waved farewell in their direction as he walked off. "You could always ask him."

Brand grunted. "Fair enough. I'll have the whole trip back for that, however, and I've promises to keep!"

She quirked a smile. "Sounds good. After I deal with this."

Millennial Mage 1 - Mageling

Trent, Atrexia, and Renix all moved off to the side, where they settled in to discuss the next few days.

Tala stepped forward.

"Name and position."

"Tala, Dimensional Storage Mage."

The man grunted. "You're the source of all this complexity, then."

Tala frowned. "What?"

He spun a slate around, showing her an itemization:

Five-and-a-half ounces gold for services rendered as a Dimensional Mage. One ounce gold for helping to deal with two threats to the caravan. Less two ounces silver for services rendered by Mage Trent. Less one ounce silver for equipment requisitioned from Head Cook Brand.

"Does that look correct?"

She frowned, thinking back. "Yeah. I believe so."

"You authorize the funds mentioned to pay the debts described, and you'd like the balance deposited into your account?"

"Yes, please."

He took the tablet back and made a couple of notes on it. "Very good. Blood here."

She took the tablet back and pricked her finger, letting a lightly infused drop vanish into the stone.

"Very good. Six ounces gold, forty-seven ounces silver has been credited to your account. Is there anything else I can assist you with today?"

"Actually, yes. I need to add an addendum to my field log to inform my guild contact of a few things."

"Such as?"

"One is a communication for the Wainwright's Guild, who are currently building out a set of cargo-slots for me."

The man grunted. "Very well." He handed her a blank slate and a stone cylinder that was similar in size and shape to a pencil.

Tala quickly used them to scribe a note to Lyn, asking her to deliver messages to both the Wainwright's Guild and to Holly, and then she quickly wrote out those missives. As the stone pen moved across the slate, it was as if darker rock bled up through the tablet, leaving her words incorporated into the very nature of the stone. "Thank you." She held it out to him.

He touched it to another tablet that he'd been working on, and a new square darkened. "Blood here."

She repeated the confirmation process, and the slate faded back to blank.

"Now, if that is all?"

"It is, thank you." She bowed slightly, walking to the side, where Brand was patiently waiting. "Shall we?"

Chapter: 37
A Spinner of Tales

As Tala walked up to Brand, ready to depart the workyard and truly enter the city of Alefast, Renix came over as well.

"Mistress Tala?" He seemed mostly better, but he still had a bit of a far-off look in his eyes.

"Yes?"

"Master Trent asked me to give this to you." He held out a rolled piece of thick paper.

Tala unrolled it and identified it as a map with a small patch of trees emphasized. "Ahh, yes. Thank you." She turned to look around, but Trent and Atrexia were already gone. *Looking for an available flesh worker?*

"I'm also to tell you that we will be staying at the Wandering Magician, and you can find us either in residence or leave any of us a message in the next couple of days. If you need lodging, it is also a reasonable place for a reasonable price."

Brand interjected. "He's right. It's one of the better-valued establishments in the city. They'll treat you right."

"Thank you, Renix, and you, Brand."

Renix bowed with a smile. "Absolutely. We're going to go get my head looked at now." He smiled ruefully. After that, he hesitated for a moment, glancing at Brand, but Renix seemed to decide against saying anything further, except for, "Good evening, Mistress. I look forward to seeing you again."

"Good evening, Renix. Take care."

With nothing further, Renix turned and departed as well, even as Tala turned her attention to Brand.

"So, your contact?"

"Let's grab your stuff, first." He led her over to a hand cart, which was propped to one side, and they took it back to the cargo wagon. Den's wagon was in a state of complete dismantlement, from the wagon bed up. The cargo-slots had been lifted free and were arranged for easy unloading the next day. The roof and sides had been disconnected to allow those cargo-slots to be removed, and the pieces lay neatly stacked off to one side.

Together, Brand and Tala quickly emptied her rather full box into the hand cart.

"One more stop." He led her to the chuckwagon, where he called over one of the warehouse workers to help him move a medium-sized, but obviously rather dense, package and add it to the cart. Brand thanked the man and turned back to Tala. "You didn't think I'd forgotten your jerky, did you?" He smiled. "Alright! Let's go."

Tala kept her eyes sweeping over their surroundings as Brand led her a couple of blocks to an open-air market. He had tried to insist on being the one to pull the cart, but she had flatly refused. He was not her porter.

The streets were wide, but not so wide as to feel cavernously empty with the diminished population.

There were people going about their daily lives, though they seemed more hardened folk than the average in Bandfast had been. *They're on the tail end of civilization and are holding on for profit and glory.* They were likely among the hardiest of humanity.

The architecture was functionally aesthetic. While it was beautiful to behold, all details and embellishments had been designed so that they would, and obviously had, survive the ravages of time and centuries of weathering, thus they were not as intricate as they might otherwise have been.

The market was a large, open square with temporary, sturdy stalls erected and manned by more of the hardened citizenry.

Brand helped her navigate the late afternoon traffic. The space wasn't packed, but it was still a bit crowded. Before they entered the market proper, Brand had advised her to turn the cart around, to push in front of herself, and he walked beside her. As they walked, he was clearly keeping a close eye on anyone who got too close to the handcart.

"Would someone really steal from a Mage?"

Brand huffed a laugh. "If they thought they could get away with it? Yeah."

"Huh…"

Near the far side of the market from where they'd entered, Brand led her to a stall, which was set up in front of the open front of a clearly well-established shop.

"BRAND!" A boisterous, slightly rotund woman strode forth and scooped him up in a voluminous hug. "I didn't expect you back until next season. What changed?"

Tala tried to direct her attention elsewhere, away from the private moment. Brand's muffled response came from within the embrace. "We decided we wanted to get the kids something special for their name-days this coming year, and an opportunity came up to head this way."

"Well, that makes vastly too much sense." The big woman placed him back on the ground. "How's Lissa? The kids?"

"Very well, thank you. Is Adrill still alive?" His eyes flicked towards Tala. She was inspecting the contents of the cart.

"Ahh, the old goat's still living. He's down in his workshop, searching for new ways to destroy my store." The woman turned to Tala. "Good day, Mistress. I am

Artia, owner of this fine store. If you need anything pertaining to magic, I would recommend a Mage such as yourself seek out the Constructionist Guild, three streets to the north."

Tala glanced to Brand, who was out of Artia's line of sight, and he made his thumb and forefinger into a circle. Tala frowned slightly. He mouthed, "Token."

"Oh!" Tala reached into a pouch at her belt and pulled out the iron coin, upon which was stamped a scythe. "I believe this would mean something to you."

Artia looked hesitant but still took the offered coin. Immediately, she froze in evident shock, looking back and forth between Tala and the token. "Well"—she glanced to Brand, who was beaming—"in that case…" She cleared her throat and put on a smile. "This is the best and only place in our fine city to find items of magic."

Brand cleared his throat, and Artia turned a raised eyebrow his way.

Finally, she grunted. "There are several *lesser* merchants of arcane-related items, but they will never have what you *need* and certainly not the very best!"

Tala grinned. "Didn't you mention the Constructionist Guild?"

Atria waved that off, still looking at the token. "Mage drivel. Not a decent merchant among them."

Brand cleared his throat. "You might be a bit biased."

Tala found herself grinning. "I am Tala." She held out her hand, and Artia took it in a firm grasp.

"A pleasure, Mage Tala." The larger woman seemed a bit uncertain if she truly believed that. "I suppose we should get your cart out of the street and learn a bit more about each other. Shall we?" She handed the token back.

"I'd be delighted."

They took her handcart down a small side alley and tucked it into a walled, back courtyard, where it would, ostensibly, be safe.

As they walked back to the storefront, Tala cleared her throat. "Actually, I am in desperate need of a blacksmith. Would it be possible for me to quickly swing by one nearby, while the two of you catch up? I shouldn't be gone more than half an hour."

Artia gave her a quizzical look, then shrugged. "Works for me, dear. There's a good one about five blocks that way." She pointed south.

Tala gave a slight bow and strode off in that direction without a backward glance.

As she walked, she heard Artia turn to Brand and whisper, "What does a Mage want with a blacksmith? Why did you bring her here? Why does she have a Harvest token?"

"I've learned it's best not to ask. As to the other questions, we'll resolve that soon enough."

"Hmmm... odd girl." Artia tsked. "Should be an interesting evening, though. A Mage! And she's not trying to unravel the Order?"

"I genuinely think that she isn't."

"Good, but I'll have to—" The rest was lost as Tala continued to move farther away, not giving any indication that she heard or even knew that they were speaking.

Interesting. It should, indeed, be a fun evening.

Tala found the smith exactly where Artia said it would be, and the sound of hammer on iron drew her on for the last couple of streets. She came up to the entrance of the work area and called out. "Ho, in the smithy!"

The hammering didn't slow, but she saw other movement within the workshop as a middle-aged man walked out. "Well good day to you, miss-"—his eyes

501

widened as he got a better look at her—"-tress. How can this humble smithy serve, this day?"

Tala quirked a smile. "No need for that, good master. I have a commission for you if you feel up to finishing by early tomorrow."

The man frowned, glancing behind himself. "No good blade will be made in an evening." He hesitated. "Not one that I'd be confident to sell in any rate."

She held up a hand. "It is much simpler than that, sir. What I want can be likened to a simple woven basket on a pole."

He scratched his head. "Like a fruit picker? Aren't those usually woven out of reeds or wooden slats?"

She clapped her hands together and grinned. "Oh! You've seen them. That makes this so much easier."

He nodded. "My gran had a couple of orchards, and we used the tools quite extensively when I was a boy."

"Then you are a better workman than I could have hoped for. I want one of iron, not steel, with holes small enough that it can catch small pickings, say a small cherry?"

"Yeah… we can do that. By tomorrow morning?"

"Yes, please. And I'd appreciate two pairs of iron pliers if you have them on hand."

He looked at her again, clearly assessing her. He paused and brief confusion flickered across his features as he noticed her shoeless feet. *I guess he doesn't see many Mages.* "Umm… A silver each for the pliers, and four for the iron picker."

She grinned. "And you haven't even given me your name." She shook her head.

The man paled, then reddened. "My apologies, Mistress! I'm Pedrin."

"Good master Pedrin. I will happily give you a silver for the two pairs of pliers, and another for the picker."

He opened his mouth to object, but she held up a hand to forestall him.

"I will, of course, pay in advance, and you will receive an additional silver in the morning, upon my receipt of the tool." She pulled her hand out of a pouch, holding up two silver, one-ounce coins. "I will be paying in hard coinage." She smiled, noting the slight additional widening of his eyes. "Naturally."

She watched him do the quick math, and he obviously realized that the total value of her offer was still below six ounces of silver, but not egregiously so, given the extra value of the metal itself. So, he nodded. "I think we can do that, Mistress."

She held the coins out towards him. "I request the pole be at least ten feet long but no longer than you feel reasonable, given your experience, and of a sturdy, solid hardwood. Additionally, I request the right to collect some of your iron dust, should I find the need."

Pedrin blinked at her in confusion. "Iron... dust?"

She shrugged. "I simply mean the dust that covers this very smithy. I've no need for anything else, and I will warn you beforehand. You can even watch my collection of such if you so desire."

After another hesitant moment, he nodded and took the coins. "Do you want the pliers now or in the morning?"

"I will trust in your good name, master Pedrin, and I will pick up all three tools tomorrow."

He gave a slight bow. "As you say, Mistress. Have a wonderful evening."

"And you as well."

With that, she turned and strode back for Artia's shop, leaving a somewhat stymied, but happy, smith in her wake.

*   *   *

Millennial Mage 1 - Mageling

Tala returned to Artia's store to find the woman and Brand sitting behind the stall in two comfortable chairs, sipping from earthenware mugs and chatting amiably.

As she walked into view, Artia stood, smiling, and gestured at a third chair. "Come, sit! Did you find the blacksmith to your liking?"

"I believe so. Thank you. I can now focus on our conversation without feeling the need to run off."

Artia bowed slightly before returning to her seat.

Tala sat as well and smiled. "So, have you two caught up, or should I make myself scarce, again?"

Artia handed her a drink, and Tala accepted it gratefully. "Why don't you expose the Order of the Harvest and have them disbanded?"

Tala hesitated for a moment, then sipped the drink. "Mint tea, chilled, right?"

Artia nodded.

Tala smiled. "What would I gain?"

"Excuse me?"

"For shutting you down. What could I possibly gain?"

Artia seemed taken aback. "I don't pretend to know the minds of Mages."

Tala snorted a laugh. "That's exactly what you're doing. You assume that, because you've had bad experiences with Mages in the past, all Mages will be the same." She quirked an eyebrow questioningly.

"Well... I suppose..."

"You spoke to one Mage, who made a sweeping judgment without all the facts. What you're doing sounded dangerous, because it is, and he erred on the side of caution, as Mages are wont to do. It was your ill fortune that caused the Mage in question to have enough authority to issue a wide-ranging edict that enforced..." Tala trailed off, realizing something. "You've never checked..."

Artia and Brand looked at each other, then back to her. Brand frowned. "What do you mean?"

Tala laughed. "You got the response of one Mage, and he was so forceful in the response that you assumed he was speaking on behalf of all. Do you know if your work is actually forbidden, or do you just assume so?"

Brand opened his mouth, then closed it, looking puzzled. Artia took a drink, then shook her head. "It's been more than a hundred years, dear. It is *known* that we cannot speak to Mages on this. Every initiate to our Order is sworn to keep this from Mage eyes and knowledge. We have extensive guild contracts in place to keep Mages from poking into the businesses of guilds associated with the Order."

"Yet, I've never heard of eating arcanous meat as being barred." Tala hesitated. "Granted, that could just be me, but I can certainly look into it. The other Mages in the caravan didn't really have an opinion on it, one way or other, when I spoke to them before asking Brand." *A hundred years?* She hadn't realized that the notes had covered that long of a timeframe.

Artia paled, slightly. "There are more?"

Tala shrugged. "They know they were fed arcanous meat, and that's it. I shared nothing further after I learned it, as it wasn't mine to share."

Artia and Brand shared another look.

"So… are the surprise questions out of the way, or…?"

Artia smiled broadly. "I think I like you, girl." Her eyes widened fractionally. "Ummm… Mistress."

Tala waved her down. "Tala is fine, and I am a girl, so…" She shrugged again. "Fair assessment, I suppose?" She looked down at herself, noting the red-dipped sleeves and spotted front. "I really should see a tailor, though…"

Brand perked up. "I can recommend a good one."

"I'd appreciate that, but for now"—she turned to Artia—"I need to sell some arcanous parts, and I need some dimensional storage." She quirked a smile. "My handcart should bear witness to both of those things."

Artia glanced to Brand, who nodded encouragingly. "Very well. Come on into my shop."

The three stood to walk inside. Before they entered, Artia called out, "Brandon!" and a young man, likely a little older than Tala, came from the darkened interior. "Brandon, be a dear and mind the stall, would you? If Master Brand is correct, the newly arrived caravan guards might be coming by to sell some harvests. Call me if they do and you need me. Yes?"

"Yes, Mother." He turned from her and froze, staring at Tala.

Tala smiled as she walked past, but otherwise, she didn't acknowledge him. There was something… off about him. Her magesight didn't give any clues on casual inspection. If anything, something seemed missing, but she couldn't really place it. She didn't want to deal with the oddity at the moment, so she chose to ignore it.

From inside the shop, she heard Brandon whisper to his mother.

"Who is she?"

"A Mage, obviously."

"A beautiful Mage."

"Brandon! Mind the stall."

"Are you sure? I could…"

There was the sound of a light slap to what Tala presumed was the back of Brandon's head, and she grinned without turning around. *It is nice to be appreciated for me, I suppose.*

Brand and Artia followed shortly thereafter, and Artia cleared her throat. "Well, apologies for the delay, Mistress. Shall I show you around?"

Tala turned her attention, for the first time, to the interior of the large but well-filled shop around her.

One wall held racks of weapons, and the opposite wall held packs and bags, belts and straps. Tables and cabinets neatly arranged in between held every manner of item from eyes in clear jars of pickling juice and fur pelts to razor blades and spoons.

Every item gave off an aura of magical power, whether she could see an inscription on the surface or not.

She let out an involuntary gasp of amazement. "What…?"

Artia walked forward, clearly pleased with herself. "These are our wares, dear. Items of magic and power. There are some arcane or magical beast harvests, some artifacts of earlier eras, and the rest are constructed and empowered items, awaiting use by Mage or man." She grinned. "What do you desire?"

Tala immediately walked over to a short-bladed knife that spoke loudly to her magesight about sharpness and durability. The magic around and throughout the piece was twisted in and through itself in strangely familiar, yet somehow entirely alien patterns. "What is this?"

"Ahh! Good eye. That is an artifact blade. It never chips or shatters, never needs cleaning, and is always as sharp as a razor."

Tala frowned. "I don't see any inscriptions. No source of power. There aren't any arcane or magical parts sealed inside, either." She couldn't fully pierce the steel of the knife's construction, but she could see well enough to determine that the material was uniform and solid the whole way through, as were the magical loops and knots woven through the material.

"As I said, an artifact blade. Never needs to consume harvest parts and never has to be refreshed. It simply is."

Millennial Mage 1 - Mageling

Tala turned a deeply skeptical look towards Brand. "You promised me a solid contact, not a spinner of tales."

Brand paled. "Mistress Tala!"

Tala held up her hand. "There is no way that this would just be sitting here if it had such power."

Artia laughed. "Calm down, Brand. She's both right and wrong." She turned to look Tala in the eyes. "It is as I said, and just as I said. It won't pierce magical defenses, and is no more than a simple knife." She smiled. "Sure, it's a nice knife, and you never have to sharpen it or worry about it breaking, but given a normal, very serviceable knife can be purchased for less than a silver, and one such as that is not hard to keep sharp, buying this one for half a gold isn't really something most people will care to do."

Tala glanced back at the knife. "A half-ounce of gold?"

"A real bargain." She chuckled. "But not worth it to most. I picked it up from a hunter, assuming some well-off patron would find it interesting and not mind the cost too much."

Tala's frown had returned. "Why wouldn't the Mages want this to study?"

"Never been to a waning city, have you?"

Tala shook her head. "What's that got to do with it?"

"The way it's been explained to me is this: as magic gathers around a waning city, it bends the world, drawing in all sorts of things of magic. Most are creatures, large and small, but some are items like this knife. It doesn't draw them in in the sense of moving them, but it does, somehow, make it more likely that hunters will find them in the ruins scattered all about." She patted Tala on the arm. "Oh, sure, you can hunt ruins anytime if you want to put your life in your hands, but those around a waning city?" She stepped back and gestured around her shop. "Those always seem to have more despite centuries of hunters combing through them first."

Chapter: 38
Little Shop of Wonders

Tala grunted, looking around at the magical items filling Artia's little shop. *What if artifacts really do show up more often, here?* "Huh... Well, assuming it's true"—she looked at the knife again—"and I can't see any reason to put that to lie, I apologize for misjudging you."

"No offense taken, Mistress."

Yeah... right... Tala put the knife down. "So, all the items without spell-lines are like that? Artifacts of magic?"

"Most of the items, yes."

Tala walked over to the wall of bags and found that many of them seemed to *warp* beneath her magesight, calling to her, beckoning her to look closer. Each of those was obviously a dimensional storage, and most didn't have spell lines.

Those without spell-lines, and some with, had a *very* familiar feel to them despite a similar looping, twisting spiral pattern that was, again, familiar but not. *The underlying magic creates an effect like the cargo-slots...* "Mages study these items to learn spell-forms."

Artia made a happy sound. "That had always been my husband Adrill's, theory, though no Mage would ever take the time to discuss it with an uninscribed."

"I'm getting the feeling that you all aren't great at finding accommodating Mages."

"With all due respect, Mistress, I think I may have met more Mages than you have."

Millennial Mage 1 - Mageling

Tala turned to regard Artia. After a long pause, she nodded. "I suppose that's probably true." She frowned. *Are Mages really so...? Yeah.* As she thought back to her time in school, she had to acknowledge that most Mages, even most Mages in training, were not very kind to non-Mages. "Fair's fair, I suppose. I never really got on well with most Mages anyways..." She felt a sadness flick through her but suppressed it. *Now's not the time.* "So, these bags...Why are *they* here? No downside I can imagine. So, why haven't they been snapped up?"

"Ahh! Yes. They degrade quickly once taken outside of the high-magic region around a waning city unless consistently fed large amounts of magic." After a moment, Artia amended, "At least, that is what I understand, not being a Mage myself."

"Really?" Tala smiled. "That's quite interesting." She picked one up, keeping watch on Artia from the corner of her eye to ensure the woman didn't object to her doing so. She didn't. "Does it simply take a raw power dump, or is it like empowering a storage wagon?"

Artia shrugged. "Not a Mage, dear." After a brief pause, she added, "My husband would know more, and if you choose one of the bags, we can discuss a trade for any information he can offer."

Tala quirked a smile. "Fair enough. Even so, I'd think these would have substantial use around your fair city. Why do you have..." She did a quick count. "Ten? Why do you have ten in stock?"

"That is a similar situation to the knife, dear. Sure, dimensional storage is useful, but they are *very* expensive for simple, local use. Even so, they really aren't that rare, so those who want them, buy them." She shrugged. "We've enough travelers that come through and want to rent them while in town that it pays to keep them on hand and not lower the price. That and locals rent them out, too, on occasion. Most folks don't need to have a dimensional storage of their own."

"And that price is?"

Artia looked at Brand, and he nodded. "Well, as a member of the Order of the Harvest, we will bundle your purchases and give you a discount."

"…But I won't know what I can afford unless you give me a starting price."

"To rent one of those bags would be ten ounces silver per day, and the policy is: if you rent it for a year, it's yours."

Tala blinked. "There is no way you charge almost forty ounces gold for one of those."

"No? They never need to be reinscribed, and they never need new power sources, so long as you stay local. A standard dimensional storage would cost you five ounces gold, plus another ounce for a power source. Then, you'll need to reinscribe it every three months or so, to be safe, for another four ounces gold, and you'll need another power source every four months or so. When a year has passed, you've spent, what? Twenty-five ounces gold? And you'll have to spend another nineteen, give or take, every year, forever, or the item loses all power and value. That isn't even factoring in the increased cost of magical metals in a waning city. I think forty to never concern yourself with that is a bargain."

Put that way, it was quite hard to argue with. "I don't have forty ounces gold…"

Artia patted her on the shoulder. "I assumed not, dear. You haven't any shoes."

Tala glared, but there wasn't any malice behind it. "I prefer to be barefoot." *She really doesn't interact much with many Mages.*

"Sure you do, dear. I understand."

"You know, you're a bit of a—"

"Um…" Brand stepped forward, quietly cutting her off. "I believe that this is going off track. Mistress Tala, there are likely arrangements that could be made, in lieu of monetary payment. You do, for example, have quite a few harvests to trade with, yes?"

Tala looked away from Artia and deflated slightly. "You are right, as usual, Brand." She glanced back at Artia. "I do not appreciate condescension. I am aware that many of your clientele are of the type to loosen their purses simply to prove you wrong. I am not one of them, and I would appreciate it if you'd forgo such tactics, for the sake of our amicable relationship." *There. Maturely handled, Tala.*

Artia smiled slightly. "Very well, *Mistress*. I will not attempt to maneuver you. Shall we look at what all we have to interest you here?"

Tala nodded her agreement. Then, an oddity struck her. "Wait…"

Artia paused, looking quizzically in her direction.

"If the bags degrade in normal or low-magic areas, how could they be found in ruins? This area is only high magic because of the waning city, and thus the bags couldn't have remained intact for the centuries since their creation."

The shop owner stared at her. "That… is an excellent question, actually." She frowned. "It is possible that the item is an artifact, and the magic inhabiting it is new?" She thought for a moment. "That does actually align with more of the details that I know." She turned back to fully face Tala. "I suppose that I should express a couple of things about artifacts because you are new to them."

Tala tried not to give a frustrated sigh. "Any information would be appreciated."

Artia nodded, consolingly. "First, artifacts… change over time. They seem to adapt to the uses they are put to and the peculiarities of their owners." She hesitated, then shrugged. "This is speculation, but I've heard of some…

older Mages whose use of artifacts seems to have modified them far more heavily than in other cases. I don't know why."

"Hmmm. Interesting. And the second thing?"

"Artifacts can be dangerous. There haven't been too many incidents in recent memory, but anyone who deals in artifacts is trained to look for certain things. There are storage bags that look like other dimensional storage artifacts but have a tendency to… eat their user."

Tala blinked several times. "What."

Artia held up her hands placatingly. "All those have some commonalities, and we watch for them carefully. All the storage I have, I've rented out hundreds of times, and they are tried and true. There were also early instances, hundreds of years ago, and in other cities, obviously, where some knives would be found in their owners' hearts, driven clean through the bone. Could have been foul play, but they have similar… threads? Yes, threads, which can be seen with magesight or items that allow similar sight."

"So… none of your items will kill me."

"They shouldn't. Though clean items have been observed to develop in that way if their owner harbored suicidal tendencies. Again, the items seem to mold to their user over time."

"So, be careful what you wish for, and don't be depressed."

Artia snorted. "Sure, if that's what you want to take from it. Also, if you ever come across an artifact, whether in the Wilds, ruins, or in this city, have a reputable dealer examine it for you. I am happy to do it myself, free of charge. I don't wish harm to come to you."

"In the Wilds? The city? Madam Artia, how could unknown artifacts simply be laying around?"

Artia shrugged. "No idea, but it happens. Some claim to have seen artifacts appear from nothing or a burst of magic to manifest atop an item, rendering it an artifact, but I've never put much stock in those rumors or tales."

"But you pass them on?"

She shrugged again. "I'd rather share hearsay than allow you to be taken unaware. I'm glad that you will exercise caution."

Tala grunted. "Fair enough. Thank you."

In the end, Tala had a moderately sized pile of items on the shop counter, which included a theoretically permanent storage bag. It was the shape of a belt pouch and roughly as large as her two fists pressed together but could hold as much as a large storage closet.

She'd picked it for several reasons: First, it could only open to just over a foot and a half in radius, and thus was restrictive in what could be stored inside. This made it seem to be the least valuable of those Artia had on hand.

Second, its twistings of dimensional magic seemed to include defensive measures—unlike any other that she'd seen. If she understood them correctly, and that was a big if, the bag could subtly shift space around itself to be out of the way of any but a direct attack on the pouch. She didn't know how it would respond to area attacks.

Artia did not seem to realize this added effect, and Tala was not about to enlighten her. Third, more than any of the others, its warping of space reminded her of her own mental constructs for dimensional reshaping. It simply felt *right* to her. It practically *called* to her.

I'll have to experiment with it a bit.

Aside from the pouch, Tala grabbed a drop-point artifact knife of the same kind as the short-bladed one she'd examined earlier. This handle fit her hand better, and the blade was a bit longer, lending utility without becoming unwieldy. The metal of the knife she chose looked like standard steel, which was not the case for all those available. The scales of the handle were what looked and felt like smooth, cool stone, pinned in place with bright, silver rivets.

Despite the apparent slick smoothness of the surface, the handle felt incredibly secure in her hand, almost as if it were clinging to her, as well. The stone was a lovely grey, white, and red-flecked black, and it reminded her of a hazy night's sky.

As she'd examined the artifact knives on display, she'd noticed that each had an odd *depth* to their magic, as if there were far more within each knife than the simple, surface enchantments. There was also a small pocket of emptiness, where something seemed to be missing from the magic, or where it could have something added but didn't have to have such. It was a fairly odd thing to see.

To the knife and storage, she added three artifacts that she'd picked almost at random but without letting that show—to the best of her ability. One was a wooden comb that untangled hair with a single stroke. The second, a whistle that only those friendly to the blower could hear. Third, a simple stone coin that always landed face up when flipped and would cool water to just above freezing when placed within it. Artia made sure she understood that it ceased to work in any liquid other than pure water. Tala acknowledged that and took it anyways.

There were supposedly a whole host of other items that Tala could look through, but she already suspected that she was well past her budget.

Therefore, that done, the three of them went out to Tala's handcart and looked over what she was willing to sell.

She had eight talons and six leg bones from a blade wing and one horn from the thunder bull. She'd prefer to keep two of the leg bones, and she additionally had right around a hundred pounds of thunder bull jerky if she needed to tip the scales.

Millennial Mage 1 - Mageling

You know, I think I'd prefer to keep the jerky than the leg bones if it comes down to it.

Artia pulled out a small eyepiece, and Tala immediately focused on it, seeing within it a magic akin to her own magesight, if more limited.

Another artifact? She wasn't lying when she said they were everywhere, it seems. Tala almost laughed at herself. *That? That's what convinces me?* She'd just been searching through a store *filled* with such items, but it seemed that this casual display was what tipped the scales in her mind.

Artia picked up one of the talons and examined it through her eyepiece before sighing. "I'm sorry, Mistress, but these are useless. All traces of power are utterly gone. I've never seen them fade so fast, but it must just be bad luck."

Brand seem flabbergasted. "What? That's impossible! It's only been a few days since those were harvested."

Artia shrugged. "I don't know what to tell you."

Tala smiled. "I do. They haven't degraded."

Artia gave her a long-suffering look. "I'm not seeing any magic."

Tala took out her own knife and took the talon from Artia. Then, as the woman watched through her eyepiece, Tala scraped her knife along the talon's surface, removing most of the layer of iron salve, which had set as an outer layer.

Artia almost gasped as she snatched the talon from Tala, examining the small opening through which magic poured. She rubbed her thumb across the surface, working the surrounding salve into movement to re-cover the small hole, and the magical light faded to Tala's magesight.

"Sealed, somehow? You coated them with something to contain the power and keep it from degrading?"

Tala nodded.

"Then, these are all as potent as if just harvested." The woman looked utterly astonished.

Tala made a hesitant sound. "I'd say they are as fresh as if harvested within the last few hours. Likely less, but I don't wish to oversell."

Artia cocked an eyebrow. "Really? After that little demonstration?"

"It is what it is." But Tala was grinning.

"Well, if a hunter brought in a fresh harvest, I'd likely be able to give a gold per talon, and three per bone." She lifted a finger. "Honestly, the larger pair would fetch four, and the smaller pair two each, but it still averages to three, which is the value of the middling set." She glanced to Brand. "As Brand stands for you, I do not need to verify the source of your goods, and I can trust that they are what they appear. The thunder bull's horn is an interesting find, as the power it contains is mainly used for shattering defenses, though some fools take that power and invert it to heal maladies of the skeletal system." She shook her head. "Why they don't use the beast's bones is beyond me, but Mages are an inscrutable bunch, and I suppose I'm no Constructionist."

Tala cocked an eyebrow but didn't comment.

Artia cleared her throat. "The horn is easily worth four or five ounces gold. Now, normally, I'd have to pass on some of these as I have no ready buyers, and everyone knows that harvests kept out of an iron box degrade quickly, and even in one they don't have an eternity to wait. I was going to make an exception, but it seems I don't have to." She looked up to the left for a moment, seemingly to do some calculations. "So, all told, that puts the valuation of your harvests, generously, at thirty-one ounces gold. I could never give you that much if I simply bought them from you, but as part of an exchange, I think we can consider that full valuation. The value of the items you selected inside is still higher, though."

Thirty-one ounces! Rust keeping two bones as fighting sticks, I'm selling all of it. She nearly had a fit of joyous dancing but did her best to keep it hidden. She remembered how her father would alter prices based on the cut and quality of a customer's clothing, and she'd needed to not only keep the numbers straight but not let on that it was anything other than the ordinary price. Tala nodded. "Shall we return inside?"

Artia had been about to continue but frowned slightly before nodding. "As you wish."

They walked inside, returning to Tala's small pile. Tala looked around at the merchandise once more. "Wait. The harvests are sitting out…?"

Artia smiled. "These are past the point of selling—too degraded, unfortunately—and they are simply out for display purposes, demonstrating the type of thing we can acquire. It takes a very long time for the last vestiges of power to finally leave an item, and until then, the type of power they have is still easy to verify."

Tala nodded. That made a good deal of sense. She gestured to her small pile, turning away from the shop at large. "What is the value we have here?"

Artia looked at Tala with suspicion but continued. "Well, that is the least of our bags, so I'd normally part with it for thirty-five gold, the knife is half an ounce, and the coin is one ounce, the whistle two, and comb really should be three, but I'll part with it for two."

Tala nodded but didn't say anything further, simply flicking a glance to Brand before returning her focus to Artia.

The shopkeeper sighed. "Because you are at least working with the Order, I'm willing to bundle these all together and part with them for an even thirty-five ounces."

Tala almost grinned. *She must rarely have use for this smaller dimensional storage bag. She's willing to be quite flexible on the price.* "So…?"

"So, if I take all your items, and you wish all of these, the balance would be four ounces gold, from you to me."

Tala nodded. "That seems quite fair."

Artia smiled broadly, opening her mouth to conclude, but Tala continued.

"Unfortunately, I'm not in a place to spare four ounces gold at this time. While the coin would provide many pleasantly cool drinks, I do not think I can justify it at this time." She moved the stone coin aside.

Artia nodded, opening her mouth, but again, Tala continued.

"And the whistle could be a boon in a pinch, but it really isn't an effective use of my resources at this time." Even as she placed the whistle with the coin, she tittered a laugh as if to herself. "And if I can't justify such an obviously helpful item, I certainly can't allow myself to splurge on a comb." She nodded, as if conceding a point, and moved the comb over to beside the other two items. "And as you said, those together were valued at…" She paused as if she hadn't calculated beforehand. "Five ounces gold."

"I did say that, but—"

Tala continued as if she hadn't heard the woman. "Thus, if my figuring is correct, I'm asking for thirty ounces of product, and I have offered thirty-one ounces in payment. I do hope that it won't be too much trouble to transfer a gold ounce to my account?"

Artia blinked at her a few times, then sighed. "You planned that, right? You preselected those three items to nudge the numbers around."

Tala shrugged. "Yes and no. If it had worked out, I'd have loved to get every item here, and those stood out as interesting, for one reason or other. I'm sorry that they won't come into my ownership at this time."

Artia huffed a laugh. "Fine, girl. It's not worth fighting you. But no, I'll not transfer the ounce. We'll do an even trade, and we'll both be happy about it. Yes?"

Tala thought for a moment, then nodded, extending her hand. "Very well. Thank you." She had to contain her excitement, partially at her exchange and partially at what a piece of her mind had just discovered, or thought that it had. While most of her attention had been taken up with the transaction at hand, a small portion of her mind had been puzzling over the mysterious, miniature void in the pommel of the various artifact knives, the place where the magic seemed to be waiting for something. In truth, such was evident in most of the artifacts, though the positioning and ease of finding the small voids varied from type to type.

And a possible answer had just clicked.

Tala concluded her business with Artia. Part of that was getting assurances that nowhere south of the pass, within a day's walk, would have low enough magic to harm her new pouch. She promised to return the following evening to discuss dimensional storage with Artia's husband and join them for dinner.

Without further delay, she shoved her remaining things, including her backpack, satchel, and jerky, into her new belt pouch and departed.

Chapter: 39
The Wandering Magician

Tala glanced up as she walked back out into the market, noting the ever-present dome of magic above her head. She'd decided that she liked the view from this side much more and found herself smiling as she basked in the magical glow that few, other than she, could easily see. *What Mage would spend their inscriptions to stare at the sky?*

Despite her revelry, she walked quickly through the market, looking for her final purchase of the day.

She found a barrel seller near the western end of the market and was able to purchase a small, iron-bound keg and two glass jugs for two silver. The keg was just small enough to fit into her belt pouch and had a top ready to hammer into place, once it was filled. It was advertised to be able to hold just over two gallons, and that was *perfect*. The jugs were each just over a gallon, so the contents of the two would fill the keg quite nicely. Until then, they had sturdy, swing-top closures to seal openings that were almost wide enough for her to fit her hand in.

Those purchases complete, via stone slate rather than coinage, she moved towards the inn in which the others were staying. *No reason to take the time to hunt up accommodations when others have done the work in advance.*

Millennial Mage 1 - Mageling

She asked several people that she passed where she could find the Wandering Magician, and she was given unerring directions.

She'd almost asked Brand for his tailor recommendations, but she could deal with that tomorrow when she got back. Right now, she wanted nothing more than a meal and her own room.

The streets were busy but not crowded, and she enjoyed people-watching as she moved through the city.

There were definitely a higher proportion of Mages, or at least people with some inscriptions, than she was used to. She had to remind herself that while most people got inscriptions of various kinds at some point throughout their lives, only Mages were devoted to perfecting the magical arts, and only they received a keystone inscription. More than half her time at the Academy had been devoted to her understanding of that one complex spell-form. It was what truly set Mages apart and allowed the truly impressive magics to function.

She smiled, bringing herself back from her musing. The amount of magic in the city, and the area at large, was staggering. *I could get used to it, here.* That was, if she didn't have a job... *There are caravans to and from this city once a month, or so. I could come here quite often if I wished.* And that was just from Bandfast. *I could go through other cities, as well...* It bore considering.

Finally, she arrived at the inn and found it to be a four-story, sprawling complex set within small, but well-appointed, grounds. "Inexpensive, huh?"

The sign over the gate proudly proclaimed the name of the establishment, along with an iconograph: a simple image of a staff with a star shining from the top.

An Archon Star? That was unlikely. It was probably just an easy way to symbolize power.

Before passing under the archway, she noted a guard standing to either side, watching her.

Tala passed under the sign and heard someone call out to her. "Oy! State your name and business. We've no use for vagrants, here."

She turned to the man, frowning. *I'm obviously a Mage. Why can't he…? Oh…* She hadn't really noticed the fading light of early sunset because her eyes didn't need nearly as much illumination and adjusted so smoothly it didn't merit her attention. Now, in moderate twilight, she would be little more than a vague shape to their eyes. *A tattered shape, at that.* "I am Mistress Tala, Mage of the Caravanners' Guild."

That earned a surprised exclamation.

"I am here in search of food and lodging. Have I come to the right place?"

"Let me get a look at you." The man who had spoken pulled out a round bit of wood, and Tala saw power swirling around it, evoking the concept of light. Sure enough, as the guard moved his finger across the item, light blossomed forth.

Wonders never cease. It appeared to be an artifact, as no inscriptions were ready-to-sight.

"Oh! My apologies, Mistress, we didn't see you very clearly and…"

Tala grinned. "I look a bit like a vagrant in the dark?"

The man cleared his throat. "No offense intended, Mistress."

"None given. I've had a long week, but my wardrobe has seen the worst of it. I'm just glad I didn't have to walk in here naked."

The guard colored just slightly. "Yes… well, that would have been… bad."

Tala paused for a moment before shifting slightly. "May I…?" She glanced farther into the complex.

Millennial Mage 1 - Mageling

"Oh! Of course. You have a wonderful night, Mistress. Welcome to the Wandering Magician."

Tala gave a nod of acknowledgment and strode up the path to the main building. It was a grand structure, clearly built to weather the centuries, but it maintained a sense of elegance despite its age. The massive double doors opened as she approached, and she found herself walking into a quiet lobby, what looked to be a pond taking up one side of the relatively large space.

She focused briefly, scanning the water, and saw that there were, indeed, many fish. In fact, if she understood her sight properly, some were quite old but still vital. She wouldn't be surprised to find out that some of the fish had been there since the founding of the city. *What a horrible existence... But probably really nice for a fish? No predators and all.*

She didn't give it further thought.

An older woman with silver-white hair and a straight, strong posture stepped forward to greet her. The matron scanned Tala with discerning eyes before nodding. "Mistress. Welcome to the Wandering Magician."

Tala gave a slight bow. "Thank you, Matron."

"A room for one?"

Tala thought for a moment. "Yes, please. Something on the ground floor would be preferred, on the exterior of the building's east side, if it's available at no extra cost." After a moment, she continued, "I would deeply appreciate a bath if one is available, and food."

The matron nodded to each request. "Could I send for a seamstress, and commission some garments on your behalf?"

Tala hesitated. What she was requesting already felt *very* expensive, and someone else doing her negotiating felt more so. "I am still a new Mage and..."

The matron held up her hand. "I am familiar with the... constraints felt by many new Mages and magelings. We will consider cost in all our services to you and keep you apprised of anything that may not be in keeping with this aspect of your desires."

Tala blinked at her. *That was quite politically worded.* "Thank you. If I may, so I have a basis for comparison: what will three nights here cost?"

The Matron smiled. "A room is five ounces silver per night, and use of the baths is an additional one ounce silver per night. Meals are two for a silver, though, if you wish, we will sell you one at no markup."

Tala nodded. *Tonight, tomorrow, and the night after; baths, obviously; dinner tonight, breakfast and dinner tomorrow, three meals the next day, and breakfast my final morning is seven meals... twenty-one-and-a-half silver. I can do that.* It was expensive, but it should be worth it if she used her time effectively.

As Tala was thinking, the Matron waited patiently, and when Tala seemed to return her attention to the older woman, the woman spoke again. "There are, of course, the additional facilities available to our guests. We have several training rooms and courtyards, as well as quite a number of peaceful places for meditation. These are complementary, and any of our staff would be happy to point them out or help you find one that best suits you."

Tala nodded, smiling. "I think that sounds wonderful. Thank you. I would like to stay for three nights and have use of the baths for all three nights. I'll start with four meals and go from there."

"Very good, Mistress. Would you care to pay now or upon departure?"

Tala hesitated for a long moment. "You let people pay afterward?"

The Matron nodded. "Mages often earn their way, while here, and only have the funds for their lodging after their work is complete."

"Huh… I'll pay upfront, thank you." *That seems open to abuse, but I suppose it works for them.* They likely required a binding contract, so the danger would be minimized somewhat.

"Currency or account?"

Tala quirked a smile. "Account, please."

"And were you interested in speaking to a seamstress?" The Matron pointedly did *not* look over Tala's state of dress again.

Tala hesitated.

"It would be no charge for me to set up a meeting."

Finally, Tala nodded. "Tomorrow evening, after supper? Would that work?"

"It can. I could also have her drop by after supper tonight, if you prefer." The Matron pulled out a stone tablet from her pocket and manipulated it briefly before handing it to Tala. "Acceptance at the bottom, if you please."

Tala glanced over the contents of the slate, verifying that they were correct, and pricked her finger, allowing a drop of her blood to vanish into the stone. She was getting very used to pulling her defenses back in order to confirm such transactions. "I think I can do after dinner tonight. Thank you." *Twenty silver, gone in an instant.*

The Matron likewise pricked her own finger to certify the transaction and smiled after the confirmation turned the stone briefly green. "Welcome, Mistress…?"

"Mistress Tala."

"Oh! Welcome, Mistress Tala. I believe that you have companions who are staying here as well?"

"I believe so, yes."

"They asked that you join them in the dining hall upon your arrival. Shall I notify them that you will join them promptly, or do you wish to bathe first?"

She briefly contemplated delaying, but her stomach rumbled rebelliously. "I think I should eat now, assuming I'd be allowed in the dining hall as I am?"

"Our guests are allowed to come as they are, Mistress."

"Thank you. Can you lead the way? I assume I can go to my rooms after?"

"That can easily be arranged. Right this way."

Tala followed the matron down a side hall and to a large, vaulted room with many varied tables artfully placed throughout. Each was both easy to see and retained the privacy of a bit of distance, occasionally utilizing a support column or half-wall to add to the separation.

"I trust that you wish dinner, now, to be one of your meals?"

"Yes, thank you."

"I will have it brought to you." She pointed towards one corner, where four figures sat at a table built for six. "Your companions are there."

"Thank you. I hope that you have a good evening."

The Matron paused for a heartbeat, then smiled. "Thank you, Mistress. You as well."

Tala nodded her thanks, turned, and strode across the room towards where Trent, Renix, and Atrexia were sitting with a stranger.

Renix saw her approaching first and waved. "Mistress Tala! Welcome. I'm glad that you could join us." He looked fully recovered from the concussion. *Glad to see that.*

The stranger glanced her way, then to Renix, and finally, he met gazes with Trent before cocking an eyebrow.

Millennial Mage 1 - Mageling

Trent rolled his eyes before turning to wave to Tala as well. "Come, join us."

Tala smiled. "Thank you, I will." As she pulled up a chair, she regarded the stranger, obviously a Mage, but found herself unable to interpret his spell-lines.

"You know, young Mage, it is rude to use your magesight on another without permission."

She hesitated for a moment before sighing. "I can't actually turn it off. What sort of defense is that? I've never seen anything, save iron, that was impenetrable to my sight."

The man grinned widely. "No deception? No arguing?"

She shrugged. "What's the point? You are clearly knowledgeable, and unless you were fishing, which I don't discount, you already knew the answers anyways. I try not to burn bridges before I know if I'll need to cross them."

"That is almost wise, Mistress Tala." He stood, holding out his hand across the wide table. "But I have you at a disadvantage. You may call me Grediv."

Tala pulled out a glove and slipped it on as she stood before taking Grediv's hand. "Good to meet you, Master Grediv. I assume that's your name... or?"

Grediv was giving her hand a strange look. "Yes, it's my name. Why the glove? Do you fear I will cast something through contact?"

You can do that? She supposed that made sense, but she hadn't really considered it before. *More the fool, me.* "No... I've just been told that contact with my skin is... unnerving for my fellow Mages."

"Really?" He tilted his head quizzically. "May I?" He offered his hand again.

Feeling a bit hesitant again, Tala pulled the glove back off. She started to reach for his hand, then paused briefly. *Well, in for a copper...* She clasped his hand, and she felt a mild spasm in his fingers in response.

"Fascinating. You are somehow reflecting the lingering traces of magic present in my body back into my fingers." He frowned. "But only from the back of your hand?"

Tala nodded. "That was my understanding. Then, are you a lightning Mage as well?"

Grediv bobbed his head noncommittally. "I've been using lightning magics of late, given the saturation of such in the region. I imagine that is why your friends, here"—he indicated Trent and Renix—"were recruited for the voyage to our fair city."

She nodded. "So, a Guide, then. Material?"

"Just so."

They both returned to their seats. Grediv was sitting between Trent and Atrexia, and Renix was sitting between Tala and Trent. "So... to what do I owe the pleasure?" She looked to Trent.

"He is the head of the local Archon Council, and we have requested he meet you and examine your... creation."

Tala gave a slow nod, silently making an 'oh.' She'd been expecting this—if not quite this quickly. "Well, no time like the present." She stuck her hand into her belt pouch, reaching in up to her elbow.

The others at the table gave her an odd look as the pouch was clearly not large enough for how she was using it, but they each almost immediately realized what it was.

As before, even through the iron vials, she could feel an odd connection to her Archon Star-like creations, and so she was able to find the vials without issue despite not actually looking into her pouch. Though, she'd thought the storage would be deeper. *I'll examine it more closely later.*

She pulled both out and handed them to Grediv.

He frowned, taking the vials. "What is this?"

Tala gave Trent a long-suffering look. "Didn't you tell him?"

Trent shrugged. "I figured it would just start an argument, which could be avoided by him seeing for himself."

Grediv sighed. "Please, just tell me what these are?"

Tala pointed to the one to which she could feel a slightly greater connection. "Those are both stars. That one is stronger, the other weaker, about half the strength, give or take."

"I know you didn't make an Archon Star out of an iron vial. So, why are they in iron vials?"

"Two reasons. First, safety: I've really no idea what they are, and I don't want them affecting the environment as such."

"Wise enough, given your lack of knowledge. The second reason?"

"They are liquid. I have to have them in something."

"Impossible…" Grediv trailed off, then glanced to Trent. "This would be that argument, yes?"

"Pretty much."

Grediv grunted. "I suppose it's easiest for me to look." He looked between the two, then gave a little shrug, setting aside the vial containing the smaller star. He took a breath, and Tala felt power moving across his face at the activation of his magesight. She still couldn't see it, which was a bit unnerving, and she realized that this was likely how other Mages felt around her.

Huh, who knew?

Thus prepared, Grediv pulled the cap off the vial he still held and looked inside.

There was a long moment, during which he just stared. Then, he moved the vial in a circular motion, clearly swirling the drop around. "It's liquid."

Tala smiled. "Seems to be, yes, though the surface tension is unbelievably strong."

He grunted assent. His eyes flicked over the table, and he reached out to pick up a spoon before tipping the vial and pouring the drop of magic-infused blood onto it. Once it was there, he continued to examine it, his gaze occasionally moving to her before returning to the blood. "This is... odd. You made it with your own blood?"

Tala nodded. "That's right. Though that one is a combination of two, which I made separately... Oh! And they absorbed another drop of my blood that I had previously infused with my power as for a magic density test."

Grediv's mouth opened, as if to object, then closed. It opened again, then he glanced down at the spoon in his hand. "You're serious." He glanced to the other vial, then back to her. "Do you mind if I pour the other onto this spoon, as well?"

Tala shrugged. "Sure. I can make another if I need to, but I still don't actually know the purpose of these."

Grediv chuckled. "I'm glad for that, at least. We can discuss it, later, along with *many* other things." He carefully set down the spoon and opened the other vial, glancing in to confirm its contents before pouring it out into the bowl of the same spoon.

The two stars moved towards each other like magnets, and as they contacted, there was a flickering flash of both power and visible light. It wasn't bright, no more than would have come from striking a flint with iron. When it passed, there was a single, marginally larger, drop of blood.

"Fascinating. It must be a property of the medium in which it was created." He looked up to her. "May I use my magesight on you?"

She nodded. "But I don't think you'll see much."

He shrugged, and she felt the power moving around his eyes once more. "You do have a layer of... something encasing you. It is quite resilient." The sense of power coming from him increased, and she thought she saw flickers in the air around him. *Green? It seems similar to the glimpse I got of Holly's yellow.*

Tala felt her skin heating up under his intensifying gaze and realized that it had something to do with his magesight interacting with her iron salve. "That's actually a bit uncomfortable."

He seemed genuinely surprised. "Really? I apologize."

The feeling both of heat on her skin and of power coming from him vanished immediately. All flickering traces of green in the air around him vanished.

"The little I was able to see tells an interesting story. You can perceive inside yourself with your magesight, correct?"

Tala squirmed a little. "Are you going to leave me any secrets?"

Grediv held up a hand. "My apologies. I am simply intrigued. I've never seen magesight scripting that detailed and powerful before." He hesitated. "Well, I've never seen them on a subject that lived through their activation."

Tala snorted. "It was *not* pleasant, that's for sure."

He smiled wryly. "I'd imagine not." He looked to the others at the table, who'd been listening closely. "Mistress Tala is right, however. I've been too free with her secrets, and I think that should cease. Thank you, Mistress Atrexia, Master Trent, for bringing this to my attention. It is, in fact, an Archon Star, though not of sufficient power to qualify her for raising." He glanced down at the spoon. "Though, with this oddity, she could get there fairly easily." He chuckled as if to himself. "I can imagine some of the oldest on our Council would be… obstinately cross about the method, however. They'd also refuse to believe it possible, so it wouldn't be too much of a hurdle. Bandfast *might* be better if she had a local sponsor…" He seemed to have devolved into talking to himself. He also seemed to notice that and brought his attention back to the table at large. "Apologies, again. Ah! Dinner is here. Mistress Tala, would you do me the honor of a short walk, after we eat? I think there are few things I should convey." He tipped the spoon, dumping the blood drop into one of the vials before sealing it and returning both to her.

She smiled. "That sounds wonderful. Thank you, Master Grediv."

As he'd said, dinner was indeed ready, and three servers brought out their food. It turned out to be a quite extensive four-course meal that reminded her of something Brand and his cooks would have made if they expected a city lord in attendance.

It was delicious, filling, and utterly satisfying. So much so that conversation virtually died while they ate, each new course coming out precisely when it was most anticipated, keeping the meal flowing smoothly.

In the end, Tala pushed herself back, sighing contentedly. "That was well worth the price." *There is no way I could get a better meal for half a silver.* She briefly considered seeing if she could take some with her but thought better of it. *I'm full enough.* She'd have to content herself with the single bottle of unopened wine she'd slipped into her belt pouch when she was fairly certain no one was watching. The others had drank the bottle brought for them, individually, so she was sure it was meant for her in any case. *Not stealing if it's mine.*

Chapter: 40
The Beginning of True Magehood

Now that everyone at the table had finished eating, Tala was becoming increasingly aware of their attention on her. Finally, as that tension threatened to break into conversations, or at least questions, she stood. "Archon Grediv, would now be a good time? I'm afraid that I need a bath after the week on the road, as should be apparent, and I have other appointments this evening after our discussion. With that in mind, I'd be grateful for some of your time, now."

Grediv took her flood of words in stride and stood as well. He swept his gaze over the other three. "Thank you, again, for the information and for allowing me to join you for dinner. I will take my leave."

The three nodded, giving Tala furtive glances.

Tala smiled and waved slightly. "See you all around, yeah?"

Nods were her only reply as she and Grediv walked towards a door in the outer wall, through which they could see a small walking garden.

The night sky was stunning overhead, as the mostly cloudless expanse gave Tala a clear view of the jewel-like stars. There was very little light pollution, even in the heart of the city, so she was easily able to pick out familiar patterns in the sky. *It has been a bit unseasonably cloudless of late. We're probably in for a dark, cold winter...*

Millennial Mage 1 - Mageling

Her magesight responded to her focus, and the city's defenses sprang into view, blocking out the stars.

She sighed, returning her eyes to the garden around her.

It was well-maintained and beautifully cultivated. Several fountains were strategically placed both to hide any noise, which infiltrated from the surrounding city, and to give any in the garden a measure of privacy from any other guests.

"I've always loved these grounds."

Tala regarded Grediv. Now that he was walking nearer to her, she could see that he was quite a bit taller than her, though that wasn't too odd. He had wings of white in otherwise blond hair, and she could see his spell-lines in amongst the roots.

He was clean-shaven, to the point that she suspected he'd shaved shortly before dinner. His clothes were fairly standard Mage's robes, loose and flowing. Though, they seemed of high-quality fabric and deep, rich colors. Primarily, they were an emerald green and deep, dark amethyst purple. It was an odd combination, but not jarringly so.

"Have you come here often?"

He chuckled lightly. "Since they were built."

She cocked her head. "I was under the impression that this inn has stood since the founding of Alefast."

"Your information is accurate."

"Care to explain?"

"Most Mages live far longer than most Mages realize that they will. Powerful, careful… beings of magic can expect millennia, though that happens with sad rarity."

He didn't say 'Mages' but that is clearly what he meant. Dancing around a rule, compulsion, or enforced edict? She had no way of knowing, and asking would be pointless. So, she didn't respond, instead simply walking beside him in silence.

He glanced at her from the corner of his eye. "Not going to ask?"

"You'll either tell me, or you won't."

He laughed again. "True enough. Unfortunately, as you are not an Archon yet, I can only share so much. I will give you one tidbit, which is only mildly taboo to share."

Again, she waited.

"You know, sometimes it is more fun when the other person asks."

"Would you like me to be more inquisitive?"

He huffed a short laugh. "I suppose not, though it does disappoint."

"Oh, don't mistake me, if I thought I could get away with it, I'd literally pin you down and wring ten thousand answers from you, but I doubt I'd even be able to inconvenience you."

"Fair enough." He grinned broadly. "Here's the tidbit, then: Archon is only the beginning. In truth, it *is* the beginning of true Magehood. Just as your time as a mageling revealed things a hundred times more expansive than you'd thought possible while at the academy. Just as your master filled in the gaps your highly focused, quadrant-specific academy education left behind, so it is when you are raised to Archon."

Tala cleared her throat. "Well… about that…"

Grediv cocked an eyebrow her way. "Yes?"

"I sort of…" *What are you doing? Why would you tell him this?* Because he seemed to want to help, and his not knowing might actually get her killed. "I never apprenticed under a master. I graduated less than a month ago and have never spent any time as a mageling." She let the words spill out of her before she could stop herself and didn't look at him for reaction.

Grediv, for his part, burst out laughing.

Tala turned to regard him then, incredulous.

Millennial Mage 1 - Mageling

He continued to laugh, moving over to sit on a bench, tucked beside a particularly lovely fountain.

She sat beside him but just more than an arm's length away.

Finally, he reined himself in. "And here I was, wracking my mind to think of what master would have let you try all that I've seen from you in just the last couple of hours." He snorted. "Mistress Tala, you are in *very* dangerous waters. You are swimming admirably, but you could easily get yourself killed."

She sighed. "Don't I know it. I've been doing what I can to catch up with books on theory."

"You're an avid reader, then?" He looked a bit surprised.

"Aren't all Mages?"

He scoffed. "If only." He scratched his chin. "I think I can help you, then. I've a few volumes that I usually give to first-time masters when they take on a mageling, but they should serve as good primers for you."

Tala felt an exuberant smile break out across her face. "That would be amazing! I can't convey how much that would help me." She hesitated. "You know, I'm also looking for texts on determining the specific modifications for spell-forms for use in unique materials, as well one on elucidating the uses of Archon Stars, and then specific techniques for Mage meditation and training… And I'm curious about time-related spell-forms." She smiled brightly, then. *Oh, please, please, please!*

He blinked at her for a long moment, then shook his head, a smile plain on his face. "The meditation and training techniques will be in the primers I get for you. I believe I have an extra copy on the tests for new material inscription, but I'm almost afraid to ask why you want them…" He didn't give her a chance to respond. "Time magic: that's a flat, emphatic *no*. The short answer is that your soul is inseparably tied to the flow of time, so if you do almost anything wrong, the result is you ripping out your own soul. No. Maybe, *maybe* once you reach Archon, but not a moment before." He hesitated. "In fact, even when you become an Archon, you should wait at least a decade before beginning that kind of research."

When I become an Archon... That floored her. This ancient Mage was telling her that she would be an Archon.

"As to the uses of an Archon Star?" He sighed. "Please, be very, very careful."

"What is their purpose?"

He hesitated. "This... isn't supposed to be shared with any who is not an Archon, yet, but no non-Archon is supposed to be able to create one, so..." He shrugged. "An Archon Star is a touchpoint for your soul."

"...What."

He grinned. "It is the first step to expanding your sway over the world around you." He gestured to himself. "The reason your magesight can't penetrate to see my magic is that I am in control of the magic around my body. Some call it a shroud, some an aura, some a field of influence." He shrugged again. "The name isn't really important."

"But humans can't control magic outside of themselves."

"Correct. But Archons can. An Archon Star is the first step towards that... in a sense. They are like... a practice sword for your soul? No, that's a terrible analogy." He scratched his chin and muttered under his breath, "I miss my beard." Finally, he let out an explosive sigh. "I can't think of a good metaphor. Needless to say, the Archon Star is an anchor for your soul, to help you exert your influence outside of your own body. Eventually, you could say that that will allow you to expand that influence into the world around you, in general, not just to the star." He snapped his fingers. "It's like the breathing apparatus at the academy for swimming underwater. It helps Mages learn what it means to breathe underwater so that their mental construct will accurately work when they use that magic for themselves."

"Huh... I never used those myself, but I think I understand what you mean. They are a crutch."

"More like a bow? To shoot you farther than you'd ever get on your own." He groaned. "This is why I'm not a good teacher... Without the Archon Star, you will never learn to exert your will outside your body. That's actually good for a whole host of reasons... But!" He held up a finger, drawing her attention sharply to him. He had correctly guessed that she'd been letting her mind run rampant at the various implications. "But, I will not tell you how to use it until you are an Archon, and I ask you to keep this information to yourself."

Tala thought about the opening she'd sensed in the magic of the artifacts she'd seen and *almost* asked, but something held her back. *I'm going to experiment, and he might stop me.* She swallowed. *Tala, this has to do with your soul... Just ask the man.* She was set on this. *No.* She'd shared enough, already.

After a long silence, he lowered his finger. "That's about all I can tell you and likely much more than I should have. My recommendation would be to work on improving the power of the stars you can create. Once you can make one... forty? Almost forty times as powerful as the one you have now, present yourself to an Archon, and you will be evaluated. I'd recommend you wait until you can do that in one go, but I can't force you to that."

"Won't that be on the higher end of usual?" *Who mentioned something like that... Atrexia?*

"So, someone has been explaining some things." He leaned back, stretching out his arms and resting his elbows on the back of the bench, still not too near her, though.

"That's true, but much of your early days as an Archon are influenced by how you are perceived at your evaluation. I could likely force your admittance with that little drop of blood, but you would be dismissed as a weakling, if an odd one, and it would take you decades to recover. In the worst case, someone would fixate on you and try to experiment upon someone so unusual. But"—he turned back to her, a smile tugging at his lips—"you come forward with an Archon Star in the upper reaches of the required power level? Made in blood? No one will discount you, then."

She was nodding. "That's a lot to think about... Thank you, Master Grediv. I do appreciate the time that you've taken." *Great... abduction...*

They stood, and Grediv gave her a slight bow. "It was a genuine pleasure, Mistress Tala. When you get to be my age, very little surprises you, and most surprises are unpleasant. Thank you for being a pleasant surprise, through and through."

Tala bowed in turn. "You are too kind. I look forward to the books...?"

He laughed again, short and merry. "Yes, yes. I'll have them delivered to you tomorrow evening. I have to ensure that I'm not breaching protocol too much in giving them to you, but I don't see that being an issue."

"Thank you." She hesitated, thinking for a moment. "If I may ask one parting question?"

He quired an amused smile. "Yes?"

"Why don't you have an Archon Mark?"

He looked at her for a moment, then snorted. "Ah, that. The specifics are decidedly outside what you should know..." He seemed to consider for a moment, then shrugged. "What many think of as an Archon Mark is actually an item used to aid a new or... deficient Archon in certain required tasks. I will not say more."

"So, those with Archon Marks, as I understand them, are the least of the Archons?"

He shrugged. "More or less accurate."

She opened her mouth to ask another question, but he raised a hand, forestalling her.

"I do have to go, Mistress Tala, and I've already said more than is generally allowed. I'll see what I can do about that, but I make no promises."

She sighed but nodded in resignation. "I understand. Thank you, once again."

They shook hands and parted ways. For Tala, that meant walking back towards the inn complex. For Grediv, that meant a wink and vanishing on the spot, without a trace of where he had gone.

Oh, Tala. How much bigger is the world than you ever realized? She was finally beginning to find out.

*   *   *

It had been easy for Tala to find a member of the staff and ask to be led to her room.

As it turned out, she would be staying in a beautiful space, twice the size of her room in Lyn's house. Apparently, because she'd opted to pay for use of the baths up front, and for every night of her stay, she'd been given one of the rooms with a private bath. To her joy, the attendant had explained that there were both cold and hot running water—the latter of which Tala had heard of but never experienced.

I wonder how they do that… Probably an artifact now, but before the waning? Might be worth investigating.

The room was simply furnished with a moderately sized bed, a writing desk and chair, and a reading chair. The lighting throughout the space was linked sets of artifact lights, similar to the one the guard at the inn's entrance had used. When she asked, the attendant explained that for most of the inn's history they'd used inscribed lighting, but as the city was now waning, they'd been able to slowly replace those expensive, costly-to-maintain devices with the more prolific artifact lights.

Also, yes, the hot water was currently supplied via artifacts, but she didn't know off-hand how it had been handled before. *Maybe similar to the artifact coin, which lowered water temp.* That would probably be a much more useful item. *Probably why she didn't have one in stock.*

Artia's warnings about evil artifacts made Tala a bit wary, but she supposed that the Wandering Magician was quite motivated to keep their guests safe and happy.

After confirming that the accommodations were acceptable, and that she didn't want or need a larger bed, the attendant departed, wishing Tala a good evening.

Tala was about to dive into the evening's work when a knock came at her door.

"Yes?"

"Mistress Tala?"

Tala frowned, walking to the door and pulling it slightly open. "Yes?"

A short, plump woman waited outside, carrying a small pack and a stepstool. For her to appear short to Tala, she was quite a bit shorter than average, indeed.

"Can I help you?"

"I was told you requested a consult from a seamstress."

"Oh! Yes, come in." Tala opened the door wide, allowing the woman entry and closing the door once she was inside.

As they both walked into the center of the room's open space, the seamstress looked her up and down. "I can see why you called for me." She tutted to herself. "Let's get a look at you." She grabbed Tala by the belt and turned her around, looking her up and down. "No, this doesn't suit you at all, and that's ignoring the state of the thing!" She tsked to herself. "I just couldn't live with myself if I didn't fix you up." She stopped Tala's movement and glared up at her. "You, child, are an affront to anyone who has to look at you."

Tala blinked, feeling as if she'd been slapped. "Excuse me?" She was starting to feel quite hurt and not a little angry.

The seamstress waved a hand. "I cannot. You are too beautiful to be dressed like an urchin boy, begging for his next meal."

Tala really didn't know what to do with that, so she just waited.

"Yes, yes. I will do one outfit for free, and after you wear it, you will be desperate for more!"

Free? "Deal."

"Hmmm? Oh, yes, of course you'll agree. No one would want to look like that." She gestured to Tala, generally.

Tala sighed. "So, what are my options?"

"Options? Silly girl, you have no options. I will measure you and make you an outfit. I will be in charge of all the choices. Tomorrow, late afternoon, you will put it on and fall in love. You will never want to wear anything else, and you will buy an entire wardrobe."

"And if I don't?"

The seamstress regarded her, again. "Not likely, but I suppose it is possible." She shrugged. "If that is the case, you can throw my work in the fire and go back to wearing flour sacks—or whatever other rubbish you find in local alleys."

Tala sighed. "Fine."

The seamstress nodded once. "Then, let me get to work."

It took surprisingly little time for the diminutive woman to take all of Tala's measurements, using the stepstool where appropriate, even though it was *all* of them. The seamstress left Tala alone and feeling only slightly violated. Even so, she was hopeful. *If nothing else, it will be interesting to see what she brings back.*

In the renewed silence, Tala pulled the curtains closed and moved through her stretches, using her magesight, directed inward, to target each muscle and ensure that those that were most sore got extra attention. It was not a fast process, but she took her time.

Quality requires patience.

That accomplished, she stripped out of her clothes and moved to the bathroom. She ran the hot water, as the attendant had shown her, and quickly filled the tub.

She took almost as long in the tub as she had stretching, soaking and then scrubbing off the grime accumulated through her travels.

That done, she reapplied her iron salve, using her magic detector to verify there were no gaps.

There, busywork complete.

She turned her attention to her gear, emptying out her new pouch and spreading her stuff across the floor and bed. She took the time to organize her items for easy access, in preparation for their return to the dimensional storage.

When that was complete, she regarded the open belt pouch. Stretched as wide open as she could make it, there was a hole just large enough for her to slip through if she were so inclined.

From the back side, the pouch looked like nothing so much as a smooth circle of leather, only made less so by the heavy cord that wove in and out around the rim. There was also a buckled strap, used to affix the whole thing to her belt.

Artia did promise that this wasn't a bag that ate people... She *really* needed to know what the inside looked like if she was going to arrange it effectively. Simply looking in had revealed nothing, even when she'd brought the bag near a light. It still simply looked black within, utterly empty.

Cursing herself as a fool, she placed the open dimensional storage on the ground, took a deep breath, and hopped in, tucking her arms in close and pointing her feet straight down to allow her to drop straight in. *All or nothing!*

She dropped down, bending her knees to land softly on a dark, even surface. She looked up, and saw the opening still there, just within reach of her upraised arms.

Around her was only blackness, though as she looked, she got the odd feeling… not of being watched, but of being held? It was a strangely comforting sensation and oddly disconcerting for that comfort. *You make no sense, Tala.*

She looked around, then sighed. *I wish I could see.* She reached out to try to touch a wall, and suddenly one was there. Under her hand, gray blossomed outward, quickly painting the entirety of the space. *Did it hear my thoughts or intuit my need from the fumbling?*

As the change occurred, she felt a small vortex of power and looked up. Above her, over the opening to the bag, her magesight let her see a short burst of magical energy moving in a swift current. It flowed into the bag for less than a second, then vanished from her sight. *Coloring the walls used energy, and it's refilling itself.* Interesting. How had it found free power, within the city's walls to draw upon? *More to ask Adrill about…*

She decided to speak out loud, just in case the bag could hear her. "If the entrance could be near one wall, with a ladder up out of it, and shelves around the outside of the top, that would make arranging this much easier." True to Artia's word, the inside of the dimensional storage was like a large closet, if with a low ceiling. *Is that because of my height? So, I wasn't trapped?* An interesting thought.

She pointedly did not think about how easily she could have been trapped if the pouch had been a bit deeper. *This was a pretty foolish thing to do, wasn't it...?*

She didn't see anything happen in response to her words, but she *felt* something. It wasn't a hunger, so much as a request? It had a similar feel to the magic which surrounded a transaction slate awaiting her blood, but without that being the exact desire.

Waiting. Did it need more power?

"Sure. Let's see what you can do now that you're owned by a Mage." It was time to give this artifact some power to work with.

Tala felt giddy. I'm a Mage. I'm really a Mage.

She had been recognized by others as a Mage.

She'd completed her first contract and been paid in gold. *Well, in the value of gold, not hard coinage.*

Now, she had her own magic items to explore and exploit.

By every hallmark of true Magehood that she'd striven to achieve, she was finally, fully a Mage.

No one would ever be able to find reason to call her a mageling again.

And the best part?

This was only the beginning.

Author's Note

Thank you for taking your time to read my quirky magical tale.

If you have the time, a review of the book can help share this world with others, and I would greatly appreciate it.

To listen to this or other books in this series, please find them on mountaindalepress.store or Audible. Release dates vary.

To continue reading for yourself, check out Kindle Unlimited for additional titles. If this is the last one released for the moment, you can find the story available on RoyalRoad.com for free. Simply search for Millennial Mage. You can also find a direct link from my Author's page on Amazon.
There are quite a few other fantastic works by great authors available on RoyalRoad, so take a look around while you're there!

Thank you, again, for sharing in this strange and beautiful magical world with Tala. I sincerely hope that you enjoyed it.

Regards,
J.L. Mullins

Printed in Great Britain
by Amazon